Irish author **Abby Green** ~~w~~ career in film and TV—w~~h~~ a lot of standing in the rain outside actors' trailers—to pursue her love of romance. After she'd bombarded Mills & Boon with manuscripts they kindly accepted one, and an author was born. She lives in Dublin, Ireland, and loves any excuse for distraction. Visit abby-green.com or e-mail abbygreenauthor@gmail.com.

Maya Blake's hopes of becoming a writer were born when she picked up her first romance at thirteen. Little did she know her dream would come true! Does she still pinch herself every now and then to make sure it's not a dream? Yes, she does! Feel free to pinch her, too, via Twitter, Facebook or Goodreads! Happy reading!

Discover more at millsandboon.co.uk.

CLAIMING HIS WEDDING NIGHT CONSEQUENCE

ABBY GREEN

SHEIKH'S PREGNANT CINDERELLA

MAYA BLAKE

MILLS & BOON

First Published in Great Britain 2018
by Mills & Boon, an imprint of HarperCollins*Publishers*
1 London Bridge Street, London, SE1 9GF

Claiming His Wedding Night Consequence © 2018 by Abby Green

Sheikh's Pregnant Cinderella © 2018 by Harlequin Books S.A.

Special thanks and acknowledgement are given to Maya Blake
for her contribution to the Bound to the Desert King series.

ISBN: 978-0-263-93547-9

MIX
Paper from
responsible sources
FSC
www.fsc.org   **FSC** C007454

This book is produced from independently certified FSC™ paper
to ensure responsible forest management.
For more information visit www.harpercollins.co.uk/green.

Printed and bound in Spain
by CPI, Barcelona

CLAIMING HIS WEDDING NIGHT CONSEQUENCE

ABBY GREEN

This is for Franca Poli,
for all of her wonderful support
and very generous help.
Grazie! X

CHAPTER ONE

'I AM VERY sorry to be the bearer of such bad news, Signorina Caruso, but the fact is that your father had borrowed for years to keep the castello *afloat and the bank is threatening to take possession of it now, unless you can buy it back at market value—which I'm afraid is impossible, considering the lack of funds in your family bank account...'*

Chiara stood at the huge window of the drawing room where she'd had a meeting with the family solicitor after her parents' double funeral just a couple of days before. Her arms were wrapped around herself as if that might offer some comfort.

For the last two days and sleepless nights the words had swirled in her head in a confusing painful jumble: *bank, take possession, lack of funds.* And she was no nearer to seeing a way out of this mess that didn't end up with her losing everything.

The family *castello* was an imposing centuries-old castle, set dramatically on the southern coastline of Sicily. Prime real estate that had once functioned and thrived as a farm, growing and exporting lemons and olives. Staples of Italian agriculture.

But once the recession had hit, and the market had taken a nosedive, their crops had all but dried up and died due to lack of demand. They couldn't afford to keep staff on and, while her father had done his best, clearly it hadn't been enough. Chiara had offered help time and time again, but her father—old-fashioned and conservative—hadn't deemed it 'appropriate work' for a girl. And she hadn't realised just how much he'd been borrowing to keep their heads above water.

She castigated herself now. She *should* have known. But her mother had been ill with cancer, and Chiara had been preoccupied with caring for her. The only reason Chiara was alive today and her father wasn't was because he'd decided to take his wife to her weekly chemotherapy appointment at the hospital in Calabria.

That morning a week ago he had said to Chiara, *'You need to go down to the village and see if you can get a job. It's not enough to just care for your mother any more.'*

His tone had been sharp. He'd never made any secret of the fact that he was disappointed Chiara hadn't been a boy, and that after suffering complications with Chiara's birth her mother hadn't been able to have any more children.

So Chiara had gone down to the village—to find that there were no jobs available. She'd never been more aware of her lack of qualifications, and the looks she'd received from the locals had made her feel paranoid.

As a child she'd been sickly, so her mother had home-schooled her. But even when she'd recovered and become strong they'd kept her at the *castello*. Her father had always had a paranoia about privacy and security, forbidding Chiara to bring anyone back to the *castello*—not that she'd had any friends! And then her mother had fallen ill, and Chiara had become her carer.

After humiliating herself in the village, looking for work, Chiara had returned home to find her parents still not returned from the hospital. So she'd gone down to her secret place—a small beach tucked out of sight of the *castello*—

and indulged in her favourite pastime, daydreaming, unaware that her parents were breathing their last in a tangle of metal after a catastrophic car crash.

What had made her feel even guiltier afterwards was the dream she'd indulged in—the same one she'd always had: leaving the *castello* and travelling the world. Meeting a handsome man and finding love and excitement. Yearning for...*more.*

Now Chiara's guilty sense of entrapment mocked her. She was finally free, but at such a cost that it left her breathless. She'd lost both her parents, and now it would appear she was about to lose the only home she'd ever known.

It was at a time like this that she felt her isolation even more keenly. Chiara had always lamented her lack of siblings, and had promised herself from an early age that she would have a large family one day. She never wanted any child of hers to feel as alone as she had, in spite of her mother's love and affection which had never quite made up for her father's disappointment.

Except now, if the bank took possession of the *castello*, the least of her worries would be a sense of isolation. She'd have much bigger concerns. Where would she go? What would she do? Her fruitless search for a job in the village was surely the tip of the iceberg when it came to finding work.

The truth was that she wasn't prepared for life beyond the *castello* walls at all. In spite of her dreams, she'd always counted on the *castello* being the anchor of her life, so that no matter where she went or what she did it would always be there to come back to. And eventually—some day—she'd hoped to fill it with a loving family.

The thought of having to leave her home now was agonising...and more than terrifying.

She felt a nudge at her leg and looked down to see their ancient family dog, Spiro, a Sicilian Shepherd. Shaggy and big. He looked up at her with mournful eyes and whined. He'd melted Chiara's heart when he was a pup, almost fifteen years ago, the runt of the litter and almost blind.

Chiara stroked his head and murmured soft words, wondering what on earth she would do with Spiro when she had to leave.

Just then she heard a noise coming from outside, and Spiro tensed and let out a feeble-sounding bark. Chiara looked out of the window to see a very sleek silver sports car prowling its way up the drive. The automatic main gates had stopped functioning years ago, in spite of her father's attempts to fix them.

Belatedly she recalled the solicitor saying something the other day about a businessman who had a proposition to put to her. She'd barely taken it in at the time, too overwhelmed with all the other news. But this could be the man he'd been talking about.

The car drew to a halt in the main courtyard, which suddenly looked very shabby and rundown next to such gleaming perfection. Feeling a spurt of irritation that a complete stranger thought it would be okay to discuss anything just days after a funeral, Chiara made reassuring noises to Spiro and then turned from the window and went through the *castello* to the main door, fully intending to tell whoever it was to come back on a more suitable day.

She doused the feeling of panic that there might not *be* a more suitable day. She had no idea how fast banks acted in this scenario when taking possession. She could be tossed out by the end of the week.

Feeling more vulnerable and raw than she'd ever felt in her life, Chiara pulled open the massive oak door. For a second she was blinded by sunlight, so all she had was an impression of a very tall dark shape climbing the steps.

She was about to put her hand over her eyes to shade them when the visitor stepped into her eyeline, blocking the sun with his height. Chiara blinked, and blinked again, her hand dropping to her side ineffectually as she took in the sight before her.

It was a man. But such a man as she'd never seen before. The kind of man she'd only seen in her fantasies or read about in stories.

Thick black hair, slightly messy, framed the most savagely beautiful face Chiara had ever seen. High cheekbones and an aquiline nose lent it more than a hint of regality, and his tall, proud bearing reinforced the impression. His mouth was as sculpted as the rest of him—firm and strong.

An intriguing air of decadent sensuality and steeliness made a quiver of something very feminine go through Chiara, all the way to the centre of her being.

She struggled to rouse herself out of the strange lethargy that seemed to have taken hold of her, hindering her ability to function. 'I'm sorry…can I help you?'

The man's eyes narrowed on her and Chiara saw they were a very dark brown—and totally unreadable. Something cool slid down her spine and she unconsciously felt for Spiro's reassuring presence behind her, even though he was so old and blind he was totally ineffectual as a guard dog.

The man looked emotionless, but Chiara sensed something almost volcanic under the surface and it was very intimidating. Strangely, though, she didn't fear for her safety. It was a much more ambiguous fear. A fear for something deep within her that was coming to life…*desire*.

'I am here to see Chiara Caruso. Maybe you would be so kind as to fetch your mistress for me.'

His voice was deep and gravelly, tugging on Chiara's senses. He hadn't posed it as a question. She realised that he must think she was the housekeeper. They'd let the housekeeper go a long time ago. Hence the general air of decay and dishevelment in and around the *castello*. But, effectively, she *was* now the housekeeper, so it was silly to feel something shrivel up inside her that he might assume her to be menial staff.

She was very aware of her plain black mourning dress, make-up free face, and long unruly hair. She knew she was no great beauty, with her unfashionably full figure and average height.

She tipped up her chin. '*I* am Chiara Caruso.'

His eyes narrowed even more and a look of sheer incredulity crossed his face. 'You?'

Tension and self-consciousness stiffened Chiara's whole body. 'I'm not sure exactly what you were expecting but, yes, I can assure you that I'm Chiara Caruso. Who, may I ask, are *you*?'

Those eyes seemed to get even colder, if that was possible. 'I am Nicolo Santo Domenico.'

He seemed to be waiting for some kind of response—as if his name should mean something. But it didn't.

Chiara prompted, 'And…? How can I help you?'

Confirming her suspicion, he said, 'You don't know who I am?'

Chiara felt bewildered now. 'Should I?'

The man emitted a sound like an incredulous laugh. 'You're seriously expecting me to believe you don't know who I am?'

The man's arrogance was astounding!

Chiara took her hand off the door and folded her arms

across her chest. 'No, I don't know who you are. Now, if you have nothing better to do than interrogate me on my own doorstep then I'll ask you to leave. We had a funeral here this week—it is not an appropriate time.'

His eyes gleamed. 'To the contrary…now is the *most* appropriate time for this conversation. May I?'

He sidestepped her neatly and was walking into the vast stone hallway before she could stop him.

Spiro whined and Chiara whirled around. 'Excuse me, what on *earth* do you think you're doing? This is my property!'

Except it's not really, reminded a little voice.

The man turned around to face her and Chiara got the full impact of him. It was almost too much. He made the majestic reception area seem small. He had to be well over six feet, and broad with it. He wore a dark suit that could only be custom-made as it clung to his well-honed physique like a second skin. His air of intense physicality made Chiara think of bare-knuckle fighters she'd seen in a documentary once. It was as if his suit was just a flimsy concession to urbanity.

His gaze slid down to beside Chiara and his lip curled. 'What is *that*?'

Chiara glanced down to see Spiro, looking in the general direction of the man and emitting a low growl. She put her hand on his head and looked at her uninvited guest. 'He's my dog and you're upsetting him. This is my home and I'd like you to leave.'

His gaze came back to rest on her and Chiara fought not to fidget under that exacting expression.

'This is precisely what I've come here to discuss—the fact that this home is not actually yours at all.'

Chiara's insides seized. Was this man from the bank? She forced herself to ask, 'What are you talking about?'

He didn't answer right away. Instead he put his hands in his pockets, drawing Chiara's eye to his mid-section. Heat climbed up her neck and face and she diverted her gaze before he might notice. But he didn't notice. He was looking up at the walls and turning around in a small circle.

He said, as if to himself, 'I've waited a long time to be here…'

Then he started walking towards the reception room Chiara had just vacated. She went after him. 'Excuse me, Signor Domenico…'

He turned to face her from the middle of the room and Chiara had the strangest sensation that *she* was the guest—and not a very welcome one.

'It's *Santo* Domenico.'

Chiara bit out the name. 'Signor *Santo* Domenico. I insist you tell me what on earth this is all about or I will call the police.'

Now she was beginning to panic. He *must* be from the bank. But were they allowed to show up like this? Why had the solicitor not warned her this might happen so soon?

Chiara's head was starting to hurt again.

He looked around. 'Where are the staff?'

Chiara felt defensive and wasn't sure why. 'There are no staff—not that it's any business of yours.'

He looked at her, incredulous again. 'How have you kept this place?'

Chiara knew that was also none of his business, but this whole meeting had taken a surreal turn and she found herself saying, 'We closed up the rooms we weren't using and just maintained the few we needed.'

'You and your parents?'

'Yes. They were buried in a double funeral two days ago, in case you weren't aware.' She was hoping to shock him into some kind of realisation that he was here at a very inappropriate time.

He nodded his head. 'I am aware, and I'm sorry for your loss.'

He couldn't have sounded less sorry.

Before Chiara could formulate another word he said, 'You had a meeting with your solicitor the other day?'

'Yes,' Chiara said faintly. 'How did you know?'

'It's customary to have the reading of the will and such after the funeral.'

'Of course.'

She cursed herself for feeling paranoid. She had no reason to feel paranoid. If he wasn't from the bank then he had to be the businessman her solicitor had mentioned. She forced herself to calm down. There would have to be due process before anyone evicted her from her own home.

'So you will now be aware that this *castello* is in danger of being possessed by the bank unless you can drum up the necessary funds.' Here he stopped, and looked around again before saying, 'Forgive me if I'm speaking out of turn, but I don't think that's likely.'

Chiara wanted to point out that he'd been speaking out of turn since the moment he'd materialised on the doorstep, but that wasn't the issue here. 'Are you from the bank?'

He shook his head and a small smile played around that disturbing mouth, as if her question was amusing for some unknown reason. It made her want to slap him when she'd never before felt violent towards anyone in her life.

'So how do you know that information, then?'

He shrugged minutely and looked back at her. 'I have my sources and I've had a…a keen interest in the *castello* for some time now.'

'A keen interest…?' Chiara struggled to make sense of his cryptic response.

He faced her squarely then, and she had the uncomfortable sensation that he was about to be a lot less cryptic.

'Yes, a keen interest. For my whole life, in fact. Because, you see, the truth of the matter is that this *castello* actually belongs to *me*. To my family, specifically—the Santo Domenicos.'

Nico looked at the woman standing just a few feet away. She couldn't be more nondescript, in a black shapeless dress, with long light brown hair and not a scrap of make-up. His first impression of her had been that she had to be the housekeeper, but now he noticed the proud bearing of her form. Spine straight, shoulders back...

His conscience pricked—her parents had just died. But he quashed the spark of compassion. This day had been coming for decades and now it was finally here.

His father had died a bitterly disappointed man, and countless other members of his family had suffered as a result of this woman's family's actions. He'd suffered too, enduring jeers and taunts his whole life.

'You're not one of the powerful now, Santo Domenico— you're nothing...'

But he wasn't nothing any more. He had singlehandedly pulled himself out of the streets of Naples and achieved stunning success, and now he was finally ready to reclaim his family's heritage from the people who had stolen it so many years ago.

His one regret was that his father hadn't lived to see the *castello* returned. That he hadn't lived to see where his ancestors were buried and pay his respects. His father had come here once, with his own father's ashes, and asked if he could scatter them in the family plot, but he'd been turned away like a beggar.

Nico would never forget the humiliation etched into his father's face and the rage burning in his eyes.

He'd said to Nico that day, *'Promise me you'll walk through those gates one day and reclaim our legacy... promise me.'*

And here he was, finally on the verge of fulfilling that promise—except much to Nico's frustration he wasn't feeling exactly satisfied. He was distracted by the realisation that Chiara Caruso's eyes were a very light green. And that she wasn't perhaps as plain as he'd first thought. She was...intriguingly fresh-faced. Untouched. He was used to women covered in so many layers of artifice, or filled with so many chemicals, it was hard to know what they looked like underneath it all.

She shook her head now, frowning. 'What are you talking about? This *castello* can't belong to you. It's belonged to my family for hundreds of years.'

Anger made Nico's voice tight. 'Are you sure about that?'

Suddenly she seemed hesitant. 'Well, of course...'

'Perhaps you're an expert denier of history, like your father was. Are you really expecting me to believe that you aren't aware of what happened?'

She went pale. 'Leave my father out of this. How dare you appear on my doorstep with some fantastical tale?' She stood back and extended her arm towards the door. 'I'd like you to leave now. You are not welcome here.'

For a moment Nico's conscience pricked again, he thought that perhaps he should leave and at least allow her a period of private mourning before returning in a couple of days. But then he registered her words: *you are not welcome here.* Exactly the same words her father had said to *his* father when he'd tried to gain access to the family burial plot.

Nico planted his legs wide. He wasn't going anywhere.

The dog standing beside her emitted another pathetic growl.

He said, 'I'm afraid that it's *you* who is not welcome here. Not for much longer anyway. It's merely a matter of time before the bank moves to take possession.'

Chiara stared at this man who looked as immovable as a stone statue. Against every instinct, her curiosity was aroused. Maybe he wasn't mad—maybe he believed what he was saying.

'What gives you the right to say such things…that the *castello* belongs to you?'

'Because it's true. My family built it in the seventeenth century.'

Chiara wanted to shake her head, as if that might make order out of what he was saying. She'd known the *castello* was old—especially some parts of it—but not that old.

He went on. 'At that time the Santo Domenicos owned this estate and all the land and villages from here to Syracuse.'

What he was talking about was a huge swathe of land, and if it were true— Chiara shook her head. It couldn't be. 'My family have been the sole owners of this castello for as long as I know—our name is above the door, etched in stone.'

He dismissed that with a curl of his lip. 'Anyone can carve words into a slab of stone. Your family took ownership of this *castello* before the Second World War. The Carusos were the Santo Domenico family's accountants. When we were in financial difficulty they agreed to bail us out, using the *castello* as collateral, the agreement being that as soon as we had the money again we would buy the *castello* back at an agreed price. Then came the war.

'After the war, your family made the most of the chaos at that time. They claimed to have no knowledge of the agreement and destroyed all the paperwork, saying our claims were bogus. So many people were trying to reclaim ownership of land and possessions after the war that the authorities chose to believe that we were being opportunistic. We were a powerful family, and some were only too happy to see us brought down and destroyed.'

He continued.

'The war decimated our savings—we lost everything. We became destitute. Your family refused to negotiate or to give us a chance to regain our property. Our very proud Sicilian family was scattered. Most emigrated to the United States. We ended up in Naples. My grandfather refused to leave Italy, always hoping he'd see our lands returned before he died. As did my father. Both were thwarted.'

Chiara struggled to take this in. 'You *can't* have proof of this. I've never heard mention of the Santo Domenicos in my life.'

He cast her a jaundiced look. 'I don't believe that. Our story is part of local legend around here.'

Chiara flushed when she thought of her very sheltered upbringing. Their housekeeper—before she'd been let go in recent years—had done all the shopping, and her father had gone into the village for supplies since then. Whenever Chiara had ventured out she had noticed the way people looked at her, and she'd burned with self-consciousness because she'd assumed they were judging her less than fashionable clothes and figure.

However, if there *was* any grain of truth to this man's claims, perhaps they'd been judging more than her appearance.

Feeling very exposed, and more vulnerable than ever, she repeated, 'You have no proof of this.'

He arched a brow. 'Come with me.'

He strode out of the room, and Chiara just looked after him stupidly before she kicked into gear. The sensation that he somehow belonged here struck her again and it wasn't welcome.

He walked out of the main door and Chiara had the urge to slam and lock it behind him. But something told her that this man wouldn't be so easily locked out.

He stopped in the main courtyard of the *castello* and looked left and right, as if trying to figure something out, and then strode confidently to the left, towards where the family church and graveyard were situated. The graveyard she'd only walked away from a couple of days ago, after seeing her parents interred.

When she realised where he was headed she hurried to catch up and called out, 'This is ridiculous—you must stop this!'

But he didn't stop. It was as if he couldn't hear her. He got closer and closer to the graveyard, but at the last moment veered away from it and walked to another gate nearby, overgrown with foliage.

She arrived behind him, slightly out of breath. 'What are you looking for? That is the old family plot.'

A place she'd never been into herself, because the housekeeper had used to tell her that it was haunted. A shiver went down Chiara's spine now. Had the housekeeper known something of this man's fantastic claims?

He thrust aside the foliage and located the latch on the gate. At this moment he barely resembled a civilised man. She could see his muscles moving under the material of his suit and felt another disconcerting pulse of awareness in her lower body. Totally inappropriate and unwelcome.

He pushed open the gate and said in a grim tone, 'Come on.'

Chiara had no choice but to follow him into the shadowed and dormant graveyard. Sunlight barely penetrated through the gnarled branches of the trees overhead and it was very still. She picked her way gingerly over the uneven ground, not even sure what she was walking on, hoping it wasn't graves.

He had reached the far corner and was pulling leaves and branches away from something. When she got closer she saw that it was a headstone. He turned to face her with an intense look on his face, and for a moment she was almost blinded by his sheer raw beauty.

Then he took her arm and said impatiently, 'Look.'

Chiara stood beside him, very aware of his hand on her arm and the disparity in their sizes. It took her eyes a moment to adjust, but when they did she could make out faint writing, her heart stuttered and stopped as a dawning dread moved through her.

There, etched in the stone, was the following:

Tomasso Santo Domenico,
born and died at
Castello Santo Domenico,
1830-1897

She couldn't believe it. Castello *Santo Domenico*. Not Castello Caruso.

'He was my great-great-grandfather.'

Chiara looked around, and now she could see the unmistakable shapes of headstones underneath foliage all around her. They seemed to loom at her accusingly in the gloom. The space closed in on her and claustrophobia rose swiftly. She pulled free of Nicolo Santo Domenico's grip and turned and made her way out, her skin clammy with panic.

She almost tripped over a mound, and a small sob came

out of her mouth, but then finally reached the gate and stepped into bright comforting sunshine, her head reeling.

Nico stood in the overgrown graveyard, only vaguely aware that Chiara had all but run out of the graveyard. This proof of his family's legacy was almost too much to take in.

Standing in that grand room just a few moments ago, facing a stricken-looking Chiara Caruso, he'd actually felt a sliver of doubt. Could this grand, crumbling estate really have belonged to his family? Had they truly once been the most powerful family in southern Sicily? It had seemed almost too much to believe when all he could think of was his grandfather's bitter countenance and then his father's. Maybe they'd dreamed it up, frustrated by the struggles they'd faced. Their fall from grace.

But, no. This graveyard was cold, hard evidence that that they had existed in this place. That they had once lived, loved and died here. His ancestors had built it, stone by stone.

A cold sense of satisfaction filled Nico's bones. He had a right to claim this place now. He was right to be here.

He knew it wasn't necessarily compassionate to confront Chiara Caruso just days after her parents' funeral, but he'd never been accused of having compassion.

Faced with this knowledge of how his family had been left to rot in an overgrown graveyard, on land that should have been returned to them decades before, he felt even less inclined to be merciful.

He walked out of the graveyard into the sun, undoing his tie, feeling constricted. Chiara Caruso had disappeared, and yet strangely he found that her stricken expression and those unusual green eyes stayed with him.

He could still feel her arm under his hand. It had been

supple and slim, hinting at a more defined body beneath the shapeless clothes. To Nico's shock, the awareness had exploded into more than a frisson, and still hummed in his blood. Disconcerting and not welcome. He put it down to his heightened emotions.

He walked over to the edge of a large uncultivated lawn that rolled down to the sea. There were pine trees along one side and gnarled bushes on the other.

His land.

It beat in his blood now, gathering force. Anger was still high as he thought of his ancestors lying in their cold graves, ignored and left to moulder.

It was one thing to have an intellectual knowledge that something belonged to you, but another thing entirely to experience it. From the moment he'd driven up towards the *castello* he'd felt a sense of ownership that went deeper than the sense of injustice he'd grown up with.

He wasn't usually one to give any credence to intangibles, but right now, for the first time in his life, he felt a sense of *home*. It was as disconcerting as the awareness he felt for Chiara Caruso. It was also something he'd never thought he'd experience after growing up in Naples and being constantly reminded that it wasn't his home.

But as he looked out on this view that the Carusos had stolen from the Santo Domenicos, things didn't feel as clear-cut as they had just a short while before. Nico didn't want to admit it, but Chiara Caruso's reaction to the news had seemed like genuine shock. Either that or she was an undiscovered acting genius.

He'd come here today to present her with a deal she couldn't refuse. A deal that would get him the *castello* within as short a space of time as possible: offering her enough money to sign over the *castello* to him and then go far away, somewhere she, the last of the Carusos, would fade into obscurity.

But that growing awareness of her in his blood and in his body was blurring the lines and making him hesitate for a moment.

A recent conversation with his solicitor came into his head, a well-worn refrain...

'Nico, you're an outsider, and that has served you well. You've made your fortune by upsetting the status quo and punishing those who've underestimated you. But now it's time to consolidate and expand. It's all very well to be the rogue operator once you have a more respectable life in the background. Right now you're losing out on deals because people feel they can't trust you. You've no family, nothing to lose...'

Nico scowled at the view. He'd been at an exclusive charity event in Manhattan recently, discussing a deal with one of Manhattan's titans of construction. The man's wife had come on to Nico, making her attraction obvious. And, even though Nico had rebuffed her advances, the next day when he'd followed up on a promise to meet and discuss things further, the construction giant had cut off all contact and Nico had lost out on a potentially hugely lucrative deal.

The truth was that he'd had marriage on his mind for some months now. Before his solicitor had even had to say anything it had become evident to Nico that the absence of a wife by his side was damaging his reputation amongst his more conservative peers. And so he'd been facing the unpalatable fact that he should make some adjustments to his very free lifestyle.

To his surprise, the prospect hadn't been totally repugnant. Nico had lived a hedonistic existence for a long time and, to be perfectly frank, he'd been feeling more and more jaded. Tired of the games women played. Tired of the avaricious gleam in their eyes. Tired of not knowing what their agenda was.

While he might once have appreciated the need for a wife who knew how to navigate that world, the thought of a woman like that made something curdle inside him now. As did the idea of growing old amidst the soaring soulless buildings of New York or London.

That might have been where he'd made his fortune, and restored the Santo Domenico pride and name, but standing here on Sicilian land—the land of his ancestors—he knew that the final piece had to be in this place. Nowhere else.

With the evocative scent of the sea and earth all around him, he found that a new vision was coming to life inside him.

A vision of a future that would help him to achieve the kind of success that he'd only dreamed of up to this point. A vision of a future that included a wife who would give his reputation the sheen of respectability he so badly needed. A wife who would give him a family and breathe the life force back into the Santo Domenico name. A wife who would complement him…who knew the value of legacy.

What he needed was as clear to Nico now as the glittering sea in front of him. It was totally audacious, and contrary to his original plan, but it was taking root inside him and would not be dismissed.

After a few more long minutes Nico turned around to face the *castello*. The only person who had been standing between him and his future—Chiara Caruso—was now the only person who could make sure it happened.

CHAPTER TWO

CHIARA TOOK A sip of the dark golden brandy and winced as it burnt her throat. It was her first time ever taking a drink from the walnut drinks cabinet in the main reception room and she could understand the appeal now, as the alcohol settled in her stomach and radiated a warm, comforting glow.

Her hand still shook, though, and when she heard determined footsteps coming across the stone hall floor beyond the room she put the glass down on a silver tray.

By the time Nicolo Santo Domenico entered the room Chiara's hands were behind her back and she was as composed as she could be, considering she felt as if she'd just been body-slammed by a ton weight.

He stopped in front of her, too close for comfort.

'Well? Is that enough proof for you? A graveyard full of my ancestors?' His voice rang with cold condemnation.

He towered over Chiara and she moved away, across the room, Spiro trotting loyally beside her. She put her hand on the dog's head, as if he could offer protection or a way out of this madness.

Eventually she said truthfully, 'I... I don't know what to say. I had no idea about any of this...'

He lifted a hand. 'Please. I don't know why you insist on this charade of ignorance, because it serves no purpose.'

He dropped his hand and his gaze narrowed on her. 'Unless, of course, your parents warned you that this could happen. That once the *castello* was vulnerable again the Santo Domenicos might return to stake our claim...'

Chiara shook her head, feeling sick, wondering just how much her parents *had* known. 'No, they never said anything. I never heard anything.'

He sounded disgusted now. 'That's impossible—unless you were a total recluse.'

Chiara wanted the ground to open up and swallow her whole. His words cut far too close to the bone.

She forced out, 'Whether or not what you say is true... and I have to admit that the graveyard does support your claim...the *castello* is out of your reach as much as mine now. Shouldn't you be talking to the bank instead of me?'

She couldn't stop the bitter note to her voice, still coming to terms with this news herself, so soon after her parents' deaths.

Nicolo Santo Domenico looked at her for such a long moment that Chiara almost snapped at him to stop. She felt like a specimen on a laboratory table, never more aware of her drabness next to his glorious vitality. She would bet that he'd travelled all over the world and probably hadn't been that impressed by it.

And then he said abruptly, 'I presume if you had a choice you would prefer to retain ownership of the *castello*?'

The sharp pang of loss just at the thought of leaving struck Chiara right in her heart. 'Of course. It's my home— the only home I've ever known. My whole family is buried here.'

Like his. Her conscience pricked.

'The only thing standing in your way of retaining the *castello* is a lack of funds.'

Chiara curbed her irritation. 'I'm aware of that, but unfortunately I don't have the funds.' She had nothing.

'I *do* have the funds.'

Chiara looked at him trying to ascertain where he was going with this. 'Is that why you've come? To humiliate me on behalf of your family by pointing out that you now have the power to buy the *castello*?'

He shook his head, still looking at her with that disconcerting intensity. 'Nothing so petty as that. What I'm saying is that I could give you the funds to pay off the debt and retain the *castello*.'

'Why would you do that?' He didn't strike her as remotely charitable. Certainly not to his family's bitter enemy. He'd been barely civil since he'd arrived.

'I would do that because if *I* was to engage with the bank to buy the *castello* it would be a lengthy and tedious process. The *castello* needs serious refurbishment, and the sooner this happens, the better. I've waited a long time for this opportunity.'

Chiara struggled to try and understand. 'But how do *I* fit into this?'

'Until the bank takes possession you're still the owner. If you pay off the debt you retain the *castello*. I am offering you a deal to do that on your behalf.'

She looked at him suspiciously. 'Why would I agree to that?'

'Because you'd get to remain at the *castello*. You wouldn't have to leave your home. Isn't that what you want?'

Chiara felt seriously confused now. 'Yes, but…how on earth would that work?'

His dark eyes seemed to bore all the way through her. 'It's very simple, really. You would marry me as soon as possible.'

* * *

Chiara looked at Nicolo Santo Domenico in shock. Eventually she managed to formulate words. 'Why on earth would you want me to marry you?'

Apart from anything else, she had to be a million miles removed from the type of woman a man like this went out with. She'd pored over glossy magazines for years, lamenting her untameable hair and full figure. Not to mention her zero fashion sense. She knew her limitations.

'Like I told you, dealing with the bank would be tedious and time-consuming. It would take months—maybe even longer. Through marriage to you the *castello* will become mine within a much shorter space of time.'

Understanding finally sank in. So that was why he wanted to marry her. He was so arrogant and preposterous she could barely take it in. The thought of even considering any kind of intimate relationship with someone like him was totally ludicrous. And yet... She couldn't deny the very illicit beat of awareness deep within her. It shamed her. She wanted his disturbing presence gone.

'I think you've said enough. Your proposal—' She stopped for a second as that word rang in her head. 'It's not even a proposal... What you've just said is frankly ridiculous. I have no desire to marry a complete stranger—for any reason.'

For a moment he looked at her, and then he turned abruptly and went to the window. Much to her disgust, Chiara couldn't stop her gaze moving over his broad shoulders, where the material of his jacket moulded to hard muscles.

He turned back to face her and she lifted her gaze guiltily.

'I should have expected that you would take this as an opportunity to thwart the Santo Domenicos one last time, but you should know that my acquisition of the *castello* is going to happen—with your help or not.'

Chiara felt frustrated. 'I told you—I had no idea about any of this. Why would I want to *thwart* you? What happens to the *castello* once the bank takes possession is out of my control!'

'Not if you marry me.'

He really was serious.

For a moment Chiara let herself imagine what it might be like not to have to leave the place where she'd just buried her parents and a wave of emotion nearly felled her. But at such a cost!

It was all too much.

Chiara felt Spiro nudge her thigh and she went over to sit down in a chair, afraid her legs wouldn't keep holding her up.

She looked up at Nicolo Santo Domenico. 'You can't possibly mean to marry me. You despise me. My family. And why would I agree to such a union? With a man who has married me solely for the *castello*?'

Faced with Chiara Caruso, back in this room, Nico was more convinced than ever that his plan was a good one. He knew exactly why she should agree to such a union. To give him what he wanted. To repay some of the huge debt her family owed *his* family. What better wife could he choose for himself than a traditional Sicilian woman? And one who was indebted to him.

'You owe me. You are the last Caruso, and I am the last Santo Domenico.'

She stood up, agitated. 'I don't owe you my life!'

'My deceased ancestors lying outside in the graveyard have had *their* lives all but wiped out of history.'

Nico realised that if they married the Caruso name

would disappear for ever. It called to the devil inside him. Karma.

Chiara's hands were clasped in front of her and Nico was aware of her breasts, full and high, moving rapidly under her dress. A spike of arousal went straight to his groin and he had to control his response with an effort that was surprising.

He had to admit that this attraction he felt was unprecedented, and had inspired this audacious plan even though she wasn't remotely his type. But something about her lush and curvy body called to a very base part of him that seemed biologically programmed to recognise a mate, regardless of what his head might want.

He'd done some research on Chiara Caruso before this meeting and had found no pictures and little or no information. She didn't appear to have done much at all. Not attended university nor worked.

She was looking at him now with wide, clear green eyes and he felt very warm all of a sudden. It was as if she could see all the way through him and right into his mind. Read his thoughts. It was a very disconcerting sensation for someone who kept his innermost thoughts private.

But it wasn't disconcerting enough to make him change his mind. He'd come to Sicily to reclaim his family's legacy and he vowed right now that he wouldn't be leaving without making this woman his wife. Whatever it took.

He said, 'What I'm proposing is a marriage of convenience. A business transaction. I will put up the money to pay off the bank and in return you will marry me and sign a contract that gives me sole ownership of the *castello*. However, through marriage to me, you will have the right to live here for the rest of your life.'

She went pale. 'Are you totally out of your mind?'

'Not at all. In case I'm not making myself absolutely

clear, I don't see this marriage as anything more than a business merger and a way to have heirs. Through them, the Santo Domenico name will flourish again after being all but decimated.'

Heirs? Chiara barely registered that as shock reverberated through her body. 'But me... Why would you want to marry me when you could marry any woman in the world?'

'Like I said, I have no desire to deal with the bank on this matter. And as I never intend to marry for love—'

'Why not?' she interrupted, momentarily distracted enough to want to know if there was some reason for his cold-bloodedness.

Nico's insides clenched. Because his mother had abandoned him and his father when Nico was just weeks old and left his father a bitter, broken man all his life. Because people used love as a way to manipulate and distract. Nico had almost lost everything he'd built up because he'd fancied himself in love with a woman. Thankfully he'd come to his senses just in time. It was a lesson he'd never forgotten.

He looked at Chiara. 'Because I don't believe in it. As for choosing you as my wife... Marriage to you gets me the *castello* and, on a practical level, you have grown up on this estate. You're part of it and you know it. I plan to do extensive renovations, and as I have offices in New York, London and Rome it will help to leave the project in the hands of someone who cares about the estate.'

Chiara shook her head as if to try and clear it. 'You're talking about a project manager, not a wife. How could you propose to bring heirs...*children*...into a loveless marriage like that?'

Something caught his eye behind her and he strode over to a small table and picked up a framed photo of her and her parents. He held it up, his lip curling contemptuously. 'Are you expecting me to believe you were a bliss-fully happy family?'

Chiara squirmed inwardly. She and her mother were smiling, but her father had that look of perpetual disappointment on his face.

Hating Nicolo Santo Domenico with a ferocity that shocked her, she went over and took the picture out of his hand, saying, 'We weren't perfectly harmonious, but we were happy in our own way.'

Liar, whispered an inner voice.

Chiara put the picture down and moved out of the man's dangerous proximity.

He said coolly, 'You've just proved my point. There's no such thing as a harmonious family. Surely it's better for children to grow up in an environment where they see their parents working as a team, with mutual respect, rather than something as ephemeral as *love*?'

'But how can you say you'd *respect* me?'

'I personally have no grudge against you, Chiara, in spite of what you may think. My father and every generation before him grew up despising the Carusos for what they did. They were emotional about it and that's why they failed to get anywhere. *My* success came from taking out the emotion.'

He'd cut out emotions long ago. The day he'd found his lover in bed with his best friend.

Nico and his friend had been about to sign a lucrative deal with one of Naples's biggest entrepreneurs, but his girlfriend had believed his friend to be the one instrumental in the deal and so had seduced him in a bid to feather her nest.

She'd begged forgiveness when she'd realised her mistake, but Nico had cut her out of his life and embraced that cold focus ever since.

Chiara Caruso was not the kind of woman who would arouse disturbing emotions or passions. She was perfect.

He said, 'As much as I'm restoring the Santo Domenico name to where it belongs, I'm also proposing this for sound business reasons. This region of Sicily has been woefully neglected and is full of potential. My plans go far beyond this estate. I've already bought all the neighbouring land. I see you as an asset to this estate, Chiara. You'll be invested in it and in its success in a way that no other woman could be.'

Chiara looked at the man and realised the extent of his ruthlessness. Even if she didn't agree to marry him—*and of course she wasn't going to marry him!*—she had no doubt he would do everything he'd just said. Including marrying someone for convenience and heirs. All she represented to him was a means to get to his destination faster.

She stood up. 'I don't understand why it has to be marriage—you could offer me a deal to buy the *castello* before the bank gets involved.'

'That was my plan originally. But since coming here... meeting you...it's changed. Now the stakes are higher, and I'm offering you an opportunity to stay in your home.'

As your chattel, thought Chiara, shocked at the lengths to which he would go, the depth of his need for vengeance.

She refused to let him see how intimidated she was. 'Well, as of this moment, I'm still the owner of the *castello*, Signor Santo Domenico, and quite frankly you're the last man on this earth I'd ever think about marrying.'

He looked completely unperturbed. 'So you're willing to walk away and never see the *castello* again? You strike me as the kind of woman who dreamed of getting married and having a family here.'

Chiara flushed all over. Was her innermost fantasy of dispelling the loneliness of this place with a large and loving family so painfully obvious? But in her fantasy she'd meet the love of her life, go travelling, and then return to the *castello* to live out the life she'd never had here, filling the place with happy sounds and not the echoing silence of her youth.

Feeling exposed, she said tightly, 'You have no idea what kind of woman I am, *signor*. Now, if you've said your piece, please leave.'

Once again Nico's conscience struck when he thought of the freshly dug graves he'd seen in the newer graveyard just a short while before. Perhaps this was evidence of what a life denying your emotions did to you. You became numb to everything except the goal. And the goal was almost in sight.

But something about the shadows under Chiara Caruso's eyes and the way she held herself made him feel uncomfortable. She looked delicate all of a sudden. Very alone in this huge room, with only an ancient dog for company.

Maybe she *was* a recluse?

He ignored the spark of curiosity—she was perfect for what he needed in his life, and that was all that mattered.

He took a business card out of his pocket and held it out. With palpable reluctance she reached out and took it from him. Nico noticed that she had small graceful hands. Unvarnished practical nails. His body stirred against his will, an image of those hands reaching out to touch his naked flesh surprising him with its vividness.

He gritted his jaw. 'Those are all my numbers, including my private one. I'm staying at a villa not far from here till tomorrow lunchtime. You have until then to consider my offer. If I don't receive a call I'll assume you're not interested.'

Chiara's head was bent down over the card as if she was studying it intently. A lock of long hair trailed over one shoulder and it gleamed a light mahogany in the light. His eye was drawn to her waist. Once again he could sense that her clothes were disguising a very classic feminine shape. The kind of shape that had been out of fashion for years but which was proving to be potent enough to snare his interest.

For a moment he hesitated, wondering if he was crazy to seek commitment with this woman. She intrigued him now, but could she sustain his interest for the length of a marriage? His sexual interest?

If the strength of his attraction was anything to go by, his body was telling him *yes*. And he was reminded of how little had sparked his interest in recent months. Certainly none of the tall, angular women he'd favoured before.

His wife would also be the mother of his children, and Nico surprised himself with a surge of conviction that he wanted a woman who would care for her children and not abandon them as he had been abandoned.

He couldn't trust any woman not to abandon her children, but at least Chiara Caruso knew about legacy—even if it hadn't been rightfully hers. She understood it. And evidently, if the state of the *castello* was any kind of indication, she was a woman who had been deprived of the better things in life. In Nico's experience it wouldn't take much to accustom her to the kind of luxuries he could provide.

But she was refusing to meet his eye now. Nico was used to women gazing at him with naked adoration and a lust that barely masked their instant summing up of his net worth. It was a silent dialogue he knew well and which he welcomed—because there was no game-playing or pretence of emotions that weren't there.

He wasn't used to this…this uninterest. Or antipathy. And he found that, refreshing as it was, it irritated him.

'Chiara.' His voice sounded tight.

Eventually she looked up and he saw fire in the depths of her eyes, making them glow. 'I did not give you leave to call me by my name.'

His pulse throbbed. A sizzle of something deeper than arousal infused his blood. Nico had to admire her spirit. Not many had the confidence to speak back to him and he realised that he'd underestimated her.

He dipped his head slightly. '*Scusami*. Signorina Caruso. I am offering you an opportunity to stay in your family home, which is more than anyone in your family ever did for anyone in mine. Think about it.'

Chiara desperately wanted to look away from those deep-set dark eyes but she couldn't. It was as if his gaze was winding a spell around her, holding her captive. The air vibrated with a kind of electricity between them.

She wanted him gone, so she could try and process everything that had just happened, so she said the only thing she knew that would make him leave. 'Fine. I will consider your offer.'

Nicolo Santo Domenico inclined his head and then he walked out.

Spiro trotted after him, as if to make sure he really was leaving.

Only when Chiara heard the powerful throttle of his car's engine did she move and go back over to the window, catching a flash of silver as it disappeared down the drive. She shivered, as if a cold finger had just danced down her spine.

The first thing Chiara did was to ring her solicitor and ask him for the deeds of the *castello*.

His sharp response—'Why do you want to see them?'—merely heightened the churning in her gut.

She asked him bluntly, 'Is it true that this *castello* once belonged to another family?'

The man was silent for a long moment and then Chiara heard muffled sounds, as if he was instructing someone to close a door.

He asked again, 'Why are you asking for this information now, Signorina Caruso? All you need to know is that the *castello* belongs to you until such time as the bank takes possession.'

'Please tell me the truth.' Her hand was gripping the phone receiver.

He sighed. 'Yes, I believe so—the *castello* did belong to another family, but they lost it around the time of the Second World War. The deeds have been in the Caruso name for decades... I really don't see how this has anything to do with—'

Chiara let the phone drop back into its cradle.

It was true.

When she was small she'd been fascinated by history and she'd used to beg her Papa to tell her stories about the *castello* and who had built it centuries ago. She'd wanted to know all about her ancestors—had they been Arab Moors? Or maybe marauding Greeks? Her father had used to laugh off her questions, telling her that her imagination would get her into trouble one day... She saw now how he'd neatly avoided telling her anything about the history of the *castello*.

Because he hadn't known? Or hadn't he wanted to admit the truth—that it didn't really belong to them?

Chiara felt the *castello* closing in on her, as if now that she knew, it was silently condemning her.

She walked outside, needing to shake off that uncomfortable feeling, Spiro loyally following at her heels. It was cool in the January sunshine and she drew in deep breaths of air infused with the evocative scents of the earth and sea. She'd often thought that if she could bottle this scent she would wear it for ever. It was *home*.

A home she was about to lose.

She'd spent so long yearning to see the world, but she'd never expected to be thrust out into it so precipitately. She didn't feel ready.

Chiara avoided the area near the small chapel and the graveyard and went down to her private place by the shore. It was a tiny sandy cove, sheltered on all sides by rocks. She sat on the rough sand and pulled her knees up to her chest, wrapping her arms around them. Spiro sank down beside her.

It was only now that she could let the tears flow—for her parents and for the shock of learning just how precarious her position was. She cried for a few minutes, until her face started to feel puffy, and then she forced herself to stop, wiping at her cheeks with the sleeves of her dress. She never usually indulged in self-pity.

She thought of Nicolo Santo Domenico in his bespoke suit, oozing sophistication and success. Arrogance. Retribution. Threat and a kind of redemption all at once. She'd never met anyone so ruthlessly compelling.

Giving in to an urge to find out more about the man who had just blown apart what little security she'd felt she had left, Chiara went back into the *castello* and fired up her father's ancient desktop computer.

Eventually it came to life, and she sat down in a worn leather chair to search for information on the Santo Domenicos.

The first thing to come up were pictures of *him*, looking even more astoundingly handsome than she remembered, dressed in a tuxedo at glittering functions. And in each one there was a stunning woman on his arm. Blondes, brunettes, redheads. He didn't appear to have a preference. They were all tall, slim and intimidatingly beautiful.

He wasn't smiling in any of the pictures. He looked driven. Stern.

Chiara quickly clicked on some other links that told the fabled story of how Nicolo Santo Domenico had displayed his entrepreneurial skills from an early age in Naples. He'd honed those skills and at the tender age of twenty-one had gone to New York and become a millionaire. Within five years he'd become a billionaire and a legend.

She unearthed a very old article from an Italian newspaper, asking what had happened to the once all-powerful Santo Domenico family from Sicily. There was no mention of the *castello*, just a general reference to the fact that they'd once owned huge tracts of land in Sicily but had lost it all. The implication was that perhaps the Santo Domenicos had run foul of the mafia.

Chiara shivered again, absorbing the information. Of course all this didn't mean that Nicolo Santo Domenico would have a leg to stand on if he was to challenge ownership of the *castello* in a court, but the fact was that the bank now owned the *castello*—or as good as. Nicolo Santo Domenico was merely capitalising on the fact that the *castello* was now available to him in a way it had never been before.

She stood up and walked slowly through the *castello*, noting how many of the rooms had long been shut up, with their furniture covered in dustsheets. Everywhere was crumbling and falling apart. It had been in disrepair for as long as Chiara could remember. The truth was that they'd never really been able to afford it—even when their crops had been providing an income.

The *castello* deserved to have new life breathed into it.

Chiara's heart squeezed to think that she wouldn't be here to see it. And then she realised she also wouldn't be here to tend her parents' grave. Or her grandparents'.

It was unutterably cruel to think of the *castello* being shut to her when her own family were laid to rest here.

As Nicolo Santo Domenico's were.

But, reminded a small inner voice, *Nicolo Santo Domenico is offering you a chance to stay.*

Through marriage.

The thought of marrying a man like him left her breathless with a number of conflicting emotions.

She'd never in a million years imagined that the faceless man she'd fantasised about all her life would actually appear on her doorstep, but as soon as she'd seen Nicolo Santo Domenico's hard and beautiful features she'd felt a pull of recognition deep inside, as if finally she had a face to put to the handsome prince of her dreams.

She felt disgusted at herself now. At the years of naive dreaming in a home that hadn't even been rightly hers.

And Nicolo Santo Domenico hadn't come for *her.* He'd come for the property, she reminded herself soberly. She was just a convenient by-product. Or a bonus. She shivered again, but this time it was in reaction to imagining what sharing intimacies with Nicolo Santo Domenico would be like.

Chiara saw her reflection in the window. She knew how she looked—plain and boring. Unvarnished. She'd inherited her large breasts from her paternal grandmother, along with her average height and the hourglass shape which had gone out of fashion about fifty years ago.

One day Chiara had heard her father say to her mother, *'Our daughter won't turn heads, but she'll make some man a fertile wife.'*

Her cheeks burned again as the humiliation came back.

And then she crushed the thought. She shouldn't be thinking ill of her father. But he had grown bitter after his wife hadn't been able to have any more children and he'd been denied the son he'd desperately wanted. Chiara wondered now how much of that had had to do with his knowledge of the provenance of the *castello*.

Had he wanted a son to ensure the Caruso name stayed alive within the *castello* because he'd known of the history?

Chiara let herself consider Nicolo Santo Domenico's… *proposition*. Surely he couldn't really mean to marry her? Was he really ruthless enough to convince himself that marriage to an unsophisticated Sicilian woman was worth the price of regaining his family inheritance?

Anger rose inside Chiara at the thought that he could treat her like a pawn. And that he'd assumed to know her, based on what he had judged of her appearance and demeanour. The fact that he hadn't been completely wrong made her pride smart. But there was so much more to her than a mere dream to marry and love in this place.

No matter what he'd said here today, he couldn't truly mean to go through with a marriage to a complete stranger.

Chiara thought of Nicolo Santo Domenico's expression when he'd left—almost smug. As if he'd achieved exactly the outcome he'd expected and knew she'd come around in the end, in spite of her refusal.

She wanted to dent that smugness. She wanted to shock him as he'd shocked her. She wanted to see him look as surprised as she must have looked this afternoon. She wanted to call his bluff and witness his panic when he really thought through the repercussions of his arrogant assumptions and demands.

CHAPTER THREE

NICO DIDN'T LIKE the sense of anticipation he felt as he waited for his driver to return with Chiara Caruso. When she'd rung him earlier that morning he'd offered to meet her at the *castello*, but she'd told him she'd prefer to meet him at his villa, so he'd sent someone to fetch her.

He paced back and forth on the terrace that wrapped around the side of the modern villa with its stunning view of the sparkling sea. From here he could see the land around the *castello* but not the actual building, which was a mix of architectural styles dating all the way back to his early ancestors, who had been Spanish. There were elements of Moorish architecture, and then more classical bits had been added over the years.

The effect was a snapshot of Sicilian history—a potent symbol of longevity and survival which had withstood the ages on its dramatic promontory overlooking the sea.

The emotional punch from his first view of the *castello* and his visit to the graveyard yesterday still lingered. The sense of urgency to reclaim what was his was even stronger now. As was his urge to claim Chiara Caruso. Last night he'd found her image stealing into his brain with a vividness that had unnerved him. He'd told himself it was only due to the fact that he'd decided to include her in his plans. Not because he hungered to know the secrets she hid under her shapeless outfit. Not because base instincts he hadn't indulged since he was a teenager had resurfaced. He was more than that now.

He heard a noise behind him and turned around to see the uniformed housekeeper leading Chiara out to meet him. He settled back against the wall and watched her walk towards him, unconsciously tensing himself against those base instincts she'd ignited so effortlessly within him.

But it was no use. In spite of the fact that she looked as if she belonged to another era, wearing a starchy white shirt with a big collar and a boxy dark jacket, arousal hummed in his blood. It was almost galling. A calf-length skirt did nothing to enhance her figure, and nor did practical flat shoes. Her hair was pulled back from her face and left loose and wavy around her shoulders.

It had been a long time since Nico had had any woman presented to him who wasn't coiffed to within an inch of her life. If he hadn't been so unnerved by the strength of his attraction to her he might have found it refreshing.

She walked out into the sunshine and he saw she was pale. The vivid green of her eyes stood out, unusual and arresting. He fought not to let his gaze drop to the full line of her breasts and straightened up, indicating for her to take a seat at a table nearby set with coffee and tea and small cakes.

She looked at the table, and then back at him. 'I'd prefer to stand.' She held a capacious black bag in front of her like a shield.

He faced her. 'Very well. Have you thought about what I said?'

Chiara could hardly breathe. Nicolo Santo Domenico was—unbelievably—even more gorgeous than she remembered. With his back to the astounding view, dressed in a

white shirt with its top button open and sleeves rolled up
and dark trousers, he could have stepped directly from the
pages of a fashion magazine for men.

The villa was breathtaking too, in its modern simplicity, built into a cliff overlooking the sea. A total contrast to
the *castello* and its ancient crumbling history. She'd never
seen so much pristine white furniture.

It hurt to look directly at the man, but she forced herself to meet his dark gaze. She'd felt full of bravado yesterday, but right now that was in short supply. Why had
she thought it was a good idea to come here? What had
she wanted to prove? She couldn't turn back now—he expected her to say something...

And then she remembered. The shock and humiliation.
The desire to see him lose some of that cool sense of en-
titlement.

She took a breath. 'I have thought about what you said,
Signor Santo Domenico, and I've decided that I'll accept
your offer.'

Chiara's heart was beating so hard she felt light-headed.
She waited for Nicolo Santo Domenico to register what
she'd said and then panic. Except he didn't look like a
man who would ever panic about anything. He looked
supremely assured. Not a flicker of reaction crossed his
face. Had he heard her?

She felt panicky. 'I said—'

'I heard you,' he said. 'Are you sure about this?'

Chiara had a sickening sensation that she'd misjudged
how to handle this situation badly. She forced herself to
nod. 'Yes. I'm sure. I want to marry you.'

'Va bene.'

He pushed himself away from the wall and strode back
into the villa. Chiara turned to watch him, her panic intensifying. She followed him inside. He picked up a mobile

phone and made a call. She heard him speak to someone on the other end.

'We will proceed with drawing up the contracts. Chiara Caruso has consented to be my wife.'

When he'd terminated the conversation he looked at her and frowned.

'What's wrong? You look like you've seen a ghost.'

'I thought… I thought if I said yes that you'd come to your senses.'

His frown grew deeper, and then something flickered in his eyes. Surprise? 'You called my bluff? You didn't think I really meant it?'

Now Chiara flushed. 'I just thought that when it came to it…to the prospect of taking me as your wife…' She stopped.

He shook his head and walked towards her. 'Oh, no, *cara*, you need to realise that I *never* make empty propositions.'

Chiara saw it then—the steely determination in his eyes. He wanted the *castello* badly enough to marry her. He really was that ruthless.

Feeling desperate, she said, 'But I'm not the kind of woman a man like you marries.'

'You do yourself a disservice, Signorina Caruso.'

His gaze flickered over her and her father's words came back to mock her, *'She'll make some man a fertile wife.'*

She didn't want to be a brood mare! She wanted to be loved passionately. This had been a really stupid idea. She should never have thought she could goad him.

She stepped back. 'I'm sorry. I've changed my mind. I can't do this.'

Chiara had started to walk out of the vast open space when she heard him.

'Signorina Caruso, wait.'

She stopped reluctantly. Nicolo Santo Domenico walked around her to stand in front of her. He looked incredulous.

'You would really prefer to walk away with nothing when I can offer you a life of ease and luxury? I am a very wealthy man, *cara.*'

Chiara didn't need to be reminded of his single-minded pursuit of success. She was watching it in action. 'I know. I looked you up.'

'Well, then, you know I am not making empty promises. I have homes in New York, Rome and London, as well as an island in the Bahamas.'

Chiara's heart squeezed. She'd longed to see those places all her life. But not like this. Not via a marriage of convenience to a cold-hearted vengeful titan of industry. She couldn't even begin to imagine what such a thing would be like. Day to day. Waking up next to a man who seemed far too powerful and dynamic to need something as banal as sleep.

She realised to her horror that she must have articulated something of her thoughts out loud when he folded his arms and answered her.

'I work mainly at my office in Rome, but I travel frequently to the States and London. You would be expected to accompany me when required, for necessary functions and social events. But in the main I see the *castello* as being my base—which is where you will reside when I don't require you.'

When I don't require you. Like an employee.

His arrogance was astounding. And yet the thought of leaving the *castello* behind for good was excruciating. *This can't be my only option,* she thought a little desperately.

'If I don't agree to marry you, would you allow me access to the *castello*? To visit my parents' and grandparents' graves?' At least if she had access she might not feel as if all links had been be severed.

A hard expression settled over Santo Domenico's features. 'Why would I when your own family didn't ever allow that basic access to us?'

Her insides tightened. Her father had been zealous about privacy and had only let staff or estate workers enter the *castello* grounds. She had a suspicion now that it had been a reflex, handed down from generations, dating back to when they'd had reason to be paranoid about intruders. *The rightful owners.*

'In answer to your question, I would afford you the same respect as was afforded to *my* family—so, no, you would not be granted access. Within a very short space of time, Signorina Caruso, your claim on the *castello* and this place will be gone for ever. It will be as if you never existed.'

Nicolo Santo Domenico's words were horrifyingly stark and brutal. Emotion rose. Terrified he would see it, Chiara whirled around and went back outside to stand at the terrace wall. Her eyes stung and she blinked rapidly.

The view was a view she'd looked out on herself many times, and yet she knew she'd never get tired of it. The scents...the sounds of this place...they were as much a part of her as her own flesh and blood.

She'd actually been born in the *castello*, because her mother had gone into labour three weeks before her due date. The housekeeper had helped her to give birth, but due to complications after the birth, and the delay in getting her to the hospital, her mother had not been able to have more children.

In spite of that, Chiara had always secretly loved the fact that she'd been born within the *castello* walls. As if she was as much a part of its fabric as the stones. She'd often wondered how many babies had been born there.

As much as Chiara had always wanted to travel and see the world, she knew she wouldn't last long unless she could return to this place. It fed her soul. The thought of leaving here and never being able to return was more than she could bear.

Nicolo Santo Domenico would take ownership no matter what—she didn't doubt that—and soon there would be fancy electronic gates permanently locking her out from her past and her ancestors. Removing her from the anchor of her life.

Chiara forced herself to try and cut through the emotion to think clearly, and her first thought was a churlish one—she'd only known Nicolo Santo Domenico for less than twenty-four hours and already he had an influence on her.

She'd called his bluff and it hadn't worked. Clearly he was willing to go as far as marriage.

Chiara looked out over the view and realised there was nothing between her and a precipitous drop to the sea except the terrace wall. She felt dizzy for a moment, as if the wall had suddenly disappeared and she was teetering on the edge of a vast void.

The question slid into her mind and she couldn't stop it. *What if you said yes? What if you just said...yes?*

She wouldn't have to take that leap into the void. She wouldn't have to face the heartache of never being able to pay her respects to her parents...her grandparents. She would see the *castello* restored to its former glory. A glory she'd never really witnessed.

Nicolo Santo Domenico might be willing to go as far as marrying her *now*, but once he saw how lacking she was in social graces and worldly sophistication—once he saw how unsuitable she was to be his wife—surely he'd realise that he'd made a huge mistake and call it off, move on to a more suitable woman?

A seed of hope bloomed in Chiara's gut. If they got divorced wouldn't she then have a chance to negotiate terms for access to the *castello*? At least visitation rights? It wouldn't be lost to her for ever.

For the first time since she'd heard his outrageous proposal, marriage to Nicolo Santo Domenico didn't seem like such a ridiculous suggestion.

Chiara heard a noise behind her and tensed—as much against the noise as at the way her blood leapt and her skin grew hot. It was disconcerting to find herself reacting like this. Disconcerting and galling that her own body could let her down so easily.

'Signorina Caruso?'

Chiara took a deep breath and turned around. She wasn't ready to leave her home. Her life. Not yet. Not until she'd negotiated terms to gain access. It was clear he wouldn't give her an ounce of leeway unless she agreed to marry him. But at least if she could do it on her terms then it might be worth the upheaval.

She looked at Nicolo Santo Domenico and told herself that if he wanted to insist on entering into a legally binding state to further his own interests then she would at least ensure that it would protect hers, too.

She lifted her chin. 'I will agree to marry you—but on one condition.'

There was a long beat of tense silence and then he inclined his head slightly and said, 'Not that you're really in a position to negotiate…but I'm listening.'

Chiara nearly crumbled at the last second, but she knew this was the only way she'd have a chance of keeping any kind of claim on the *castello*.

'My condition is that after six months we review the marriage and see how it's working. And there will be no question of having children until after the six-month trial period.'

As Chiara didn't expect Nicolo Santo Domenico to be remotely interested in giving up the parade of beauties in his life any time soon, she felt fairly confident that in spite of his pronouncement about heirs he hadn't actually planned on having them *now*.

He was silent for a long moment, that dark gaze far too assessing. Chiara fought not to squirm.

Eventually he said, 'That's actually *two* conditions. But very well. I agree.'

Chiara felt light-headed, and her heart palpitated madly as the enormity of what she'd just agreed to sank in, but she told herself she was doing the right thing. The alternative—walking away and never seeing her home again—was unthinkable.

Chiara held out her hand, 'In that case, you may call me Chiara.'

Nicolo Santo Domenico took her hand in his and Chiara almost jumped out of her skin at the electric shock.

He squeezed her hand firmly and said, 'And you may call me Nico. I look forward to getting to know you, Chiara.'

Chiara pulled her hand free abruptly, terrified he might see how he affected her. She knew there was a wall behind her, but suddenly she felt as if she took a step back she would be freefalling over that precipice with nothing to hang on to except the triumphant gleam in Nico's dark eyes.

And it was too late to do anything about it except go forward. And pray that she hadn't grossly underestimated him. *Again*.

* * *

A week later, Chiara's head was still spinning. As soon as she'd made it clear that she would marry Nico, the true extent of his wealth and privilege had become scarily apparent.

There had been a flurry of meetings at the villa with his legal people and her solicitor, who had pulled her aside and wondered if she was quite all right. She'd ascertained that, yes, the bank would take possession of the *castello* as soon as possible, so she'd found out all she needed to know—this was indeed her only option of retaining any contact with her home. Doing a deal with Nicolo Santo Domenico. A devil with the face of an angel and the body of a bare-knuckle fighter. A self-made billionaire who'd lived a life in pursuit of vengeance. Against *her* family.

Contracts had been drawn up and signed, and Chiara's life had been sent spinning in a direction she hadn't ever anticipated.

She looked at herself now, in the mirror of her bedroom at the *castello*. She was wearing the wedding dress that had belonged to her paternal grandmother, whom Chiara had loved dearly. Her *nonna* had shown her the dress before she died and then laid it carefully in its custom-made box, telling Chiara that she would love to think of her wearing it on her wedding day, even though she wouldn't see her.

Chiara had inherited her body shape from her grandmother so the dress fitted almost perfectly. It was a little threadbare in places, but it was still surprisingly pristine. Made of Sicilian lace, it had long sleeves and a high collar. It was demure, and yet Chiara felt very exposed when she noted how it clung almost indecently to her body, showing off her too large bust and hips.

But there was nothing she could do about it now. She was due to go to the *castello* chapel and marry Nicolo Santo Domenico at any moment now.

He had offered to buy her a dress and hire professional stylists, but she'd refused. She'd eventually agreed for him to enlist the help of a couple of local girls, and one of them approached Chiara now with the matching veil for the dress. She'd pulled her hair back in its habitual style and it fell loose and wavy down her back—she'd given up any attempt to tame it.

They attached the veil low on the back of her head and pulled it over her face, almost obscuring her vision.

Chiara had seen the looks the girls had exchanged as they'd helped her dress, but she didn't care. She knew this wasn't a real wedding, and if her aim was to make Nico regret marrying her as soon as possible then this was the way to go.

They'd barely exchanged two words all week as the preparations had taken over and Chiara had felt ridiculously relieved—even though she knew it was futile to think she could avoid her husband once they were married.

But, thankfully, it looked as if he was as reluctant as she for them to spend any time together. He'd told her as much during one of their brief conversations, saying, 'I will have to return to New York almost immediately to oversee a merger. There won't be time for a honeymoon.'

She'd responded with relief. 'I don't expect a honeymoon—this isn't a real marriage.'

He'd looked at her for a moment, as if he was about to say something else, but then they'd been interrupted and Chiara had taken the opportunity to escape.

Soon, she reassured herself, he would be back in New York, where he would be indelibly reminded of the kind of woman he preferred. By the time he returned to Sicily he would have decided to divorce Chiara and she could negotiate her terms.

She'd already checked with her solicitor and he'd assured her that once they were married, no matter what the contracts said, she would have rights as Nico's wife. That was all she needed to know.

The two girls stepped back. There was a knock on the door and a voice.

'*Signorina*, they are ready.'

Chiara sucked in a breath and tried to quash the ominous feeling that her confidence in predicting the swift demise of this marriage was all too shaky. She'd underestimated Nico before. But this was her only option—unless she wanted to take off the dress, pack it up and walk out of the *castello* for good.

She closed her eyes briefly, sending up a swift plea for a speedy resolution to all of this, and then she opened them again and turned around to face her destiny.

Nico was surprised at how on edge he felt as he waited for Chiara to appear at the entrance to the *castello* chapel. There was only a handful of guests. Her solicitor and his own legal team. There was no great pretence that this was anything other than a marriage of convenience.

Chiara had been surprisingly co-operative once she'd agreed to marry him, signing every contract put under her nose after brief consultation with her solicitor. In fact she'd been so amenable, particularly about the clauses that dictated how much of his fortune she'd receive if they ever divorced—she'd barely even looked at that part—that he'd had to instruct his own team to go through them again with a fine-tooth comb in case they'd missed something.

He'd given in to her demand of a six-month trial period, but he was confident enough to presume that by the time six months had passed she would be reluctant to give up her new lavish lifestyle.

But a small, annoying inner voice reminded Nico that Chiara had turned down all his offers for clothes, a dress... stylists. How ironic, he thought now, to have apparently found the one woman in the world who truly appeared to have no designs on his wealth—a member of the very family that had stolen his birthright!

There was a movement at the doorway and he narrowed his gaze. When she appeared, though, he wasn't prepared for the punch to his solar plexus. She should have looked ridiculous in the old-fashioned wedding dress, so traditional that it must have been made in the last century. And yet its sheer simplicity robbed Nico of any coherent thought for a moment as Chiara started to walk down the aisle.

Unaccompanied.

And if there was something about that lonely image that sparked some answering echo inside Nico, he denied it immediately.

Quite frankly, he was too distracted by the way the dress effortlessly showcased the full extent of Chiara's curves. The Venus de Milo made flesh. He even saw one of his legal team's eyes widen at the sight of her, and felt a rush of something very hot and possessive. *Crazy.*

If Nico hadn't been so acutely aware of what he was doing and where he was, he might have imagined himself to have slipped back in time some hundred years.

An ornate lace veil framed her face and dark hair. There was a small bouquet of flowers in her hands. When she finally reached his side he caught the delicate scent of wild flowers and earth...the sea. It was evocative and surprisingly sensual.

He turned to face the altar and was reminded again of how petite she was next to him. She reached his shoulder at the most. The priest started to speak, but the words washed over Nico as he realised that he had to restrain himself from reaching out to pull the veil up to see her face.

'I now pronounce you husband and wife. You may kiss your bride.'

Nico turned to face Chiara, overcome with a sense of anticipation he never would have expected to feel for his convenient bride, no matter how much she might stir his blood.

Her head was down-bent and he reached for the veil, pulling it up and over her head. He willed her to look up at him and finally she did. He sucked in a breath. No make-up. Just clear fresh skin and those remarkable eyes. Long dark lashes. And her mouth… Had it always been so full?

He'd never have expected it, but right now all he could think about was how much he wanted to kiss his bride. He caught her chin between his fingers and thumb, angling her face up to his. The church, priest and witnesses were forgotten as he fixated on that lush mouth. As lush as the rest of her, it trembled slightly, and he saw the tiniest hint of a pink tongue. A wave of need rushed through him.

His mouth was on hers before he could stop himself and this was no chaste kiss, mindful of where they were. This was fuelled by unexpected lust and desire. He gathered her to him, feeling those abundant curves press against his body. Soft where he was hard and aching.

It took a long second for him to realise that his brand-new wife wasn't responding as he'd intended. She was like a taut bow against him, quivering but not acquiescing. Her mouth trembled under his but didn't open.

With the utmost reluctance he pulled back and saw those wide green eyes as startled as a fawn's. Her cheeks were flushed. Her breasts moved rapidly against his chest.

He trailed his thumb down and along her delicate jawline, touched the corner of her mouth, making it open slightly. Right now there was nothing else in the world but this.

Nico said roughly, *'Baciami.'*

Kiss me.

Chiara's whole body was on fire. She was pressed so tightly against Nico's body that she could feel the delineation of every hard muscle under his suit.

This wasn't how it was meant to be! She'd been expecting a peck on the cheek. Nothing more. Then leaving the chapel. Enduring a couple of hours of their pseudo-happy wedding breakfast with total strangers before Nico left in his private jet to get on with his life and his work. Leaving Chiara at the *castello*, to come to terms with her new situation and the hope that she'd be served with divorce papers as soon as possible.

But she couldn't think about any of that now. All she could think of was Nico's firm mouth and how it had felt on hers. Like a brand. A hot brand of ownership. As if he didn't already own her, thanks to the price he'd paid. As if he had to kiss her like that to really stamp his mark on her.

He was still holding her and saying *'Kiss me.'* As if she hadn't just—

His mouth touched hers again, chasing away all coherent thought. And if she'd thought that last kiss was a brand then this was a brutal awakening.

Nico's mouth moved over hers, insistent, masterful. She had no choice but to open up to him, and when his tongue touched hers she almost lost the power of her legs, her insides turning to hot liquid jelly.

She'd longed her whole life to know the power of a transformative kiss. But this didn't feel transformative— it felt cataclysmic. Earth-shattering. Nothing so banal as merely transformative. This was scorching along her insides and lighting a fire deep within her that begged for *more*.

When he finally lifted his head again Chiara was aware of a vague sound and realised it was the priest, clearing his throat with increasing vigour. She felt undone...turned inside out.

She looked up into her husband's dark eyes and realised she hadn't a clue who this man truly was. And yet she'd just allowed him to breach defences she hadn't even been aware she'd erected over all the years of her isolation here at the *castello*.

She pulled back so abruptly she almost fell, and only Nico catching her arm stopped her. She glared at him, not even sure why she felt so angry. He'd just kissed her. So why did it feel like more than a kiss?

He held her arm and they walked back down the aisle. Chiara's face was flaming. When they stepped out into the bright morning sunshine she was momentarily blinded, but she rounded on Nico anyway, pulling her arm free of his grip.

She opened her mouth, about to demand to know why he'd kissed her like that, but then their guests walked out behind them and she had to close her mouth again. It felt swollen.

Nico led the way back to the *castello*, where he'd hired a local catering company to set up a wedding breakfast.

There she endured the further humiliation of making small-talk with one of Nico's legal team, aware every second that everyone knew this was just a business agreement.

Finally, when everyone had gone—including the caterers—Chiara pulled the veil off her aching head and massaged it with her fingers. She walked downstairs into the kitchen, Spiro at her heels, and for a moment felt grateful that at least she hadn't been separated from him.

After she'd fed Spiro she went back upstairs, wondering if Nico might have already left for New York. But when she walked into the drawing room, he was there, looking moodily at a family photograph of Chiara and her parents, holding a crystal glass in his hand.

She was very aware of the jump in her pulse, reminding her of that kiss and also of that secret part of her which didn't necessarily want to see the back of him so quickly. She was very aware that he'd divested himself of his jacket and waistcoat and she could now see that he wore a close-fitting shirt that left little to the imagination.

Once again she had the realisation that, even though she knew superficial facts about him, she didn't really know him at all.

He turned and saw her, where she stood in the doorway. He put out a hand. 'Welcome, *mia moglie*, would you like a drink?'

My wife.

The *castello* was now his. *She* was now his. The only thing protecting Chiara from being thrown out on her ear was the fact that she'd married him.

Panic mounted inside her as she questioned if she'd done the right thing. But she'd had no choice! she assured herself, trying to quell that panic.

'Yes, I'd like a drink.'

She walked into the room, trying to appear as nonchalant as possible, as if it was every day that she wore a vintage lace wedding dress that felt glued to her body like an indecent wrap. She'd caught his eyes on her at various times during the day and had wanted to squirm with embarrassment. No doubt he'd been sending up thanks that their wedding wasn't more public. *His unfashionable bride.*

He uncorked a bottle of champagne that had been chilling in a bucket and presented her with a glass of the sparkling golden liquid. She took it from him just as a fresh rush of humiliation landed in her belly as she recalled the kiss they'd shared. She had a suspicion that he'd been toying with her in some way.

She clutched the glass tightly. 'Why did you have to kiss me like that in the chapel, in front of everyone? The only person who doesn't know the truth of this marriage is the priest.'

He looked at her steadily. 'Maybe because I wanted to.'

She stared at him as something indefinable zinged between them. Not possible. Her and him. No way.

'You really didn't need to pretend to fancy me. We both know the kind of woman you prefer.'

He put a hand in his pocket. He couldn't have looked more louche. 'Oh, really? And what kind of woman would that be?'

Chiara's face grew hot. She took a quick sip of her drink, regretting opening her mouth. She tried not to cough as the bubbles fizzed in her mouth and down her throat. When she risked looking at Nico again he raised a brow, still waiting for her answer.

She paced away from him towards the window. Dusk was claiming the sky. How had the day slipped by so quickly? Why was he still here?

She turned around to find an arrested expression on Nico's face and she wrapped her arm around her middle in a subconsciously protective gesture. 'I've seen pictures of the women you like—tall, willowy. Beautiful.'

His dark gaze rose to meet hers. 'I might have agreed with you—until you appeared today looking like the most innocent temptress ever created.'

Reaction set into Chiara's bones and she started to tremble slightly. Nico put down his glass on a side table and moved towards her across the room. He looked as if a civilised layer had been stripped back from his urbane surface and Chiara found it more mesmerising than she wanted to admit.

The air between them crackled. The room suddenly felt sweltering. She might almost have sworn that a fire burned in the massive fireplace just feet away, but a fire hadn't been lit there since Christmas.

He stopped in front of her. She couldn't seem to form a coherent thought. 'I don't... Why are you still here? You were supposed to be getting on a plane to New York.'

He frowned. 'This is our wedding night—why would I be getting on a plane?'

Chiara's head started to throb. 'But it's not a normal wedding.'

He stepped closer. 'This was the perfect wedding. No false declarations of love, no heightened emotions. Just two people coming together for a mutually beneficial cause. To save the *castello*.'

'Which you would have done in any case.'

He shook his head. 'I'm not a patient man, Chiara. I wasn't prepared to wait to regain my inheritance.'

'An inheritance you had to *pay* for.'

It seemed to be important to goad him right now, to keep him back—because she was very afraid that if he came any closer he'd see just how brittle she felt right now. How ready she was to shatter into a million pieces if he touched her again.

This was where her real vulnerability lay. In this space between them that shouldn't exist. Because he shouldn't be looking at her as if he wanted to...to devour her.

He shrugged one wide shoulder. 'The money I couldn't care less about. The *castello* is mine now, and that's all that matters. And into the bargain I have you as my wife.'

'But you don't want me…not like that. You should go… your business must need you.'

If Chiara could just get him to leave now, he'd go to New York and realise that whatever he was feeling for his convenient Sicilian bride was a total aberration. He was a highly sexed man—it oozed from his every pore. He needed to be reminded that she wasn't his type.

But Nico looked straight into her eyes and said, 'On the contrary, I find that I *do* want my wife. Very much.'

CHAPTER FOUR

'*ON THE CONTRARY, I* do *want my wife. Very much.*'

Chiara could barely breathe through the palpitations of her heart. Nico's gaze left hers and moved down. He reached out and took a tendril of her hair that trailed over her shoulder. He twined it around his fingers and tugged gently, so that she had to move forward.

She could feel the heat of his hand through the delicate material of the dress. Her nipples peaked into two hard points and she bit her lip, praying he wouldn't look down.

He said, almost musingly, 'It's been a long time since I saw a woman with hair as long as yours.'

Chiara answered quickly, 'It's not fashionable. I should get it cut.'

He speared her with a dark look. 'Do *not* get it cut.'

Her heart palpitated at his authoritative tone. 'You can't order me not to cut my own hair.'

Nico gritted his jaw for a second, as if biting something back, and then he said with faux politeness, '*Please* do not cut your hair. I like it.'

Chiara knew she was fighting a losing battle. To have all this man's attention focused on her...she'd have to be made of stone not to react.

She was melting into a puddle of lust. Her body felt painfully alive and sensitised. She ached in secret places—

between her legs. Her wedding dress suddenly felt constricting, and all she wanted was to feel a cool breeze on her bare flesh. She imagined Nico's big hands reaching for her, pulling the dress apart...baring her to his dark, hungry gaze.

That lurid thought was like a bucket of cold water landing on Chiara's head. *What was wrong with her?*

She jerked away from Nico so fast that her hair pulled and she winced. She realised she was still holding her glass with a death grip and put it down on a nearby table.

She sucked in a breath. Nico looked unperturbed. She gestured between them. 'I don't know what this is... I barely even know you.'

'And yet we're married.'

She glared at him. 'Only because you made sure I was between a rock and a hard place.'

His mouth tipped up slightly and he drawled, 'Believe me, *cara*, I know how *hard* it feels.'

She couldn't stop her gaze from dropping and she saw the bulge pressing against his trousers. She glared at him again, even as her body quivered in reaction to this evidence of his arousal. 'That is disgusting.'

'That is chemistry—and we have it, whether you like to admit it or not.'

Desperation mounted. 'We don't! It's only because you're highly sexed and you probably haven't slept with a woman since you arrived here and—'

He held up a hand. 'Stop. I have been with enough women to know that true chemistry is a rare thing. I haven't wanted a woman this much since—' He stopped at that, his face darkening. 'That's not important. What *is* important is that I want my wife, as unexpected as that fact might be, and I have every intention of consummating this marriage tonight.'

In spite of her instincts, which were screaming at her not to let this happen, for reasons she wasn't even sure she fully comprehended Chiara was intrigued. She wanted to know more about the other woman he'd wanted as much. She wasn't as intrigued by the dart of dark emotion that thought engendered. This man shouldn't be provoking her emotions.

'You're little more than a stranger!'

'And yet I'd say we know more truth about each other than most couples who get fogged up by emotions that aren't real.'

He closed the space between them and Chiara's already weak resistance got even weaker. She'd never experienced such a compelling pull towards another human being. And she hated herself that it was for someone who was so singularly ruthless. That it was for someone who saw her only as a pawn.

He reached for her, placing his hands on her waist and tugging her towards him. She put up her hands, but all that did was bring them into contact with his chest—a wall of hard muscle.

God help her, but she felt it in her bones. The inevitability of what was to come. Because she *wanted* it. Though every self-preserving instinct was screaming at her to run, there was also something rebellious within her stirring to life after all these years, willing her to do the most audacious thing she'd ever done...

Maybe they *did* know more about each other because of the lack of emotion? But in spite of that she desperately needed to know that there was more driving his ruthlessness than just a need to succeed where others had failed.

'Why was it so important to you?' she blurted out.

He frowned. 'Why was *what* so important?'

'The *castello*—getting it back. You said yourself that

you felt more detached about it than your ancestors and that's why you were successful. So would it have really mattered if you hadn't got it in the end?'

He tensed, his hands tightening on her waist. 'Why are you asking me this now? It's done.'

'Because I just...need to know.'

His eyes bored into hers. 'I did it for my father, who wanted it for his father, who had memories of this place. It was his dying wish that I return this land to our name and I will always regret that I wasn't able to do it in time. I grew up in Naples, but it was never home. We were reminded of that by the gangs who ran our neighbourhood. We were never welcome. I've never felt at home anywhere. You'll probably think this sounds ridiculous, but as soon as I walked into the *castello* it felt like home...'

Chiara's chest felt tight. She recalled having that impression when he'd arrived—as if he belonged here more than she did. She understood the concept of *home* all too well. She'd been lucky enough never to question hers. Until now. And she knew what grief felt like and had an insight into what it must have been like to want to fulfil a parent's dying wish.

She had a sense that Nico was already regretting saying what he had. She could see his expression closing, becoming impenetrable. Acting on instinct, she put her hand up to his face, tracing his hard jaw.

'I'm sorry your father died before he could come back here.' Her voice was husky. For the first time since she'd met him she felt a moment of affinity with him.

The tension she'd been holding on to eased inside her. Nicolo Santo Domenico wasn't as cool and impenetrable as he appeared.

His hands were still tight on her waist. 'I don't want to

talk about that. In fact I don't want to talk at all. I want you, Chiara.'

I want you.

The words sent a thrill of excitement through Chiara. In spite of the fact that everything about this whole situation was unorthodox, and had morphed out of all sense of control, she knew she didn't want to be anywhere else right now.

Trembling from head to foot at the strength of the feelings and desires building within her, she said, 'I want you too.'

Nico's eyes flashed. He pulled her to him, spearing a hand into her hair at the back of her head and curving his other arm around her waist.

When his mouth met hers Chiara almost combusted on the spot. Her fingers clutched at his shirt. She could feel his arousal digging into her belly and it made her ache even harder. The kiss was wild and hot, too consuming for Chiara to wonder if she was doing it right or wonder what Nico would do when he discovered his very traditional Sicilian wife was a virgin.

She had no time to think at all, because Nico broke off the kiss and swept her up into his arms, striding out of the room and up the stairs. He stopped in the corridor and she felt the tension in his bunched muscles.

'Which way?'

Chiara's old bedroom lay to the right, but the master bedroom, which she'd prepared while fully expecting it not to be used, lay further down to the left. She lifted a hand and pointed in that direction and Nico moved, all coiled power and intent.

He strode through the door, kicking it shut behind him. The moon was rising outside, bathing the room in a silvery glow. Nico let her down beside the bed. Her shoes had fallen off somewhere along the way, unnoticed.

She looked up at him, breathless with desire and a kind of wonder that this was actually happening. To someone like *her*. Who had harboured fantasies like this all her life. But the feelings fluttering inside her were too dangerous to try and analyse now—because how could she be feeling anything for someone she hardly knew?

For a taut moment neither one moved, and a sudden cold dread moved through Chiara at the thought that Nico was coming to his senses and wondering what on earth he was doing.

It was the very thing she'd wished would happen. But then he said, 'Turn around.'

Chiara turned around, and the relief rushing through her was more than immense. It was dangerous. Because she knew she should let Nico know just how innocent she was. But she was afraid he'd stop looking at her as if she was the only woman in the world. She wasn't ready for this moment to end. And so she said nothing.

Nico brought his hands up to move Chiara's long hair over one shoulder. He noticed they were shaking. *Dio.* What was wrong with him? He was behaving like a virginal groom who had never undressed a woman before. But he couldn't remember the last time he'd been so hard and aching. He scowled at himself. *Not even then.*

Her hair was heavy and silky. He pulled out the tie holding it back from her face and pushed it aside over her shoulder, to reveal the bare back of her neck. He had an urge to press his lips against that spot and so he did, noticing that her petite frame shuddered slightly.

Who would have known it? he marvelled. That he would have considered marriage to a woman like this and that he would want his convenient wife so much? When he'd first thought it through he'd fully intended for this to be a traditional marriage in all aspects, but even he had considered giving her some space before making this a marriage in bed.

But from the moment he'd watched her walk down the aisle earlier he had known there was only way this day was ending. In this bedroom. *Right now.*

He found the top of her dress and the long line of buttons that ran down her spine. A bead of sweat broke out on Nico's brow, as he painstakingly undid every button until the last one, just above her buttocks. It was a surprisingly erotic experience when he was used to women leaving little to the imagination. The dress gaped open to reveal her pale back and the clasp of her bra.

He undid that and felt her go very still. Giving in to an uncharacteristic moment of conscience, Nico put his hands on her shoulders and asked, 'Okay?'

The fleeting thought occurred to him that maybe she was innocent, but he dismissed it. In this day and age? No matter how sheltered someone might be, it was nigh on impossible to hang on to any kind of innocence or purity.

He was surprised at how that thought made him feel. Almost disappointed...

She nodded her head and he heard a faint, 'Yes, I'm fine.'

Nico slipped his fingers under the dress and pushed it over each smooth shoulder and down her arms. Now she was bare from the waist up, her back a sinuous curve that made his blood sizzle.

His voice was unbearably rough. 'Turn around, Chiara.'

She waited an infinitesimal moment—enough to have Nico's nerves screaming with tension and need. He almost laughed at the notion that she was innocent now. This women was a siren and she knew exactly what she was doing! She had to! He was on fire.

Chiara's heart was beating so fast she felt light-headed. No one had ever seen her naked before. She'd never even inspected herself in the mirror, shying away from looking at her too pronounced curves.

And yet something new and bold within her compelled her to turn, and when she did an intense heat flooded her whole system. Nico's eyes widened and colour slashed across his high cheekbones. His chest moved rapidly, as if he'd been running.

Chiara's bare breasts felt full and heavy. Nipples tight and stinging. Nico reached out a hand and cupped one full weight in his hand and little beads of sweat broke out on Chiara's brow.

He shook his head, as if dazed. 'I want to see *all* of you.'

Chiara put her hands to the dress, where it hung precariously on her hips, and pushed so that it fell down. Now she wore just her panties.

Nico's hand dropped to his side and Chiara saw him curl both hands into fists, as if to stop himself from reaching out again.

He said, 'I never thought a woman like you could exist.'

Intense self-consciousness flooded Chiara and she brought her arms up to cover her chest and between her legs. 'I'm too big—'

Immediately he stepped forward and took them down, saying, '*No*. You are beautiful. You embody pure sensuality, Chiara.'

She kept her gaze lowered, feeling even more self-conscious now—because she was practically naked while he was still fully clothed.

As if reading her mind, Nico took his hands from her again and started to undo the buttons on his shirt. Now it was her turn to look as bit by bit his chest was revealed, broad and powerful, with a smattering of dark hair that led in a line down his flat muscled abdomen and underneath his belt.

His hands were there now, and he undid his belt and trousers. With an economy of movement he pushed them down, taking his underwear with them. She sucked in a breath, taking in the majestic power of his aroused body, rising proudly from the dark curling hair between his legs. Her mouth watered and she wanted to taste him. It shocked her how carnal she felt. And, how right it felt.

'Chiara…don't look at me like that.'

She looked up, her face burning. He smiled and there was a falling sensation in her tummy—he'd never really smiled at her before.

'I won't last if you look at me like that.'

Oh.

He took her hand to lead her to the bed behind them and she stepped out of the dress which had pooled on the ground in a mound of silk and lace.

She desperately resisted the urge to believe this moment was special, but it felt significant. She was about to give herself unhesitatingly to a man who had swept into her life and turned it upside down in the space of a week. A man who had behaved in an unbearably ruthless manner but who had shown her that there was something running deep under the surface.

There was more to Nicolo Santo Domenico—Chiara knew it.

He laid her down on the bed and looked at her for a long moment. Then he came down beside her. She desperately wanted to explore his body but she didn't have the nerve. Any anyway he robbed her brain of any power to think when he started to touch her, saying, 'I want to explore every bit of you, taste you…'

He encouraged her to lie back and do nothing as he proceeded to do just that. He started with her mouth, drugging her with deep kisses, while his hand explored her breast and pinched her nipple, making her turn to liquid and squirm against him, silently pleading for more.

Then he moved down, taking his time, teasing her until her nerves were screaming and she was begging for mercy. When he finally surrounded her nipple with his mouth and sucked it into the hot wet cavern she screamed.

His hand moved down, over her belly and to the juncture between her legs. He pushed them apart with gentle force and Chiara held her breath. He lifted his head and watched her as his fingers explored the place where she ached the most.

She turned away, embarrassed at how turned-on she was, but Nico turned her back to face him as his fingers explored all the way into the heart of her, where she was hot and wet.

'You are so ready for me… It's incredibly sexy, *cara*. And it's the same for me.'

He took her hand and wrapped it around him, exactly as she'd wanted to do herself before. She was awed by the feel of him, steely strong and covered with hot silky skin. He felt so vulnerable and yet never more powerful.

'I need you *now*.'

She looked at him and the moonlight glazed his features with a silvery hue. His expression was stark. She nodded her head and he moved over her body, pushing her legs further apart with his thighs.

She could feel him press against her and had an urge to push her hips up, instinctively seeking that deeper union. He huffed out what sounded like a tortured chuckle, and once again she was struck by this lighter version of Nicolo Santo Domenico and how he made her heart swell dangerously.

He put a hand under her buttocks, angling her up towards him. She was totally at his mercy, and yet she had never felt more powerful than right at this moment. She trusted him implicitly. It came from deep inside her.

And then, with a surge of his body against hers, he thrust deep inside her. Her body bowed in shock and awe at the intrusion. There was a moment of red-hot pain and tears stung her eyes.

He stopped and looked down, the shock she felt mirrored on his face, '*Chiara?* You're a...*virgin?*'

She nodded miserably, all her self-confidence draining away. She fully expected Nico to pull back, disengage, look at her with disgust. But he didn't. Instead something ferocious lit up his expression and he put a hand between them, his fingers touching the point where their bodies met.

'Bear with me, *cara*, it won't hurt for much longer. Trust me.'

She held her breath as Nico started to move again, slowly this time. His fingers moved against her, making her feel something besides pain and discomfort—a burgeoning pleasure.

And then, miraculously, the pain diminished and the glide of his body in and out of hers took on an ease that hadn't been there before. She could feel her body adapting to his and a whole new set of sensations took over. Aligning them. Making her seek a deeper connection.

Instinct took over. This was an age-old dance and Chiara found herself succumbing to its rhythm. She wrapped her legs around Nico's hips and felt him slide deeper. She silently urged him to go harder, faster, as tension mounted in her body and begged for release.

He was remorseless, though, refusing to give in to her demands, eking out her pleasure, until Chiara had to bite into his shoulder to stop herself begging out loud.

And then something snapped inside him…some control he'd been clinging on to—*for her benefit?* The thought was too fleeting to hang on to because Chiara got a sense of how restrained he'd been when his movements became wilder and less controlled, pushing her higher and higher. Finally she climbed to the top of the peak and her whole body tautened like a bow against his for a long, infinitesimal moment, until finally she fell over the edge and into a sea of pleasure more exquisite than she'd ever known, so exquisite that she never wanted it to stop.

Nico's huge body went still and she felt the rush of his release deep inside her—she was too stunned to consider what that meant. He sank over her, deep shudders racking his body, and she could feel her own body still pulsating, milking every last ounce of pleasure from him.

Nico stood under the pounding shower spray as dawn spread across the sky outside the bathroom window. His body felt wrung out. Weakened from an overload of pleasure.

He braced his hands on the wall, bending his head against the sluicing water as if it might wash away the memory of how completely he'd lost it.

She'd been a virgin. *A virgin.* Nico had never made love to a virgin before—not even when he'd been one himself.

And, to Nico's disgust, his first reaction had been one of very carnal male satisfaction. To know that he was the only man she'd known intimately. To be the first man to wring that unbelievably sensual response from her lush body. To be the first to see her orgasm and feel the contraction of those tight muscles around his—

Dio. He cursed again.

He could still see the look of wonderment on her face after they'd made love. It had taken him completely unawares. He was used to women feigning emotion, not really feeling it. It had to have been because she was innocent. She wasn't like his other lovers. World-weary and jaded. Cynical.

Never in a million years had he imagined that the attraction he felt for Chiara would be so all-consuming and intense. To the point where he hadn't even thought of protection. Something he'd never failed to do with any other lover.

But she's your wife.

That might be so, Nico thought grimly, and he had fully intended theirs to be a marriage that would produce heirs. It was part of his plan. He'd told her that. But he'd also promised to honour the six-month trial period. Even he had thought that wasn't such a bad idea.

But any kind of coherent rational thinking had gone up in flames as soon as he'd seen her naked body.

He tried to curtail the resurgence of desire just from thinking of her. He reassured himself that it was highly unlikely that one night would have got Chiara pregnant. And next time he wouldn't forget.

Next time.

His body reacted forcibly to the thought of introducing his very innocent Sicilian wife to all the pleasures lovemaking had to offer and he cursed through gritted teeth as a slew of X-rated images flooded his brain.

He switched the water to cold.

When Chiara woke it was bright. She could feel a soft cool breeze skating over her skin. The window must be open. She felt incredibly…at peace. Sated in a way she'd never felt before. Even though when she moved experimentally her body ached all over. But not with pain. With remembered pleasure.

And then it all came rushing back—every Technicolor moment of her awakening. She looked round but she knew she was alone in the bed. The sheets were creased. She saw her wedding dress draped carefully over a chair. Nico must have done that, because *she* certainly hadn't given it a thought last night. All too eager to strip off.

She pulled the sheet over her face for a moment, groaning softly. Who had she been last night? A total wanton. A sensualist in training. No inhibitions—or too few to mention.

After that first time Nico had only had to touch her for her to be eager to experience that extreme pleasure again. She had a vivid memory of him moving down her body, pushing her legs apart and putting his mouth on her *there*.

She pulled the sheet down from her face and blinked, trying to will away the rush of heat sweeping up through her body, which was still tender. And yet she knew if he was here right now, looking at her and touching her, she'd probably give in all over again.

Where was he?

She sat up, the sheet falling away from her body. She looked down and could see marks on her breasts. Faint and pink. Evidence of his touch. Mortified, Chiara scrambled from the bed and found a robe to pull on. She belted it tightly and made her way downstairs.

Spiro appeared at the bottom of the stairs, tail wagging. She patted him on the head. There was no sign of Nico in the main rooms or in her father's old office, which she presumed he would take over.

She found him in the massive kitchen. He was dressed in dark trousers and a light shirt, and he was drinking coffee and reading something on a tablet. Chiara felt a rush of self-consciousness as she stood in the doorway.

He glanced up and saw her, and indicated with his head towards the stove. 'I made fresh coffee.'

He looked back down at his tablet again. 'The first thing we'll have to take care of here is the WiFi—it's ridiculously slow. And then we need to hire staff. A housekeeper and a maintenance person to start with.'

A lead weight sank into Chiara's belly. She'd had no idea what to expect the morning after a night such as she'd just experienced, but it wasn't this: Nico speaking to her as if she was some kind of assistant, not the woman he'd made love to all night with an ardour that had made her feel—

She slammed a lid down on that thought, terrified that it might show on her face. She shouldn't be feeling anything.

But you are, whispered a little voice.

Chiara walked into the kitchen, acutely aware of her naked body under the robe while Nico was fully dressed. She needn't have worried, though, because he wasn't looking at her. She poured herself some coffee and brought it over to the table, sitting down at the opposite end to her husband.

He was pristine and cool. A million miles from the passionate lover of last night. He looked up at her and finally something seemed to register.

He put down the tablet. 'How are you this morning?'

Solicitous. Impersonal.

Chiara struggled to keep her frayed emotions in check and to be as cool as him. 'I'm fine, thank you.'

'Bene.' Nico stood up. 'I've made a change in my plans. I'm going to go to Rome today for some meetings and I'll go to New York next week instead.'

Chiara put down the cup, a tiny spurt of excitement making her pulse jump. 'Will I be coming with you?'

He frowned. 'Why would you come with me for business? No, you'll stay here unless there's a social function that requires your attendance. There will be enough for you to do, preparing the *castello* for its refurbishment.'

The spurt of excitement sputtered, but a tiny flickering flame of hope refused to die. She said, 'I thought… after last night…that perhaps our marriage might not be so…businesslike.'

Nico's face was unreadable. 'You were a virgin, *cara*, it's natural for you to confuse lust with emotion. I married you for the *castello*, and because I need a wife and heirs. Nothing has changed in that regard.'

Oh, God. She thought of the things he'd told her about fulfilling his father's dying wish and how the *castello* had felt like home. Meaningless platitudes. Humiliation was immediate and acrid in Chiara's gut.

She went cold as the true enormity of her naivety sank in. What for her had been a deeply transformative experience evidently hadn't been anything of the sort for Nico. How could it have been? She'd been a virgin.

Then something else struck her and she went even colder. She stood up, barely aware of the clatter of her chair on the stone floor. 'We didn't use anything…protection.' It hit her—she could be pregnant right now.

Something flashed across Nico's face. He said heavily, 'I know.'

Panic gripped Chiara, twisting her insides. 'You did it on purpose—you took advantage of my inexperience so that you could try and get me pregnant.'

Nico's face tightened. 'Your opinion of me isn't very high.'

Chiara waved a hand. 'Can you blame me? All I've seen is evidence of how ruthless you are. But even I hadn't considered you could be *this* ruthless.' She could feel hysteria building and had to breathe to calm herself.

Nico started towards her and then he stopped. Colour slashed across his cheeks and to Chiara's eternal shame, in spite of her anger and humiliation, she could feel her body yearning for his again.

'Last night... I wasn't thinking clearly. Of course I didn't intend for you to get pregnant. But as we are married, and I told you part of our deal was having heirs, it wouldn't be the worst thing in the world, would it?'

Yes, it would, thought Chiara. Because even though she knew she would feel a fierce love and protectiveness for her baby, she didn't want it to happen like *this*. In a confusing blur of lust and mindlessness. She hadn't intended for that to happen at all! And yet it had...

She said starkly, 'Last night was a mistake. It shouldn't have happened.'

'I never lied to you about wanting a real and practical marriage, Chiara.'

She backed away from the table, thinking of all the emotions that had been flowing through her the previous night. Thinking of how she'd felt when she'd woken. At peace. Sated. *Optimistic.*

Her grand plan that he would be in New York by now, realising what a mistake he'd made, lay in tatters at her feet. Thanks to her weakness and susceptibility. Her deep-seated wish to believe in some romantic fantasy.

'I should never have agreed to this marriage. It was a mistake.' Feeling desperate, she added, 'I want an annulment.'

He shook his head. 'It's too late. The marriage is consummated.'

Chiara's gut churned as suspicion turned to certainty. 'You seduced me on purpose.'

Of course he had! He was ruthless enough to cover all the bases. All he'd had to do was compliment her once or twice, make her feel as if she was the only woman on the planet, and she'd melted in a puddle at his feet. He'd played her like a fiddle, and her virginity had made it so much easier.

His expression was closed off. 'I seduced you because I wanted you.'

Chiara emitted a semi-hysterical laugh. 'Conveniently enough on our wedding night.'

And without using protection!

Nico picked up his tablet. 'My plane is waiting to take me to Rome. We can continue this discussion later.'

When he would undoubtedly try to seduce her again?

Chiara mocked herself. He wouldn't have to *try*. If he so much as touched her she'd go up in flames.

He started to leave the kitchen and then he turned to face her. 'Chiara, there will be many more benefits to this marriage than most. We are under no illusions about feelings and we both share a love for this *castello* and want to see it restored. The fact that we have chemistry is a bonus and will make this easier.'

And then he was gone.

Chiara heard the faint roar of an engine throttle and then silence. She sat down heavily in the chair and stared into the space he'd just left unseeingly.

She couldn't believe she'd been so utterly naive. And yet how had her life in the *castello*, being sheltered and overprotected, ever prepared her for something like this? For a man like Nicolo Santo Domenico?

She had to face the very stark fact that she'd merely replaced her parents as gatekeepers with her new husband, who clearly had no intention of letting her have a life outside the *castello*.

Her hand went to her belly again. *She could be pregnant. Already.* And she could imagine him greeting that news with a smug satisfaction that the Santo Domenicos were on their way back to domination.

All Chiara was to Nico was a pawn. And the worst thing about it was that he'd never tried to dress it up as anything else.

But last night had given Chiara a glimpse into another part of herself. She'd become a woman. And for a moment she'd believed there was something between them. She'd indulged in a vision of a *real* marriage. And she'd been utterly, astoundingly naive.

Last night might have been a sensual revelation for Chiara. But for Nicolo—no matter what he'd said about chemistry—it had to have been a very pedestrian experience. She'd given him a tool with which to coerce her to commit to this marriage fully. And that tool was her own weakness.

Chiara could see the future stretching out before her. She would be endured. Much as her father had endured her, disappointed that she wasn't a boy. She realised now that her fear of leaving the *castello* was far less than her fear of getting lost completely in the whirlwind of Nicolo Santo Domenico's life. Of finding herself pregnant and trapped for ever with a man who saw her only as a pawn. Never mind herself—she couldn't do that to an innocent child.

A sense of panic gripped her. *She wasn't pregnant. She couldn't be.* Life wouldn't be so cruel.

But she had to seize her chance now, before Nico came back. Before he touched her again and saw that he'd touched her emotions as much as her body.

She should never have thought she could manipulate Nico by marrying him. She'd underestimated him at every turn. She wouldn't make that mistake again.

CHAPTER FIVE

Five months later

'I THINK WE'VE found your wife, Mr Santo Domenico. I'm sending you over some pictures so you can see for yourself. She's in Ireland, working in a restaurant in Dublin. Also, there's something you should be prepared for... She's pregnant. When you confirm it's her you'll have her back within twenty-four hours.'

Nico's private investigator's words rang in his head. One word in particular: *pregnant.*

Nico got up from behind his desk and walked over to the window, which showcased a titan's view of Manhattan here at the heart of his global corporation which encompassed everything from real estate to media and tech industries. Enough to keep ten men busy, never mind just him. But his mind hadn't been focused on his businesses for weeks now. *Months.* Five months, to be exact.

He scowled, still incensed that his very meek and innocent Sicilian wife had had the temerity to leave him and disappear into the ether like a ghost the day after their wedding night.

His satisfaction that Chiara had been found was eclipsed by anger, because she'd put him in a very awkward position for these last few months. All his peers knew that he'd married, and yet he had no wife to show for it. His explanation that she was renovating the *castello* in Sicily was beginning to wear thin. Only a week before, at an exclusive charity auction, one of his adversaries had slyly questioned if his wife was, in fact, real.

Oh, she was real all right.

The erotic charge of their wedding night lingered in Nico's blood, much as he wanted to deny it, and the thought of having her back in her rightful place was precipitating a very unwelcome sense of anticipation.

For a man who didn't dwell on his past actions—and certainly none involving his lovers—their wedding night and the following morning had played ad infinitum in his head for the past five months.

Specifically, that first image of his wife naked. That memory was burned into his brain like a provocative brand. He could still see the luscious curves, the heavy breasts, the tiny waist and full hips. Her hair long and wild. She'd looked like a beautiful nymph.

He hadn't considered that she might be so innocent, in spite of her being so unsophisticated. An anomaly in this day and age. It was no wonder that she'd been so affected.

But it had been a mistake to give in to his hormones like that. It had exposed him. And it was only because she was so inexperienced that she hadn't capitalised on his momentary weakness, like another, more cynical woman might have.

When she'd appeared in the kitchen the following morning and he'd seen the look on her face—shy, and still suffused with the same wonder he'd seen the night before—he'd felt a lead weight sink into his belly.

He hadn't tried too hard to refute her accusation that he had deliberately tried to get her pregnant because it was better that she think him capable of that rather than reveal that he had lost all sense and reason.

Coward... whispered a snide inner voice. He ignored it.

As much as he wanted their marriage to be a real and practical one, he didn't want her to develop feelings for him—because he would never return those feelings and it would make the marriage untenable. And so he'd left her under no illusions that there had been anything remotely romantic about their wedding night.

If Nico hadn't learnt to divorce himself from his emotions he would still be in Naples, hustling to make a few euros from stolen phones, or seducing rich and lonely female tourists.

He would never have fulfilled his father's dying request—to reclaim the Santo Domenico rightful inheritance and bring respect back to the name. *Finally.*

But now, even though he'd achieved what he'd set out to do—and much more besides, having created a vast personal fortune in the process—Nico couldn't rest. He had an errant pregnant wife to track down.

She'd left him a note, the contents of which were also burned into his memory—much as he didn't like to admit it.

Dear Nico,
As you will no doubt have noticed, I have left. I made a mistake in agreeing to marry you. We are not suited to each other. I only agreed to marry you because I felt it would be one way of securing my right to retain contact with the castello *and the burial place of my family.*
I think you would have to agree that you can find someone eminently more suitable than me. I don't

*want any of your money. I just want a divorce and
access to the castello a couple of times a year.*

*Please take care of Spiro. He is old, and probably
won't live much longer, but I'd like to think of him
enjoying his last months in comfort. I've left instructions for his care and the details of his vet.*
Yours,
Chiara Caruso

Chiara Caruso. Not Chiara Santo Domenico. As if they
hadn't even married! And she cared more for that dog than
him. That stung.

Her solicitor had got in touch after she'd disappeared,
asking if Nico would grant her a divorce. He'd flatly refused.

What irritated Nico, though, was the fact that it hadn't
been the possibility that she might be pregnant that had
made him refuse—it had been a knee-jerk instinctive reaction. *He didn't want to let her go.* And he wasn't even
sure why. He had the *castello* now, he could divorce and
remarry—someone eminently more suitable. Exactly as
she'd suggested.

But Nico had never been good at taking other people's
suggestions. Especially when he didn't want to do something.

None of the women he'd met in the last five months had
interested him in the slightest. He'd found himself comparing their sleek thoroughbred thinness with the lush curves
of the women he'd married.

Damn her.

Nico heard the distinct *ping* of a new email from behind
him and went back to his desk. He sat down and clicked
on the link. Images filled the screen. Images of his wife.
Entering and leaving what looked like a small, intimate

Italian restaurant on one of Dublin's leafy city streets. The same kind of Italian establishment that populated cities the world over. This one was called Bella Toscana. Unoriginal and utterly pedestrian.

She was dressed in a black top and trousers and a white apron. He tensed as his gaze narrowed on the very evident swell of her belly. *Pregnant.* She'd be five months pregnant now. That small waist had stretched to accommodate her pregnancy.

Nico had always seen having a family as an abstract thing. A promise to his father. A duty to fulfil. A burden, almost. But now, as he looked at the image of his pregnant wife, he didn't feel abstract or dutiful... He felt a surge of something very primal. Possessive.

Mine. My seed.

Nico was shocked at this evidence that their wedding night had borne fruit. *If you're the father,* said a snide inner voice. Who was to say Chiara hadn't slept with another man just after him?

The thought of her sharing that look of wide-eyed wonder with another man made something even more primal and possessive beat through him. She wouldn't. But then... what did he know? He barely knew her. But she had a hold on his libido he didn't like.

He ignored the snide inner voices and let the prospect sink in for a moment. *He had a family.* The revelation sent conflicting emotions through him.

He immediately thought of his father, heard his gruff voice... *'Nicolo, you have to have a family or our name will be gone for ever. You are all that is left of what was once a great and powerful dynasty. The Santo Domenicos cannot be allowed to fade away with such a stain on our name. You cannot let that happen... Promise me, Nicolo... Promise me.'*

And he'd promised him. Just as he'd promised him to regain the *castello*, whatever it took, along with restoring their fortune and good name.

Nico looked at the pictures again and focused on Chiara's face. She looked much the same. Her long hair was pulled back into a ponytail that swung over her shoulder. She still wore no make-up. She looked pale. Tired. That realisation made him feel uncomfortable.

He recalled the unusual light green of her eyes all too easily. And the way they had glowed like translucent emeralds as he'd joined their bodies. His gaze caught on her full breasts, pushing against the top she wore.

His body rose to rampant life.

Inferno!

He closed down the images and picked up his phone. When the call was answered at the other end he said tersely, 'It's her...yes. Definitely.'

Nico stood up again and walked back over to the window, the lingering heat in his body being replaced with icy cold resolve and anger.

'No, that won't be necessary,' he said. 'I'll go and get her myself.'

'They want the short pasta, Tony. Not the linguine.'

Chiara stifled a smile as the head chef scowled and made a rude comment about people not knowing how to eat Italian food properly. She put a hand instinctively on her neat bump, rubbing it distractedly. The baby hadn't moved in a while, but she wasn't concerned. It usually seemed to sleep when she was active, and then bounced around when she was trying to sleep—which didn't help her energy levels.

All she wanted to do was sleep...except sleep let the demons take over her mind. The nights were the hardest...

when she couldn't block out the memories of *him*. Her husband. The man she'd left after one night of marriage.

One night had been enough to tell her that she was way out of her depth. She'd known she was out of her depth but she'd ignored the voices telling her so, too greedy to experience what he was offering. And it had burnt her. Badly.

She'd spent the first couple of months cursing herself that she hadn't tried harder to negotiate a deal in which marriage hadn't been necessary. Surely he would have agreed to *something* if she'd pushed him enough?

Now she'd never know. *And you would never have had that night,* reminded an inner voice. The night that had changed her life. Literally.

At first she'd tried to ignore the signs that she was pregnant—missed periods—telling herself it was stress. And it *had* been stressful. Her first time out of Italy, living in a foreign country with minimal English. But she'd done well, and she was proud of how she'd survived and thrived.

If you could call waitressing *thriving*.

She could imagine the scathing look her husband might give her. Because he *was* still her husband. He'd comprehensively rebuffed any overtures from her solicitor to agree to a divorce. *Why?* She kept circling back to that question.

And then her conscience struck with the other constant refrain. *You have to tell him about the baby.* She knew she did. Some time. But not right now. When she felt ready.

Heartburn crept up Chiara's oesophagus just at the thought of initiating a meeting with Nico. Coming out of her hiding space...seeing him again in the flesh...

'*Chiara*... Earth to Chiara.'

Chiara blinked and the restaurant came back into focus.

One of her fellow waitresses was standing in front of her with her hands full of plates.

She jerked her head towards the door. 'Someone has just come in…can you seat him?'

Chiara lambasted herself for spacing out and snapped into action. 'Of course—sorry, Sarah.'

She grabbed a couple of menus and turned around to greet the new customer, planting a fake smile on her face. But it soon slid off.

Recognition was swift and brutal, because this customer stood head and shoulders above all other mere mortals. The menus fell out of her nerveless fingers.

It would appear as if she didn't have to worry about initiating contact with her husband. Because Nicolo Santo Domenico was right here. In the flesh.

Somehow Chiara managed to form some words. 'Can I help you?'

Those dark eyes flashed. 'I've found what I'm looking for, but I'll take a black coffee. Strong.'

Chiara's brain felt sluggish with shock. Her husband was here, in this small, unremarkable restaurant. *I've found what I'm looking for.* He'd been looking for *her.*

She could feel the simmering tension. The barely banked anger. She saw it in his eyes and fought against putting a hand on her belly, where his dark gaze had just rested. She'd felt it like a physical touch. Or the lash of a whip. Censorious.

She finally kicked into gear—before her boss came over to see what the stand-off was about. She picked up the menus and said, 'Of course. Please take a seat and I'll bring your coffee right away.'

Nico was lowering his tall, broad frame into a chair as she turned away, her heart palpitating. She felt sick. Clammy. She was all fingers and thumbs at the coffee machine, cursing herself for not thinking more clearly. She spied the open back door nearby and for a second thought wistfully of making a run for it. But at that moment she looked back into the restaurant and caught her husband's eye.

He shook his head very slowly and deliberately. *Don't even think about it.*

Chiara finished making the coffee and carried it out from behind the counter, praying she wouldn't spill it all over the floor. She put it down in front of Nico with a clatter, belatedly taking in his pristine suit and tie. His clean-shaven jaw. Ridiculously, she found herself wondering if he had to shave twice a day or once? She'd slept with him but she didn't even know that useless information.

She was about to turn away when a large warm hand clamped around her wrist. The shock of his touch was blistering. A rush of X-rated memories filled her head, making her dizzy.

'Sit with me, *mia cara moglie.* It's been so long since I've seen you.'

Beloved wife. She was no beloved wife. She'd been a means to an end and she'd walked herself into the situation, believing that she could somehow emerge unscathed. She was far from unscathed now, at five months pregnant. And, as much as she knew this wasn't the ideal situation for a baby, from the moment she'd had to accept she was pregnant she'd felt a fierce love and protectiveness for her unborn child.

A child that didn't deserve to be born into this mess.

Anger rose and she welcomed it, pulling her hand and wrist free of his hold. 'What do you want, Nico? I'm working.'

He cast a disdainful look around the restaurant and then looked back to her. He said coolly, 'No wife of *mine* needs to work.'

Feminist hackles Chiara hadn't even known she possessed rose. 'I like working and I need to survive.'

'Because you ran away.'

'I told you—the marriage was a mistake.'

His eyes narrowed. 'Ah, yes, your kind note. I never lied to you, Chiara. I never pretended emotions were involved. I thought you understood it was a logical business agreement. A marriage of convenience.'

Chiara tensed. She was giving too much away. 'Yes, I did understand that. But I changed my mind.'

Now he was accusing. 'You married me just so you would be in a better position to negotiate terms?'

She sat down, defeated by Nico's presence. 'Can you blame me? You weren't giving me any options.'

Nico regarded his wife across the small table and felt the pull of desire in his groin. He cursed silently. He couldn't remain unaware of how lush she looked. Her breasts were bigger, straining against her top. And suddenly he thought of other men looking at her fertile body. Desiring her earthy beauty.

Because he could see it now. She *was* beautiful—in spite of her lack of adornment. She had stunning bone structure and a wide lush mouth. He had to fight off the memory of how swollen it had looked after his kisses. And those unusual light green eyes that seemed to change colour every second. They were like rare jewels.

He forced his attention away from her body and the desire she was sparking with an effort he resented.

He drawled, 'There are plenty of women who wouldn't consider marriage to me such a chore.'

Chiara sat back and folded her arms. 'Well, by all means divorce me and marry a more willing woman. I won't stand in your way.'

Nico let his eyes drop expressively to the swell of her belly. 'I think it's a bit late for that.'

She blanched, as if she'd forgotten for a moment. 'How do you know it's yours?'

Nico looked up again at her tart tone and assessed her show of bravado. It was all too flimsy. He felt the truth in his bones. This baby was *his*. A sense of satisfaction he couldn't ignore rippled through him.

'You were a virgin. I can't really see you hopping into the next available bed.'

She bit her lip and said, 'Maybe I didn't—but don't underestimate me.'

A cold fury swept through Nico at the thought of her in another man's bed. He said, with quiet but lethal economy, 'You will never be unfaithful to me, Chiara.'

Chiara felt the intensity of Nicolo's steely tone. A little shakily, she said, 'I presume that works both ways? Or am I to be subjected to a series of mistresses kept in luxury apartments in every major city of the world?' Though, she had to admit that the few times she'd looked him up on the internet since she'd left, he hadn't appeared with another woman. She didn't like to admit how relieved she'd felt.

'We are married. I see no reason not to remain faithful if my...appetites are satisfied.'

A sizzle of something hot arced between them and shock slammed into Chiara to think that Nico might— She shook her head mentally. She had to be imagining it—he couldn't *possibly* fancy her like this. She'd lost whatever small waist definition she'd ever had!

She'd never really believed him when he'd said they had chemistry. Not on *his* side, anyway. She believed that he'd wanted her enough to sleep with her, but no more than that. He hadn't felt the all-consuming desire she had.

The morning after their wedding night had shown her

in no uncertain terms that he'd been as strategic about seducing her as he had been about everything else. Cutting off any chance she might have to escape their vows by claiming non-consummation. By not using protection.

Chiara opened her mouth to remind him of that, but then a shadow loomed over their table and she looked up to see her boss, a barrel-chested man called Silvano, who was also from Sicily. He was looking from her to Nico and then back to her.

'Your break isn't for another hour, Chiara.'

Nico stood up, rising to his full height of six foot three. He topped her boss by some inches, and the man immediately looked ineffectual. It almost made Chiara giggle, and she realised she was close to hysteria.

'Not that it's any of your business, but this woman is my wife and she no longer works for you. I have come to take her home.'

Her boss looked at her. He was a nice man, and he'd been quite protective of Chiara since he'd realised that she was pregnant.

'Is this true?' he asked.

She stood up, more conscious of her ungainly belly now than ever, and feeling very flustered after what Nico had just revealed. *He wanted her.* She hadn't been prepared for that.

She nodded reluctantly, knowing there was no way out of this. 'Yes, it's true. I'm sorry.'

The man shrugged. 'Mondays are always dead. If you need to leave I won't stop you… Unless you want me to?'

He shot a look at Nico, but Chiara didn't feel like giggling any more.

She avoided her husband's eye. 'It's okay, Silvano.' Her boss was a traditional Italian man, after all, and he no doubt welcomed someone turning up to claim her.

He stood back. 'Get your things, then. I'll send on whatever wages you're due if you give me a forwarding address.'

Chiara shook her head and felt a part of her lament that her brief taste of independence was to be over so soon. 'No, share them out with the staff. I won't need them.'

He put up his hands. '*Va bene*—whatever you wish.'

Silvano stepped away, and Chiara turned to go into the staff room at the back of the shop. A hand caught her arm and she reluctantly looked at Nico. He seemed taller and broader than she remembered.

'One of my men is round the back.'

He thought she was going to run again. She pulled her arm free and glared at him. 'I don't think I'd get anywhere very fast, do you?'

'How many women were sharing that room?' Nico's voice rang with condemnation.

He was referring to the room she'd been renting, in a big house carved up into numerous flats. Salubrious, it hadn't been.

'There were eight of us.'

'In bunk beds!'

'Rent is expensive in Dublin. They were nice girls.'

She fought not to sound defensive. They'd mostly been Brazilian students, in Ireland to learn English. And Chiara had found the communality of their living quarters—while not ideal, obviously—a novelty after living in the *castello* for so long, with all that space to herself.

'We looked out for each other and they helped me with my English.' She was proud that she was almost fluent now. She'd discovered an unknown aptitude for languages.

Nico made a rude sound, and then he said, 'If it had ever got out that you were there, living like that... You could have put the baby in danger.'

Chiara hid a dart of hurt. 'Don't pretend that you care about the welfare of the baby. All you care about is that you have an heir—which you planned all along.'

For a moment he said nothing, and all Chiara could hear was the hum of the private jet's engines and the soft muted murmurs of the staff at the other end of the plane. Then he turned towards her, and she could see his strong hard features tighten with some expression she couldn't decipher.

'The truth is that I had no intention of not using protection that night. No matter what you might believe about my ruthlessness.'

She was surprised he remembered what she'd said. 'What do you mean?'

His jaw clenched, and then he said with palpable reluctance, 'By the time we got up to the bedroom protection was the last thing on my mind. It's something I've never done before. That night... I wasn't capable of thinking straight.'

The fact that his tone was almost accusing led Chiara to believe him. She hated the betraying quiver of awareness deep down between her legs. He wasn't telling her he wanted her *now*. How could he when she looked like a beached baby whale?

Then he asked, even more accusingly, 'Would you have told me?'

Chiara's hand instinctively went to her bump, and his eyes followed it and then moved back up. There was a wealth of emotion she hadn't expected in his expression for a moment, before it became a stern mask again. And she wondered for a second if she'd misjudged his ruthlessness when it came to having children.

She took a breath. 'I know I wouldn't have been able to keep it from you. But I'm not sure when I would have told you…before or after the birth. I did believe that you deserved to know, at least.'

He frowned. 'What's that supposed to mean?'

'I was going to tell you that I fully intended bringing up our child on my own. I still believe that a loveless marriage is not a good environment for a child.'

Nico turned to face her more fully. The awareness deep inside her grew more acute. He dwarfed the chair he sat in. And the whole plane.

'That family photo in the *castello* showed a seemingly content family, yet you admitted yourself that it wasn't all that harmonious.'

Chiara wanted to ask him why he was so cynical, but she felt suddenly shy. Which was crazy. He'd all but barrelled back into her life and kidnapped her! Even if she *had* come willingly. Because she really had no choice. Not any more.

'We weren't perfectly harmonious, no,' she admitted reluctantly. 'I was close to my mother, but after she had me there were complications and she couldn't have any more children. My father… He was disappointed he didn't have a son. He didn't think a farm was an appropriate place for a girl, so I wasn't allowed to get involved in the business, and then it all collapsed anyway.'

'Why were they so protective of you?'

Chiara felt like squirming under Nico's scrutiny. He hadn't been so curious about her when he'd been railroading her into marriage. So why now?

Reluctantly she answered. 'I was sickly as a child. Nothing specific, but I was prone to picking up infections. I grew out of it, but by the time I did my parents were used to home-schooling me and keeping me close.'

She opened her mouth, then closed it again. She felt deceitful, but she really didn't want to admit that her parents' marriage hadn't been a truly happy one. It would only confirm his cynical beliefs.

A steward approached and interrupted with a discreet cough. Nico tore his gaze away from Chiara to look at the man.

'Excuse me, sir, but we'll be on our final descent into Rome shortly.'

'Rome?' Chiara asked when the steward had walked away. She'd only been to Rome once before, on an educational tour with her parents.

Nico looked at her. 'Yes, I've been invited to a formal dinner tonight, at the French ambassador's residence. It's the perfect opportunity to show everyone that my wife isn't a figment of my imagination.'

Chiara felt the lash of his censorious tone again. It made her hackles rise. 'I'm nothing to you but a pawn. You *bought* me along with the *castello*.'

'You allowed yourself to be bought,' he pointed out in a drawling voice. 'You wouldn't have lasted two minutes outside the gates of the *castello*.'

Chiara flushed at that. 'But I did last. I lasted five months.'

'Your place is by my side, as my wife and the soon-to-be mother of my child.'

Nico looked away from her then, and down at his palm tablet. Chiara felt like a child. As if she'd been summarily dismissed. She bit back a growl of frustration and looked out of the window as the plane landed in Rome.

The irony wasn't lost on her. She was fulfilling her fantasy of travelling and having new experiences while she'd never been more trapped.

'I didn't know it could look like this!'

Chiara stared at her reflection in shock. Her unruly hair

was tamed into sleek shiny waves for the first time in her life. She had cheekbones. And full red lips. Her eyes were huge. She looked like a different person. Like the kind of person she saw in magazines.

'You have beautiful, naturally wavy hair, Mrs Santo Domenico, you just need to use the right products to make it look its best.'

Mrs Santo Domenico. The use of her married name broke her out of her uncharacteristically self-absorbed reverie. Since they'd landed in Rome it had been a whirlwind. Nico had been on his phone for the entire journey to his apartment, situated in one of Rome's most beautiful buildings, in one of its most exclusive areas.

He had the top apartment, with an outdoor terrace that offered breathtaking views over the ancient city. There was even a lap pool. And the Colosseum was within spitting distance.

On arrival, he had handed her over to a team of stylists to get her ready for the function. Chiara might have been insulted if she hadn't been so relieved.

She'd barely had time to draw breath, never mind let her new reality sink in. *Nico had found her and within four hours she'd been returned to Italy.* If she thought about it too much she felt dizzy.

'How many months pregnant are you, Mrs Santo Domenico?'

Chiara looked at the stylist, who had replaced the hair and make-up girl behind her.

'Five months.'

'Come with me. I've chosen a few dresses that should suit.'

As Chiara followed the very slim and sleek woman into a bedroom suite that had lots of wardrobe rails stuffed with clothes she tried not to feel totally intimidated. Her experience of shopping for clothes was via online bargain websites.

About five glittering dresses were hanging on a rail nearby and the stylist had started looking at them and looking at her.

Chiara said apologetically, 'I'm sorry I'm not very tall.'

The stylist smiled conspiratorially. 'Don't worry. Most people are about your height, and designers cater for normal women these days.'

Relief washed through Chiara as the woman pulled out a black dress and said, 'I think this one will be perfect. Try this on. I'll help you with the zip.'

Chiara went into the bathroom, and just as she was ruminating on her very plain white underwear, and how it would look under the dress, there was a knock on the door and the stylist handed her a box.

Chiara opened it to find the most beautiful underwear under layers of tissue paper. Black lace. And surprisingly practical. In exactly her size. Her cheeks flamed as she put it on, wondering how they had known her size. Had Nico told them? She wouldn't have credited him with remembering, but then she couldn't ignore the sizzle of awareness that had been between them since the moment he'd appeared in the restaurant.

When she was dressed she came out, and the stylist turned around and exclaimed, '*Bellissima*, Mrs Santo Domenico!'

Chiara didn't believe her, and reluctantly looked at herself in the full-length mirror. She sucked in a breath. The dress had a wide vee neck and then fell in soft flowing layers of chiffon to the floor. Her pregnancy was unmistakable, but the clever cut of the dress managed to flatter and make her look almost petite.

There was a knock at the door at that moment and then a voice. 'Signor Santo Domenico is ready to leave.'

The stylist jumped into action, giving Chiara a wrap and a bag and helping with her shoes—a pair of black strappy sandals. At the last moment Chiara remembered her plain gold wedding ring and slipped it onto her finger. It was snug; her fingers had swollen slightly with her pregnancy.

And then, when she was ready, she took a deep breath and steeled herself to greet her husband.

CHAPTER SIX

NICO WAS HAVING a hard time focusing. He put it down to the fact that he had his wife by his side for the first time since they'd married and he wasn't used to being at a function with someone. But that wasn't it. The reason he couldn't focus was because when Chiara had appeared in the drawing room of the apartment a short time before she'd looked endearingly shy and uncertain. And...*gorgeous*.

She was a sleek and coiffed version of the woman who had walked down the aisle to marry him. Unrecognisable as the woman who had come to him that day in the villa in her boxy shirt and jacket and calf-length skirt. He wanted her just as much, if not even more, because he knew exactly what she was hiding under all that elegant packaging. A raw and earthy sexuality.

They stood amongst a throng of Rome's elite society now, and more than one man's glance had lingered on Chiara.

Her hair was pulled back on one side and coiled over the other shoulder in a shiny Hollywood wave. The vee of the dress drew the eye to her creamy cleavage. Nico had had to restrain himself from demanding she wear something less revealing, because he knew that she was probably the most chastely dressed woman in the room right now. And yet he looked at her and all he could think about was sex and how his body ached for her. *Had been aching for five months.* He'd never denied himself the pleasures of sex for that long.

He felt almost angry that the neat plan he'd devised to marry Chiara Caruso had all but blown up in his face.

Her arm was linked in his and he realised she was gripping him so tightly she was almost cutting off his circulation. He looked down at her and could see naked terror on her face. 'Are you okay?'

She looked up at him and all he could see were those huge green eyes. How had he ever thought her nondescript?

'I've never been to something like this before. I don't know what to do or say.'

Nico's conscience pricked. He could see the faint shadows under Chiara's eyes. He'd whisked her out of Dublin, put her on a plane, and now she was here, at one of Rome's highest society events of the year. There weren't many who could swim easily in an environment like this.

And he could remember all too well what it had been like when he'd attended his first such event. He'd felt raw and uncultivated, and he'd been sure people were looking at him expecting him to steal the silver.

'When was the last time you ate?' He'd noticed that she hadn't eaten on the plane. In fact he noticed now that apart from her bump she'd lost weight. She looked delicate.

She blinked. 'Breakfast... I think.'

Irritation surged. 'You're not looking after yourself—or the baby.'

She turned to face him, pulling her arm free of his, eyes flashing. 'I'm not the one who arrived like a whirlwind and gave me hardly enough time to pack, never mind eat.'

Nico's conscience smarted even more. He took Chiara's elbow and led her into the dining room, where the rest of the guests were heading. 'There's a five-course meal this evening so make sure you eat. Tomorrow we'll set up an appointment with a specialist and make sure everything is all right with the baby.'

Chiara felt prickly, and completely out of her depth. She'd never been in such an opulently decadent place before. Glittering chandeliers and hundreds of candles bathed the guests in a honeyed glow inside the huge ballroom of a medieval Italian palace—the home of the French embassy.

Chiara was nearly blinded by the jewels hanging off necks, ears, throats and wrists. Each woman was more beautiful than the last and the men were handsome and statesmanlike.

Sleek waiters in black and white uniforms moved among the guests with exquisite canapés and champagne.

It was seriously intimidating, and Chiara felt absurdly self-conscious in her dress.

Nico had looked at her earlier as if she'd had two heads. When she'd asked if she looked all right he'd just said a gruff, 'You're fine. We should go.'

She also felt far too jittery and far too aware of him. It was the first time she'd seen him in a tuxedo, apart from in photos on the internet, and she still hadn't got her breath back fully. How could one man be so distractingly gorgeous?

She was the only pregnant woman here. Every other woman was about a foot taller than her and the size of a stick.

'Everything *is* all right with the baby, if you must know. I was seeing a very nice doctor in Dublin.'

Nico made a non-committal sound. 'We'll still see a specialist here, and I'll make sure we have the best doctors available on stand-by in Sicily.'

They reached their table and Nico pulled a chair out for

Chiara. 'I'm not due for another four months,' she pointed out as she sat down.

Then she noticed that Nico was walking away and a spurt of panic gripped her. Wasn't he meant to be sitting beside her? He took a seat directly opposite, but as the table was about six feet wide he might as well have been on the moon.

She noticed that he was in between two very beautiful women, a blonde and a redhead, who both seemed to be vying for his attention. She felt a spurt of dark emotion. Something she'd never experienced before—jealousy.

He looked across at her and raised a brow. She forced a smile, determined not to let him see how affected she was.

She felt very exposed and gauche, and at that moment a tall and very regal-looking woman took the chair on Chiara's right-hand side, while an ancient-looking man took the seat on her left.

To say Chiara was dreading the ordeal ahead was an understatement, and when the scary-looking woman asked, 'Well, then—who are you and what do you do?' Chiara's stomach fell to the floor.

She said truthfully, 'I'm no one important at all. I'm here with my husband—Nicolo Santo Domenico.'

The woman immediately perked up and looked Chiara up and down, taking in her protruding belly. '*Very* interesting. First of all, *never* tell anyone you're not important—because it's simply not true. Now, you must tell me all about yourself because if you're Santo Domenico's wife then I'm sure you have an interesting story… You know everyone used to call him "the man who can't be tamed"?'

The woman glanced across the table to where Nico sat and then winked at Chiara, saying, 'I'd say you've put the cat among the pigeons this evening, my dear.'

'What did Princess Milena say to you?'

Chiara looked at Nico, sitting in the back of the car in shock. 'She was a *princess*?'

He nodded. 'Princess Milena of Genoa. One of the oldest royal lines in Italy.'

Chiara absorbed this. 'But she was lovely...we had such a nice conversation.'

Nico sounded sceptical. 'She's famously taciturn and intolerant of people, and yet every time I looked over at you she was laughing.'

Chiara shrugged. 'We were talking about everything and anything.'

'Did she ask about me?'

Chiara raised a brow, intrigued by this glimpse of a less arrogant Nico. 'Paranoid?'

His jaw clenched. 'I went to her looking for investment once and she refused to see me.'

'She was curious as to how we met.'

'What did you tell her?'

'The truth...that it was through the *castello*. I see no point in hiding the facts. Obviously I didn't elaborate on the business end of our arrangement, but I don't think she believes it's a romantic match.'

'*No* marriage in that world is a romantic match. It's so rare you'd be more likely to see a unicorn at one of those functions.'

'I don't believe that. Why are you so cynical?'

'Because in my experience love is a myth peddled by writers, poets and artists to distract from the reality of life—which is that inevitably you're on your own.'

'What happened with your mother?'

Nico turned his face towards her. It felt as if they were

in a cocoon as Rome flashed past them outside, its lights winking and fading.

'What's my mother got to do with this?'

Chiara heard the warning in his voice but ignored it. She was carrying this man's child. She needed to know who he was. 'A lot. She was your *mother*.'

'No, she wasn't. She gave birth to me, but that's about it. She left when I was only a few days old. Abandoned me and my father.' He sounded harsh and he turned away, presenting her with his profile.

Chiara's heart squeezed. She could hear the hurt in Nico's voice even though she knew he probably wasn't even aware of it. 'You never saw her again?'

He was silent for so long she thought he was going to ignore her question, and then he said, 'She turned up at my office here in Rome a few years ago, asking to see me. I refused.'

Carefully Chiara said, 'I can understand why you reacted like that…but she might have had something important to say…wanted to explain why she did what she did.'

He turned to look at her again and Chiara almost shrank back at the harsh expression on his face, lit up by the neon lights outside. 'I have no interest in her explanations, whatever they might be. She is dead to me. This subject is closed.'

She might have had something important to say.

Chiara's words scored at Nico's insides like blunt knives. He hated it that he'd felt compelled to respond. To say something. He hated it that he was now thinking of that day when his assistant had come into his office, frowning and saying, 'There's a Signora Santo Domenico here to see you—she says she's your mother.'

At first Nico had been too shocked to respond, and then

a sense of sheer anger and hatred had rushed through his system so strong that he'd shaken with it.

He'd stood up and said, 'Tell her I'm not available and tell her never to return.'

He hadn't slept properly for a couple of months afterwards, and part of the reason was the guilt he'd had no control over. Exactly the emotion Chiara was provoking now. If anyone should be feeling guilty it was his mother, not him.

They arrived back at Nico's apartment and he felt wound up in a way that only one or two things could alleviate. Physical exercise or sex. He stood beside Chiara in the lift and saw how she was avoiding looking at her reflection in the mirrored doors.

'Why won't you look at yourself?'

She met his eye and he could see her blush. How could she blush? *Because she is still little more than a virgin.* That thought did not help Nico's levels of tension. Nor did the confined space, the scent of Chiara's evocative perfume or her lush body just inches from touching his.

'I've never liked looking at myself. And now... I don't feel like myself.' She gestured with a hand to the dress and styling. 'This isn't me.'

Tension made Nico's voice harsh. 'You're my wife—this *is* you now. You'll just have to get used to it.'

He saw how she paled when the doors opened. Nico felt dangerously close to losing the veneer of civility he'd grown over the years; dangerously close to the raw uneducated teenager he'd once been. All he wanted to do now was to lift Chiara into his arms, strip off that flowing provocative dress and lay her down, bare, on his bed, and then sink into her hot tight body and lose himself in oblivion until he felt focused again.

But she was pregnant. She was out of bounds. He had

given her a separate bedroom. He didn't know if they could make love without harming the baby—this was uncharted territory for him. The fact that he found her even more attractive now was something he had not expected and didn't know how to navigate. He wasn't used to holding back.

She turned to face him in the marbled hallway, avoiding his eye. 'Goodnight, then.'

She turned to leave and Nico said, 'Wait.'

She stopped and turned around.

Gruffly, he said, 'You had Princess Milena eating out of the palm of your hand and she's one of the toughest nuts to crack. You looked beautiful this evening.'

A little flare of pink came back into her cheeks and Nico felt ridiculously light for a second.

'Thank you.' She turned around again and left, and Nico stood watching the empty space for a long moment. Then he went to his bedroom, found some sweats and went to the gym and exercised until he couldn't breathe. Then he took a cold shower.

Only then, when he was utterly exhausted, did he feel some of the tension leave his body.

'You looked beautiful this evening.'

Chiara lay awake for some time. She blamed the baby for starting its nightly Samba routine, but really it was due to everything that had happened that day.

That morning, waking up in the overcrowded room she'd shared with all those girls, she'd never have guessed she'd be ensconced in Nico's luxury apartment in Rome by midnight. After having attended her first high-profile social event as a married woman.

In a way, she could admit that she was relieved Nico had found her, because telling him about the baby had been weighing on her mind more and more. And now it was done. The only thing she had to come to terms with now was how her life would fit in with his.

Did they have any kind of a future at all? Would Nico ever make love to her again? A shiver went through her, just remembering what it had felt like to stand next to him in the confined space of the lift. She was so *aware* of him. Would it ever diminish?

But as much as she craved his touch again she also feared it, because their wedding night had broken her apart—so much so that she'd had to put thousands of miles between them. If he touched her again, how would she be able to hide what she was feeling?

Her pregnancy didn't help matters. She felt as if a layer of skin had been removed, baring her emotions even more.

Chiara put her hand on her belly and felt the baby kick. She couldn't stop a smile, even though she didn't feel like smiling. She hoped for their baby's sake that there was *some* kind of a future for them.

She just couldn't fall for him… Because if she did making a life with Nico would be excruciating. He was not a man who would ever love her back.

His attitude to his mother was chilling, even if she *could* understand how resentful and hurt he must have been after being abandoned by her. When Chiara had heard the pain in his voice earlier she'd wanted to soothe it. And that scared her because she should be remaining detached.

Then the baby kicked again and Chiara cursed herself for being selfish. As long as Nico loved their child, that was all that really mattered. She didn't want her child to experience what she had—feeling *less* than, or not enough. And that would be her priority—this baby. Bringing it safely into the world and ensuring that he or she felt loved and wanted, no matter what was going on between her and Nico.

* * *

'Do you want to know if it's a boy or a girl?'

The doctor looked from her to Nico and Chiara held her breath. She was flat on her back on a table, her belly exposed and smeared with cold jelly. They'd just been reassured that everything was fine with the baby. And now there was this question.

Chiara said, 'I don't care as long as it's healthy.'

She looked at Nico, who had been transfixed by the image on the screen ever since it had appeared. He looked pale. Then he said, 'I'd like to know.'

He looked at her. 'If that's okay?'

Chiara figured that for a man who ran a huge global enterprise, comprising myriad businesses and thousands of employees, it made sense for him to leave little to chance.

She shrugged. 'I don't mind.'

The doctor pressed down again on Chiara's belly and then she said, 'Okay, I just wanted to be sure… I'm delighted to tell you that you're having a baby girl.'

An instant sob of emotion came out of Chiara's mouth before she could stop it as she looked at the screen and saw the tiny heartbeat pounding away. *Her daughter.* She put a hand to her mouth.

It took her a second to realise that Nico hadn't said anything, and when she looked at him his expression was shuttered. Instantly she felt trepidation.

The doctor seemed to sense their need to absorb this alone and wiped the gel off Chiara's belly and pulled her robe down. 'I'll be outside when you're ready, but be reassured that all is well. Congratulations.'

The doctor left and silence filled the small room. Chiara pulled the robe down over her belly a little more and sat up. Nico was still standing beside the bed, dwarfing the small space.

Chiara forced herself to look at him. His expression was still a little shell-shocked.

A bitter sense of disappointment made her belly sink. 'You don't want a daughter.'

He seemed to come out of the reverie he'd been in and he looked at Chiara. He frowned. 'No… I mean…*yes*. I just hadn't really thought about it in terms of a he or a she yet. And now…'

He sat down on the chair looking a little bewildered. It was the first time Chiara had seen any kind of chink in his indomitability.

'Are you disappointed? Would you have preferred a boy?'

Of course he would, crowed an inner voice, *he's an Alpha male!*

But Nico shook his head slowly. 'No… I want the baby to be healthy, like you. It's just hard to get my head around. I think I'd just assumed it would be a boy.'

His honesty eased something inside Chiara. After all, neither of them had been prepared for this or expected it. Or planned for it.

She plucked nervously at the bedcover. 'My father wanted a boy. I mean, he would have been perfectly happy with a daughter as long as he had a son too, but then… when my mother couldn't have any more children…he was left with me. I felt the weight of his disappointment my whole life.' She looked at Nico. 'I don't want that for our daughter.'

He met her eyes. 'I will be the first to admit that my experience at the hands of women hasn't always been positive, but I'm not going to punish my daughter for other people's actions.'

There was something fiery in his eyes, and for a moment Chiara had a vision of him with a small dark-haired girl squealing with laughter on his shoulders. In a bid to stop him seeing the emotion she felt, she said, 'You said *"women"* and *"other people"*…what did you mean?'

Nico got up and paced in the small space. He'd taken off his overcoat and wore a dark suit with an open-neck white shirt. He oozed confidence and virility. Chiara hadn't been unaware of the lingering looks from the female staff of the private clinic, and it was probably only the fact that her doctor was close to retirement age that made her somewhat immune to Nico's charms.

Chiara wondered a little desperately how any woman could ever come to terms with being with a man like this, who would be in constant demand and the object of women's lust?

He turned around and looked supremely reluctant to speak. She sensed he wouldn't. So she said, 'Nico, we're about to become parents. I deserve to know who you are.'

He ran a hand through his hair, making it messy. It only enhanced his appeal. *Damn him.*

'There was a woman…when I was much younger. I thought I was in love with her.'

Chiara's heart clenched. He *had* believed in love. Once. 'What happened?'

Nico's voice was harsh. 'I found her in bed with my best friend and business partner. She'd encouraged him to betray me by doing a deal with a client behind my back and cutting me out. She overestimated his ability and severely underestimated mine. I cut them loose and went to America, and I never looked back.'

And now he was King of the World.

Chiara was realising that Nico might put on a cool, emotionless front but he was far from being that. He'd been hurt by his mother and then this woman and it had affected him. A lot. The fact that he'd once let a woman close

enough to hurt him crushed something inside Chiara—
the seed of hope that he would one day let *her* get close.

Quietly Chiara said, 'Not all women are like that…
greedy and duplicitous. Our daughter certainly won't be.'

'If I hadn't met you I might still believe the worst of
people, but maybe you're right.'

He came to the end of the bed and wrapped his hands
around the frame. Chiara was acutely aware of his long fingers, recalling all too easily how they'd felt on her skin…
inside her. Her breathing got faster.

Just then there was a knock on the door and a nurse
popped her head around, her eyes gravitating naturally to
Nico and then widening comically. 'Your doctor has another appointment scheduled but she'd like to chat to you
before you leave.'

Chiara felt like saying something tart and snappy, to
get the girl's attention away from Nico, but he just said
thank you and barely glanced at her. He was oblivious to
his effect on women, or else just so used to it he didn't
notice any more.

He looked at her and she must have had an odd expression on her face because he said, 'What? What did I do?'

She shook her head. 'Nothing.'

He glanced at his watch. 'My plane is ready and waiting at the airport. It's time to go back to Sicily.'

He left the room so she could get dressed and Chiara
felt alternately excited and full of trepidation about seeing her home again, never having expected to be returning like this.

The first thing Chiara noticed was that there were new
gates—steel and reinforced. They opened automatically
when Nico pressed a button in his sports car, which had
been waiting for them at the airport.

As they drove up the driveway she saw gardeners working on the gardens. They'd been cleared and new plants put in. She immediately wanted to get out and inspect what they were doing, as her mother had used to love gardening before she'd got ill and the gardens had run wild. They'd even had a herb and vegetable garden outside the kitchen.

But then they rounded the last corner and Chiara's favourite view appeared—the *castello*, perched on the edge of the world, with nothing but the sparkling sea behind it.

She gasped. 'What's all that?'

'Scaffolding. The builders are almost finished doing the exterior refurbishment work.'

Chiara could see gleaming new tiles. For years they'd had leaks in various parts of the *castello*, but it had been way beyond their financial reach to try and fix them.

Nico brought the car to a stop in the main courtyard and came round to open Chiara's door. He had to help her out because the car was so low slung, and she hesitated before putting her hand in his, afraid of her physical reaction.

Nico scowled. 'I don't bite, Chiara.'

She flushed and put her hand in his, feeling it close tightly around hers. A wash of heat rushed through her whole system. She'd read in a book about pregnancy that increased hormones could make you more acutely sensitised to everything, including desire. *Brilliant.* She'd never felt more ungainly or more aroused.

It also hadn't helped to hear what the doctor had said to them before they'd left the clinic.

'I'm sure you don't need me to tell you this, but you're experiencing a very healthy pregnancy so there's no reason why you shouldn't be enjoying every aspect of your marriage—including the physical side. Some couples are afraid they'll harm the baby, but that's really just a myth... You're in your second trimester now—this is when you can

really enjoy being pregnant...before the last trimester sets in and it becomes a little more uncomfortable...'

Chiara's face had flamed bright red and she'd avoided Nico's eye the whole way back to Sicily, terrified he might be expecting her to jump on him and demand her conjugal rights.

And then a blur of fur appeared from around the corner, and Chiara dropped to her knees as Spiro all but jumped into her arms, whining with excitement and slobbering all over her. She laughed, but felt perilously close to tears to see her old friend and find that he was okay. His tail was wagging so hard she could feel the air moving.

In a very gruff voice she said, 'Thank you for looking after him for me.'

Nico didn't mention the veritable team of dog-minders and walkers he'd had to hire to keep Spiro occupied and cared for. He also didn't mention how the dog had somehow managed to burrow his way under Nico's skin, so that when he was sitting in his office and Spiro came in to lie under the desk at his feet he liked it.

'It was fine,' he said, and watched as she got up and walked away from him with one hand on the dog's head. She was more happy to see the damn animal than him. He felt irritated. She'd avoided looking at him or even talking to him the whole way here.

Actually, it had been from the moment the doctor had said that there was no reason they shouldn't be enjoying a full marriage. *Sex.*

He was one of those people who had thought it dangerous for the baby, but now... All he could think about was Chiara's lushly curved form and how badly he wanted her.

But evidently, if her reaction to what the doctor had said was anything to go by, the last thing *she* wanted was sex.

She wore the maternity clothes that the stylist in Rome

had provided: leggings, a close-fitting clingy top that showed off her neat bump and a loose cashmere cardigan. Her hair was sleek and shiny. She oozed health and vitality and an innate sexiness he knew she was unaware of.

Once again it confounded him. He had never met a woman who didn't use her assets to gain some advantage.

She disappeared into the *castello* and Nico took a moment before following her, reliving the moment when the doctor had revealed the sex of their baby. *A girl.*

Nico, in his arrogance, had assumed it would be a boy. The thought of a girl frankly terrified him. But it also sparked a wave of protectiveness so strong that he felt tremors in his body. The only other person who had come close to sparking a similar feeling was Chiara, when he'd seen those pictures of her in Dublin. The evidence of her pregnancy.

Protectiveness. A totally expected and sane response for a man to feel for his wife and the mother of his child. It didn't mean anything more than that.

'I waited until your return before hiring interior decorators as I thought you would know best what to do.'

Chiara was shocked. 'I… Thank you. I wouldn't have expected that.'

Ever since she was small, she'd often daydreamed and imagined what she would do to the *castello* if she had the freedom and the money. Her father had favoured heavy furnishings and dark colours, and her mother had gone along with it to keep the peace.

Chiara had even made a mood board of cuttings from magazines for what she'd like to do one day. Make the *castello* bright and modern and airy. Her mother had found her board and said, '*Piccolina*, don't let your father find that. But you're right, the *castello* deserves to look beautiful, so I hope you get to do this some day.'

Now, the prospect that she was actually going to get to fulfil her dream made her feel very emotional—especially since Nico would have had every right to get on with hiring an interior decorator in her absence after she'd left him. *Abandoned him.* Only now did it occur to her that what she'd done must have held echoes of his mother for him. She'd only reinforced his already healthy cynicism.

She looked at Nico. 'You must have some ideas?'

He shrugged. 'I'd like to retain as many of the original features as possible, while giving it a more open and modern air, but that's about it. I trust your judgement.'

The fact that his vision matched hers made her feel ridiculously pleased. 'But I might have awful taste.'

He gestured at the heavy dark curtains and furniture. 'Would you keep any of this?'

She made a face. 'No way.'

'Well, then, that's all I need to know.'

'Have you been living here?' Chiara asked, suddenly curious.

'Only for a few weeks here and there. I was in New York a lot. I've taken over your father's study—I hope you don't mind. And I've been sleeping in the master bedroom. *Our bedroom...*'

Chiara could feel the heat climbing up her neck and face again and cursed silently. She was hardly a blushing virgin any more!

She spoke fast, to detract from her self-consciousness. 'Of course I don't mind about the study. And the bedroom...the bedroom—' she nearly choked '—that's fine too. I can use my old room.'

There was a taut silence for a moment and then Nico said, 'No, *cara*, we will be sharing a bedroom. There's been enough speculation about this marriage without adding fuel to the fire. Unless that will be a problem for you?'

Chiara could feel her blood drain south while at the same time her pulse-rate tripled. A very disconcerting sensation. 'I can sleep in the room adjoining the master bedroom. It used to be a dressing room. That way it won't be so noticeable.'

Nico moved closer and Chiara's levels of panic spiked.

'What do you have to be afraid of? We shared a bed before...' He directed an explicit look at her belly.

Chiara was terrified that if she protested too much it would give away why she was so reluctant to expose how she reacted to him. While *he* was only insisting she sleep with him for appearance's sake.

'I'm not afraid of anything... I just don't sleep well at the moment. The baby is very active at night. I'll keep you awake.'

'Don't worry about me, *cara*,' Nico responded silkily. 'I can survive on very little sleep.'

CHAPTER SEVEN

A COUPLE OF hours later Chiara was still feeling angry and jittery at having been so neatly routed by Nico. *Sharing a bed.*

She'd felt a sense of complacency when she'd had her own room at his apartment in Rome. And now not even being back in familiar and well-loved surroundings was helping much.

She heard a noise and looked up from where she was stirring a pot at the gas stove in the kitchen.

Nico stood in the doorway, hands on his hips, frowning ferociously. He'd changed into worn jeans and a casual long-sleeved top, and it took all Chiara's control not to let her eyes drift and linger over his body.

'What are you doing?'

She lifted the wooden spoon, almost wishing she could smack him with it for corralling her into sharing a bed with him. 'I'm cooking dinner.'

'Where is the housekeeper?'

Nico had hired a middle-aged local woman—Maria—who had been bustling around the kitchen when Chiara had explored earlier.

'I told her she could go home for the evening. I usually cooked for my parents.' She was a good cook.

Nico came into the kitchen, still frowning. 'My wife

is not a cook. That's why I hired a housekeeper and why you will be interviewing more household staff over the next few days.'

The fact that she was irritating him was some balm to Chiara's own irritation. 'I enjoy cooking. It's no problem.'

He came closer and seemed to sniff the air. She saw the flare of interest in his eyes before he could hide it.

'What is that smell?'

'It's *pollo alla cacciatora*. Not very original but one of my favourites.' She stopped, and felt a bubble of hysteria mount. 'I don't even know if you're vegetarian. We've never actually shared a meal...apart from last night.' When they'd been separated by a table wide enough for a football game.

Nico looked grim now. 'I'm not vegetarian.'

Chiara gestured to where she had set the wide wooden kitchen table. The place where she'd spent most of her time growing up—learning how to cook with her *nonna*, doing schoolwork, reading...dreaming.

She regretted setting the table down here now. It felt too intimate, all of a sudden. Too exposing.

'I thought we'd eat down here, but I can set the table in the dining room if you'd prefer.'

He glanced at the table and a look of something almost like fear came over his face before it returned to neutral. 'No, here is fine.'

Chiara served the stew into two big bowls and brought them over to the table. Now she *really* regretted not going upstairs, to the more formal dining room where Nico had undoubtedly been eating for the last few months.

Nico ate some stew and tore off a piece of the crusty bread that Chiara had decided to serve with it. The ultimate comfort food. Now she felt even more exposed. Nico would no doubt be assessing her and thinking that this was where her extra pounds came from.

But then he said, 'This is very good. How did you learn to cook?'

Chiara poured a glass of Chianti for Nico and sparkling water for herself. 'My *nonna* taught me. My father's mother.'

Nico ate more of the stew, and then glanced at her.. 'How long were you without staff here?'

'For about the last five years.'

'That's a long time to be running a property this size on your own.'

She shrugged. 'We managed.'

He sat back and took up his wine glass. It should have looked ridiculously flimsy in his big hand but it didn't. 'And you really didn't know about the history of this place?'

Chiara dabbed at her mouth with a napkin and shook her head. 'No idea.'

She put the napkin down again and forced herself to meet Nico's eye.

'Although if what you say about my father turning your father away that time is true, he must have known. He was always paranoid about security and privacy. I think that was one of the reasons he insisted on home-schooling me even after I got better. Maybe he didn't want me mixing with the local children in case I heard something.'

'So you had no friends?'

Chiara felt as if Nico was pulling up a layer of skin and peering underneath to her tender underbelly. A little testily she admitted, 'Not really, no. I made friends with some of the workers' children, but their work was usually seasonal and then they'd move on.'

Nico said, 'When I was young I didn't have many friends either, actually.'

Chiara stopped her jaw from dropping. A man as dynamic and charismatic as him?

He grimaced slightly. 'Your father was secretive and overprotective—my father believed we were better than everyone else and that we didn't deserve to be where we were, in the flats of Naples. Other kids picked up on it and ostracised me. Jeered at me for believing I was better than them. Jeered at me for not having a mother. They knew about the Santo Domenicos and how far we'd fallen. It only made my father more determined that I'd succeed.'

Chiara felt a pang for Nico. She could imagine him as a scrappy kid all too well. Full of hurt and trying to hide it.

'I had one best friend I trusted with my life…'

'The one who slept with your girlfriend?'

He took a sip of wine and nodded. 'For years I blamed her for seducing him—she was very beautiful and knew how to use it.'

Chiara crushed a surge of self-consciousness.

Nico shook his head. 'But really it was him. I knew he had wanted her from the moment I introduced them. She just took advantage of his weakness for her.'

Chiara asked, as lightly as she could, 'Did you ever see her again?'

Nico avoided her eye and drained his wine. 'I've bumped into her occasionally. I believe she's on marriage number two now.'

He stood up then, and put his napkin down on the table. 'Thank you—that was delicious. Better than most restaurants I've eaten in. I have some calls to make… Leave the dishes for Maria. You don't need to do menial tasks, Chiara, not any more. And in future we'll eat upstairs.'

Moments ago Chiara had felt that black pang of jealousy, wondering if he still had feelings for his lover, and now she lambasted herself for it.

'Are you forbidding me to cook?' She forced a lightness into her voice she didn't feel.

'If I'd wanted you to cook I would have made you my housekeeper, not my wife.'

When Chiara woke the next morning she lay there for a long moment, soaking in the sounds and the smells and the warm breeze coming in through the open window. The earth smelled damp—it must have rained during the night.

The night. In bed with Nico.

Chiara's eyes opened. The bedroom was empty—she knew that much. She looked to her left and saw the covers thrown back and the dent in the pillow where Nico's head had been. She could smell his scent.

She had gone to bed last night after dinner, hoping to be asleep before he retired, but not really expecting it to happen. Her head had been whirring with everything he'd told her, and the fact that they'd shared a relatively pleasant meal together. Until the end, when he'd more or less told her to stay out of the kitchen.

But after she'd washed and changed and scurried into bed, like a terrified little mouse afraid of a predator, she'd obviously fallen asleep immediately. Tired after her two eventful days.

The baby moved now, and Chiara put her hand on her belly, smiling. *A girl.* A pang of anxiety rose up though when she thought of Nico's response to the news. But, she had to remember that he'd been brought up by a single father after his mother had abandoned him, and then his lover had betrayed him. It was no wonder he felt less than enthusiastic about a girl. He wouldn't know how to relate because his experience of women was skewed.

Still, she couldn't believe she'd slept so soundly beside the man who had driven her mindless with pleasure in this very same bed on their wedding night. She put it down to extreme pregnancy fatigue...

There was a light knock on the door and Chiara clutched at the sheet like a terrified virgin. 'Yes?'

The door opened and a smiling Maria appeared with a tray balanced expertly in one hand. She came in and put it down on the table beside the bed. The tray contained orange juice, pastries, water, fruit salad...

Chiara stuttered a greeting. It had been a long time since housekeepers had served anyone in bed at the *castello*.

Maria was now delving into Chiara's cases, which she realised Nico must have brought up to the room at some stage while she'd slept. All attempts to tell Maria not to worry fell on deaf ears as the woman pulled out all the clothes that the stylist had packed and proceeded to hang them up or put them in drawers.

Chiara's belly sank. So much for hoping she could make some excuse not to sleep with Nico. Not only had she slept like a log, but apparently she'd be checked up on first thing every morning by Maria.

After Chiara had showered, and dressed in a pretty floral maternity dress, she went downstairs to find Nico. It felt strange in the *castello* now. But good. There was an air of activity that hadn't been there for a long time.

She found him in her father's study where, instead of her father's ancient computer, there was now a state-of-the-art desktop computer and two laptops. A TV was high on a wall in the corner, showing rolling footage of a financial channel.

Nico heard a sound and looked up. Chiara stood in the doorway in a dress that was all at once positively nun-like

and yet more provocative than the most barely-there lin-
gerie Nico had ever seen on a woman.

There were two straps showing off Chiara's toned arms
and delicate collarbone. Her breasts were barely contained
by the bodice, full and ripe. The dress had an empire line
and flowed out over the bump and to her knees. Her legs
were bare. So were her feet. And her nails were painted
a coral colour that seemed absurdly provocative to Nico.

Her hair was long and loose, and he wanted to grab it
and wrap it around his hand so he could tug her onto his
lap, where she would feel for herself how hard it had been
for him to sleep beside her last night while, unbelievably,
she'd snored gently.

It had been a total novelty for Nico, to come to bed and
find Chiara curled up on one side, already asleep, with the
sheets pulled up to her chin. He had never slept beside a
woman before without seduction and the pursuit of pleasure being involved. He'd half expected her to be naked
and waiting.

He'd found it curiously disturbing at first, until he'd
fallen into a fitful sleep, populated by X-rated re-runs of
their wedding night, and then woken with a raging erection as dawn broke outside.

Chiara had been on her back by then, one hand thrown
above her head, the sheet down around her waist. Her
chest had been rising and falling gently as she slept. Her
thin nightdress had done little to disguise the press of her
nipples against the fabric. It had taken all of Nico's will-
power not to lean over and put his mouth there, encircling
the peaks and bringing them to hard life...waking her up
and seeing those green eyes widen with sensual appreciation and desire...

Instead he'd taken a cold shower and checked in on the

markets waking up across the world, and now he felt thoroughly disgruntled and had no one to blame but himself.

'You slept well?'

Chiara nodded, her face pinkening slightly. 'Like a log. I must be more tired than I thought I was. In truth, the room I shared with the girls was like a train station—it was almost impossible to get a good night's sleep.'

Nico put down his pen. 'Why did you put yourself through that? Why did you leave so suddenly? Didn't I at least deserve a conversation?'

The pink leached out of Chiara's cheeks and he had the impression that she was ready to bolt. So much so that he got up and took her by the arm, leading her into the office and closing the door.

He let her go and sat on the edge of the table. She was skittish, avoiding his eye. And then he saw it—the delicate flush on her face, and the pulse beating hectically at the base of her neck. A surge of triumph went through him. *She wanted him.* She might have slept through the night in the bed beside him, but she wasn't immune.

'You owe me an explanation, Chiara.'

Chiara felt like a nervy foal. Why had she come looking for Nico again? She cursed herself now. She could be down in the kitchen baking a cake, or checking on the herbs and vegetables. Or taking Spiro for a walk. Anything but this.

'I told you in the note. I thought it was a mistake for us to marry.'

'Why? You got what you married me for—keeping your life at the *castello*. What changed between the wedding and the morning after?'

Everything! cried a voice in her head.

And suddenly, in that moment, Chiara knew it. Somehow—pathetically—she had fallen for Nico, and she'd used the wedding night and their passionate combustion as an excuse to run. Not wanting to deal with the fact that she never would have allowed someone such intimacy, no matter what the circumstances, if she hadn't already been falling for him.

'I… I just changed my mind.' It sounded pathetically weak to her ears.

'After a night like we had? I remember how you responded, *cara*. What we shared is rare. Maybe it scared you a little?'

Chiara looked at Nico. He was so close to the truth that it shocked her. And it terrified her that he might realise. He was an astute man.

'Don't be ridiculous. I told you—I married you because I thought it would be the only way I could negotiate terms to keep access to the *castello*. I didn't marry you for…' Chiara felt breathless '…for what happened.'

Nico stood up, and he was so close now they were almost touching. Chiara had to tip her head back, and she was suddenly bombarded with memories of just what *had* happened. How good it had felt.

His eyes were intense. 'What happened,' he breathed, 'was amazing. I haven't been able to get it out of my head for the past five months. I've cursed you every night when I couldn't sleep, reliving that night.'

He was echoing her thoughts like a sorcerer. 'But you don't want me… How can you…?' She made a half-hearted gesture to her bump.

'Because you're pregnant?'

She nodded.

'It may surprise you to know that if anything I find you even more attractive. The sight of your body…ripening with my seed…is unbelievably erotic.'

Chiara wondered dimly how she was still standing. She couldn't feel her legs. All she could feel was an urgent spiking of delicious tension deep in her groin, where her intimate body was responding, getting hotter, damper. Aching.

'You want me, Chiara.'

It wasn't spoken as a question, but Chiara heard a question. She also saw something in Nico's eyes—a hint of uncertainty. She would bet that he'd never stood in front of a woman before and felt unsure if she wanted him.

Chiara knew she could lie. She knew he wouldn't push it if she insisted she didn't want him. She could blame the pregnancy. Step back and break the tension. Leave. But an excitement she hadn't felt in months was coursing through her veins, making her feel alive. *She didn't want to lie.* Or leave. She wanted to experience that sublime union again.

'Yes,' she said simply. 'I want you.'

A shudder seemed to go through Nico and he stepped up to Chiara, spearing his hands into her hair, tilting her face up to his.

'I meant what I said before…about the wedding night. I'd never wanted anyone as much. I wasn't capable of being rational. And I still want you like that…like a fever in my blood.'

He bent his head and claimed her mouth in a kiss that showed her in no uncertain terms the truth of his words. It was heady and intoxicating to think that he'd been thinking of her, wanting her. That she'd driven him to the edge of his control.

The kiss was all-consuming, and Chiara was slipping down into a vortex of heat. She dimly wondered how she'd survived for all these months without this. The solid wall of his chest was under her hands and desperately, not even aware of what she was doing, she searched for buttons, undoing them, ripping them apart in a feverish desire to touch his bare skin.

Nico broke away from the kiss, breathing harshly. It took a second for Chiara's eyes to focus again. His shirt was open and her hands were splayed across his pectoral muscles. One of her straps had fallen down and her breasts were straining against the bodice of her dress.

They were so sensitive it almost hurt. *Now* she understood what the doctor had meant with that conspiratorial smile. Chiara's whole body felt like an erogenous zone.

Nico went over to the door and locked it and then came back, putting his hands under Chiara's arms and manoeuvring her so that she was sitting on the edge of the desk.

His eyes were so dark they glittered like black jewels. With his hands still under her arms, touching the sides of her breasts, he said, 'I need you *now*.'

She bit her lip to stop herself from sounding too eager. 'Okay.'

He kissed her again, moving between her legs, pushing them apart. The height of the table aligned her body with his perfectly. She could feel the potent thrust of his body through their clothes and, acting totally on instinct, she reached down and undid his trousers, finding him and pulling him free of his clothes.

He drew back, a breath hissing out of his mouth. Chiara looked down, and the sight of her hand wrapped around all that majestic masculinity almost undid her.

Nico caught the front of her dress and pulled it apart, baring her lace-clad breasts to his gaze. He pulled the straps of the dress down, found the clasp of her bra and pulled it off and threw it aside. Now she was bared to his gaze, and breathing so fast she was almost hyperventilating.

Nico cupped her breasts, his thumbs grazing her nipples. 'I've dreamed of this...of you...so many times.'

For the first time Chiara felt a pang of regret that she'd

run. But then any coherent thought fled as Nico bent and sucked one hard nipple into his mouth, tonguing and nipping at the sensitive flesh.

Chiara squeezed the stiff column of flesh in her hand. She could feel the tension in Nico and knew she wouldn't be able to hold on. She was too close.

She took her hand from him.

He lifted his head and looked at her.

'*Now*, Nico.'

Nico reached under her dress and found her panties, pulling them off and down her legs till they dropped to the floor. He spread her legs even further and positioned himself between them.

Chiara was panting. On some level she wondered what on earth she was doing, sitting on Nico's desk in broad daylight, about to— But then he joined their bodies in a smooth but cataclysmic thrust and she didn't care about any of that. She only cared about *this*. The inexorable glide of his body in and out of hers and the exquisite climb of tension, higher and higher.

She pushed his open shirt off his shoulders, exploring his chest, wrapping her hands around his neck, pressing her body even closer. Nico put a hand under her bottom, lifting her so that he could go even deeper. Chiara bit his shoulder to stop herself from crying out.

Her belly was pressed against him and Chiara felt him touch the very heart of her as she shattered into a million pieces within seconds, every part of her pulsating and contracting as she drew every ounce of his own climax from his body.

They were sweating…shaking…breathing like marathon runners. When Nico could move, he extricated himself from Chiara's tight clasp and stood up. He felt dizzy. Undone. But also regenerated.

Her face was flushed and her hair was wild. Her nipples were wet and her breasts were pink from where he'd touched her and from the hair on his chest. She looked up at him. Eyes huge and dazed.

A feeling of intense satisfaction rushed through him. He couldn't even feel regret that he'd taken her on his desk like an animal. He'd never taken a woman with such urgency. *Not even her.* The thought was fleeting and he batted it away, not wanting to look at that significance now.

He tipped up Chiara's chin so she had to look at him. Her eyes were too big, seeing too much. Nico felt exposed.

'There will be no running away again, *mia cara moglie*. And you don't need to cook for me and create some domestic idyll. I'm not interested in that. I'm interested in *this*, and in having you by my side when I need you, and in you being the mother of my children. *That's* why I married you.'

When Chiara woke the shutters were closed in the bedroom and the light was dim. She was totally disorientated. Her body felt heavy and lethargic. The baby moved and she put a hand on her belly—and then it all came rushing back, because she remembered Nico splaying a big hand across her belly and saying, *'There will be no running away again...'* and *'*That's *why I married you.'*

He had married her to be his trophy wife...when she was the most *un*-trophy-like wife in the world. And to be the mother of his children. Not to cook or create a cosy domestic home. Which was exactly what Chiara had wanted to create here all her life, in this huge place that had always felt more like a mausoleum than a home. And that was because it had never been *theirs*.

Nico had left her under no illusions that things would

be different now. He'd reminded her all too brutally, albeit pleasurably, of her role.

She rolled over on her side and then realised that she was naked under the sheet. She went hot all over, belatedly remembering how Nico had had to carry her upstairs to the bedroom, and how he'd laid her down, taken off her ruined dress, before pulling a cool sheet over her still tingling body.

She got up, pulled on a robe and opened the shutters, noticing the setting sun. She'd slept through the whole day. He'd put her into a pleasure-induced coma.

Feeling thoroughly discombobulated, Chiara took a shower and dressed in leggings and a maternity shirt—nothing that could be considered remotely provocative. She twisted her damp hair back and up and secured it onto her head with a clip.

When she went downstairs Maria was walking from the dining room. She saw Chiara and smiled. 'I was about to come and wake you. Signor Santo Domenico said you weren't to be disturbed till dinnertime. He's in the dining room.'

Chiara forced a smile while feeling out of place, because *she* was usually the one making dinner and serving it up. With a pang, she realised that that was unlikely to happen again. And then she mocked herself. She had to be the only woman on the planet who felt hard done by for having *less* work to do.

She steeled herself to see her husband again and went into the dining room. He sat at one end of the imposingly large table. There was another place set to his left, and Chiara went over and sat down. He put down the paper he was reading and watched her the whole way. She felt acutely self-conscious, wondering if he was thinking, *What is it about her?*

'You had a good rest, *cara*?'

Chiara felt prickly. He was so smooth. So used to these post-sex situations. 'Fine, thank you. You should have woken me earlier. I didn't need to sleep the day away.'

'Clearly you did. You've been overdoing it.'

Chiara heard the censorious tone in his voice and opened her mouth to say something, but a young girl came into the room with their dinner. A pasta starter. By the time she left Chiara had forgotten what she'd wanted to say.

She asked, 'Who is she?' as Nico filled her water glass and poured some wine for himself.

'She's Maria's daughter—helping out until we hire more permanent staff. Actually, I've arranged for someone from a local recruitment firm to come and speak with you to-morrow, so you can let them know what we need and the kind of people you want. We'll also need a nanny for after the baby is born.'

Chiara nearly choked on her pasta and put her fork down. This was what he'd done after their wedding night—made love to her with a zeal that had turned her inside out and stirred up all her emotions, only to behave as if nothing extraordinary had happened. And for him evidently it hadn't. He'd merely been scratching a physical itch.

Chiara knew she wouldn't survive unless she could channel the same kind of detachment—but not right now. Her anger bubbled over. She looked at Nico. 'I am *not* handing my baby over to a nanny.'

He put down his own fork. 'We will have a busy social schedule and I will expect you to be by my side. You'll be traveling abroad with me when I require it.'

When I require it.

Chiara's appetite disappeared. 'I am not your employee, Nico. I'll be the mother of your daughter and *she* will be my focus—not you or your career.'

Upset at this reminder that for Nico this marriage was very much just a business transaction, Chiara stood up and left the room as elegantly as she could, feeling Nico's eyes boring into her back the whole way.

She passed Maria, who gave her a startled look. 'The food...is everything all right?'

Chiara took her hand and said truthfully, 'It is delicious. I'm afraid I'm just not hungry.'

The women patted Chiara on the shoulder and glanced at her belly before saying something sympathetic about knowing how she felt. She obviously assumed Chiara had some kind of morning sickness.

Spiro appeared at that moment and came up to Chiara, nudging her thigh. She patted his head and then instinctively went to one of her favourite secret spots in the *castello*. The old library—a huge, cavernous room with hundreds of floor-to-ceiling bookshelves.

She pulled one of her favourite books off a shelf, as familiar to her as her own face, and then curled up in one of the big high-backed chairs and opened it. She was hoping it would help to give her back some sense of equanimity and control, when she felt as if she was in deep water and in serious danger of drowning.

Nico threw down his napkin and stood up. He'd just endured a hurt look from Maria after telling her he wouldn't eat any more dinner. He sighed. Since when had he grown a conscience and cared about people's feelings?

He took his wine glass over to the window. The view took in sweeping gardens all the way down to the sea. It was majestic. And *his*. Finally.

He should be feeling extremely satisfied right now. He'd achieved it all. But he *didn't* feel satisfied. He felt unsettled. As if the world to which he'd become accustomed, where everyone said *yes* and success begat success, just wasn't functioning any more.

Actually, there was only one area where he seemed to be misstepping all the time. *Chiara*.

He scowled, thinking of the dinner she'd prepared the previous evening. He'd literally never tasted anything better. And yet at every moment he'd resisted the urge to sink into that cosy scene with every fibre of his being.

The disturbing thing was how alluring it had been.

He wasn't stupid—he knew it stemmed from having grown up with a single father, and because their lives had been as far from a cosy domestic scene as possible. In a very secret place he'd always envied harmonious family units, so he'd told himself that it was all just an illusion, hiding the cracks in unhappy families. Something he would never indulge in because it wasn't real.

But it had felt real last night. Sitting and talking to Chiara…

Women had tried to seduce him over the years by creating something similar, believing *they* could be the ones to heal his fractured soul, but in every instance he'd walked out, earning himself a reputation as being cold-hearted. Impossible to please. Impossible to tame. As if he was a wild animal.

He'd felt wild earlier, when he'd made love to Chiara. She *made* him wild. She made him forget everything. She made him *want*…want things he hadn't thought of in years. Things he hadn't even known he missed. Or needed. Things that would make him weak. Make him lose his edge. Because if he didn't have his intense hunger to succeed and restore, what would be left?

And that was why it was important to keep her back. Make sure she knew where the boundaries were. *Make sure she doesn't get too close?* asked a jeering inner voice.

Nico ignored it and drained his wine. She would soon adapt to his life, he assured himself. She would grow used to the ease and luxury he could provide.

Her fierce assurance that their child would be her priority had made something dark spike inside Nico—something almost like jealousy. He told himself he was being ridiculous—that if anything it was a good thing that she felt so strongly about their baby.

Nico left the dining room and went to find Chiara. He was about to give up when he saw the door to the library partially open. He saw her straight away, curled up asleep on a chair, legs tucked under her. A book open, resting on her bump.

He reached down and picked it up. *The Collected Poems of William Wordsworth*. Nico put it down on the table beside the chair, and when Chiara showed no signs of stirring he reached down, slid his arms under her and lifted her up into his arms.

Chiara was wide awake—she'd been awake from the moment Nico had come into the room, albeit dozing. She'd actually sensed him before he'd appeared, the tiny hairs going up on her arms. Her body the traitor.

Now he was carrying her up the stairs with that awesome ease and strength. It took immense effort not to turn her head into his neck and breathe in his scent, reach out her tongue and taste his skin. But she was still feeling raw and insecure, and she knew if Nico seduced her again she wouldn't have the strength to say no, and then he would have chipped away a little more at the walls she had left around her.

So when he laid her down on the bed and pulled a cover over her she kept pretending to be asleep, and only opened her eyes when he'd left the room...like a coward.

* * *

The following morning when Chiara woke she was alone. She saw a sleek-looking mobile phone and a charger by the bed on the table with a note on top.

She picked it up.

Call me when you wake, Nico.

Chiara dialled the number that was on the note, and it connected straight away—almost as if he'd been waiting. A silly idea.

'Morning, *cara.*'

Chiara wished he wouldn't call her *cara*—it felt like a lie. She sat up and made her voice brisk. 'Good morning. Where are you?'

'I'm at the airport, about to fly to Rome for some meetings. But I'll be back this evening. There's a charity function we've been invited to in Syracuse. We'll leave at seven p.m. One of my assistants will meet you at the *castello* this morning to go over hiring staff, and also an interior decorator.'

Chiara desisted from saying *Aye-aye, sir,* and just responded, 'Fine, I'll see you later.'

She cut the connection and lay back on the bed for a moment. This was her new reality and she would just have to get used to it.

CHAPTER EIGHT

'THANK YOU SO MUCH, Carmela.'

The young girl smiled prettily. 'No problem. It's good for me to have someone to practise on!'

Maria's daughter was training to be a beautician, and she had helped Chiara to get ready for the function this evening.

She stood back now. 'You look beautiful, Signora Santo Domenico.'

Chiara grimaced, 'Please, call me Chiara.'

The girl gathered her things and left and Chiara sucked in a deep breath. She still wasn't used to seeing herself like this. Dressed up. The only time she could really remember dressing up had been on her twenty-first birthday, when her parents had taken her for dinner in Catania, just a few months before they'd died. Her mother had been so ill, but she'd insisted on going.

Thinking of the dress she'd worn made her cringe now. It had been so old-fashioned and unflattering. She could still remember the sniggers from a crowd of girls they'd passed.

This evening's dress was dark green, with a sweetheart neckline and a high waist just under her breasts. The top of the dress was lace, with a short lace sleeves. It was elegant and classic and it skimmed over Chiara's bump, which seemed to be getting bigger by the day now. Carmela had pulled Chiara's hair back into a low, sleek bun, and make-up made her eyes look huge.

She was just stepping into matching shoes when there was a knock in the door connecting the dressing room with the bedroom.

Nico came in, adjusting his cufflinks. He wore a white tuxedo jacket and a black bow tie, black trousers. And he was breathtaking. Hair still damp from the shower...

He looked at her and stopped moving, an arrested expression on his face. Chiara's whole body tingled with awareness. That black gaze raked her up and down, and then he met her eyes. She could see the heat in his gaze and it echoed the building heat inside her.

'You look...stunning, Chiara.'

Unused to compliments, she said, 'I... Thank you.'

And then he came closer and took a box out of his jacket pocket. A small navy velvet box. She looked from it to him, not understanding.

He made a small grimace. 'I know this was never a traditional marriage, but I should have given you an engagement ring. I'd like to rectify that now.'

He opened the box and Chiara looked inside and gasped. It was a beautiful emerald, baguette cut, with smaller diamonds either side.

He took it out and held it up. 'Shall we see if it fits?'

Feeling a prickle of superstition, and almost hoping it wouldn't fit because that might mean something and it was too beautiful, Chiara held her hand out. Nico took it and slid the ring down her finger so it nestled alongside her wedding band. Her heart clenched. It fitted perfectly.

Weakly she said, 'You shouldn't have bought this. It must have cost a fortune.'

Nico's hand tightened on hers and she looked up at him. He was shaking his head.

'Seriously? Most women would be asking for a bigger gem.'

Chiara felt gauche. Stiffly she said, 'I'm not most women.'

'No,' Nico said, 'you're not.'

Chiara pulled her hand back, avoiding Nico's dark eyes that seemed to see too much. 'It matches my dress.'

'It matches your eyes.'

Chiara looked at Nico again and the electricity flowed between them. A delicious coil of tension knotted deep down inside her.

Nico took a step towards Chiara and she saw the intent in his eyes. She could feel herself softening, moving towards him almost helplessly, as if he were a magnet. But she put her hands up to his chest, saw the emerald glinting in her peripheral vision like a beacon. A reminder not to let him get too close.

'Wait…my make-up…' she said half jokily. 'I'll never be able to re-do it on my own.'

Nico's jaw clenched. 'You don't need make-up. But you're right—we should leave.'

Chiara followed him out, feeling wobbly in the high heels after what Nico had said. Did he mean she didn't need make-up in a *good* way? Or because it didn't make any difference? But then she thought of how he'd just looked at her and her heart skipped a beat. Maybe he meant it in a good way.

A driver was waiting to chauffeur them the short distance to Syracuse, and as Chiara slid into the luxurious confines of the back of the car she realised that she couldn't keep pushing Nico back for ever. She would have to learn how to disguise the way she felt when he touched her or she wouldn't survive this marriage.

* * *

'Don't *touch* me. You disgust me.'

Chiara tried not to let her jaw drop as the very tall, very glamorous woman they'd just been talking to, with her husband, stalked away and into the crowd. She and her husband had just had a very brief but vitriolic row, sparked off by him making a snide remark about her shopping habits.

Her husband, an equally tall, grey-haired gentleman, didn't even look surprised. He said lightly, 'Excuse my wife. She likes to air our grievances in public—it adds an extra dimension to the torture that is our marriage.'

He walked away, leaving Nico and Chiara staring after him. Chiara was in shock. When she looked at Nico, though, he didn't appear to be too perturbed.

'That was...*horrible.*'

The whole time they'd been talking there had been a brittle tension between the couple. And the wife had flirted outrageously with Nico, precipitating her husband's snide remark.

Nico looked down at her. 'Was it? Maybe they were just being more honest than most of the people here who can't stand each other. They're probably already re-enacting that exact scenario they just played out with us. Couples like that get off on public displays of aggression.'

Chiara shivered. She felt cold all of a sudden. And disheartened by Nico's persistent cynicism. The room was too hot and Chiara saw open French doors nearby. Muttering something about needing air, she put her glass of water down and made her way through the glitterati of Syracuse.

When she got outside the terrace was mercifully empty and a cool breeze was coming in off the ocean in the distance. It was dusk and lights were twinkling on, lighting up the stunning Syracuse cathedral nearby. It was magical. *Romantic.*

Chiara put her hands on the stone wall and looked down at her ring, glittering as brilliantly as the rest of the jewels she'd seen in the room. Was that why Nico had given it to her? To keep up with his peers? Had he noticed that Chiara wasn't adorned enough?

Here she was, married, with a beautiful engagement ring and pregnant. She'd always imagined in this scenario that she'd be with someone she loved. Who loved her. She'd seen the lack of love between her parents and had always yearned for something more. That was why she'd devoured romances all her life, stuffing them behind other books in the library so her father wouldn't find them.

Was it really asking too much to love and be loved in return? She hated it that the world Nico moved in seemed to be populated by cynical people.

She sensed him behind her and tensed, not ready to see him. But when was she *ever* ready?

'Are you okay?'

There was concern in his voice and Chiara turned around. She waved a hand. 'I'm fine—it was getting stuffy in there.'

His eyes dropped to the swell of her belly. 'We need to set you up with a doctor—we'll do it tomorrow.'

She put a hand on her belly. 'I'm fine.'

The baby gave a vigorous kick at that precise moment and Chiara let out a little *oof*.

Immediately Nico put his hands on her arms. 'What is it? The baby?'

Chiara shook her head, something quivering inside her at the concern in his voice, even if it *was* only for the baby.

'She's moving.' Acting on instinct, Chiara reached for Nico's hand and placed it firmly on her belly, with her own hand on top. 'She'll do it again…just wait.'

It seemed very important to Chiara right then that Nico

should experience this moment, amidst all the cynicism, and feel something very *un*-cynical and pure. His daughter.

For a heart-stopping moment nothing happened. Chiara was about to apologise but then the baby kicked again, even harder. As if she *knew*.

Chiara held her breath as a look of pure wonder came over Nico's face and his eyes widened on hers. Her chest swelled and she felt a swooping sensation. He was *getting* it. The baby kicked again and Chiara couldn't help a small laugh escaping. Pure joy in the moment. In new life. In *hope* that maybe, just maybe—

'Well, well, isn't *this* a cosy scene.'

Nico's whole body went rigid and he lifted his hand off Chiara's bump. Chiara looked to her right, to see one of the most beautiful women she'd ever seen in her life. Flawless bone structure, enviably smooth olive skin, full pouting lips and long sleek black hair. She was poured into a midnight-blue glittering gown that was slashed all the way to her navel, displaying the perfect globes of her breasts.

Her dark and dramatically kohled eyes were on Chiara—specifically on her bump. 'Ingenious…' she purred. 'To trap Nico by getting pregnant. Maybe I should have thought of that myself.'

And suddenly Chiara knew who this was. *The woman who had broken Nico's heart.* How could she not have? She was perfection.

'That's enough, Alexandra. Chiara does not deserve your spite.'

Nico's voice was taut with anger, but that did little to assuage Chiara's growing sense of insecurity.

The woman wouldn't stop looking at Chiara, her dark eyes raking her up and down. 'Are you seriously telling me that you *chose* to be with this woman? I can't believe you could bring yourself to—'

'Enough!'

Nico's voice rang out like a pistol shot. But Chiara put up her hand when she thought he was about to say something else. His ex-lover's words were cutting far too close to the bone for Chiara's liking, but she wasn't going to stand meekly by and let Nico defend her.

She was blisteringly angry that a precious moment had been ruined—infected by the cynicism she hated so much.

Chiara walked up to the woman—so close that her belly was almost touching her. She had to look up because she was so much smaller, and some part of her delighted in seeing the woman swallow nervously.

'My marriage to Nico is none of your business. You gave up any right to know *anything* about my husband when you slept with his best friend. You are not a nice person. And yet I wish you well, because everyone deserves a chance.'

Before Chiara could lose her nerve, she turned and walked back into the party, through the throng and all the way down to the foyer, which was empty. She paced there for a few moments, sucking in deep breaths to try and diminish the rush of adrenalin.

Nico appeared at the top of the stairs and Chiara watched him come down. His face was expressionless, but then when he got closer she saw that there was a small smile playing around his mouth.

'Well, I think you handled Alexandra pretty well. But you didn't really need to jump to my defence.'

'I didn't want you to jump to *my* defence. I'm not sorry about what I said.'

Nico's smile faded. 'You shouldn't be. She owes you an apology. She was unbelievably rude.'

Chiara looked at the wide marble stairs behind him. 'Do we have to go back in there?'

Nico almost shuddered. 'God, no. I'm done.' He surprised her by taking her hand. 'Are you tired?'

There was still too much adrenalin pumping around Chiara's body. She shook her head.

'Good. I'd like to show you somewhere—it's not far.'

Chiara groaned appreciatively. 'This is amazing.'

'I know. Have you ever tasted better gelato than this?'

She shook her head, then said with a rueful smile, 'But I haven't exactly travelled a lot.'

'You'll have plenty of opportunities to travel with me.'

Chiara looked at him. 'We'll have to see how that works with the baby... I'm not leaving her for any length of time, Nico.'

He took a sip of his espresso and inclined his head. 'I know, and I have to commend you for it. I haven't had the benefit of selfless maternal love, so I'll have to trust your judgement.'

'I'm sorry that you didn't know your mother.'

Nico shrugged. 'You can't miss what you don't know.'

Chiara did not agree, but she didn't want to shatter the peace so she took another piece of ice cream, relishing its tart lemon taste as it slipped down her throat. The gelato parlour was right on the seafront and very busy, mainly with groups of laughing joking teenagers.

Nico had given Chiara his jacket against the breeze coming in off the sea, so she sat there now under the fluorescent lights in his jacket and her evening dress. She loved it. And she loved it that he had brought her here, away from that stuffy party. Away from *her*.

'How did you know about this place?'

Nico looked around. 'My father told me about it. He used to come here on boat trips from Calabria with his father when he was small.'

They sat in silence for a moment as the gang of teenagers moved off down the seafront. Chiara envied them their light-hearted ease and friendship.

Nico put down his small espresso cup and leaned forward. He had undone his bow tie and opened the top button of his shirt. He looked rakish and sexy.

'I know you want more, Chiara.'

Chiara looked at him, shocked. Had he seen into her mind?

'I saw your collection of romance novels, hidden behind other books in the library. Unless they were your mother's?'

Chiara knew she could laugh breezily and lie, but she didn't want to. 'Yes, they're mine. What do you mean by knowing I want more?'

'Just that I think you were hoping for love...and romance. Not a marriage of convenience.'

Chiara shrugged and played with her ice cream spoon. She was terrified he'd make the link between her running away after their wedding night and her deepest most secret dreams. Nonchalantly she said, 'I'm not a total fantasist, Nico. I know life doesn't always turn out how you expect it to.'

He sighed. 'I just wanted to say that while I can't give you everything you want, I promise to do my utmost to make you as happy as I can.'

Chiara looked at him, and the little flame of hope that had sprung up when he'd felt the baby kicking withered a little inside her.

'I appreciate that.'

'I like you, Chiara. I respect you... You helped me to achieve a long-held ambition and dream—to restore the *castello* to the Santo Domenico name. You're giving me a child. We have insane chemistry, and we want each other—

which is more than can be said for a lot of those couples we saw at the party this evening. I think we have a lot going for us. I think we can be happy.'

Chiara sucked in a deep breath. She hadn't been expecting Nico to be so honest. It was heartening and also quietly devastating. He was telling her not to get her hopes up. Not to wish for more.

That woman Alexandra had hurt him a long time ago, and maybe seeing her again this evening had reinforced his own walls of defence. They were impenetrable.

What could she say? Except, 'Okay...we'll do our best to make it work.'

Nico reached across the table and took her hand, lacing his fingers through hers. In spite of the heaviness in her heart Chiara felt the familiar burn of desire and saw it in his eyes too. She knew that no matter what he said, or how hard she tried, that little flame of hope wouldn't die out completely...not yet.

Her emerald engagement ring glinted at her mockingly and Chiara turned her hand away so she couldn't see it.

Chiara had taken off her shoes in the car on the way back and when they reached the *castello* Nico insisted on carrying her from the car, in spite of her sleepy protests. But by the time they reached the bedroom Chiara was wide awake—and very aware of Nico, and the way his jaw was stubbled after a day's growth.

Nico put her down and turned on a couple of lamps—just enough to see. He came and stood behind her in front of the mirror, where she was trying to reach the back of the dress.

'Let me.'

She took her hands down and felt him find the zip and pull it down to just above her buttocks. She shivered minutely.

'Cold?' he asked disingenuously. It was the height of summer.

She wanted to scowl, but when she looked at him in the mirror her heart stopped. He was so dark…and towering over her. She shook her head.

He smirked. 'I didn't think so.'

He pushed the dress off her shoulders and then tugged it all the way over her hips, so it fell to the floor in a *swish* of silk and chiffon. Now she wore only a strapless bra, that barely contained her breasts, and panties.

Nico undid her bra and that fell away too, releasing her breasts. Chiara wanted to turn her head away, but she couldn't take her eyes off him. He was bending his head now, pressing a kiss to where her neck met her shoulder, and she shuddered as a wave of desire raced through her body.

He stood up and put his hands on her shoulders. 'Look at yourself, *cara*, you're beautiful.'

Reluctantly, Chiara looked at herself, and watched Nico undo her hair and loosen it so that it fell over one shoulder, almost touching her breast.

His hands came around and cupped her breasts and she caught her breath. She could see her nipples peak into hard points, her skin flushing with arousal.

Her belly was a perfect rounded curve and Nico's hand moved down, over her belly and lower, under her underwear. She couldn't breathe.

'Keep looking at yourself.'

It was a command that Chiara had to obey. One of Nico's hands was on her breast, kneading the tender flesh, finding a nipple and tweaking it, and his other hand was between her legs, fingers seeking and exploring right into the heart of her, where she was hot and damp and aching.

Her legs opened to give him more access. She groaned

and bit her lip, unable to take her eyes off what he was doing to her. He was winding her tighter and tighter, his clever, merciless fingers moving in and out until she couldn't stop a gasp of shock as she exploded in a spasm of pleasure so intense her legs turned to jelly.

Nico finally turned her quivering body around and hauled her into him before kissing her senseless.

After a long moment, when she aftershocks of pleasure had finally diminished, Nico pulled back. He smoothed Chiara's hair back from her brow and said, 'See? This... this is all we need.'

Chiara was too spent to argue, and when he laid her down on the bed and pulled the sheet over her she let sleep claim her, obscuring the fact that she knew pain would be an inevitable part of living with Nico because she was in love with him.

Nico looked down at Chiara sleeping, and even though his own body throbbed with sexual frustration he didn't mind. It had been intensely erotic, watching her fall to pieces around his hand and fingers like that, through the mirror.

Seeing Alexandra earlier had been a shock. It was always a shock. Except this time Nico had truly resented her intrusion on a private moment. And when she'd started to attack Chiara it had taken him a couple of seconds to realise that Chiara had stepped up to her, confronted her. He hadn't noticed because he'd been so blinded by rage.

A kind of rage he couldn't remember feeling before. Not even when he'd found Alexandra in bed with his friend.

No one had ever defended Nico like that.

He could remember being beaten by a group of lads when was a young teenager. His father had found him, bruised and bleeding on the ground, with the boys standing around him jeering. His father had just stood there and said, *'Get up, boy. You're a Santo Domenico. Show them!'*

And Nico had somehow hauled himself up and limped home.

When Chiara had walked away earlier, Nico had been aware of a load lifting off his chest. As if he'd finally broken free of some shackle. He'd barely even glanced at Alexandra's stricken face as he'd gone after his wife.

His wife. His lover. The mother of his child.

Nico felt a surge of protectiveness race through him. He knew he couldn't give Chiara everything she wanted—not even for *her* was he willing to expose himself to the vulnerability of loving someone again. Seeing Alexandra was a sign he couldn't and wouldn't ignore.

But he and Chiara had all they needed. They didn't need anything deeper.

CHAPTER NINE

CHIARA FLIPPED ONTO her back and lazily moved her arms and legs, just enough so that she didn't sink like an over-inflated beach ball to the bottom of the pool. It was late summer and she loved the evenings, when the intense heat was lessening and she could go down to the newly installed infinity pool and cool off.

She looked up into the azure blue sky. There was only the sound of the sea water lapping against the shore nearby, and the call of the birds. The workmen restoring the out-side of the *castello* had finished for the day, as had the interior decorators, who were moving through the *castello* room by room, accompanied by someone from the Italian National Heritage Trust to make sure none of the original features were damaged.

Chiara sighed. She felt…*restless*. In spite of the sooth-ing surroundings. Content…but not happy. And then she castigated herself. She had it so much better than many people. She had no reason to complain.

Her husband was unfailingly solicitous. He was con-siderate. He never spent more than three days away from home. And when he was at home… Chiara blushed even now to think of how intense the attraction still was be-tween them. In spite of her pregnancy.

Since she'd turned eight months pregnant he'd decided

not to go back to New York for work until after the baby was born, and he'd promised that once Sofia was old enough to travel they would all go as a family.

Sofia.

They'd already agreed on the name.

Sofia, after Chiara's beloved *nonna*.

Maria was now living in at the *castello*, along with two other permanent household staff. Chiara had little to worry about except for the fact that no matter how considerate Nico was, how solicitous, it was as if a glass wall separated them. She could get close, but not too close. He maintained a distance that she couldn't seem to breach, no matter what.

The only time she seemed to get closer to the man behind the wall was when they made love. No matter how 'pregnant' Chiara was feeling—fatigued, et cetera—as soon as she laid eyes on Nico it all fell away and she became a mass of needy hormones.

'*Here* you are…'

Chiara stopping moving in the water and promptly sank like a stone. She popped up again quickly, spluttering and blinking to clear her eyes of water, to see that Nico's voice hadn't been an aural hallucination. He was standing at the side of the pool in short swimming trunks, holding a towel and looking too gorgeous for words.

It was so unfair. As her body got progressively rounder, his body remained as beautiful as ever. Lean and hard-muscled. Not an ounce of spare fat. And that tantalising hair on his chest, leading down to the line dissecting his six-pack and then disappearing—

Chiara forced her eyes up to see an amused expression on his face. She scowled. He was disturbing her peace. 'You're back early.' He hadn't been due back from Rome till tomorrow.

An expression she couldn't decipher crossed his face fleetingly before he dropped the towel and dived gracefully into the pool, surfacing just inches away from Chiara.

Predictably, her body was already responding, tingling. Every cell was aligning with his, like magnet filings finding true north. He reached for her, his hands finding her arms and pulling her towards him until her belly touched his.

She put her hands on his arms, feeling the muscles bunching under his skin. He smiled and it made him look ten years younger. Carefree.

'You *can* admit you're pleased to see me.'

When he was like this—charming—it was almost impossible to forget that she had to keep her guard up: the final bastion of her self-protection.

'Fine,' she conceded. 'It's nice to have you home.'

He winced. '*Nice?* Now, that is *not* a word levelled at me too often.'

Chiara's legs touched his as she trod water. He didn't have to—he was so tall. He started to move backwards, though, taking her with him as he moved down the pool.

'Nico…' She groaned, hating it that he could manipulate her so easily.

He ignored her, lazily pulling her along as if she was learning how to swim. Chiara gave up and let him tug her. She could feel the damp tendrils of hair where they'd fallen out of her high bun, clinging to her cheeks.

And then he stopped and stood, and Chiara could stand too, now it was shallow enough. He looked at her for a long moment, and there was something almost desperate in his gaze that made Chiara's heart hitch, but then it was forgotten when he kissed her, and tingling awareness exploded into full-on arousal.

Nico's hands traced Chiara's body through the swimsuit, cupping her breasts, her bottom. She ached for him. Every time. He walked her back to the wall and she leant against it, looking up at him, breathing fast. Her peace was well and truly shattered, but she didn't care any more.

He looked down at her, rivulets of water running down his chest and face, hair flopping forward damply, making him look endearingly young.

She could feel him against her. Hard. Potent. She reached down under the water and pulled down his shorts, taking him in her hand. It was the only time she felt marginally powerful in this relationship—when he looked at her as he was looking at her now, slightly dazed. Flushed.

'Turn around,' he said.

She took her hand from him, turning around to face away from the house out towards the sea beyond. Her heart was drumming with excitement. He peeled the straps of her bathing suit down and freed her breasts, reaching around to cup them and tease them to hard, aching points.

Chiara leant her head back against him. She sensed his desperation as he pulled down her suit over her hips and her legs. He was naked behind her, and then he was pushing her legs apart, pulling her back so that he could thrust into her in one smooth but cataclysmic thrust.

Her body clenched around him in need as he slowly began to thrust in and out, building up an inexorable rhythm until Chiara was biting down on her hand to stop herself from screaming out loud. Nico slammed into her and sent her body flying into an orgasm so intense she thought she might pass out.

He wasn't far behind her, and he collapsed over her back, shuddering his release deep inside her for long moments.

After a few minutes he pulled free and turned her around. She was still dizzy.

'What do you *do* to me?' he asked hoarsely. 'I didn't intend on ravishing you in the pool, but I get near you and...'

She looked up at him, the aftershocks of pleasure still coursing through her system. 'I could say the same of you,' she said shakily.

It was in these brief moments, in the aftermath of pleasure, that there was some demolition of the wall between them. But soon Nico would recover and return to his cool, solicitous self. She could see it happening now. The raw, open look was fading from his face and he was stepping back.

She felt very naked—because she *was* naked, she realised. Her swimsuit was somewhere at the bottom of the pool.

Nico said, 'Stay here. I'll get you something.'

He waded out of the pool, his body gleaming, muscles rippling, and went up the steps, totally and unashamedly naked. He went into the small cabana by the pool, which held supplies, and when he re-emerged he had a towel hitched around his waist and was carrying a terrycloth robe for her.

He held it out at the top of the steps and Chiara crossed her arms over her breasts self-consciously. 'I can't walk out like this—what if someone sees?'

'They're all having dinner in the kitchen on the other side of the *castello*. I was just in there.'

Chiara glared at him. He was daring her. Something rebellious rose up within her—a wish to try and unsettle him, break him out of that cool, impersonal place he went back to whenever they'd been intimate.

So she waded out too, and went up the steps, aware of the water sluicing off her body, which still felt too sensitive.

Nico's eyes were dark by the time she reached the top,

his mouth a tight line. She stood in front of him for a long moment, for once revelling in her nakedness.

Nico bitterly regretted goading Chiara. He should know by now that she was never to be underestimated. She stood before him like a beacon of fertile sensuality—heavy breasts, wide hips, her rotund belly carrying their child. And suddenly *he* was the one afraid of people looking out of a window and seeing her. He didn't want anyone else's eyes on her. *Ever.*

He put the robe around her shoulders, waited till she'd fed her arms through and then belted it firmly.

He might have thought she was unaware of her power over him—the insanity that consumed him until he was buried inside her and the world returned to sharp focus—but after watching her sashay up those steps like a fertile warrior goddess he knew better.

He could feel himself drawing back, to the place inside where he didn't feel so raw. He took a step away and saw some of the light in her green eyes fade. He ignored the pang in his chest. He didn't need that.

'Maria said dinner will be ready when we come in.'

Chiara forced down the frustration to see Nico so utterly in control again. 'Fine. I'll take a shower and clean up.'

Chiara watched as Nico strode back up the garden towards the *castello*. For a moment she could almost imagine he was one of his ancestors —a marauding Greek or Moor.

The truth was that Chiara wouldn't ever have got close to a man like Nico if it hadn't been for extraordinary circumstances. She was average in height, and looks, and was becoming more like a beached whale with every passing day.

Yet, remarkably, they still had insane chemistry. Which was all very well—for now. But what would happen when Nico's desire for her fizzled out, as it invariably would?

And what would happen when the baby was born and they had to deal with a whole new reality? Babies tested the best of relationships.

Would she have the strength to keep up the pretence that she was okay with just this and not *more*? Or would the huge cracks that she knew were ever-expanding just below the surface of their relationship appear and tear them apart completely?

She couldn't imagine a man like Nico settling for life with a wife he no longer found attractive, and she wouldn't be able to bear it if he took mistresses.

She was going to have to talk to him. But while the after-effects of his lovemaking still flowed through her blood like nectar she thought *Just not yet*.

A week later

Nico leant against the door that led outside from the kitchen, where a small vegetable and herb garden was laid out. Chiara was on her knees, planting something in the ground, wearing a huge sun hat to keep the sun off her face. Her hair was long and tangled down her back, and with irritating predictability all Nico wanted to do was go over, wrap her hair around his hand and tug her head back so she presented her lush mouth to him.

Irritating because he couldn't see an end to this desire that seemed to pulse through his system with growing force. Not less force. It wasn't that he didn't *want* to find his wife attractive, but her role as his wife of convenience wasn't meant to include making him feel insatiable lust.

At least if that diminished Nico might feel some semblance of control returning. Right now, control was an elusive concept.

She must have sensed his presence, because she turned

around and looked up. Her face was flushed and she smiled and Nico found it hard to breathe.

He said, '*What* are you wearing?'

The smile slid off her face and Nico could breathe again—but he felt like a heel.

'They're old dungarees belonging to my father. I thought they'd be perfect for doing some gardening.'

Nico couldn't take his eyes off her. She shouldn't have looked remotely sexy in a sleeveless vest and cut-off voluminous dungarees, but right then he was hard pushed to drum up a sexier image.

Chiara clambered to her feet, which were in bright pink flip-flops. Today her toenails were painted purple. Desire hit Nico directly in his solar plexus and moved down lower.

She said, 'Actually, I'm glad you're here—there's something I want to show you.'

Nico saw how flushed she was and said, 'When was the last time you drank some water?'

She blinked. 'Um…lunchtime?'

He made a disapproving noise and called back into the kitchen for some water. Maria came out with a bottle, clucking like a mother hen. Chiara took it and rolled her eyes at Nico before taking a few big gulps. It didn't help Nico to cool down when he saw drops dripping down her chin and under the neck of the T-shirt.

Dio. He was a walking hormone and *she* was the pregnant one. Pathetic.

'You said you wanted to show me something?'

She nodded and started to walk out of the small garden towards the area where the chapel and graveyards were situated. He stopped in his tracks when he saw that the old graveyard, full of his ancestors, had been completely cleared of foliage and that men were working on the gravestones, cleaning them and re-engraving them.

He could feel Chiara's eyes on him and his skin prickled.
'When did they start this?' His voice was sharp.

Chiara sounded nervous. 'When you went to Rome. I
asked the landscape gardeners to look at it and one of them
knows someone who cleans headstones. Do you mind?'
she asked.

Nico felt as if a layer of skin was being peeled away
to reveal the tender underside of a wound. It was disconcerting. 'Why would I mind? The truth is that it should
never have been allowed to become overgrown in the
first place.'

'No, it shouldn't,' she said quietly. 'And I thought that
this would at least go some way to rectifying the situation.'

What Chiara had done cut right to the heart of him. Nico
knew his reaction was irrational, but he couldn't control
it—there was much he couldn't control at the moment. He
felt as if his heart was expanding in his chest, cutting off
all the oxygen, making it hard to breathe. He also—ridiculously—felt his eyes stinging.

All he could think of to counteract his reaction was to
push Chiara back to where he might be able to breathe
again.

He turned to her. 'Cleaning a graveyard won't do much
to rectify the fact that your family wilfully denied us our
home for generations. The only thing that *will* is when our
daughter is born, and then a son, to breathe life back into
the Santo Domenico name indelibly.'

Nico walked away from Chiara, but her stricken, hurt
expression was burnt onto his brain. He told himself it was
for the best. The sooner she remembered why they were
married, the better.

'You haven't forgotten about the charity ball tonight in
Naples? We'll be staying over, so you need to pack a bag.'

Chiara closed the book on pregnancy she'd been reading in the library and looked up. Hurt at the way Nico had reacted to the graveyard yesterday was still fresh in her stomach, making her feel ill, but she suppressed it.

'I've packed a bag. I'm ready to go when you are.'

He looked at his watch. 'We'll leave in an hour.'

Chiara didn't pick up her book again when he'd left. She couldn't concentrate. She rubbed her belly distractedly. The baby had been restless over the past few days. She figured it was just because she was getting closer and closer to her due date.

The cracks that she'd envisaged as being just below the surface of her marriage with Nico were becoming more apparent. And even though he'd shown her again and again that he wasn't ready to give *more*, that little kernel of hope inside her wouldn't die.

She hated herself for it, but sometimes she saw an expression on Nico's face, or in his eyes, before he blanked it, that made her heart thump hard and made her think there might be a chance he could feel something for her.

But yesterday had been a brutal lesson in remembering her place. She had thought the restoration of the graveyard would please him, but maybe inadvertently she'd reminded him of his priorities.

She levered herself out of the chair to go and gather her things, telling herself that what she had to focus on was the baby—that had to be her priority for now, not wishing for things that would never happen.

Nico knew he was behaving like a boor, but he couldn't seem to help himself. They'd taken his private jet for the short flight to Naples, and he'd booked them into one of Naples's most exclusive hotels to get ready.

When Chiara had emerged from the dressing room he'd

wanted to march her right back inside and peel the grey Grecian-style dress from her body. It was one-shouldered, and totally modest, but it seemed to cling indecently to every rounded curve.

She'd left her hair down and coiled it over one shoulder in a loose plait, and it glowed with brown and faint auburn highlights. She looked young and modern and fresh—and far too sexy for Nico's equilibrium.

He'd said nothing, though and they'd left, with the tension that had been between them since the graveyard incident yesterday still simmering. Nico knew he should apologise—Chiara was not to blame for the decisions made by her family many years ago, and he'd told her from the start that he didn't hold her personally responsible. And yet he couldn't bring himself to do it because he was afraid of the softening he'd see in those green eyes. He was afraid of how badly he wanted to see it. To have it soothe something ragged inside him.

When they'd arrived at the function he'd been cornered by some business associates who had been chasing him for weeks and Chiara had said, 'Go on—I'll find a drink and a seat.'

And now he couldn't see her, and frustration was prickling over his skin. He was feeling claustrophobic.

And then finally he *did* spot her, over in the corner, and hated how his heart-rate immediately eased.

He kept her in his sights after that.

'Do you mind if I join you?'

Chiara looked up to see a tall and very elegant grey-haired woman dressed in black hovering over the chair beside her.

She put out a hand. 'Not at all. I'm afraid I'm not being

very sociable. High heels and swollen ankles don't really mix very well.'

The woman sat down.

She looked familiar to Chiara, and she asked impulsively, 'Have we met before?'

The woman shook her head. 'No, my dear, we haven't. I'd remember you—you're one of the most naturally beautiful women I've seen in these circles in a long time.'

Chiara blushed, embarrassed by this compliment from a stranger. 'Thank you—what a nice thing to say.'

The woman looked at her bump. 'Due soon?'

Chiara put a hand on her bump. 'In a couple of weeks. But I've been warned it could go over—most first babies do.'

Then the woman said, 'I'm sorry—how rude of me. I'm Patrizia Sorellani. Pleased to meet you.'

Chiara took her outstretched hand. 'Chiara Santo Domenico.'

The woman held on to her hand. 'You're married to Nicolo Santo Domenico?'

Chiara nodded. 'Yes. Do you know him?'

The women pulled her hand back and nodded. She looked sad. 'Yes, I do…in a way. I'm his mother.'

Chiara absorbed the shock. 'You knew who I was before you came over?'

The woman nodded unhappily. 'I'm sorry. I hope you don't mind. I've been trying to get him to meet me for some time now, but he keeps rebuffing me. I thought that maybe—'

'What are you doing here? You are not welcome.'

Both women looked up to see Nico towering over them. He was glaring at his mother in a way that Chiara recognised from their first meeting. She barely knew the other

woman, but she knew instinctively what she should do—
even though it would incur Nico's wrath.

She stood up. 'Your mother is here because she wants
to speak with you.'

Nico turned his glare on Chiara, but she met it full-on.
'Can't you give her just five minutes?'

For what seemed like an aeon Nico said nothing, and
then, finally, 'Very well. Five minutes. Come with me.'

He turned and stalked off. Patrizia turned to Chiara
for a moment, saying emotionally, 'Thank you so much.'
Then she hurried after her son.

Chiara sat down again, a little shell-shocked.

It was about fifteen minutes before Nico reappeared,
and he looked grim.

Chiara put down her glass. 'What is it? Is everything
okay?'

He took her arm. 'We're leaving.'

He all but marched her out of the function room to
where his car was waiting outside. Once in the back of
the car, and when it was moving Chiara said, 'How did it
go with your mother? She seemed…nice…' she finished
lamely.

Nico was looking out of the other window, his whole
form tense. 'I listened to what she had to say.'

'Nico—'

He turned to her. 'Something else has come up. I'm
going to drop you at the hotel and then I'm going to fly to
Rome tonight. The plane will return to take you home in
the morning. I'll be back tomorrow evening.'

In other words he wasn't going to discuss his mother
or whatever else was going on.

They were pulling up outside the hotel now. Nico got
out and came around to let Chiara out of the car. He escorted her inside and left her at the lift. By the time she

was in the suite and kicking off her shoes frustration was bubbling up inside her.

Maybe Nico did have a crisis to attend to—maybe he didn't. But one thing was clear: she was not welcome to stray out of the clear boundary zone he'd put her in all those months ago.

Chiara undressed and undid her hair, cleaned off her make-up. Then she pulled on a thick robe and went on to the outdoor balcony, leaning on the railing, drinking in the view of Naples at night, this thriving, hectic, chaotic city.

She sucked in a deep breath. It was time to face facts. Nico wasn't going to miraculously fall in love with her. He was going to continue to operate like a lone wolf and punish her for getting too close by shutting her out.

The future she faced was stark. It was also lonely. And Chiara needed to figure out what was best for her and her baby.

By the time Nico returned to the *castello* the following evening—late—Chiara was waiting. Nervous but composed. She had let all the staff have a night off, because there was a fête in the local village, so there would be no interruptions.

He came into the reception room and saw her straight away. 'You shouldn't have waited up.'

Chiara noticed that he looked tired and her silly heart clenched. His jaw was stubbled. 'Was everything okay?'

He moved over to the drinks cabinet, pulling at his tie as he did so. He poured himself a shot of whisky and downed it in one. And then he turned around.

'There was a fire at a tech plant I own outside Rome.'

Chiara gasped, and immediately felt guilty for having thought he was just trying to avoid her. 'Was anyone hurt?'

He shook his head. 'Thankfully there were no employees there—just security guards, and they raised the alarm. It'll be covered by insurance.'

Chiara said, 'You should have told me, Nico. I want to know when things like that happen.'

'But it's nothing to do with you.'

'Of course it is! I'm your *wife*.'

For a long moment he said nothing, and then he said, 'Fair enough. And I owe you an apology. I handled the graveyard thing badly. It was a shock to see it like that… exposed, and being taken care of, after all these years. I shouldn't have taken it out on you—you did a good thing.'

'I wanted to do a good thing. I never meant anything else. But maybe I should have asked first. After all, this isn't my home any more.'

He frowned. 'Yes, it is, Chiara—you're having my child.'

She felt desperation rise in the face of Nico's infuriating calm. This was what he did—retreated to that civil place. No emotion.

'But it's not really my home, is it? I'm here mainly under sufferance—because you didn't want to wait until the *castello* was in the bank's hands and I didn't want to let it go. And then I got pregnant. We both know I wouldn't be here if it weren't for that sequence of events.' She continued painfully, 'I know you wouldn't throw me out…but I'll never be anything more than a glorified guest.'

'What are you talking about?'

'I'm talking about the fact that you are determined to shut me out at all costs, Nico. Whenever I stray too close you push me away. And I know you told me you can't ever give me *more*, and I know I thought I could deal with that, but the fact is… I can't.'

He just looked at her.

Chiara kept going before she lost her nerve.

'The truth is that I fell in love with you, Nico, way back… I think on our wedding night. And when you were so clinical the next morning, so unmoved, I realised that I had it all wrong. It had just been a physical thing for you, while for me…it changed my life. *Me*. I was so terrified you'd notice that I ran away, hoping I'd never see you again. But then I became pregnant. And you brought me back.

'Even then I tried to tell myself it wasn't love. That it was infatuation because you'd been my first lover. But it wasn't. I *love* you, Nico, and I do want more, and I won't survive with you unless you can give me that… So I think the best thing, once the baby comes, is if I move somewhere else. We can talk about custody arrangements at a later date.'

She finished speaking and felt her heart beating wildly. Nico looked stunned. As if someone had just punched him.

'Why are you telling me you love me? Is it because you're hoping it might get you back on the deeds of the *castello*? Is that what this is all about?'

Chiara should have known to expect Nico's ever-present cynicism, but it was still a shock.

She shook her head. 'No, it's not about me trying to get anything. It's about self-preservation.'

His eyes were burning. 'You're having my child. You can't leave.'

Chiara tipped up her chin. She felt as if her insides were being lacerated, and there was a dull pain at the base of her spine. 'Nico, after the baby is born I'm going to ask for a divorce.'

He shook his head and put the glass in his hand down with a clatter on the drinks tray. 'Chiara, this is crazy. You know what we have…'

He started walking towards her and panic galvanised Chiara into action. If he touched her she'd crumble.

She put up her hand. 'Please—don't. I don't want you, Nico. Not like that. Not now.'

Liar. You'll always want him.

She saw that look in his eye—the look that told her he was thinking that all he had to do was touch her and she'd acquiesce.

Her panic intensified. 'I'm sleeping alone tonight, Nico. I need some space.'

The intense expression on his face and in his eyes faded, to be replaced with the mask Chiara recognised well.

She was doing the right thing. She had to do this.

The tone in Nico's voice when he spoke was ominous. 'We'll talk in the morning.'

Chiara had said her piece and now just wanted to escape, so she could lick her wounds. She left Nico behind in the reception room and went up to the bedroom. The pain in her back had intensified and she was feeling crampy. She put it down to emotional stress and got ready for bed.

It was when she was about to get into bed that the first crippling spasm of pain hit her—right across her belly. It was so strong she couldn't breathe for a long moment. When it had passed she gasped for air, and it was only then that she noticed she was wet. She looked down and for a horrific moment thought she'd wet herself, But then she realised what it was and said wonderingly, 'My waters have broken...'

A wholly different kind of panic surged as reality set in and Chiara rushed out of the bedroom, cold and clammy. She went back down to the reception room, but Nico wasn't there. He wasn't in the study either.

By now Chiara was sweating, and she felt another wave of pain about to hit. She doubled over at the bottom of the stairs, groaning. This spasm was longer and more painful. She was also feeling an urge to push, which terrified her.

She forced herself to breathe deeply and calmly as she checked all the bedrooms, and she was almost giving up hope when she saw a light coming from under the door leading to the gym that Nico had had installed. She pushed open the door and he was there, dressed in sweats, punching a bag with a ferocity she'd never seen him exhibit before.

She collapsed to her knees as another contraction hit and Nico saw her. He threw off his gloves and rushed over, crouching down.

She gripped him and got out, 'Waters broken…contractions…the baby is coming.'

He looked at her stupidly for a moment, and as the contraction died away Chiara gripped his hand.

'This is what happened to my mother, Nico. She had me here at the *castello*…then there were complications…she couldn't have any more children… I'm scared.'

Nico rose to his feet in a smooth movement, lifting her into his arms. He said grimly, 'That won't happen. I'm going to put you in the car and take you to the hospital.'

Chiara could feel the next contraction coming and said urgently, 'There's no time, Nico. She's coming… I need to push. You have to call an ambulance—they'll tell you what to do.'

After Nico had laid her down on the bed he got someone on the end of the phone—a paramedic—and it all became a blur to Chiara. She was in the grip of an elemental force and just had to hang on for dear life.

All she could do was focus on Nico and do as he told her to do. After what felt like hours of excruciating pain she felt a rush of energy between her legs—a great release—

and then she had an image of Nico's awestruck face as he held his tiny daughter in his hands. There was an impression of flashing lights before she slipped into blessed darkness and relief from pain.

CHAPTER TEN

'I'M VERY HAPPY to be able to tell you, Signora Santo Domenico, that all is well. There is no reason why you can't go home tomorrow.'

Chiara couldn't stop the knot of anxiety tightening inside her even though she held her perfect sleeping baby in her arms. 'There were no complications?'

The hospital doctor glanced at Nico, who was also in the room. 'Your husband did tell me what happened to your mother, but, no, happily things have moved on from those days, and there is nothing to worry about. You had a textbook birth—thanks to your husband—and the only reason you fainted was because of pain and shock.' He patted her hand reassuringly and said, 'I'll come back later to check on you, but please don't worry. Everything is fine.'

Chiara forced a smile and felt relief wash through her. She knew that everything *wasn't* fine, though. She had told Nico that she loved him and it hadn't precipitated a declaration of anything from him except that she couldn't leave. She could still recall finding him in the gym, punching that bag with all his might...

'Chiara...'

She looked at Nico reluctantly. He was still in his sweats, hair messy.

'You should go home, Nico.' Her conscience pricked.

'Thank you for what you did—you were amazing. I don't know what I would have done if you hadn't been there.'

His face darkened. 'I'm your *husband*, dammit, you don't have to thank me. It was the most profound experience of my life.'

Chiara's heart clenched. She could still recall seeing the awestruck look on Nico's face just before she'd lost consciousness. She'd never seen that look before.

'Chiara, we need to talk.'

She shook her head, not at all ready for their inevitable conversation. 'I'm tired, Nico. Go home. We can talk another time…'

He looked obstinate for a moment, as if he was going to refuse, but then he sighed and said, 'Fine, I'll come back later.'

Chiara wanted to tell him not to, but he was already walking out of the room. When he was gone she turned her head away from the door and let a tired tear slip out of her eye.

These last few hours had been a rollercoaster, and she needed to conserve her strength if she was going to do battle with a man who wanted to insist they stay together even though he didn't love her, and who would use his seductive wiles to manipulate her.

She turned her attention to their daughter and let a rush of maternal love and gratitude for her healthy baby distract from everything.

When Chiara woke later that day she opened her eyes and automatically checked the cot beside the bed—but it was empty. She lifted her head, panic gripping her for a moment.

But then she saw where her daughter was and blinked. And blinked again. She was cradled in Nico's arms, and one of his fingers was clutched in a tiny fist. He'd obviously gone home and showered and changed. His hair was still damp and he wore jeans and a polo shirt, and he looked gorgeous.

There was a look of such naked wonder and awe on his face that Chiara almost felt like a voyeur. Still raw after the birth, she had no defence for seeing Nico like this, with their baby. No defence for the evidence that he *could* feel emotion. Clearly he was in love. Just not with Chiara. And it shamed her that she felt jealous.

She wondered if perhaps she'd been too hasty. Surely if he could love their daughter then she had a duty to try and make their marriage work?

He must have heard her move because he looked up and caught her eye. Immediately his expression blanked. And Chiara knew in that moment that she wasn't strong enough to do it. To spend a lifetime with a man who didn't love her. No matter how much he might love their daughter.

All Nico could see was Chiara's bright green gaze. It left him nowhere to hide, and he wondered if she had witnessed the moment when his heart had swelled so much he'd almost been afraid it would burst, as he looked down at the fragile perfection of his daughter.

Catching her tiny slithery fragile body in his hands when she'd been born had been a truly magical experience—which had turned to one of sheer horror when he'd realised that Chiara wasn't conscious.

He never wanted to go through that stomach-curdling feeling of terror again. He'd lived and died a hundred deaths in those moments as he'd knelt there, holding the exquisite miracle of his daughter, while also contemplating the bone-numbing terror of Chiara's unmoving body.

All the emotions he'd shut off for years had come bursting out of his heart, cracking it open and blasting down the walls he'd erected around it to keep himself safe for years. He'd been an idiot to think he could hold back the dam which had been building inside him from the moment he'd laid eyes on Chiara Caruso.

A God he hadn't acknowledged for a long time had kept Chiara safe. And his daughter. And had answered his fevered prayers.

Feeling more raw than he had ever felt in his life, Nico stood up with Sofia and took her over to Chiara. He desperately felt the need to articulate what was inside him, but didn't know where to start.

As he handed Sofia into Chiara's arms he said, 'Chiara...'

But she looked up at him and said, 'I need to feed her and then change her.' She looked down again, dismissing him.

Her words were like a slap. It reminded him painfully of the day when he'd come to the *castello* to proposition her. When she'd held his card in her hand and refused to meet his eye. He could see now that that had been the moment when she'd touched something much deeper inside him than mere intrigue. He'd been fooling himself all along.

He tried again. 'Chiara...'

She looked up. Her face was expressionless. 'We're fine. You should go. It's late.'

Nico felt a very uncharacteristic sense of defeat. He'd met his equal in Chiara, there was no doubt about that. But he also felt a sense of renewed purpose. Now came the most difficult part. Convincing Chiara to listen to him. And, more, to *believe* him.

The next day Chiara was let out of hospital with Sofia. Nico took them home in a brand-new family-friendly car, with a newly installed baby seat in the back, where Chiara sat beside Sofia to keep an eye on her.

She knew that sooner or later they'd have to talk. When she felt stronger, she told herself weakly.

When they returned to the *castello* Chiara felt ridiculously emotional to see all the staff lined up to greet them. Maria was beaming and clucked over Sofia, and even the gardeners looked suspiciously dewy-eyed.

Spiro, faithful as ever, just came up and nudged Chiara's thigh, telling her he was there. She had noticed that he would invariably gravitate to Nico's study if she wasn't around, and she'd often find him there curled up under the table.

Chiara took Sofia up to the nursery they'd set up directly across the hall from the master bedroom. It was a beautiful sunny room, with brightly coloured furniture and murals on the walls. She stopped in the doorway when she saw the new additions. Stuffed toys of every description were dotted around the room and in the cot, and there was a gorgeous upholstered rocking chair with a foot-rest and wide arms, perfect for nursing.

She could sense Nico behind her and asked faintly, 'Did you do this?'

He sounded wary. 'I just got a few extra things.'

His thoughtfulness made her feel vulnerable, and she knew she wasn't strong enough to look at him, so she half turned and said, 'Thank you, they're lovely. I'm going to change Sofia and feed her now—can you give us some privacy?'

There was a taut moment, and Chiara almost lost her nerve, but then Nico said, 'Sure,' and shut the door.

Chiara felt awful, and hated herself for feeling awful. But she *had* to shut Nico out of these tender, vulnerable moments or she would break completely.

* * *

'Chiara…wake up.'

Chiara's eyes flew open and she sat up. The chair rocked, pitching her forward.

Nico caught her, holding her by the arms. 'You were asleep. Maria will have dinner ready in half an hour, and I've run you a bath.'

Chiara looked over to the cot to see Sofia sleeping peacefully. 'Sofia—'

'Is fine,' Nico said firmly. 'I burped her and changed her.'

Chiara was suddenly wide awake. 'You did all that?'

'Maria showed me how.' He held up a baby monitor. 'We'll hear her if she needs anything.'

Chiara felt a pang. *She* should have been the one to show Nico how to care for Sofia and she couldn't believe she'd slept through it. She realised she was still in the clothes she'd worn home from the hospital, and also that she was starving. She felt thoroughly dishevelled.

Assuring herself that Sofia was fine, she followed Nico into the master bathroom, where a fragrant steaming bath was waiting. Chiara wanted to dive in and never come out again.

He closed the door and Chiara saw that he had laid out clean clothes—soft leggings, a long, loose cashmere top and underwear. Comfortable clothes. *Thoughtful.*

She sank into the bath, groaning in appreciation as the warm water soothed the parts of her that were still tender after giving birth.

She would have fallen asleep again if it hadn't been for Nico knocking on the door a short time later.

After washing, she got out and changed, not wanting to admit that she felt like a new woman. She avoided Nico's eye and tried not to notice how gorgeous he looked dressed in dark trousers and a long-sleeved top.

He led her downstairs after she'd checked again on Sofia, who was still sleeping soundly, her rosebud mouth in a little moue. Her lashes were long and dark. Taking after her father.

Maria served up a delicious hearty Sicilian stew, and it was only when Chiara sat back, replete and relaxed, that she saw the calculating gleam in Nico's eye and realised how cunningly he'd manipulated her.

'Chiara…we have to talk.'

She immediately tensed. 'We have nothing to talk about.'

He fixed her with those dark eyes so like his daughter's. 'We have *everything* to talk about.'

Chiara felt panic rise. She stood up and put down her napkin. 'I don't want to do this now.'

He put out a hand. 'Okay, let me just tell you about my mother, can I? I couldn't tell you that night because it was a lot to process, and in all honesty I had trouble articulating it even to myself…'

Chiara sat down again, reluctant but curious. She hadn't expected him to mention his mother. 'Okay…'

Nico sighed. 'She told me that night at the party about why she left. She had suffered from a mild form of bipolar disorder since her teens. When she got pregnant with me it exacerbated the condition and she couldn't take her medication. My father was unsympathetic, not understanding mental illness. By the time my mother gave birth she was terrified she was going to do something drastic, like run away with me. She knew enough to know she couldn't do that to me, so she left—and left me behind. She told me that she came back a couple of years later, when she was stable again, but my father refused to hear her explanation. He said she had shamed him and he told her to leave and never come back.'

Chiara couldn't stop her heart aching for Nico and his mother. 'I'm so sorry…'

Nico shook his head. 'I always blamed her, but it was my father who refused to give her a chance. She had no money, no resources to try and mount a legal battle—and anyway, they would have made mincemeat of her in a court once they knew about her illness. So she left and got on with her life… But she told me she never forgot about me. She sent me letters but they never reached me—my father must have destroyed them.'

Chiara curled her hand into a fist to stop herself from reaching out to touch Nico. 'I'm glad you know now. Are you going to see her again?'

He nodded. 'Yes, at some stage. But it's thanks to you, for pushing me to listen to her…otherwise I would have cut her off again.'

Chiara shook her head. 'I'm sure you would have listened to her eventually.'

Feeling even more vulnerable after hearing about Nico's mother, Chiara put down her napkin. She was about to make her excuses and leave when Nico said, 'Wait, I need to say something else.'

She stopped, her heart pounding. She desperately wanted to escape Nico's inexorable pull, but she forced herself to ask. 'What?'

'I love you.'

He was looking directly at her, his eyes never darker or more intense.

Chiara couldn't breathe. 'What did you say?'

His jaw clenched. 'I said, I love you.'

A surge of hope so strong that it made her tremble, galvanised Chiara to move up and away from the table. Out of Nico's orbit.

She hugged herself. She couldn't believe this…the risk was too great. He'd told her about his mother just to play on her emotions. He had too much to lose now if she insisted on divorcing him. He loved his daughter. Of course he was going to do his utmost to convince her otherwise.

'You don't have to say this just because I said it to you, Nico.'

He stood up. 'I'm not. I mean it.'

Chiara shook her head, refusing to allow herself to believe. 'What we went through the night Sofia was born… You delivered her into your own hands. It's natural to associate strong emotions with an intense experience like that.'

'Don't patronise me, Chiara. I know what I feel.'

She desisted from reminding him that he'd said more or less the same thing to her about losing her virginity.

'Then it's very convenient that you had this revelation *after* I told you I want a divorce and after the birth of your daughter—which is perhaps making you realise more than ever that you want to promote a united family front to your peers.'

He shook his head. 'You didn't used to be cynical.'

Chiara responded tartly, 'I wasn't, until I met *you*.'

She stopped and bit her lip. He was right, damn him. This wasn't like her.

'I'm tired, Nico. I'm going to bed. Sofia will be awake again for a feed shortly.' She stopped at the door and looked back. 'I'd appreciate it if I could sleep alone. I'll take Sofia into the bedroom in her Moses basket…'

Nico's jaw clenched visibly, but then he said, 'Of course. I'll sleep in a guest suite.'

As she went upstairs she told herself she was doing the right thing. Nico was ruthless—she'd seen it at firsthand. He wasn't above doing whatever it took to get what he wanted…even telling her he loved her.

* * *

When Chiara woke at dawn the next morning she found a note on the pillow beside hers. She picked it up, recognising the slashing writing instantly.

Chiara,
I have to go to Rome on business for a couple of days.
We will talk again when I get back.
Nico

An incredible sense of disappointment flooded her. She'd refused to believe Nico last night, but she'd woken with that eternal flame of hope inside her, and before she'd seen the note she'd thought to herself that if he said it again...tried to convince her...she might just believe him.

But she'd been right. Evidently he'd given up the pretence and gone back to work. Maybe he was with his solicitors right now, drawing up papers for their divorce?

Just then Sofia awoke, making small mewling sounds, and Chiara reached over and plucked her out of the Moses basket, plumping up the pillows behind her so she could get comfortable for feeding. As Sofia latched on to Chiara's breast with unerring accuracy and suckled strongly Chiara once again reminded herself that the most important thing was this small baby, and protecting her from whatever fallout lay ahead.

Nico looked across the lawn to where Chiara was lying in the shade on a sunbed, with Sofia in a pram beside her and another umbrella shading her. She was wearing a strapless swimsuit and she'd never looked more beautiful.

He felt an incredible sense of vulnerability and trepidation. It this didn't work he truly didn't know what he would do—for the first time in his life.

Chiara was drowsing in the late-afternoon sun when she sensed Nico's presence. Just like that. For the first time since she'd given birth there was a stirring deep inside her, and the small hairs stood up on her arms. She opened her eyes and saw he was approaching where she lay, looking fiercely determined.

She scrambled up to a sitting position, pulling a shawl across her bare shoulders.

'Nico. You're back.' He must have been back for a while, because he was dressed in worn jeans and a loose shirt. Rolled-up sleeves. Hair damp from the shower.

He sat down on the lounger beside hers. Too close. Chiara couldn't breathe for a moment. She wasn't ready to see him. He'd caught her unawares.

'I said we'd talk when I got back.'

Chiara scooted back nervously. 'Sofia is due a feed... she'll wake in a minute.'

'Stop using our daughter as a defence, Chiara. I'm just asking you to listen to me for a few minutes—is that too much to ask?'

There was a bleak tone to Nico's voice that she hadn't heard before and she went still. 'No, of course not.'

He relaxed marginally and Chiara realised how tense he was.

He ran a hand through his hair and muttered something like, *'God, this is hard.'* Then he looked at her. 'I told you I loved you the other evening. And I meant it.'

Chiara opened her mouth but he put up a hand.

'No. Let me finish. I can appreciate that you might not believe me, given the nature of why and how we married. Given the fact that I've done my best to keep you at a distance... But the truth is that I didn't know how to let you get close. And every time you did it repelled me— because that's how I deal with *any* kind of intimacy. My father never showed me affection. My relationship with Alexandra was immature and incredibly selfish. I thought I loved her, so I associated being betrayed with being in love. It took seeing her again—next to you—for me to realise that I'd felt nothing for her. She wounded my ego, nothing else.

'I think that's when I fell in love with you—not that I was ready to admit that then. No one had ever defended me before, until you literally stepped in front of me and confronted her. But I wasn't ready to admit to any feelings other than *like* and *respect*. That's what I told myself when I laid out the reasons why I thought this marriage could work.

'I knew you wanted more, Chiara, and on some level I think I knew you were in love with me. But in my arrogance I thought that was a *good* thing—you feeling more for me than I did for you. Which was a joke, because while I was telling myself you loved me I was falling for you and not even aware of it. All I knew was that if I left here for more than two days I had to get back. I couldn't contemplate desiring another woman ever again. I couldn't understand how my desire for you got stronger and stronger…why I was falling deeper and deeper.

'You did beautiful things—like the graveyard, and forcing me to confront my mother. But the emotions you stirred terrified me. It was easier to push you away. So I can understand why you won't believe me when I say *I love you*.' He sighed heavily. 'And, yes, it *did* take Sofia's birth and the terror of thinking I'd lost you to make me finally come to my senses… I needed to almost lose you to find my heart…'

Chiara was stunned into speechlessness. Nico drew a rolled-up sheaf of papers out of his back pocket and handed

it to her. She went clammy at the thought that it was divorce papers. That he might have given up on hoping he
could convince her.

She said, 'Nico—'

He put up a hand. 'Just take a look before you say anything.'

She unrolled the papers and it took a second for her
eyes to make out the ornate calligraphy. Slowly she said,
'These are the deeds to the *castello*…in the Caruso name.'
She looked at him, not understanding.

'I needed to do something to convince you. The *castello* is back in your name. It's yours. I couldn't care less
any more about my claim on it, because it's just bricks
and mortar. What I care about is here in this garden, not
on those deeds.'

And then he pulled a small box out of his jeans pocket.
Chiara saw that his hands were trembling. He opened the
box and revealed a plain gold band inlaid with tiny glittering emeralds.

'It's an eternity ring. Because I want to spend the rest
of my life with you, Chiara, being your husband, partner,
lover. I want to take you to all those cities and show you
the world…'

Chiara was overwhelmed. She shook her head. 'I
don't….' She couldn't speak. Her throat was too tight
with emotion.

She saw Nico's face fall, the light in his eyes fade. He
closed the velvet box and put it down before standing up.
She realised that he was misreading her reaction.

'I'm sorry, Chiara, I never meant to hurt you. If you still
truly want a divorce then you can have it.'

He had turned to walk away before Chiara could make
her body work. She stood up and called out hoarsely,
'Stop!'

Nico stopped, his back to her.

She started towards him, her legs like jelly. 'You didn't let me finish…'

He turned around and she saw the pain etched into his features. She took a deep shaky breath. 'What I was going to say was that I don't know what to say—except I love you with all my heart, and, yes, I want to spend the rest of my life with you too…'

The dawning relief on Nico's face told Chiara better than anything just how much he'd been holding back for so long. She wasn't sure who moved, but they were in each other's arms, mouths fused in a desperate kiss of love and reunion.

When they broke apart Chiara looked up in wonder and traced Nico's mouth with a shaking finger. 'I love you so much. You deserve to be happy, Nico.'

His eyes were suspiciously bright. '*You* are my happiness—you and Sofia. I love you both. For ever.'

Chiara looked deep into Nico's eyes and saw his soul reflecting back all the passion and emotion he'd been denying himself. She took a deep breath and allowed herself to believe. *Really* believe.

As if reading her mind, he said, 'You deserve to be happy too, *cara*.'

She smiled tremulously and nodded. 'I am—finally.'

Just then a mewling cry sounded from the pram and they both smiled.

Nico traced Chiara's jaw and whispered, 'Later, *mio amore*, I'll show you just how much I love you…'

Chiara took Nico's hand and led him to where the pram sat in the shade. She took Sofia out, and as she nursed their daughter Nico picked up her hand and placed the eternity ring on her finger. He pressed a kiss to her hand before interlacing their fingers and letting the peace that had eluded him his whole life infuse every bone in his body.

He'd never believed in love…but now it was all he could see.

EPILOGUE

CHIARA FELT ARMS slide around her midriff from behind and the intimate contact of her husband's hard body against her back as he settled behind her and stretched his legs alongside hers, where she sat on the sand in the shade.

As it always did without fail, her pulse sped up and her body reacted to his proximity. She leant back against him, letting him take her weight. She sighed happily. 'You're home.'

'I told you I'd make it back before dinner.'

She craned her head to look at him. 'You're not missing the buzz of Rome or New York too much?'

Nico had moved his main office from Rome to Syracuse, and he commuted in and out of there every day now—apart from the occasions when he had to go abroad, when he invariably took Chiara with him.

'It's the only thing that keeps me sane, having you near me,' he'd told her.

'No way,' he said now.

Chiara felt his voice running through her body like a happy hum of contentment. She'd never have guessed he could smile so much, or laugh, but that was all he seemed to do these days.

'Did you speak to your mother?'

She could feel him nod—yes. 'She's coming at the weekend.'

'Good.' Chiara was happy for Nico that he and his mother had developed a relationship at last. Patrizia adored visiting and spending time with them.

Nico's lips feathered a kiss near her ear and he asked, 'Well, is this close to what you imagined all those years ago?'

Chiara had told him of her fantasies about the kind of life she'd wanted at the *castello*. She looked around them and smiled. Sometimes her heart felt too full, as if it would burst. Now was one of those moments, on the small beach she'd always loved so much.

Their eldest daughter Sofia was holding one-year-old Luca by the hand and encouraging him to walk in the shallows of the sea. He was squealing with delight every time a small wave washed over his feet and pudgy legs. He had a head full of thick dark hair, and sometimes he reminded her so much of Nico that it hurt.

The twins, Alicia and Alessandro, were building sandcastles nearby under an umbrella, their hair almost blonde from the sun, freckles dusting their cheeks. They both had the green eyes of their mother, while Sofia and Luca had dark brown eyes.

Happy sounds and splashing water filled the air. She nodded against Nico's chest, feeling emotional. 'This doesn't even come close…it's so much better.'

Nico laced his hands with hers and squeezed tight. 'I didn't even have this dream—you gave it to me.'

Chiara tipped her head back and Nico pressed a kiss to her mouth. It held the promise of passion to come and endless love.

And just then came an excited squeal from Alicia, '*Papa!* You're home!'

Chiara felt Nico smile against her mouth as the moment turned into happy chaos and four children aged from six to one, descended upon their parents and buried them under a sea of legs, arms and kisses.

As the sun set on the small beach Nico and Chiara gathered up their family and made their way home to the *castello*. The stone above the main entrance now read *Castello Santo Domenico Caruso*, reflecting what was on the deeds.

They passed by the two graveyards, old and new. They were one graveyard now—two families united by love in the end.

* * * * *

SHEIKH'S PREGNANT CINDERELLA

MAYA BLAKE

CHAPTER ONE

HIS EARS WERE playing tricks on him. They must be.

Otherwise they wouldn't have relayed the unconscionable message to his brain that—

No.

'Repeat yourself,' Sheikh Zufar al Khalia, current occupant of the throne of Khalia, breathed softly at the short, bespectacled senior aide standing before him.

The man shrank back, very much aware that his King's lowered, even tones were far worse than his bark. Not that Zufar al Khalia, much accomplished, master strategist and all-round frighteningly intelligent head of the exulted royal family, needed to lower himself to such unseemly actions as barking.

Marwan Farhat only managed to withstand his liege's chilling tawny gaze for a handful of seconds before lowering his to the priceless Persian rug beneath his feet.

'Now, Marwan,' Zufar insisted.

'We've been informed that your betrothed has disappeared, Your Highness. She's not in her suite, and her maidservant thinks she's been taken.'

'Thinks? So there's no actual evidence?'

'Uh… I haven't spoken to the servant myself, Your Highness, but—'

'For all you know, my betrothed could be hiding somewhere in the palace, under the pretext of the foolish, pre-wedding nerves that normally afflict women on such a day, correct?'

Marwan exchanged glances with the other aides. 'It is possible, Your Highness.'

Zufar heard the *but* not spoken, loud and clear. 'Where is this maidservant? I wish to speak to her myself.'

The senior aide grimaced. 'Of course, Your Highness, but I've been informed the girl is quite hysterical. I don't think it will be useful—'

'Useful?' The cold disbelief trapped in his chest expanded. 'Do you see what I'm wearing, Marwan?' Zufar drawled in the soft, deadly voice that usually hushed his subordinates into fearful silence, as he rounded the massive teak desk that had previously belonged to his esteemed grandfather.

Marwan's Adam's apple bobbed again as he took in Zufar's heavy burgundy-and-gold military uniform, complete with wide sash, epaulettes, and buttons made of solid gold. Where other men would have looked stiff and pompous, his King looked enviably elegant, his towering six-feet-plus height lending the uniform a regal stature few could emulate.

The accompanying cloak hung on its own specially made frame nearby. Together they formed the King's ceremonial wedding attire, commissioned on his twenty-first birthday for this one momentous occasion. Zufar al Khalia had cut a commanding figure since he hit puberty, but on this day he rose above all men into an exclusive realm of his own.

'Yes, Your Highness,' he responded respectfully.

Zufar tossed the white gloves he'd been about to put on before he was interrupted onto the desk, and advanced towards the men. He had their attention, but he needed to make sure that not a single syllable that fell from his lips would be misconstrued.

'Have you seen the dignitaries and heads of states currently making their way to the Imperial Room? The fifty thousand citizens who've been camping in the capital for the past seven days in anticipation of this ceremony? The three hundred journalists and innumerable cameras waiting on the south lawn to televise this ceremony?'

'Of course, Your Highness.'

Zufar took a deep calming breath, certain that if he didn't he would burst a blood vessel despite his supremely robust health. And that would be terribly unwise considering this was supposed to be his wedding day.

'Tell me again why you think it would not be *useful* to discover the whereabouts of my betrothed as soon as possible?'

Marwan clasped his hands before him, a gesture of supplication that did nothing to appease Zufar's rising temper. 'A thousand pardons, Your Highness,' he said. 'I merely came to inform you that there might be a delay. Perhaps we can postpone the ceremony—'

'No. There will be no postponement. You will find my betrothed immediately and this wedding ceremony will proceed as scheduled.'

'Your Highness, the guards and all the servants have searched everywhere. She is not here.'

A red haze washed across Zufar's vision. His collar began to constrict him, blocking his airway. But he didn't raise his hand to undo a button or in any way indicate his discomfort.

He was the King.

Since birth, streams of instructors and governesses had drummed long-suffering poise and decorum into him, with swift and merciless punishment delivered for stepping out of line. As for rash displays of emotion like the bellow of frustration that bubbled inside him? Those came with a week's banishment to the winter palace on the northernmost part of Khalia with nothing but the frozen mountains and endless reams of Latin recitals for company.

No, unfettered displays of emotion had been his father's eminent domain.

For Zufar and his younger brother and sister, it had been an emotionless existence in the strictest boarding schools in foreign lands. And during the holidays when they were allowed home, they would spend hours being groomed into becoming the perfect ambassadors of the Royal House of Khalia.

On the rare occasion when his temper strained and attempted to get the better of him, like today, people took notice. And fled his presence at the earliest possible moment.

Zufar gathered himself until his spine was a steel column, and fixed his eyes on Marwan. 'You will take me to this maidservant now. I wish to hear what she has to say for myself.'

The senior aide immediately bowed low. 'Of course, Your Highness.'

The palace guards stationed on either side of the door sprang forwards to open the double doors for him.

The moment Zufar stepped into the hallway, he knew something was very, very wrong. The excited buzz that had charged the air during the final preparations for the royal wedding had altered.

Several staff members of the royal palace wore anxious expressions as they rushed back and forth. And while it was respectful to drop one's gaze before the King, he noticed that every single one of the staff was actively avoiding his.

The palpable tension raised the hairs on his nape. Beside him, Marwan also avoided his gaze. In fact, the man was doing everything in his power to extend his short strides in the rush to put self-preserving space between himself and Zufar.

It would've been amusing had Zufar not felt in his very marrow that his impending nuptials were in jeopardy.

Whispers around him grew as he entered the main part of the palace. As with most royal palaces, the women's quarters were separated from the men's by several wings. His own private rooms were to the west of the sprawling palace that sat on top of Mount Jerra.

Quick strides took him across to the east wing. He ignored the bows and scrapes of his palace staff and extended family members as he walked, grim-faced, towards the guest suite that Amira, his fiancée, had occupied since her arrival at the palace three weeks ago.

She was a daughter of his father's oldest friend, and Zufar had been aware of Amira's existence since he was a boy. But she was several years his junior and had clearly found him intimidating to the point of speechlessness at the best of times. He hadn't taken much interest in her until his father had informed him of the agreement he'd made with Feroz Ghalib, Amira's father, for them to marry.

Even then, the wedding had been a distant future event, arranged by others and needing only a handful of meetings for the sake of appearances. Still, he'd taken his duty seriously and ensured during their meetings that she was at ease and not being forced into a union she didn't want. Her assurances had satisfied him enough to accept that she would be his wife when the time was right.

The medical report that had confirmed that she was healthy enough to bear his children had sealed the deal.

Beyond that, he hadn't given her much thought, although she'd been peculiarly distracted during their twice weekly dinners recently.

But Amira was close with his sister and Zufar was confident that Galila would have informed him if there'd been a problem with the upcoming nuptials.

Nevertheless, had he dropped the ball somewhere?

He frowned.

The burden of governing his kingdom was his first and only priority. It had needed to be, considering the chaos it had been left in by his father's sudden abdication.

Tight anger knotted inside him as he strode faster towards the suite of luxury rooms that were reserved for the Queen and other female members of the royal family.

He wouldn't think of his father today, or the fact that the ex-King had banished himself to the summer palace since his wife's death and hadn't spoken to his children in months. Zufar wouldn't think of the sleepless nights and backbreaking work it had taken for him to keep the kingdom that had already been woefully neglected by his father from falling apart.

Today, *this hour*, demanded his complete attention. His people yearned for a royal wedding. That was exactly what he was going to give them.

The footmen stationed outside the Sapphire Suite spotted him and immediately threw open the doors.

Zufar entered, then drew to a stop at the sight of the visibly distressed women in the living room. Two were babbling hysterically, and an older female servant was busy comforting another.

'Which one is she?' he demanded tersely. Eyes swivelled to him, followed predictably by shocked gasps and hurried comportment before the bows and scrapes and averted gazes commenced.

Marwan hushed them, and then uttered a sharp query to the junior aide behind him. The younger man shook his head, throwing a furtive glance at Zufar. Marwan approached the older attendant and questioned her. Clearly nervous, she pointed to the inner chamber.

Zufar strode towards smaller double doors, his temper frothing furiously in his chest. This time he pulled the doors open himself, bitter memories tossing themselves onto the pyre he was trying to contain as he walked into the huge, lavish chamber that had once been his mother's domain.

His gaze didn't linger on the priceless keepsakes, furniture or decoration. He didn't know which items in this room his mother had treasured and which gifts from his father and her secret admirers had been less favoured. He didn't know her favourite book or the preferred flower arrangement for her private sitting room because he had never been allowed in here.

On the rare occasions his mother had tolerated him, they had been in public where her pretended adoration could be captured for the world to see and praise and to provide moments of smugness as she perused the gossip rags. Beyond that, she'd never had a kind word for him or his siblings.

But he wasn't here to dwell on the subject of his mother.

He trained his focus on the figure hunched over near the headboard of the vast bed. She was so slight he almost missed her.

Had it not been for the drab, body-shrouding beige clothes that painfully and distastefully stood out against the gold and cream bed linen, he would've mistaken her for one of the pillows or part of the rich drapery that decorated the four-poster bed.

As he advanced towards her he noticed that her slim shoulders were shaking. Another few steps and the small sniffles of her quiet sobs reached his ears.

Zufar stifled his curse before it ripped free.

He didn't care for weak women. He cared even less for weak, *crying* women.

Behind him, Marwan clicked his tongue sharply.

The figure jumped up, stumbled over her long, shapeless skirt, and immediately tumbled to the floor in a graceless heap at Zufar's feet.

He waited, impatient breath slowly spilling through clenched teeth, for her to rise. But she didn't seem interested in regaining her feet. Instead, she was developing an almost mesmerised interest in his shoes.

He took a step forwards, hoping to dislodge her hypnosis. When that failed to work, he cleared his throat.

'If that is a shoe fetish you're exhibiting, may I suggest you indulge in it another time? When the reputation of my kingdom isn't at stake, perhaps?' Zufar drawled.

A sharp intake of breath, then, finally, she raised her head.

Large, tear-soaked dark eyes rose from his feet, and plotted an excruciatingly slow journey up his body. By the time they reached his face, her expression was creased into abject horror.

Coupled with a face blotched and bloated with tears and a mouth frozen in an unattractive O, she was the most unsightly girl Zufar had ever seen.

'What is your name?' he bit out, praying she could actually string enough words together to answer.

She didn't respond. She simply stared up at him, her horror intensifying by the second.

'Do you not hear your King addressing you, girl?' Marwan demanded sharply.

Her mouth closed. She swallowed noisily, but still uttered no word.

Zufar's fists started to curl. Almost a year's worth of meticulous planning hung in the balance because of one tear-streaked, dumbstruck girl.

About to move, he paused as her gaze darted to his fists and she recoiled.

The sight of her naked fear struck an uncomfortable chord in him. He breathed out and slowly unfurled his fingers. There would be no coherent conversation with her unless he found a way to defuse some of her fear, he realised.

He sensed Marwan moving towards her and held up his hand. 'Leave us,' he instructed.

Marwan made a small sound of surprise. 'Are you sure, Your Highness?'

Zufar's lips tightened. 'Leave. Now.'

The room emptied immediately. He kept his gaze fixed on the girl crouched before him, and slowly extended his hand towards her. Again, her gaze darted between his face and his hand, as if terrified he would do something unpredictable. Like bite. Or strike.

He frowned.

She reminded him of the skittish colts in his stable. The ones that demanded substantial time and patience to respond to his commands.

Except he was in gross negative supply of either today. His marriage ceremony was scheduled to commence in less than two hours.

Zufar leaned down and extended his hand further. 'Stand up,' he instructed, firming his voice.

She placed her hand in his, scrambled upright, and immediately gasped and dropped his hand as if she'd been scalded.

He ignored her reaction, his gaze moving over her, confirming that the drabness indeed extended from the top of the dishevelled tufts of dark hair peeking out of her beige scarf to the soles of her feet.

Except, she wasn't a girl as he'd initially surmised.

She was long past adolescence, if the pronounced swell of her chest and the hint of curves beneath the clothes were any indication. She came up to his chin in her flat, tasteless shoes, her covered arms slender and her jaw holding a delicate strength.

His eyes were drawn to her chest again. It was just her agitated breathing that was snagging his attention. Nothing else. He stepped back, folded his hands behind his back and assumed a gesture of ease that never failed to work on his horses.

'What is your name?' he asked again in a lower voice.

Her gaze dropped to the ground and she mumbled.

'Speak up,' he said.

Her chin jerked up a little, but her gaze remained, once again, on the tips of his shoes.

'Niesha Zalwani, Your Highness,' she repeated.

Her voice was soft, smoky and lyrical, if a little too timid for his dwindling patience. But at least he was getting somewhere. He had a name.

'What is your role here?'

'I—I'm… I was a chambermaid until last week, when I was added to Miss Amira's personal staff.'

'Look at me when I'm addressing you,' Zufar drawled. It

took an interminable age for her head to rise once more. But eventually, her gaze met his, then promptly flitted down to rest on his nose. Zufar prayed for strength and continued, 'Where's your mistress?'

Immediately her lower lip wobbled, her wide eyes grew haunted and her breathing turned agitated again. Zufar forced himself not to stare at the soft globes of her breasts or the pale creaminess of her throat as she trembled before him.

'She…she's gone, Your Highness.'

Zufar's fist threatened to ball again. Resisting the urge was difficult. 'Gone where?' he managed through clenched teeth.

'I don't know, Your Highness.'

'Very well. Let us try another way. Did she leave alone?'

Another frenzied twisting of her fingers, and then she cleared her throat. 'No, Your Highness. She…she left with a man.'

A detached, icy sensation stroked his nape. 'A man? What man?' he asked softly.

'He did not tell me his name, Your Highness.'

'But you are certain she has been taken against her will by an unknown male?' he pressed.

The woman before him bit her lip, drawing his attention to the plump, reddened curve of her mouth as she nodded. 'Yes…well…' Her distress grew.

'Tell me what you know,' he insisted.

'I may be wrong, Your Highness, but she didn't seem… unwilling.'

The possibility that he'd been jilted arrived with ice-cold anger. Except, curiously, Zufar wasn't enraged on his own behalf. Rather, the impending disappointment for his people, the chaos for his kingdom, was what caused his fists to clench behind his back.

'Did she say anything? Did *he* say anything to make you think this?'

'It—it all happened very quickly, Your Highness. But…' Her hand disappeared into the folds of her skirt and emerged with a folded piece of paper. 'He…he instructed me to give this to Princess Galila to hand to you.' She held out the piece of paper, her slender fingers trembling.

Zufar took it from her, his insides frozen as he unfolded the sheet he recognised as a torn piece of his own royal stationery.

He read the message once. Then again.

With a thick curse, he crumpled the heavy, embossed paper between his fingers, his fist clenched tight until it shook with the force of his emotions. The red haze of fury returned, deeper, steeping his lethal mood as he crossed to the window and pressed his fist against the wide pane.

Before him, the palace grounds sprawled in sun-dappled splendour. Beyond the windows, the muted buzzing of an expectant crowd rolled over the horizon. Excited citizens and eager tourists who'd flown in especially for this occasion were anticipating a fairy-tale royal wedding of their King to his chosen Queen. The whole kingdom had been gripped in wedding fever for months.

Only to have his heathen bastard of a half-brother claim in writing that he'd seduced and stolen his betrothed!

In another life, perhaps, that tiny sliver of emotion piercing through his fury could've been called relief from yet another responsibility. But Zufar gave it absolutely no room whatsoever, because he now faced a monumental problem. Aside from the humiliation of announcing that he was no longer in possession of his fiancée, this arrangement had held great economic advantages for Khalia.

He needed to find Amira. Confirm for himself that his half-brother's claim was the truth.

But how could he, when he had no idea where he'd gone? The dossier he'd collated on Adir when he'd first made his unforgettable appearance at his mother's funeral had revealed he had no fixed abode, or, if he did, he'd kept it very well hidden.

Even if Zufar knew his whereabouts, he had no time to go chasing after him. He acknowledged with a bitter laugh how well timed Adir's revenge had been. His half-brother knew that doing this now would cause the most humiliation. The most uproar.

Zufar wasn't about to hand him that victory. Not in this lifetime.

He whirled to face the young chambermaid. 'When did they leave?'

Her throat worked again. But this time she wasn't silent for very long. 'I brought her tea, and left her alone for just ten minutes.' Her voice was wracked with nerves and anguish. She began to wring her hands again. 'I had gone to get the royal jewellery when I heard the commotion.'

'So you saw them leave together?'

Her head moved in a shaky nod. 'Yes.'

'And you're sure he didn't harm her?' Zufar demanded.

'She—she didn't appear in distress, Your Highness. She seemed…willing.'

The tightness in his chest eased a tiny fraction. 'How did they leave?'

She pointed to the very window where he stood.

Zufar's jaw clenched tight. They were on the second floor, with nothing outside the windows but climbing vines. Granted, they were over a century old and sturdy enough to hold a horse, but had his barbarian brother really whisked his betrothed out of a second-floor window?

'Did anyone else see them?'

'Only Her Highness, the Princess, but they were almost on the ground when she came in.'

Zufar frowned. Why hadn't Galila informed him?

Had she tried to stop them and been unsuccessful? Most likely Galila was keeping well out of Zufar's way because she knew how he would take the news.

'How soon after did you raise the alarm?'

Guilt flickered across her face and her lower lip trembled once more.

'Seconds? Minutes?' he snapped.

She paled. 'I—I'm sorry… I thought… I thought it was a prank.'

'It wasn't. And your failure to raise the alarm in time may have aided his getaway.' Zufar was sure of it.

She shrank further into the wall. He whirled away, tension threatening to break his spine.

The scandal just waiting to be triggered by such a revelation struck him stone cold. But under no circumstances was he going to let that happen.

He shoved the piece of paper into his pocket and closed his mind to the burning gross insult against his kingdom and his crown. He would deal with his half-brother later. For now he needed an interim solution to this situation. One that did not involve calling off his wedding.

A quick glance around the room showed the suspended state of preparation.

The gown that should've been adorning his bride-to-be by was draped over a mannequin, the heeled slippers peeking out beneath its hem.

Detachedly, he inspected the rest of the room as he mentally ran through the list of other bridal candidates that had been presented to him when the subject of his nuptials first came up a year ago. Like most royal arranged marriages, although one choice had been favoured above the others, there were always contingencies in case of sudden unsuitability.

Three of those candidates were downstairs, ruled out as potential brides to the King and reduced to honoured guests at his wedding. Could one of them be elevated to the position that would turn out to be a dream come true for them?

Zufar's lips twisted.

There was no way to execute that plan without announcing to the whole world that he'd been jilted. That would only result in frenzied tabloid gossip the media would feed off for years.

Not that any solution he came up with wouldn't cause ripples. But keeping it under wraps until *he* was ready would control the beast.

Which meant he had to keep the circle of trust as tight as possible while he found a quieter, interim solution.

But to mitigate the uproar of impending scandal, he needed a bride; needed to ensure he was married within the next two hours before news that he'd been jilted got out.

His reason for choosing his new bride would need to be explained, of course. That would be a problem for tomorrow.

He turned away from the wedding gown and came face to face with the chambermaid. He'd forgotten about her. To be honest, she was barely breathing, striving to be as unobtrusive as possible. Zufar was surprised she hadn't fled while his back was turned.

Her wide-eyed gaze fixed on him, watchful and wary as she followed his pacing figure.

He slowed to a stop on the next pass, an impossibly ludicrous idea taking root in his brain. 'How long have you been in my palace?' he asked.

'All…um… Most of my life, Y-Your Highness,' she stammered.

He gave a satisfied inner nod. She would know his customs, know the value of discretion.

Sweet desert stars, was he really entertaining this preposterous notion? 'And how old are you?' Zufar growled.

She swallowed, her nostrils quivering delicately as she inhaled. 'Twenty-five, Your Highness.'

He stared at her for a full minute, then nodded briskly. There was neither chagrin nor prevarication in the decision his brain latched onto.

He needed a solution, and he'd found one. His gaze dropped down to her twisting ringless fingers. 'Do you have a husband?' he asked.

A deep blush flamed her cheeks, her gaze flitting away from his again as she shook her head. 'No, Your Highness, I am unmarried.'

Just to be sure, he probed deeper. 'Are you committed to another?'

Her mouth tightened for the briefest second, but she shook her head before she mumbled, 'No.'

He wanted to demand that she repeat that. To look him in the eyes while she did so. But time was slipping through his fingers.

Zufar's chest filled with grim purpose as his gaze sprang from the unsuitable woman before him to the wedding dress, and back again. She was roughly the same size as Amira, if perhaps a little bustier and wider of hip than his...*former* fiancée. Their heights too were similar and so, from what he could see beneath the blotchiness and drabness, was their colouring.

Of course, Amira had held herself with more poise than this maid, years of first-class schooling and a finishing school in Switzerland undertaken for the sole purpose of her future role as Queen. The woman in front of him was nowhere near as polished.

But he didn't need a gem, just a polished stone to pass off as the real thing until he could resolve this situation quietly and on his terms.

'Come here,' he commanded evenly as he strolled to stand next to the wedding dress. Now he'd decided what to do, he couldn't afford any more tears or, heaven forbid, tantrums that would further delay him.

She presented him with that rabbit-caught-in-headlights look again, the pulse fluttering at her throat racing faster.

Zufar bit down his exasperation. 'You're not deaf. I know you can hear me. Come here,' he stated firmly.

She jerked into movement, stumbling to a stop two feet away from him.

He inspected her, noting that her eyes were in fact a

dark amethyst, not the brown he'd thought, and that her eyelashes were far longer than he had initially noticed. Her mouth too was curved in a perfect little bow that, should it ever find its way into a smile, might salvage some of her dreariness.

His gaze dropped, took in the lines of her neck, and again experienced a tiny bolt of surprise at how sleekly it curved to her shoulders, how delicate and flawless were her collarbones and skin.

No, not a diamond, but perhaps a better quality stone than he'd first surmised.

A quality stone, but still rough around the edges, he modified, when he noticed she was still twisting her fingers into an agitated mess. 'Be still, little one,' he commanded.

She made a strangled little sound under her breath but her body stilled and her fingers stopped moving. He suppressed a need to tell her to straighten her spine and look him in the eye when he spoke to her.

Such training was unnecessary for what he had in mind. All that would be required was for her not to collapse into a useless heap before he'd achieved his goal. And he had a way to ensure that happened.

Decision made, he whirled away from her. As if they were in tune with his thoughts, a brief knock sounded on the door before Marwan and the rest of his aides rushed in.

'Your Highness? Have you any news you wish me to relay to the royal guard? A starting point for the search for your intended, perhaps?'

'We are past that, Marwan,' Zufar said coldly, noting absently again that Amira's absconding didn't sting as much as it should. If anything, it was his half-brother's insult that grated harsher.

'Oh? Does that mean the ceremony is off?'

Zufar glanced at the woman standing shell-shocked in the corner of the room.

She looked even worse, as if a fresh bolt of lightning

had hit her. His decision didn't waver as his gaze objectively raked her.

The wedding bouquet would occupy her skittish hands, veils would shroud her face, and heels would elevate her height and hopefully correct her posture.

Beyond that, very little mattered.

'No, it does not. The ceremony is still going ahead.' He slashed his hand through the shocked murmurs echoing through the room. When he achieved silence, he continued, 'I fully intend to be married in two hours' time. Niesha Zalwani is to be my bride and everyone in this room will ensure that my wishes are fulfilled.'

CHAPTER TWO

'TELL YOUR BROTHER I've not only seduced his precious bride
but that she runs away with me willingly. Tell him I'm stealing away his future Queen, just as he stole my birthright.'

Those were the most scandalous words Niesha had expected to hear today, and possibly for the rest of her days.
A day that should've been one of intense joy, but which had
taken a wrong turn to hell about an hour ago.

With the Sheikh's appearance in his intended's bedroom,
she'd harboured hope that everything would be resolved.

Except King Zufar al Khalia had just spoken words that
simply didn't make sense. For a moment Niesha wondered
whether the shock of watching Amira Ghalib disappear
from right under her nose had dislodged a few million brain
cells.

The man in front of her, the formidable, extraordinarily
captivating tower of masculinity who prowled through his
kingdom with harsh authority and power, commanding and
receiving the loyal adulation of his subjects because he was
simply that breathtaking, had just said—

No. You did you not hear him right. It was impossible.

Her thoughts were clearly echoed by Marwan, who
sprang forwards. 'Your Highness?' His voice was ashen
with disbelief.

The King—*her* King, since she too was a subject of the
Kingdom of Khalia—moved another step closer, bringing
his earth-shaking life force even more dangerously into
her space. He stalked so close she could almost see the ice
crackling in his eyes, the contained fury vibrating his body.

Niesha shrank away from the elegant folds of the wedding gown, the sheets of icy shock thawing into a cauldron

of panic. She glanced around the room, selfishly wishing Princess Galila were still here.

King Zufar's sister barely noticed Niesha most of the time, but her kind smile when she did was far better than the fiercely domineering glower of her brother, and the tableau of horrified expressions spread in panorama before her.

Perversely, those expressions were what hammered home the fact that she'd heard correctly. He'd used her full name. In connection to marriage. *His* marriage. Today. Shock gurgled in her throat.

Her fingers moved then, connected with the soft, warm folds of the most extraordinary wedding gown she'd ever seen in her life. The gown that, finding herself alone in this room three nights ago, she'd secretly indulged in one insane moment's fantasy of wearing herself to marry the ephemeral man of her dreams.

The gown that Zufar al Khalia wanted her to…to—

'I'm sorry, Your Highness…' she whispered, but his voice overrode hers.

'Time is of the essence,' he growled, without raising his deep voice. 'I suggest we begin preparations immediately.'

'Your Highness, this…this will be highly unprecedented,' Marwan said.

'I should hope so, or there would be something seriously disturbing with my reign,' Sheikh Zufar stated without looking the old man's way. 'But make no mistake. This wedding ceremony will happen. She is the one who will take Amira's place,' he uttered with a finality that drove a bolt of fear down Niesha's throat.

Aware that she had to get herself together very quickly or risk being flattened by the force of nature bearing down on her, she straightened her spine and raised her head.

He was watching her with the savage, mesmerising golden eyes of a hawk. Before she could summon any words, Marwan beat her to it. 'Your Highness, perhaps we should discuss this—'

'You are risking insubordination by questioning my command. The subject isn't up for discussion. Get the bridal attendants in here now.'

Niesha realised her head was moving from side to side, a pendulous action she couldn't stop. Shockwaves that hadn't stopped rippling through her since she witnessed Amira and the stranger's extraordinary flight now threatened to drown her. Another sound ripped from her throat.

Dark, tawny eyes zeroed in on her.

'You will not pass out,' Zufar commanded tersely, as if just by issuing the edict, her body would follow. 'Bring her a glass of water,' he tossed over his shoulder.

A cut-crystal glass instantly appeared.

With elegant fingers and an unwavering gaze, he handed it to her.

Niesha took a sip, swallowed it along with the hysterical laughter bubbling up. This wasn't happening. She wanted to go back to an hour ago, when she was the least significant person in the room, no different from the straggly orphan without a past she'd been some twenty odd years ago, the one who'd been absorbed by the state orphanage that bore the royal family's name.

The hand-me-down clothes she wore were two sizes too large, and really should have done their job of hiding her better, she mused dazedly. She'd chosen them out of prudence, not fashion. It had simply meant she wouldn't have to worry about new clothes any time soon.

Except, even covered from head to toe, she felt more naked now than she'd ever felt in her life.

'Drink some more,' he decreed.

Her hands shook wildly, but she managed to take another sip without spilling it. He promptly relieved her of the glass. Still dazed, Niesha watched as it was spirited away.

Then her eyes clashed with his, and the words he'd spoken rose like a horrifying mirage before her eyes. Beyond the space filled out by his broad shoulders and his overwhelming presence, Niesha spotted movement as the bridal attendants entered.

He flicked a wrist, and Halimah, the head attendant of the women's wing, who'd barely tolerated Niesha before today, approached.

Zufar acknowledged her presence with a single glance. 'I do not take your loyalty for granted. But I demand your discretion in this matter.'

'Of course, Your Highness,' Halimah replied.

Zufar nodded. 'My new bride has been selected. You will ensure Niesha is ready at the allotted time. Is that clear?'

Halimah's eyes widened as she stared up at her King.

'Is there a problem?' he demanded.

Her head lowered immediately. 'No, Your Highness.'

Another tremble swept through Niesha as he continued, 'You will dress her and present her to the Grand Hall ready for her royal parade in one hour.' The deep, dark, ruthless timbre of his voice brooked no argument.

No. This wasn't happening.

She was just a maidservant. An orphan with no past. A nobody. She wasn't even worthy of wearing Amira's cast-offs, never mind her wedding gown!

'Please,' she started. The word emerged as a weak, scratchy sound. She cleared her throat and tried again. 'Your Highness, I beg your pardon, but I cannot.'

Pure thunder rumbled across his impressive eyebrows. His eyes, so direct, so hypnotic, drilled right into her bone marrow.

'Yes, you will. Unless you prefer to suffer the consequences of disobeying your King you will go forwards with this.'

Niesha balled her hand and placed it over her racing heart, desperate to calm it before it burst out of her chest. A long time ago, she'd sworn allegiance to him and his family. It had been one of the conditions of inhabiting the palace, and she'd done so willingly. And although he had no inkling who she was or her very small insignificant role his life, she'd done everything asked of her, for him.

In her own way, she'd given him moments of comfort, she liked to tell herself, by making sure that the food she was tasked to serve him in his private dining room was the right temperature, by ensuring his favourite wines were on hand when he returned to his royal apartments after long days away from the palace.

On one occasion, she'd taken it upon herself to purchase a bottle out of her meagre savings when the palace delivery had been delayed.

And when his personal cleaning staff had come down with the flu, she'd volunteered to work in his private quarters. To this day, tucked away in her mind, Niesha had a memory of the scent of his sheets and the unique cologne he wore on his skin.

Those tiny, insignificant but intense moments had made her blush for weeks afterwards on recollection. Still made her blush.

So, yes, like everyone else in this room, she would do anything for Sheikh Zufar al Khalia.

But not this.

The oscillation of her head grew faster as her alarm escalated. 'With respect, Your Highness, you don't want me. I'm nobody. Th-there are others far more suitable for this role. You're making a mistake.' She was a little glad that her voice held firmer than before.

Not so glad when several gasps echoed through the room and his forbidding expression tightened even further.

'I have made my decision. You are my choice. So, do you have any other objections?' he drawled.

Niesha was stunned by his question. Did that mean he would listen if she objected? What further objection could she voice other than telling the King of Khalia that he was utterly, stark raving crazy? The mere thought of doing such a thing made the blood drain from her head.

'By your silence, I assume you do not.'

'Please, you have to reconsider,' was all she could manage.

'This discussion is over,' he declared. 'But, rest assured, you will be adequately compensated for your role.'

He turned away.

Niesha knew she shouldn't trust the tiny burst of relief that spiked through her after being released from the force field of his stare. Her emotions had been on the edge of severe agitation ever since she'd walked in to find Amira and that towering barbarian of a man climbing out of the window.

She'd lost precious minutes frozen in place, unable to believe her eyes. After she'd screamed and sounded the alarm, she was sure she'd been incoherent in the first few minutes. Guilt surged anew beneath her skin.

She should've done more to stop them from leaving. Or raised the alarm quicker, as Zufar had said.

This was her punishment for not acting swiftly enough. If she had, this...*insanity* wouldn't be happening.

Because...marriage? To him?

Sweet heaven, she couldn't do it.

She took a faltering step closer to where he stood issuing clipped instructions. 'Your Highness, please, can we talk about it?' she ventured.

'We don't have time for a discussion,' he stated. His voice was soft and even, but she wasn't fooled. He was seething. 'This is an emergency requiring an interim solution. Any long-term resolutions will be thrashed out later, including whatever concerns you might have.' He went back to issuing instructions.

Heads bobbed up and down, unlike her shaking head and her quivering body, everyone poised to move the moment he finished speaking.

Moments later, firm hands reached for her, fingers tugging insistently at her clothes. She was going to be undressed in front of him? A bolt of rebellion fired through her, and she pushed the attendants away. 'No!'

Everyone in the room froze.

'No?' Halimah whispered in horror. 'You're saying no to your King?'

A row of shocked eyes stared back at her, one in particular lasering her in place. She realised Zufar also awaited her answer. And the expression on his face was telling her everything she needed to know. There would be hell to pay if she didn't obey him. She was the one who had let Amira get away. She was the one who hadn't sounded the alarm in time. When she'd eventually done so, she'd been hysterical and inadvertently alerted the whole palace that the bride-to-be had fled.

She might not have aided his fiancée, but Amira's disappearance might have succeeded partly because of her.

Sheikh Zufar slowly retraced his steps until he towered over her. 'I too am waiting for an answer,' he breathed.

Niesha swallowed, accepting in that moment that she had very little choice. She'd helped cause this state of chaos. It was up to her to fix it.

'No,' she said. 'I… I mean yes,' she amended hurriedly when his face turned to stone. 'I will be your interim…your stand-in bride,' she whispered, her mouth bone-dry.

Niesha wasn't sure why her gaze darted to the window just then.

Sheikh Zufar followed her gaze, and, unbelievably, his face hardened even more.

'If you're thinking of going the same way as my previous bride-to-be, think again. Halimah and her companions will stay with you. They will help you to dress. You will not be left alone until you are by my side at the altar in one hour. Is that understood?'

Her world spinning ever faster on its axis, Niesha barely managed a nod of agreement.

It must've sufficed because he and his aides exited the

room, Sheikh Zufar striding with the regal, animalistic grace infused in his bones since conception. There were sources that said Zufar al Khalia carried the essence of life itself with him when he moved in and out of a room.

The truth of it hit her hard as her breath was expelled in a mighty rush.

At the outer door, he paused, slashing her with golden eyes once more. 'There will be guards placed outside the doors and along every path you take today. Just to ensure that you make it from this room to the wedding ceremony without impediment.'

Niesha wanted to laugh, but she was absolutely certain that she would end up sobbing. And even she couldn't attend her wedding ceremony in tears.

Her *wedding* ceremony!

How on earth was this happening?

She had no time to dwell on it as the women sprang into action, tugging her to the centre of the room before proceeding to disrobe her. Minutes later, she found herself immersed in the rose-scented bath she had drawn for Amira only an hour or so ago.

The water was still warm, luxury gels and shampoos uncovered and ready to be used for the pre-wedding pampering the bride-to-be deserved.

The bride-to-be. *Her.*

Niesha closed her mind to the whispers swirling around her. Her emotional tank was dangerously close to full capacity for further distress. She was fairly sure Halimah and the women were speculating wildly about her. A lowly servant without a past attracted either awkward conversation or derogatory comments, no matter one's age.

Over the years, Niesha had learned to harden herself against the pitying and sometimes callous comments, but somehow the barbs always found their way to her heart. It was why she'd stopped attempting to make friends with her colleagues.

Right now, she was rawer than she'd ever felt in her life. It was almost a relief to sink into the water and let the numbness overtake her. To ignore the awkward silences and the intense loneliness drowning her and pretend this wasn't happening.

She barely felt the hands washing her body or the fingers weaving through her hair as she was cleansed from head to toe. Somewhere in the dark tunnel of despair, she realised she was still shaking, that she couldn't stop trembling even after she was bundled into a thick, luxurious robe and seated at the bridal make-up station. She stared unseeing into the middle distance as her make-up was applied and her hair dried and fussed with.

It was as they nudged her towards the wedding gown that Niesha finally woke up.

'No...' It was a feeble attempt, one a small, wounded animal seeking a last pass for mercy would make.

Of course, there was no reprieve.

'Yes,' Halimah insisted. 'For whatever reason the cosmos sees fit, you have been chosen for this role. You will not dishonour our King by disobeying, and I will not have my head on the block because of you. Now lift up your arms so we can put this exquisite garment on you.'

Interim.

She was just an interim solution. A stand-in for today only.

Tomorrow, Zufar would go into the desert or wherever Amira had been spirited off to and bring her back.

This was temporary.

Remember this.

This time next week, she would be back in her old, familiar clothes, in her rightful place, with this terrifying incident tucked away to retell to her children and grandchildren in years to come.

They would probably not believe her, she mused numbly. She could scarcely believe it herself.

She lifted her arms and let them slide the undergarments over her body before the layers of the specially commissioned wedding gown were added. The skirt was a bit tight at the hip but the snugness wasn't uncomfortable. She held her breath as the zip was tugged up and the delicate buttons fastened.

The sensation of being sealed into her temporary prison threatened to choke her. She hurriedly blinked her prickling eyes before tears fell. Halimah wouldn't welcome her handiwork ruined, and Niesha needed to get herself back under firmer control. The quicker she was done with this, the quicker she could retreat into her shell, and life could go on again.

She placed her feet in the shoes when instructed, angled her head so the magnificent diamond and sapphire tiara could be put in place, and held her hands out for the two dozen bangles that came with the outfit. Precious gems of all shapes and sizes gleamed from her wrists, throat and ears as she was tugged forwards to stand in front of the giant gilded mirror.

Niesha only managed to hold her expression for a split second before her gaze dropped to her feet again. She didn't know the woman in the mirror. And that was a good thing. She could remove herself completely from this situation, retreat to the numb place where she was safest, away from the whispered gossip and the stunned glances. The place where the soft, kind voice lived in her head, the one she didn't recognise but had accepted over the years as her merciful companion, clinging to it the hardest when she felt her lowest.

The carers at the orphanage had offhandedly dismissed the voice she'd unwittingly confessed to as her imaginary friend. Some had ridiculed her, but Niesha had felt no shame in embracing the gentle susurration telling her she would be all right.

You'll get through this.

She was repeating those words to herself as Marwan, his

aides, Halimah, and six ceremonially dressed guards escorted her down a wide private staircase towards the Rolls-Royce Phantom idling in a courtyard at the north wing of the palace. The safety of the three veils shielding her from direct view of everyone else was a welcome presence.

Still, she heard the furtive murmurs as she slowly glided forwards. Behind her, hands fluttered over her train and helped her into the car. Niesha uttered no words as Marwan slid in beside her. The part of her brain that wasn't suspended in disbelief understood his presence.

Amira's father, Feroz Ghalib, had been primed to take this role with his daughter. Even though tongues would wag at Marwan's presence beside her, it would delay the ultimate revelation of exactly what was going on.

Nevertheless, her hands trembled around the stem of the exquisite bouquet made up of diamond-studded cream roses as the car began to roll forwards.

For a wild moment, Niesha contemplated flinging open the door and fleeing as fast as her legs would carry her. She knew every nook and cranny of the royal palace, having spent all her free time exploring it over the years. She could find a hiding place within minutes.

Even as temptation seeped through her, she was dismissing it. The recent death of the Queen had devastated Khalia. The kingdom was still in mourning when its bereaved King dropped the bombshell of his abdication. Though his people had accepted Zufar wholeheartedly, aftershocks still echoed throughout the kingdom.

He'd been right when he'd said that this wedding needed to happen. Galila had said as much last night when she'd voiced her worry over Amira's curious indifference towards her wedding, leading to an exchange of words Niesha had overheard as she'd tidied up Amira's room.

There were larger implications besides a simple marriage between two people who'd known each other since childhood.

The simple truth was that Khalia could ill afford another scandal.

'Wave,' Marwan instructed tersely. 'You need to wave to the people.'

A startled glance out of the window showed they were already on the street outside the palace. She hadn't been privy to the protocol of the ceremony but, from watching other televised royal weddings, she knew there was a brief ride to acknowledge her future subjects and show her gratitude for their goodwill, before the actual wedding ceremony began.

Slowly, she lifted her hand, her movements woefully stilted, and waved.

Screams of joy pierced the thick windows of the car, forcing home the reality that she'd become a symbol of hope to the people. She…the orphan from the poorest part of the capital, the woman with no past and no name save for the one the carers had given her.

Light-headedness clawed at the fringes of her consciousness. A garbled sound echoed from far away but she knew it had come from her throat.

'You will pull yourself together, girl,' Marwan said.

Again hysterical laughter bubbled up. How very easily everyone told her to pull herself together, to rise up to the occasion. To obey. But no one knew the terrifying depths of her emotions. No one knew how she'd secretly watched Zufar move around the palace, on TV, stared at his pictures in magazines for years. No one knew of the secret awe she held for the man who sat on the throne.

For a brief moment in her youth, she had even fancied herself in love with him! She'd grown out of that foolishness, of course, but the unfettered awareness and awe he drew from her had never dissipated.

If she'd been performing this task for any man other than the King of Khalia, she would probably have summoned something other than terror. But he wasn't any other man.

Zufar al Khalia was in a stratosphere of his own, over and above the royal blood that ran through his veins and the crown that sat on his head.

All too soon the ride was over.

Trumpets sounded as the Rolls stopped in front of the Imperial Ceremonial Room where she would be taking her vows before the hour was out. The breath she drew into her lungs did nothing to offer sustenance or clarity, and, even though the senior aide highly disapproved of what was going on, Niesha was grateful for his presence as he alighted and held out his hand to her. She was certain she would've fallen into a wretched heap if he hadn't offered his support just then.

The hand she placed on his arm trembled wildly.

Flower girls she'd never met giggled and danced in front of her, throwing handfuls of scented flowers in her path as she slowly glided up the twenty-one steps to the wide doorway and down a gold-edged, royal blue carpet towards the centre of the exquisite ballroom reserved for the sole purpose of conducting official ceremonies.

Outside, several dozen more trumpets joined the heralding around the kingdom, crowds roaring where they were watching on giant screens across the city.

Inside, Niesha moved towards the man who stood tall, regal, and devastatingly handsome at the altar, her heart firmly wedged in her throat.

When Marwan winced, she realised her fingers had dug into his skin.

An apology tripped on her tongue but was immediately strangled by her nerves.

The murmurs in the congregation escalated, heads beginning to turn as speculation grew as to why Marwan walked next to the bride.

Niesha had no chance to dwell on that. Her sole focus was on Sheikh Zufar as he swivelled on his heel to watch her progress down the aisle.

His face gave nothing away. Years under the spotlight had honed an ability to ruthlessly school his features. But the many interviews that Niesha had watched of the Crown Prince, now turned King of Khalia, had clued her into the nuances of his expressions.

Right now, he bristled with fury, still incandescent at the atrocity that had been perpetrated against him. That fury was ruthlessly caged, the greater calling of duty and responsibility taking priority. He meant to see this through, come hell or high water.

Niesha cursed her senses for choosing that moment to flare back into life. The bright colours of the Imperial Ceremonial Room, the hushed voices of the guests and the laser focus of Zufar's eyes all pierced her consciousness, grounding her mercilessly in that moment.

You will be all right.

How? she railed at the soft voice. She wanted to scream, turn and flee from the room, but there was nowhere to go. They were almost at the altar. Marwan was lowering his arm in preparation to step away.

The moment he did, Galila stepped close. Zufar's sister's face was pale, her mouth pinched as she cast a searching, bewildered glance at Niesha. Unlike the others in the room, she knew why a maidservant stood in Amira's place.

'The bouquet,' she said gently.

Niesha reluctantly handed it over, mourning the tiny support being stripped from her.

Before she could dwell on it, Zufar extended his hand. They were to take that last single step to the altar together.

Niesha stared at the long elegant fingers of her soon-to-be—temporary—husband. Automatically, she lifted her right hand and placed it in his left. She wasn't sure whether to be grateful or frightened by the pressure of the fingers that took hold of hers and nudged her forwards onto that last devastating step.

The cleric began to intone a long string of ancient words. Words that demanded obedience, fidelity, faith, companionship.

Love.

Niesha's insides scrambled over that last word. She'd known none of it in her years. The occasional kindnesses that came her way had been from strangers. In her quiet moments, she'd dreamed of such a feeling, but never in her wildest imagination had she dreamed of it being uttered in such circumstances.

A glance at Zufar showed his face was a stoic mask, the words not having any effect on him save for the façade he'd put up for the public. When it was his turn to repeat his vows he did so in deep assured tones, not hurried, not in any way nervous.

The cleric turned to Niesha. Her heart lurched frantically. Her fingers began to tremble, then her whole body was seized by vicious little earthquakes that just wouldn't stop.

'Repeat your vows,' Zufar instructed with a grave whisper. 'Repeat them now.'

Niesha swallowed painfully, forcing her dry throat to work. She opened her mouth, and with a sense of wild surrealism said, 'I, Niesha Zalwani, take you, Zufar al Khalia, to be my husband.'

Shock waves rippled through the crowd, echoed outside the palace as the true identity of the bride was revealed. Through it all, Zufar kept his gaze fixed, haughty, regal and straight-ahead.

'Proceed,' he commanded the cloaked cleric.

To his credit, the old man did not hesitate. He recited reams of archaic, binding words.

And a mere half an hour later, Niesha was officially wed to the King of Khalia.

CHAPTER THREE

A THREE-MINUTE STATEMENT was issued by the official press secretary on behalf of Sheikh Zufar al Khalia immediately following the ceremony. That was all it took for the strange tale of the swapped bride to turn the atmosphere from scandalised confusion into roars of elation.

By the time Niesha stood beside Zufar's side on the royal balcony above the Imperial Ceremonial Room, the whole kingdom was in a romantic frenzy. Social media went into meltdown at the idea that the King had followed his heart and married the bride of his choosing rather than the one arranged for him. The media, searching for dissenting views, had only been met with romantic sighs and tales about star-crossed lovers.

The little Niesha managed to catch only added to the surrealism of the whole thing.

A five-minute lesson in wedding protocol instead of the usual weeks of tutoring was all she'd been granted in between leaving the wedding ceremony and arriving on the balcony.

She was to stand to the right of her new husband, not the left. Her arm was never to rise above shoulder level when she waved to the crowd. And while she was allowed to show her teeth when she smiled, her demeanour should not in any way exhibit raucousness. Terse instructions whizzed through her brain, the dos and don'ts of being the new Queen streaking like lightning across her senses.

'Look straight ahead and smile,' Zufar instructed calmly. 'I believe this is the moment when you should go to your happy place and think positive thoughts.'

With everything that had unfolded in the last few hours,

Niesha was terrifyingly close to succumbing to hysteria. Lately, her happy place had been curling up with a book beside the fire in her tiny bedsit on the borders of the palace grounds. Oh, how she wished she were there now. Anywhere but here, where a million eyes gawked shamelessly, and the guests of honour who were no longer bothering to keep their voices down openly speculated as to how *she* had come to be in these particular shoes.

'My happy place?' she murmured. 'I don't think that's a very good idea.'

Even though she'd kept her voice low, he heard her, and cast her a brief but hard glance.

'Why not?' he enquired. 'Isn't that what women do when they wish to escape their troubles?' There was a bitter undertone that pulled her up short but his face displayed the same neutral mask he'd worn since the moment they were announced as husband and wife, and had turned to face their honoured guests.

'I'm not sure I know what you mean,' Niesha said.

'That's not important right now. All I care about is that you do not project anything other than utter bliss to find yourself in this position. Remember, the whole world is watching.'

He probably believed he was helping. This was his way of supporting her through an impossible situation. All Niesha could take in at that moment was the pounding of her heart and the boisterous jubilation of the crowd as they waved their flags and screamed congratulations across the royal park where they were gathered.

'Do your best. That is all I ask,' Zufar muttered. 'It would please me greatly if you did it now, however. The others are joining us.'

That was all the warning she had before the doors behind them parted and the rest of his extended family flooded onto the balcony to join them.

Galila slid into place beside her, while his brother, Malak, took his position next to Zufar. Aunts, uncles, nieces and nephews slotted into their allotted positions and acknowledged the crowd with regal waves and salutes honed into place since childhood.

While each and every one of them cast lingering looks her way.

Niesha felt thankful, for the briefest moment, that Zufar had kept her by his side. One bold relative had attempted to pry out the reason behind his last-minute change in brides. Zufar had responded with a stern rebuke for him to mind his own business.

'I will call a family gathering as soon as I have a moment to spare. But do not hold your breath. I intend to be occupied for a while with my new bride.'

His uncle had retreated with his chastised tail between his legs, while Niesha was left blushing furiously. Word had quickly spread that Sheikh Zufar was not to be questioned on the subject of his bride. Not today at least.

'I suppose congratulations are in order,' Galila murmured.

'Thank you,' Niesha replied.

'I would love to know how this interesting outcome transpired,' Galila continued. 'I mean, I left you a maid-servant. Two hours later, you're my sister-in-law. Not that I don't love a riveting story, but this—'

'Watch it, Galila,' Zufar warned beneath his breath, his hands positioned strategically in front of his face as he waved.

Galila easily maintained her graceful smile as she looked at her brother. 'What?' she asked softly. 'So sue me if I'm dying to know what happened. One minute I was attempting to locate your elusive bride-to-be and the next I seem to have acquired a new sister-in-law altogether. If I didn't know any better, I'd think I'd slipped and fallen into a reality TV show.'

'Enough,' Zufar growled. 'Don't forget there are lip-readers out there. If there's discussion to be had, we will get to it later. For now, remember where you are.'

Beside him, his brother Malak snorted under his breath. 'If you wanted us to behave, brother, you shouldn't have offered us this salacious piece of adventure on your wedding day. If you're trying to get into the history books, then bravo. No one will forget this day in a hurry.'

The only hint that Zufar wasn't in complete control of his emotions was the small tic that throbbed at his temple. He continued to wave and acknowledge the crowd, and even at one point slid his hand around the Niesha's waist as the royal military jets flew overhead.

Niesha was thankful for the deafening roar of the jet engines, as it swallowed the gasp that travelled through her body when his hand settled on the curve of her waist. Besides the moment when he'd helped her off the floor, and the moment he'd slid the wedding ring onto her finger, Zufar hadn't touched her.

She'd been very thankful for that, she told herself, despite the humiliating stone lodged in her stomach when he'd lifted her veils and promptly stepped away without executing the customary newly-wed altar kiss.

But now, with his touch searing through the folds of the wedding gown right into her skin, Niesha couldn't suppress the tingles that swarmed her body. The smile she'd pinned to her face froze as her every sense homed in on the sensation evoked by his touch. It was as if his hand were charged with a unique voltage that zinged through her bloodstream, firing up little explosions of fireworks. A handful of seconds passed, then more, and then all sense of time and space disappeared as Zufar looked down into her eyes.

Tawny-gold eyes seared right into her soul, as if he intended to possess her every thought. Somewhere in the distance the royal jets performed acrobatic loops, and then started their return journey. She knew it was only a matter of moments before millions of confetti pieces would be tossed from the sky and showered upon them.

It was the moment the crowd had been waiting for.

The moment when the King kissed his new Queen.

Never in her wildest dreams had she believed it would be her. Above that, never in her wildest dreams had she believed that a man like Zufar would be staring down at her with that intense look in his eyes.

It was all an act, she repeated to herself. But her hammering heart and the frenzied little cyclones whirling through her veins dared to suggest otherwise. His hand steered her to face him, an insistent move that told her that there was no getting away from this. Zufar, the man she'd harboured silly dreams about in her teenage years, was about to kiss her.

Far above her head, a gigantic burst of blues and golds rained from the sky. Niesha paid little attention. Every single cell in her body was focused on the head slowly lowering towards hers, the hand grasping her waist, and the firm, insistent tug as he pulled her close.

'Relax,' he breathed, his voice holding warning as well as rough reassurance.

But Niesha wasn't reassured. How many women dreamed that their very first kiss would be witnessed by millions, if not billions of people across the world? What if she got it wrong? What if she made a complete fool of herself, more than she had before this whole debacle started? And what if—

'Niesha,' Zufar murmured again, his warning deeper this time.

'I'm trying,' she whispered back fiercely.

'Try harder. You look as if you are heading for the gallows instead of your first kiss with your new husband. Is kissing me such a daunting prospect?' he drawled.

'Maybe it is. Have you considered that it may be the last thing I want?'

His eyes widened a touch with surprise at the spark of defiance in her voice.

Tawny-gold eyes gleamed an instant before the first shower of confetti drifted past her. Another landed on her cheek.

About to brush it away, she froze when he murmured, 'Stop.'

He captured her free hand, the one not holding the bouquet, and laid it gently on his chest. And then, with a suave move, he brushed the tiny gold piece of tinsel from her cheek. Expecting his hand to return to her waist, Niesha gave a little gasp as his fingers stroked her jaw and then drifted to her neck.

This wasn't how it was supposed to go. She'd seen more than a few royal first kisses, had dreamed many years ago of how it would feel to be the recipient of one, just like any other girl her age.

Those embraces had been chaste, the exchanged gazes nowhere near this intense.

Zufar was breaking protocol.

But, of course, she couldn't question his actions. Not without risking her lips being read. So she stood before him, attempting not to tremble out of her skin as sure fingers drew down her neck to rest lightly on her collarbone. His thumb gently tilted her chin upward, causing her shiver to intensify.

'How you tremble so, little one,' Zufar murmured.

She opened her mouth—to say what, she would never know. Because in that moment Zufar closed the gap between them and sealed his lips on hers.

The roar and the call of trumpets were for this staged show, Niesha knew. But every sound intensified the thrill and sizzle in her blood the moment Zufar kissed her. She wasn't sure why she closed her eyes, but it felt like the right thing to do. Perhaps because she was more than a little drugged from the effect of his mouth on hers.

It was like nothing she'd ever experienced in her life. Heat and magic and earth-shaking desire surged through her body, flowing from his lips right through to her very toes. He swallowed her tiny squeak of shocked delight as he deepened the kiss. His hand didn't move from her throat but the one at her waist dug deeper, searing his fingers onto her skin. That tiny moan escaped again. The crowd roared louder. All through it Zufar continued to kiss her, his tongue swiping across her bottom lip, weakening her knees so she sagged against him.

He caught her easily, held onto her as he continued to gently ravage her mouth.

'Enough, you two,' Galila said with a chuckle. 'There are children watching. Let's not turn this into an X-rated show.'

With a muted grunt, Zufar lifted his head. His face reflected a hint of surprise, then irritated bewilderment. Both were quickly masked a moment later.

If it had been anyone else, she would've believed he was experiencing the same sensations cascading through her body, but his eyes studied her with piercing speculation that added apprehension to her already jangled emotions.

What was he thinking?

As if he caught the silent question, his hand dropped from her throat, and he faced the crowd. A smile lifted the corners of his mouth, as if he was acknowledging that he'd just shared a special moment with every citizen in his kingdom, and millions more around the world. A second later, he looked down at her, his eyes telling her that she needed to also acknowledge the crowd.

Blushing fiercely, Niesha faced the crowd again. In unison, they waved, smiled, waved some more. All the while, her senses spun.

Her first kiss.

Was this how everyone felt? She was drowning in sensation, as if the whole world had tilted and taken a different course that would never be the same again. Because how could anything else compare to this?

She wasn't a romantic. Childish, fairy-tale feelings had been beaten out of her by years of hard work and the reality that only a lucky few found their happily-ever-after, most of them in the books she treasured. She was old enough to accept that those foolish daydreams needed to be set aside the moment she closed the book.

So what she was experiencing now was nothing short of a daydream she needed to put behind her as soon as possible.

This was temporary. *She was a stand-in.*

Come tomorrow she'd be back in her beige uniform, fluffing pillows and refilling shampoo bottles in bathrooms in the east wing.

The thought froze the smile on her face, even as she continued to wave to the crowd.

After an excruciating half-hour, with one final wave, Zufar steered her away from the balcony. They re-entered the small anteroom serving as a holding place before, but that was now a path that led to the banqueting hall where the formal wedding reception was being held.

'You did well,' Zufar stated as he tucked her hand into the crook of his elbow.

Despite the tersely murmured statement, a bubble of warmth speared through the sizzling shock that hadn't entirely left her.

'Thank you,' she murmured, pleased that she hadn't completely let him down.

'Of course, you could do with smiling a little bit more,' he added.

The bubble burst. 'I can't smile on command,' she replied.

'You are the Queen now. You have to learn how.'

'But I am not, though, am I?'

'That ring on your finger, my dear, is all the evidence you need.'

'You know what I mean, Your Highness.'

'Do I?' Zufar murmured even as he nodded to a guest bowing as they passed.

'Of course you do,' Niesha muttered fiercely. Why was he pretending he didn't know what she was talking about? 'I'm not your Queen. This was temporary. You said so yourself.'

His body tensed, then a muscle rippled in his jaw. 'We'll talk about this later,' he said.

A spurt of apprehension turned into full-blown alarm. 'What is there to talk about, Your Highness?'

'You calling me Your Highness, for starters. I'm your husband now. You are allowed to address me as Zufar.'

Her footsteps faltered. For as long as she could remember, he'd always been Sheikh Zufar, or Crown Prince Zufar. Not even in her dreams had she addressed him by his given name alone. It felt…huge. As if she were taking a leap into thin air. Niesha started to shake her head.

Somehow, she had to bring this back to reality, back under her control.

'You also need to stop shaking your head at every little disagreement. As my new bride, you're supposed to be glowing and blushing with happiness, not wearing an expression as if you've been led into the devil's own playpen.'

'You know why I am acting this way. I don't know why you're pretending you don't know what I'm talking about. You said this was temporary.'

'Did I?'

Her mouth parted in a stunned O.

'Remember where you are,' he warned. 'Do you really think this is the right time for this discussion?'

She didn't. And she couldn't very well demand an explanation from the King. Not with guests in earshot, and not when they were entering the banqueting hall where attendants lined the walls in their dozens, ready to serve the first course the moment they sat down.

So she walked beside him as Zufar led her to the head of the table.

His white-gloved hand gripped hers tightly where it rested on her arm, as if he was fully intent on preventing her from fleeing.

As if she would. As if she *could*. She wouldn't get very far, even on her own two feet. As he'd warned, there were guards posted everywhere in the palace. Did his warning still apply even now that they'd exchanged their vows? Most likely. But she couldn't think about that. All she wanted at this moment was for everything to be done so she could disappear into her little corner of the world and put this behind her. But he was looking at her in that way again as the guests crowded in.

The way he'd looked at her on the balcony in the moments before he'd kissed her. It was all still an act, Niesha knew. But that tiny fluttering reignited under her skin and grew into huge, wild butterflies demanding freedom.

When the room was half filled, he pulled out her chair and waited until she sat down. He remained standing, his gaze on the crowd who stood as protocol demanded, beside their seats.

Zufar's gaze effortlessly commanded their attention. 'Many of you are wondering about the turn of events today. You will have to keep wondering.' A smattering of laughter echoed through the crowd but eyes slid to where she sat, probing her every expression in the hope of accessing juicy gossip. It took every ounce of composure she didn't know she possessed to maintain a serene expression as Zufar continued, 'All you need to know is that I've made my choice, and I am extremely happy with it.'

Her pulse jumped as he redirected his gaze to her again, his eyes gleaming for a moment before he straightened. 'Now you will do me the honour of acknowledging and accepting Niesha al Khalia as my bride and your Queen.'

Thunderous applause echoed down the banqueting table. Then they took their seats and the formal reception began.

Niesha only managed to pick at a few mouthfuls of the twelve-course dinner. Aside from a few sidelong glances, Zufar didn't question her lack of appetite. She supposed it could all be slotted under the general heading of wedding nerves, even after the fact.

And almost as if he'd instituted an invisible no-fly zone around her, no one approached her even to offer congratulations.

When Galila breached the barrier, Zufar shot her a warning look.

She rolled her eyes but didn't make any more comments except to lean down and brush a kiss across Niesha's cheek. 'You and I will need to have a spa day very soon,' she whispered in Niesha's ear before straightening and walking away.

'What did she say?' Zufar asked.

'She wants a spa day with me, I think,' Niesha responded a little dazedly.

'Hmm, I believe that is code for something else entirely.'

Surprise rounded her eyes. 'What?'

'Curiosity is my sister's middle name. I will caution you to be careful around her. She has a way of prying out information that would make my own intelligence department proud.'

She reached for the crystal water glass, aware that her fingers hadn't stopped shaking. 'Well, you don't need to worry about that, do you? By the time we get around to the possibility of such a day, I'll no longer be your wife.'

For some reason her response made his features tighten. Did he not wish to hear the truth? She opened her mouth to voice the thought but he beat her to it.

'This is our wedding day. Let us endeavour to enjoy at least some of it and not give everything a sour note, shall we?'

She frowned, then quickly smoothed out her features, aware that she was still the cynosure of all eyes. 'It's not our wedding day. Not really. Is it?' she pressed, intent on making him acknowledge the transient nature of what had happened today.

It was that or… The alternative was unthinkable. No, not exactly unthinkable, but impossible for someone like her. A nobody who'd left such foolish dreams beneath the dreary pillows in her lonely orphanage bed.

'Think of it as an elaborate party then, if you must,' he bit out quietly. 'Whatever it is, I wish to enjoy at least some of it for the sake of appearances. Is that okay with you?'

Was he really asking her that when he'd all but dragged her to the altar? But the anger she wanted to summon didn't materialise. Not when she knew the true meaning behind his actions.

He'd done it for his people. So had she. She owed it to the royal family and to every citizen in Khalia not to sustain that anger. She didn't need to be in his shoes to understand it took guts to take such chaos as had been thrown at him only a few hours ago, a situation that would've left other men quaking in their boots, and turn it into a triumph.

Proving once again why he was such an effective, awe-inspiring monarch.

One who had demanded a sacrifice she couldn't in good conscience fault him for. Right in this moment, Niesha couldn't find it in her heart to begrudge the people of Khalia, who had endured the death of their Queen, and seen the kingdom plunged into uncertainty after the abdication of the King.

'Of course, if that's what you wish,' she murmured softly.

His eyes gleamed in that suspicious way again, as if he were divining her thoughts way better than she could. It made her *extremely* nervous. Niesha attempted to look away, but found herself hypnotised by the gold flecks in his tawny eyes.

'That is what I wish,' he reiterated in deep, low tones. 'Now you will smile, and nod, and pretend that this is the happiest day of your life.'

For some insane reason, that command wasn't difficult to obey.

When the corners of his mouth lifted, Niesha found herself following suit. His gaze dropped to her lips, and stayed there for an infinitesimal second, before he lifted his gaze back to hers.

'Much better,' he drawled. 'I will push my luck and request that you eat more than the few mouthfuls you have consumed so far. If the food does not suit, you only need to say and I will instruct a new dish to be brought to you.'

Her eyes widened. What would her peers—the servants—think if she made such a request? She cringed. 'No, that will not be necessary.'

'I do not do it out of necessity. I do it because you are my Queen and what you wish goes.'

What she *wished* right now was for him to stop referring to her as the Queen or *his* Queen. It would be better all round that way. *Safer*, even. The last thing she wanted was to start believing, even for a second that this temporary role was in any way real. She needed to maintain the distance to ensure she left this nightmare with her faculties intact. 'This is fine, I'm sure,' she insisted firmly.

Zufar nodded, and turned to speak to his brother, who sat to his left. The sudden bereft sensation that assailed her took Niesha by complete surprise. It took a few precious seconds to master her composure, after which she lifted her gaze to the guest seated closest by. But that chair was empty, vacated by Galila a few moments ago.

She was about to turn away, but her attention was snagged by Zufar's uncle, the same one who'd attempted to pry information from Zufar earlier. Niesha attempted a smile. He returned it with a speculative gaze, his eyes darting from Zufar and back again.

'You must come to dinner when you return from your honeymoon.'

Honeymoon?

She tried to master the shock that bolted through her.

Of course the King and Queen were expected to go on their honeymoon. She had no clue where Zufar had intended to take Amira. Was she supposed to know of the destination for her own honeymoon?

'I... I...' she stuttered. A moment later, a warm hand covered hers, the gentle but insistent pressure on her fingers applying subtle warning.

'We'll be happy to accept your invitation, Uncle, on our return. Providing of course that our schedules allow,' Zufar slid in smoothly, proving that even though he'd been in conversation with his brother, he had been fully tuned into what was happening with her.

Was he that terrified she would bungle the ruse? A spark of irritation lit up beneath her skin. When she attempted to withdraw her hand from under his, he held on firmly, turning his imperious head to look at her with what everyone else would have assumed was an adoring look from a groom to his new bride. But she saw the warning clear in his eyes. *Behave.*

She lowered her head under the guise of forking another bite of her superb sea bass. But she never lifted it to her lips, because she feared she would choke if she attempted to swallow.

'Where's the honeymoon destination?' the woman seated next to Zufar's uncle asked.

'We will spend a few days in the Emerald Palace, and then I will take my bride on a multi-national tour, ending in the most romantic capital of the world, of course,' Zufar said.

'Oh, you mean Paris, don't you? I love Paris,' his aunt exclaimed, her eyes lighting up. 'I haven't been in months.'

'And there's a reason for that,' his uncle said dryly. 'My

bank account screams in agony whenever you're in the French capital.'

Laughter greeted the response. Amid it all, Niesha noticed Zufar watching her with that same pseudo-adoring, warning look. When his uncle turned away to address another guest, she tried to withdraw her hand once again.

Even though her irritation had faded, a new sensation had taken root at his touch. He no longer wore his gloves, making the sensation even more searing. The burst of relief poured through her when he didn't restrain her. She dropped her hand into her lap, her fingers curling into her palm as her blood sang wildly.

Realising that he was still staring at her, she pinned that smile on her face again, and returned his look. 'You don't need to keep watching me like a hawk, you know. I'm not about to announce to the whole world what is happening here.'

'I'm glad to hear it, but since we did not discuss a honeymoon, I thought it best to step in. Surely you don't have an objection to that?' he murmured testily.

'But what will they say when they find out that it's not true?' she said tightly.

The taut little smile he gave her reproached her for being foolish. 'That will not happen, little one, because it's true. We are going on honeymoon.'

Zafar had never met anyone who blushed with such frequency as his new bride. Or trembled as much. He was stunned she hadn't collapsed into a heap of nerves thus far. His earlier summation that she was as skittish as one of his mares couldn't be more accurate. Even now, as they took their first dance, he sensed she was moments from tugging out of his hold and fleeing across the ballroom.

But just like before, right when he thought she would succumb to her nerves, she straightened her slender spine, raised that delicate little chin, and speared him with a look of such defiance it almost made him smile.

Almost.

Because this was no laughing matter. He had taken a complete stranger as his Queen. Granted, Amira had been little more than an acquaintance despite the arrangement to marry, but this was...unprecedented.

Just like that kiss on the balcony...

He clenched his gut as the memory drew another strange zing through his bloodstream. It had just been a kiss, nothing more. So why was the unique sensation lingering, luring him into wishing to experience it again? He wouldn't, of course.

This whole near disaster had him on edge. The adrenaline high of salvaging a situation that could've exploded in his face was what had blown that kiss out of proportion.

But it was time to wrestle *everything* back under control.

Despite the press release holding at bay the dozens of questions he was sure were coming his way, his people would need definitive answers by morning.

He'd barely been able to stop Amira's father from detonating the whole event even before it'd started. The man was rightly in search of answers for his daughter's whereabouts and bewildered at the news that Amira had jilted the man she was supposed to marry. Only by asserting his full authority had Zufar stopped his father's best friend from causing a scene. Feroz had finally realised Zufar was the wronged party and agreed to return home to await further news.

Zufar resisted the urge to grit his teeth at the thought of his half-brother's actions.

He had set his best investigators on the case to satisfy himself that Amira hadn't been taken against her will, but instinctively he knew she hadn't been abducted. In fact, in hindsight, Amira's lacklustre interaction with him lately was revelatory.

That sliver of relief slid through him again, this time arriving with a cold acceptance that perhaps he'd dodged a bullet that could've seen history repeating itself. Because a wife that could've so easily been seduced by another man, as his mother had been, was one he didn't want. Maybe his half-brother had done him a favour. Had even unwittingly ensured Zufar wasn't distracted from his duty and responsibility the way his father's preoccupation with his mother's infidelity had made him?

His teeth met in jaw-clenching grit. He wasn't so forgiving as to brush away the fact that Adir had done this *today* to extract maximum humiliation—

'Perhaps you should take your own advice, Your Highness,' his new bride stated softly.

He redirected his gaze to hers. 'Excuse me?'

'You want me to smile and not give the game away but you should see your face right now,' she said.

'And what does my face say?'

'That you are terribly displeased by something. Of course, I'm sure I don't need to guess what it is. You think you will find her soon?' she asked.

He pushed his irritation away. 'I don't wish to talk about Amira.' Further thought of his half-brother was not welcome. Moreover, Zufar found he was much more interested in the woman he held in his arms.

For the purposes of keeping in character, of course.

Because Niesha was right. He was at risk of giving the game away. He schooled his features as he continued to look down at her. As he did so, he noticed the changes in her.

The hair he'd believed to be mousy was in fact a lustrous thick chestnut, highlighted with dark gold strands he was sure didn't come out of a tube. Her eyelashes were unbelievably long, fanning almost hypnotically against her cheeks when she lowered them. Lips painted a deep peach drew his eyes consistently to the soft, plump curve of her mouth.

Her eyes were wide and alluring pools edged in kohl that emphasised the amethyst depths.

In her heels, she came up to his chin, bringing him that much closer to the lips he had tasted all too briefly on the balcony outside. Lips that his own thirsted to taste.

The zing threatened to spark into something else, something *more* as his recollection deepened.

She wasn't experienced, that much he could tell by kissing her, but he had sensed an innocent eagerness in her that lit a fire in his belly. The temptation to kiss her, experience that thrill again, fanned his hunger. He curbed it ruthlessly.

He wasn't weak like his father, controlled by his obsessional urges to the ruin of all else around him. Zufar enjoyed sex, and the carefully selected women he'd indulged himself with over the years had more than satisfied his needs. But not a single time had he let his emotions overtake him.

He didn't intend to start now.

Duty had dictated he take a wife and produce heirs. That would be his end goal. And with Amira out of the picture...

He stared at his new Queen. His *temporary* Queen.

His people's reaction to her had been...extraordinary. Surprisingly so. They'd readily accepted her. So why upset the cart?

Why indeed...?

Zufar cautioned himself against revealing to Niesha that, far from thinking that this was only a temporary marriage, she was now bound to him for life. That conversation would need careful strategising.

In the same instance that he accepted his decision, it occurred to him that the idea of binding himself to a near stranger neither disturbed nor displeased him. He'd never intended to marry for anything other than ensuring lasting stability for his people after the turbulence of his father's reign.

He wasn't so weak as to give into ephemeral notions of marrying for love. That emotion was a fairy tale he'd never wasted his time seeking, and especially not once the reality of his position in life had been made clear.

His father had fallen victim to lust and obsession to the detriment of his family and his kingdom. Zufar was well aware of the whispers that had followed his father, the veiled scorn shown towards the weakness that dogged the previous King. He had no intention of falling prey to that absurd sickness.

'I'm in no hurry to locate my former fiancée.'

Her breath caught. 'And why not?'

'Because if she went of her own free will, then she's no longer of any consequence.'

She gasped. 'How can you say that? She was promised to you. You still need a bride! Your people need a queen.'

Zufar continued to look down at her as they glided across the dance floor. Absent-mindedly, he noted the grace with which she swayed in his arms, the way she held herself with careful poise. She wasn't as unpolished as he'd imagined, he mused again. In fact, with a little bit of help, she could become the diamond he sought. The diamond his people deserved.

The more he thought about it, the more the idea settled deeper inside him.

'Your Highness?' Her prompt was tremulous, as if she knew of the monumental decision he'd taken.

Her eyes were growing wide again, her lower lip set to tremble in that alluring quiver that made him want to devour her again.

'I don't need to find her, little one, because I've already found my bride. I've found my Queen. This wedding, and this marriage, will be my first and my last. There hasn't been a divorce in my family in recorded history. In fact, I'm not sure the constitution has allowances for it. So, you see, you and I are bound together for life, Niesha. Accept it.'

CHAPTER FOUR

IF NIESHA HAD been informed only half an hour ago that there was a way for her whole world to be shoved even more off kilter, she wouldn't have believed it. But she was fully installed on that wild, turbulent roller coaster now.

She stared up at Zufar, knowing that this time there was no mistaking what he'd said. Nor was there any doubt that this was an accidental revelation. They were in the middle of the dance floor, surrounded by over three hundred guests. She had nowhere to go, was unable to protest without causing the most horrendous scene.

Zufar al Khalia's diplomatic prowess and mental agility was renowned. He'd won almost every polo match since he was seventeen. The moment he'd entered public office, he'd gained a reputation as a master strategist.

That he'd brought those abilities to bear on this situation was irrefutable. Panic and anger surged in her belly, lending her vocal cords the strength to dig herself out of this hole she was disappearing into.

He shook his head. 'Not here,' he instructed tersely.

'You lied to me,' she whispered, the depth of his trap making her tone husky with shock.

His eyes grew chilly but the smile didn't fade from his face. 'I said, not here,' he emphasised with clear displeasure.

But Niesha was a little too out of her head to heed the warning. 'You planned this all along.'

'If you mean did I plan to speak to you afterwards so we can discuss this like rational human beings, then yes, that was my intention.'

Chilled through by his almost careless dismissal, she took a step back from him, but the arm banding her waist pulled her closer, the fingers curled around hers holding her prisoner. 'You will not cause a scene.'

Her King demanded obedience. But in that moment, Niesha couldn't find the capacity to fall in line like everyone else at his command.

'You keep telling me how to behave, to smile, to breathe. I'm not an object, Your Highness. I'm a human being. I chose to obey you because I thought I was doing the right thing. But you misled me. I will not stand for that.'

His nostrils flared, his whole being tightening against her as his gaze pinned her.

'What is it you're intending to do?' he questioned with a deadly smile.

'I won't cause a scene, if that's what you are worried about.'

A single tic rippled through his jaw before he regained himself. 'That's good to hear. However, I hear a *but* in there.'

'I will remain meekly by your side until this ceremony is over. And then you and I will talk.'

One corner of his mouth lifted in a hint of a smile that promised to be lethal given its full scope. 'My meek little bride seems to have a spine after all,' he mocked.

The bubble of anger in Niesha's belly grew. 'I get that way when I'm misled.'

'Be careful. Don't forget whom you're addressing,' he warned.

A chill went through her body. 'Is that a threat, Your Highness?'

'I am reminding you that we have an audience, and our every move is being watched so if you are going to be disagreeable, I suggest you wait until we are behind closed doors.'

'Disagreeable? You think I'm being—'

Before she could further vent her anger, he leaned close and brushed his lips over hers.

Like on the balcony, this was meant to shut her up. Niesha

knew that. And yet it worked like magic. The high-wattage shiver that went down her spine was so strong she thought she would be lifted right off her feet.

And that was with just a whisper of his lips over hers. She cursed her body's reaction. Continued cursing it as the song ended and she was led off the ballroom floor with suave attentiveness.

As if he knew and meant to capitalise on her reaction to his touch, Zufar didn't release her. Long fingers meshed with hers as they moved from group to group holding brief court with their guests.

For two hours she was subjected to his electrifying touch and blasts from tawny eyes that held her fraying nerves on a tight leash.

The evening culminated with spectacular fireworks on the great lawn of the palace. Across the capital city, individual households joined in, with bursts of fireworks lighting the sky across the city.

Niesha barely acknowledged them. All she wanted to do was to retreat at the earliest opportunity and guarantee her fate wasn't as final as she suspected.

Relief drenched her as her attendants materialised beside her at the stroke of nine p.m. to whisk her off. Moments later, she realised Zufar was not following as she'd expected.

She stopped. They needed to discuss what he'd said now. She couldn't bear to wait another second. 'Wait. I need to—'

He intercepted her as she headed back to where he stood with one of his ministers. 'Go on without me. We will be reunited soon enough, little one,' he said smoothly as he took her hand and brushed his lips over her knuckles.

Dear heaven, he was smooth.

And calculating.

She was struggling to find her breath when the women firmly led her away.

Niesha was so caught up in the conversation she intended to have with him that she didn't notice where they were headed until she realised that they weren't returning to the Queen's private quarters. 'What… Where are you taking me?' she blurted, although she had a fair idea.

Halimah, walking a few steps in front of her, looked over her shoulder and smiled. This time her smile was more tactful, her whole demeanour remarkably altered from this morning.

Of course, Niesha mused, she was now the Queen, and where there'd been whispered speculation and awkwardness before, there were now smiles and an abundance of courtesy and respect.

Even as a tiny spurt of resentment erupted inside her for their about-face, she wanted to blurt out that there was no need for their change of attitude. She was still one of them. She certainly wasn't going to be Queen for very long, not if she had any say in it.

The thought that her wish might not come true sent a fresh bolt of alarm through her. Zufar hadn't misspoken. Niesha didn't know the ins and outs of constitutional law, but she knew the history of the royal family enough to know that there'd been no divorce for generations.

To date, Zufar's own father had been the only one to abdicate the throne and that had sent shock waves through the kingdom.

'Your Highness?'

Niesha whirled around, expecting Zufar to be behind her. When he wasn't, she turned back around, frowning at Halimah.

'Your Highness, which gown do you prefer?' the attendant urged.

She realised that she was the one being addressed, and her heart lurched. 'Please, don't call me that.'

Halimah and the young attendants exchanged apprehensive looks. 'Begging your pardon, but that is your official title. To address you as anything else would be disrespectful, Your Highness.'

'I see,' Niesha replied. Her resentment of moments before dissipated, replaced with the stark notion that, whether she liked it or not, they truly saw her differently now. She might not feel it inside but to them she was now a rarefied species, no longer one of them. Niesha didn't know whether to be sad or to give into more hysteria. She settled for a solemn nod. 'Okay.' She knew how rigorously the rules of the palace were followed. The last thing she wanted to do was cause trouble for the staff. She would be one of them again soon enough.

'I've prepared some tea for Your Highness. Jasmine tea, to calm the nerves before the wedding night,' Halimah offered with a benign smile.

Niesha stopped herself from blurting that it was a waste of time. She didn't intend to sleep in Zufar's private quarters tonight or on any other night.

'Can you help me with my gown, please?'

'Of course, Your Highness,' Halimah sang out.

Gentle hands began undoing her clothing. She wasn't sure why she paid closer attention this time. Perhaps it was the knowledge that she would never be close to such perfect creations again that made her look down at her gown properly for the first time, noticing the precious stones sewn into the skirts swirling around her legs as it was removed, the delicate sleeves and masterful design.

An exquisite diamond and sapphire necklace gleamed against her skin, the gems in her ears and on her wrist adding to the magical quality of the wedding gown that didn't belong to her and never would.

But for one small infinitesimal moment, she allowed herself to believe that this was real.

When she finally met her gaze in the mirror, she dared to dream that when this moment was far behind her, she would one day experience a wedding day of her own.

Smaller and less spectacular, of course, but enchanted all the same.

First, though, she had to get through to Zufar. Had to extricate herself from this web of impossible circumstances closing in on her. She raised her arms as the gown was lifted over her head and spirited away.

Then Halimah was in front of her, gesturing to an array of gorgeous evening gowns hanging from a rail.

Niesha stared at the dresses in surprise. 'Are these new?' They hadn't been there this morning and she hadn't spotted them with the bridal trousseau.

Halimah nodded. 'His Highness ordered these for you himself.'

'Excuse me?' she blurted.

A smile curved Halimah's lips. 'The suddenness of the…new arrangements left you no choice but to wear the only wedding gown available. But I believe your new husband did not wish to see you in another woman's clothes on the night of your wedding. He had the royal couturier provide these for you especially.' There was wistfulness in Halimah's voice that suggested that underneath the sometimes brusque exterior lurked a romantic.

Nevertheless, Niesha was stunned Zufar had arranged all this. Should she really be surprised? If the bombshell he'd dropped on the dance floor was true, then within minutes of entering this room this afternoon he'd made a life-altering decision for her without so much as blinking in her direction.

The formidable calculation behind that staggered her.

'Which one is it to be, Your Highness?' Halimah prompted.

Half dazed, Niesha pointed to the emerald sequinned gown, made of material she was almost too afraid to touch. 'That one,' she murmured.

'A wonderful choice, Your Highness,' Halimah agreed.

That bubble of hysteria threatened again. She swallowed it down, willing herself to remain quiet as the women bustled around her again.

Her hair was rearranged, her make-up touched up, and heels presented to her.

'We thought you would prefer your tea on the terrace, Your Highness. The fireworks are still going on, and you can get the best view from there.'

Niesha trailed after them out onto a stone terrace where an elaborate tea service had been laid out. She'd barely eaten anything at the wedding banquet but Niesha knew she wouldn't be able to eat now either. She contemplated the exquisite offering, wondering whether she shouldn't try anyway to calm her nerves.

But she didn't want her nerves calmed. She'd been too dazed and confused earlier, had meekly stumbled her way through what should've been a firm refusal to succumb to his wishes. She'd gone along with the idea that she would be a stand-in, temporary bride. She intended to make her voice heard this time.

She would scream if she needed to. With a brisk nod to herself, Niesha sat down and held her hands in her lap.

'May I pour you a cup, Your Highness?'

She stopped herself from gritting her teeth at the title. It didn't belong to her and she would never get used to it.

'No, thank you,' she said. 'You may go now. I'll pour it myself when I am ready.'

'But… Your Highness, that is not protocol.'

Niesha swallowed her irritation. 'I'm quite capable of pouring my own tea, Halimah.'

The older woman gave a curt bow, and stepped back. 'As you wish, Your Highness. Will there be anything else?'

Niesha shook her head. But as the women started to re-treat, she turned. 'Do you know when Zu—His Highness will be here?' She heard the nervousness in her own voice but Halimah's gaze only softened.

'You can expect him within the hour, Your Highness.'

Another series of curtsies later, Niesha was alone.

An hour.

She snorted under her breath. The likelihood that she would've gone completely mad by then was very real. The moment she heard the door shut, she jumped to her feet.

There had to be a way out of this, there simply had to be. She paced until her feet began to pinch, and then she kicked the shoes off. Hearing them thud against the wall brought a tiny bit of satisfaction, immediately followed by guilt at the treatment of what had to be thousands of dollars' worth of accessories.

That thought ramped up her agitation. As she turned from her pacing, another burst of fireworks lit through the sky. Niesha lifted her head to watch it, the enormity of why this celebration was happening settling on her. She raised a hand to her throbbing head and caught a spark of her wedding ring. It was unlike any ring she'd ever seen.

From the history of the al Khalia kingdom she'd devoured back in her teens she knew exactly where the ring on her finger had originated. It had belonged to Zufar's grandmother. She'd been married to his grandfather for over seventy years and had worn the ring every day of her married life. The heirloom's historical significance threatened to overwhelm her. Perhaps it was fortunate then that the hard rap on the outer door dragged her from her thoughts.

The bundle of nerves that jumped into her throat suggested perhaps not. On shaky feet, she rushed to where she'd thrown off her shoes and slipped back into the heels. Sucking in a deep breath, she walked through the living room to the doors. With one last slide of her clammy palms over her dress, Niesha opened the doors.

Zufar too had changed. Gone was the magnificent military uniform he'd worn for the ceremony. In its place was an equally captivating tunic that drew her eyes to his broad shoulders and the tapered physique that been honed from his love of polo. Dark curly hair gleamed under the chandelier lights. He'd taken a shower at some point since she'd last seen him.

Despite the emotions raging inside her, Niesha couldn't take her eyes off him. The subtle clearing of his throat embarrassingly long seconds later alerted her to her gawping.

When she met his gaze, his eyes were a touch cool, but as his gaze roved from her head down to her feet a different look replaced it. A look that sent hot tingles surging through her belly to curl low and insistent in her pelvis.

'Are you going to invite me in or do you wish to tackle me where I stand?'

Niesha cursed the blush spreading in her cheeks, and stepped back hastily. He stepped inside and shut the door behind him.

'The gown suits you,' he said with more than a hint of satisfaction.

The thought that he'd chosen it especially for her shouldn't have sent that traitorous bolt of pleasure through her bloodstream, and Niesha immediately wished it away. She didn't want to speak about clothes. Or wonder whether the unbelievably soft and silky gown that clung to her breasts, waist and hips pleased him in any way. She only wanted to talk about her freedom.

'Tell me what you said isn't true,' she blurted heatedly.

He didn't respond but his nostrils flared slightly as he looked around the room. 'Perhaps we should sit down.'

Niesha shook her head. 'No. You said this was an *interim* solution. I want to know why you deceived me,' she demanded, her voice more plaintive than she wished.

'Calm yourself.' His voice was a firm command.

'I'll be calm when you tell me that this marriage will be annulled as soon as possible,' she returned.

He didn't react to the unbecoming screech in her voice or the undeniable accusation she lobbed at him. He merely continued to stride away from her towards the living room, leaving her no choice but to follow.

She watched him lower his impressive frame into the

heavy silk armchair she was sure cost more than two years' salary, and cross one leg over the other.

'I've had you investigated,' he stated baldly. 'You do not have any family, correct?'

A bolt of pain shot through her heart, along with the shock of discovering he was changing tactic yet again.

With balled fists, she stared at him. 'You had me investigated?' she parroted.

He nodded calmly, as if her incredulity was of no consequence to him. Perhaps it wasn't. But the thought that while they'd been exchanging vows he'd been digging into her background made nausea rise in her belly. Knowing what he'd found, knowing that he had evidence that she was a nobody, literally and figuratively, sent another wave of anguish through her.

Nonetheless, she raised her chin. 'Then you'll have your confirmation that I'm unsuitable for this…this…'

'Being my Queen?' he finished softly. So softly she barely heard the words.

Why was he so calm? Why was he not doing everything in his power to be rid of her at the first opportunity?

'Yes,' she hissed, taking a step closer to him even though her instincts warned that it would be wiser to keep a sensible distance between them.

'On the contrary, I believe it is to my advantage.'

'Your advantage?' she echoed blankly.

'Precisely. I have no relatives to appease, no scandals to come out of the woodwork. There is only you to deal with,' he stated with faint satisfaction.

Her heart lurched. 'What exactly do you mean by that?'

His gaze raked over her again, lingering longer this time. As if he had all the time in the world. 'You've had a challenging day, little one. Sit down before you fall down.'

Niesha barely managed to stop herself from stomping her feet. 'I'm not as weak as you think I am. I'm perfectly capable of carrying on a conversation without needing to wilt into the nearest chair.'

'But perhaps it will be more civil that way?' he parried in a mocking tone before flicking one sleekly elegant hand towards the seat next to him.

The suggestion that she was not being civilised cut her to the quick. Niesha brushed it aside. She didn't really care what his opinion was of her. All she cared about was that this evening's conversation ended with her achieving her freedom.

Nevertheless, she made her way to the sofa, acutely aware that he followed her every step until she perched on the corner of it, tucking her legs neatly to one side and folding her hands in her lap. Only then did she lift her head and meet his gaze full on. An expression passed through his eyes, gone too quickly for her to decipher.

'I'm sitting down now, Your Highness. Please explain yourself.'

He gave the barest hint of a smile, but it was gone an instant later.

'The constitution is not as backwards as I allowed you to think. Divorce isn't disallowed, but, were I to divorce, I would be the first in my family's history to do so.'

Relief surged through her, but it was accompanied by an alien, disturbing sensation she couldn't quite pinpoint. 'We can divorce?' she repeated slowly, wondering why the words attempted to stick in her throat.

He remained silent for a long moment, then he gave a brisk nod. 'Yes.' The word was uttered with a single, acrid bite. 'There is a clause that states that divorce can be initiated by either party, but there are specific circumstances under which it will be considered.'

'What circumstances?'

His nostrils flared. 'Infidelity.'

Her eyes widened when he didn't continue. 'That's it?'

'Yes,' he said.

'But—I'm not... This isn't a true marriage...not that I have any intention of doing...being unfaithful...' She shook her head to stem her babbling. 'All this is absurd. What about an annulment?' she tagged on desperately.

He shook his head. 'No history of that in my family either.' An intensely arrogant expression crossed his face. 'No al Khalia has failed to consummate his marriage.'

For some reason that statement sent a bolt of heat surging through her belly. 'But you're going to be the first though?'

Slowly, Zufar uncrossed legs, leaned forwards and rested his elbows on his knees. 'Am I?' he drawled softly, his eyes narrowed like twin lasers on her.

Niesha's fingers trembled. She clenched them tighter. 'Of course you are. That's our only choice.'

'It is not.'

The finality of those three words shook her to her very foundations. The hairs on her nape rose chillingly as he continued to regard her steadily. 'Wh-what do you mean?'

'I mean this marriage can be real.'

'Real?' she echoed as if the word were alien to her. Perhaps it was. None of what he was saying made any sense.

'Real,' he affirmed. 'I will be your husband, and you will be my wife. You will bear my children, and you will be my Queen.'

He'd said those words to her previously. And yet Niesha's jaw still dropped to the floor.

'And...why would I want to do that?'

'Because your reward would be elevation to a position very few women will ever achieve in their lifetime. You will have the respect of a whole kingdom and the adoration of millions.'

Something curled into a tight ball inside her. 'I'm not sure when I gave you the impressive that I wanted any of that. I don't.'

He sent her a disbelieving look as he leaned forwards

even further. 'You wish to remain a chambermaid for the rest of your life?'

The lash of the question was meant to wound. And it did. She didn't need reminding that she was a nobody, with no family or even friends she could count on. That all she had was the deep yearning to leave a mark deeper and more meaningful than the sad and transient childhood that had been thrust upon her.

Despite her shredded emotions, she kicked up her chin, glared down her nose at him. 'No. I have a little bit more ambition than that. But it doesn't involve sitting around basking in the adoration of your subjects.'

He nodded, as if he hadn't all but snorted his disbelief moments before. 'Very well, tell me what it is.'

'Why?' she asked suspiciously.

He levelled a shrug so beautifully arrogant and elegant she blinked a few times before she could concentrate again. 'Perhaps I can help.'

Niesha shook her head. Nothing came for free. She knew that all too well. But his eyes were hypnotising her, the gold depths drilling to the heart of her desires.

She found herself responding before she could stop herself. 'I've always wanted to work with children,' she said softly. 'I've been saving to start a course next year.'

'A tutor will be hired for you,' he declared immediately.

Her breath caught, but the reminder that nothing came for free stuck harder. 'In return for what? You want something, I know you do. Why don't you just tell me?'

His eyes gleamed at her. 'I have already told you.'

She shook her head, shaken beyond belief. 'This cannot possibly be what you want. You...you don't even know me.' Her voice was a perplexed shrill.

He shrugged again. 'Perhaps a blank slate is exactly what I need.' The hardness to his tone sent a cold shiver through her.

'That doesn't make any sense.'

'It may seem that way to you, little one.'

The bolt that went through her this time was all heat and charged electricity. 'Please stop calling me that.'

He stiffened. 'Does it offend you?'

She bit her lip but remained silent because, contrary to offence, every time he used that low, deep-voiced endearment, something decadent churned within her, something she didn't want to fathom, never mind explain.

Everything about this man pushed her severely off kilter. But it was time for her to regain her balance.

Before she could speak, he rose to his full, imperious height.

Long, elegant strides brought him to where she sat, and he lowered himself into the seat next to her.

The virile force of his masculinity hit her square in the face. Niesha attempted to swallow, and realised that even that small action couldn't be achieved with him so close.

'Today my people confirmed what I have known for a while—that they need the stability of a king who is married and stable rather than one who is not. The economic potential of my marriage is immense. To upset that turn of events will be unfortunate and unacceptable. For your part, you have been accepted into their hearts. You, a nobody from nowhere. Even if I wanted to be the first in my family to divorce, which I do not, the reaction to our union has made me rethink my decision. You will stay married to me, and in return I will give you a better life.'

Her insides shook but Niesha forced herself to speak. 'And what life is that, exactly?' She wasn't asking because she was about to accept his ludicrous proposal. She just wanted to buy herself a little time to come up with her own strategy to extricate herself from this situation.

'Any life you wish for yourself.'

'And what about Amira?'

His jaw grew rigid for one second. 'You said she wasn't

coerced into leaving. Unless you were mistaken?' he asked, one eyebrow lifted.

She bit her lip, recalling those moments in the room. As much as she wanted to deny it, the truth had been plain to see. 'No, she wasn't coerced. But don't you want to find her?'

'I know exactly who took her and why. It was meant to cause humiliation and chaos, and I've successfully averted that.'

She frowned. 'But you'll want her back, surely?'

His face shuttered. 'I spoke to her father before the ceremony. Our arrangement is broken.'

'Just like that?'

He gave a cold, firm nod. 'Yes. Besides, I believe I've already said I've made my choice. Right now, I want to discuss us.'

Her heart shuddered once more. *Us.* When had they become us?

'My people have been through enough,' he continued forcefully. 'I will not jeopardise the stability of this kingdom with another emotional spectacle like the one my father exhibited recently.' The heat behind his words shocked her to the core. As if he hadn't intended those words to slip out, his face tightened. 'I need someone with a clear head and a strong work ethic by my side.'

'But…you don't even know me,' she repeated.

'I've seen your file. Spoken to those that matter. Your work in my palace has been exemplary.'

She stared at him, stunned. 'And that's it? That's all it takes?'

'No, that's not all it takes. But it's a good basis on which to start.'

Niesha shook her head, her racing heart seeming to have no intention of slowing down. 'This can't be happening,' she said under her breath.

'Reconcile yourself to it.' The finality to the words frightened her.

'I don't want to,' she whispered heatedly. 'You said this was an interim solution,' she reminded him.

Without warning, he reached out and brushed his knuckle down her cheek. The action, electrifying and unexpected, froze her in her seat.

Several minutes passed in silence. When she chanced a glance at him, his eyes were narrowed, the look in his eyes intently calculating.

Niesha was sure that whatever was going on behind his breathtaking face wouldn't include setting her free.

'My people need us to remain married, Niesha,' he eventually said.

Her heart squeezed painfully. 'I… I don't want to make them unhappy but—'

'But what? You wish to return to a life of single servitude?'

'I want to have a choice in when and who I marry!'

His hand dropped, his expression tightening in offence. 'And I'm so vastly unsuitable?'

'I didn't say that,' she mumbled. On the contrary, he was a little too close to her ideal specification of a husband.

'What will suit you, then?' he asked, but Niesha had a feeling he was just humouring her.

Her chin went up. 'For you to honour your initial agreement, that this was only temporary.'

Again he went silent for several spine-tingling minutes. Then he nodded. 'Very well. Five years,' he murmured deeply and abruptly. 'That is all I ask. Five years.'

'I… What?'

'If a permanent marriage to me is too much for you to handle, then let's revisit our situation in five years. In the meantime, you stay by my side. Bear my heirs. At the end of it, if you still want your freedom, I will grant it to you. In return, you will have the education you want, any position you desire, the title of Queen, and riches beyond your wildest dreams.'

'Can you please stop talking about your wealth? I don't want your money.'

His forefinger tucked under her chin and lifted her gaze up to meet his. 'What about my people? Do you hate them so much that you wish to see them unhappy?'

'That's not fair,' she said.

A grim smile played around his lips. 'Get your head out of the clouds, little one. If life was fair, you would not have ended up in an orphanage.'

There was no malice in his tone, only stark truthfulness. And yet the pain was hard to block out. Although there was no record of her past, the quality of the clothes on her back when she'd been found wandering dangerously close to a ravine had indicated that she might have been cared for at one point. But this was no salve right now. Well off or not, she'd been abandoned, possibly left for dead, the orphanage matron had informed her after endless probing.

Niesha had stopped asking about her past when every query—besides those about what she'd been wearing the day she was found at just five years old—had met with a stern rebuke to look forwards not backwards. She had a roof over her head and food in her belly. She needed to be grateful for that, she was told.

Nevertheless, those questions had never left her. It was what fuelled the burning need to work with children. Especially orphaned children.

If she could at some point in the future reunite one child with their rightful past that would be enough for her. Because the pain lodged in her heart all these years later wasn't something she wanted any child to experience.

The idea that Zufar al Khalia could expedite everything she'd ever dreamed of slowly wove through the waves of pain. The other things he had mentioned—being Queen, bearing his children—sent bolts of anxiety through her. They were so impossibly far-reaching she shook her head. 'You...want me to have your children?'

His lips twisted. 'That is generally the idea when a man takes a wife. But especially so in my case since mine is a hereditary rule.'

She stopped herself from laughing hysterically. Was she even capable?

'If you're wondering if you can bear children, I've also seen your medical file. There's nothing to suggest that you may not be able to carry my children.'

Was there a square inch of her life he hadn't probed? The question was ludicrous, of course. He was the head of the royal family. It stood to reason that he would cover every base. Even though they'd been brought together by a set of bizarre circumstances, it seemed as if Zufar had every intention of making this work.

But did she?

'I need your answer, little one.' He pressed his finger still resting beneath her chin, not allowing any avenue of escape.

'Children,' she echoed, her mind darting to his face, unable to stop her imagination from running wild. Would their offspring look like him? Images bombarded her, filling her with a sudden longing that robbed her of breath.

'Many,' he echoed. 'As many as we can manage in five years.'

The prospect of marriage and children had been abstract thoughts in the daily grind of her work in the palace. It was something she had hoped would happen in the future. The reality that it was happening now, unfolding right before her eyes, was almost too much to take in.

As if he knew he had her on the ropes, that she was reeling from everything he had laid out at her feet, he leaned forwards until his mouth was a scant inch from hers. 'Do you agree?' he breathed.

Marriage. Children. Everything the foolish sixteen-year-old in her had dared to dream about as she'd thumbed through the glossy pages of the royal books in the library. Those daydreams that had followed her into her sleep now wormed their way through the dazed anxiety pressing down on her.

Zufar had spoken no words of love—nor had she expected him to. But looking into the hard contours of his face, she doubted they would be forthcoming in the future. When it came right down to it, they were strangers to one another, thrown together by harsh circumstance.

Still, she couldn't dismiss that image of her sixteen-year-old self, staring after a much younger Zufar as he strode commandingly through the palace.

He'd led a life of integrity, loyalty, absolute dedication to his people; his crown. What better characteristics to look for in a future partner than those?

The notion that she was talking herself into this struck her hard.

She attempted to move, to give herself breathing room.

He stopped her retreat by slipping his hand to her nape, just as he had on the balcony earlier. Eyes sharp with intent gazed deeper into hers. 'You want this,' he murmured. 'Think about all you stand to gain, all the children you can help. Say yes, Niesha,' he pressed deeply. Hypnotically.

Had she yearned to retreat to a life of drudgery only an hour ago? Did she really want to scuttle away to her lonely bedsit and scrimp and save for years until she could make something more of her life?

She knew without a doubt that she would kick herself from here to eternity if she refused to take the chance being offered to her on a silver platter.

His lips moved tantalisingly close, eliciting a deep craving that scandalised her. She wanted to kiss him again, she realised shockingly. Wanted the chance beyond today, beyond tomorrow, as many days as she would be granted.

With Zufar al Khalia, there would never be any doubt that her children would be nobodies like her. They would be princes and princesses, future kings or queens with centuries of history and pedigree at their fingertips. She could set a true path for her children. Perhaps even find an identity for herself that she'd been denied. Maybe that was a little bit wrong. But in that moment, it was a decision Niesha couldn't walk away from.

Her hands twisted in her lap. In the next moment, he grasped them with his free hand. He was taking control of her life, of her whole being, and she didn't even care. Her gaze dropped to the mouth she wanted to kiss so badly, before rising to meet his once again.

And then she breathed the word that seared into her heart. 'Yes.'

For endless heartbeats, he didn't move. Then, without granting her the kiss that she craved, he rose, grasped her elbow and pulled her up with him.

'You have made a wise decision,' he intoned.

'Have I, Your Highness?' she responded dazedly.

Again the corner of his mouth lifted in a barely there smile. 'You really need to stop calling me that.'

A shaky breath moved her. Then her breath stilled completely as he cupped her face in his large, warm hands. 'After all, you can hardly call me *Your Highness* when I am deep inside you,' he said in a low, thick voice.

'I…?' She stopped as heat flamed her face.

'Zufar,' he urged. 'That is my name. Use it.' His thumb caressed her jaw, rendering her speechless.

Numbly, she shook her head.

'Never fear, I will have you screaming it by the time the night is over,' he vowed deeply.

He dropped his hand and captured one wrist. The next moment he was pulling her towards the door.

'Where are you taking me?' she blurted.

'It's our wedding night, little one,' he said without breaking stride. 'Royal tradition is no different from any other. We will consummate our marriage this night. After all, if five years is all we have, then you will need to bear my children sooner rather than later, don't you think?'

The look he threw over his shoulder was filled with rock-hard purpose. There was lust in there, sure—no matter how discreet he'd been, Zufar's liaisons with beautiful women were a known fact—but it was a contained lust, one he seemed determined to keep under lock and key.

As he'd said, tonight was their wedding night. And Zufar fully intended to carry out his duty in the bedroom.

Immediately.

Heart in her throat, she stumbled after him down an endless corridor into his private bedchamber and towards the vast and solid four-poster bed that would be the venue for their wedding night.

The place where she would lose her virginity to the King of Khalia before the night was out.

CHAPTER FIVE

NIESHA BARELY ACKNOWLEDGED the magnificently appointed private suite she'd been so in awe of the handful of times she'd visited the King's bedroom as a chambermaid.

Her every sense was focused on the searing clasp of his fingers against hers. Their palms were glued together, the heat from his branding her, imprinting on her skin the same way the royal crest was embossed on the flags that fluttered along the driveway leading to the palace.

Her heart hammered loud enough to drown out any other sound in her ears, so much so that she was terrified she would hyperventilate if she didn't find a way to calm down. But how could she? How could she remain serene in the face of this earth-shaking set of events unfolding in her life?

This morning she'd woken up believing her day would be ordinary—save for the momentous event of the royal wedding, of course—but here she was on the verge of giving her virginity to the King.

Did she have to tell him? Would he know? What was the etiquette? The flurry of questions reeled through her mind, adding to the turmoil seething inside her.

As if he sensed her unsettling thoughts, Zufar stopped abruptly. 'What's wrong?'

'I… This is going too fast,' she answered truthfully.

She expected another one of his thunderous frowns, but was surprised when he studied her for a moment and then nodded. Without releasing her, he raised his other hand and gently brushed his fingers down her pale cheek. 'Do not fear, little one, I will make this memorable for you. We will endeavour to go as slow as you wish.'

A swell of relief bloomed through her apprehension. In

the next moment, it all evaporated when he cleanly swept her off her feet.

'What are you doing?' she squeaked.

'I believe this is the tradition?' he replied.

He wasn't moving. He stared down steadily, waiting for an answer. Only then did Niesha realise that they were poised outside the doors to his inner bedchamber. Beyond that, the immense emperor-sized bed waited, covered with the exquisite gold and blue coverlet she herself had laid on it only a few days ago. The insane, whirlwind journey from then to now seemed like a hallucination.

A quick swallow later, she redirected her gaze to him. 'If you believe in that sort of thing, I guess,' she murmured.

One eyebrow slowly lifted. 'Do you not believe, Niesha?'

It wasn't the first time he'd said her name, but this time the effect of the deep baritone curling around her given name sent tiny bursts of fireworks from deep in her belly, radiating outwards. She watched him track her blush, a small smile curving his lips, drawing her eyes to the sensual outline of his masculine mouth.

'I believe I have my answer,' he said.

With that, he stepped over the threshold and calmly walked her over to the bed.

Slowly he set her down on her feet, his hands trailing her upper arms to settle on her shoulders. Then his gaze raked her from head to toe, lingering at her breasts and her hips in a very frank, masculine appraisal that sent a flare of awareness over her skin.

Her nipples began to pebble, her breasts growing sensitive as he lifted eyes turned molten gold to her face.

'Beautiful,' he pronounced deeply.

No one had ever called her that. Not even close. She shook her head. 'It's not me. It's the dress and…the make-up.'

'It is also the woman wearing those things,' he declared haughtily.

Recalling that he'd been responsible for the gown she was wearing, she looked down at herself. 'Thank you for this. You didn't have to but—'

He cut her off with a shake of his head. 'You were not given a choice in your wedding gown. The situation needed to be remedied for what followed. I couldn't be so distasteful to ask you to wear another woman's clothes on your wedding night.'

A knot she hadn't even been aware of eased inside her. Consideration where there needn't have been touched a place inside her that sent prickles to the back of her eyes. 'Thank you,' she said again.

'You're welcome, but I'm afraid it's time for the dress to come off.'

Just like that the atmosphere shifted again. The purposeful heat gathering in his eyes sent similar flames surging through her body. His hands slowly drifted up her shoulders to the pulse fluttering in her neck. There he paused, his fingers lazily caressing her skin until a helpless moan drifted from her throat.

'Do you like that?' he demanded, his gaze a little too incisive, as if he was intent on learning her body language.

Molten heat flashed through her. Her tongue darted out to lick dry lips as she contemplated her answer. Would he find her daring if she admitted that she liked his touch? Did she even need to answer? Surely he could see for himself?

'This is part of the "getting to know one another" process, Niesha. There's no need to be shy. I intend to learn your body, the same way I wish you to learn mine.' His elegant fingers caressed again, slightly more insistent, his touch leaving trails of heat on her skin. 'Do you like this?' he demanded again, his imperious voice setting off deep tremors inside her.

'Yes,' she moaned.

'Good.' The satisfied sound rumbled from his throat. Then, with both thumbs resting beneath her chin, he tilted her head up, exposing her face to the golden fire of his gaze. 'I wish to taste your lips again,' he stated.

Before she could stop herself, Niesha swayed towards him. A deeper satisfaction twisted his lips before his face grew taut with a captivating look from which she could not look away.

With a rough sound under his breath, he lowered his head and sealed his mouth to hers. She had no prior experience save for their previous kiss, but even Niesha knew this one was different.

For a start, it seared her to the soul. A deeply carnal, deeply intoxicating experience, it was a statement of subjugation over her that swiftly stripped her of the ability to think.

Her every sense focused on the dark magic being visited upon her, a magic she never wanted to end. The bold probe of his tongue between her lips commanded her to open up for him. With a sigh of need, she parted her lips and experienced an even greater depth of sensation as his tongue brushed hers.

Bold. Fiery. Caught in the grip of fever she'd never imagined possible with a mere kiss, she couldn't stop herself from clinging to his waist as the ground moved beneath her feet. Hungry for more, she parted her lips wider, and moaned low and deep as he explored her with brazen thoroughness. Wave after wave of sensation swept through her, her knees growing weaker with each passing second.

At some point her eyes had drifted shut as she succumbed to the power of touch and scent. She heard his breathing grow heavy to match hers, the hands resting at her throat drifting down her back to cup her buttocks before pulling her closer into his body. No man had ever touched her so boldly. No man had ever done even a fraction of what Zufar was doing to her. It was intoxicating beyond belief.

With another helpless moan, she gave into the temptation and allowed her own hands to roam his body. The silk of his tunic heated beneath her fingers as she slowly circled his waist and tentatively explored his back. Hard muscles flexed beneath her touch, his body tensing and relaxing as she hesitantly caressed him. All sense of time faded away, the only reality in her world the utterly mind-bending sensations carrying her away to an unknown destination.

A harsh hiss issued from his lips. She blinked, then realised her nails were digging into his shoulders. At some point, his fingers had buried in her hair and he used the gentle grip to notch back her head so he could gaze down into her face.

'Do I have a little hellcat on my hands?' he queried lazily.

But there was nothing lazy in his ferocious gaze. It was determined and powerful and intent on conquering.

And she wanted to be conquered. So much.

Her gaze dropped to his lips, eager and unashamed for another taste of his superb kiss.

At her moan, his eyes glittered with an indecipherable edge that escalated her heartbeat. 'You look at me with such unfettered need,' he said. 'It is enough to lead a lesser man into dangerous waters.'

'But not you,' she observed huskily.

Because he was above the weaknesses that plagued mere mortals. Even now, he stood tall and proud and domineering, statue-like evidence that he was extraordinary in every way imaginable. And so very confident in the bold manhood that branded her belly through their clothes.

Maybe it was her imagination, and she certainly had no comparison, but the imprint of his girth was substantial enough to set off a different set of alarm bells through her system.

But alongside it, there was also a thrill, sinful and delicious, temptation at its worst. Between her thighs, liquid heat threatened to melt her into a puddle, even as a terrible hunger tunnelled inside her, demanding fulfilment. She gasped as his hands slowly explored her waist, then drifted up her back once more.

Deft fingers located her zip and pulled it down with steady purpose. The sound filled the whole room a vivid manifestation of what was happening.

The noise that emerged from her this time was less of a moan and more of a whimper.

Before her nerves could eat her alive, he was wreaking havoc again, kissing one corner of her mouth before planting decadent little kisses along her cheek, her jaw and then down her neck to the point where it met her shoulder. Merciless teeth nipped at her skin, dragging a shiver that drew a deep grunt of satisfaction from him.

'You are so responsive. I look forwards to drawing even more reactions from this body.'

The soft breeze that whispered over her skin was her first indication that her dress was undone. Still kissing her neck, he slowly drew the emerald silk down her arms until her breasts were bared to his gaze.

Alarm rushed over Niesha, dampening her desire. Her arms slammed across her chest, covering her breasts as she took a hasty step back.

Zufar froze. A thunderous frown gathered on his brow. 'Something wrong?'

She swallowed hard. 'There is…something you should know.'

A faint wave of displeasure washed over his features. 'Yes?' The prompt was a tight rumble from his chest. Even as he waited for her answer, his gaze moved over her, lingering on her shoulders, the breasts she was desperately shielding from his view, down to where her dress rested low on her hips.

She would never have believed a look from a man's eyes could evoke such cataclysmic feelings inside her. And even though Zufar seemed in complete control of his faculties, the look in his eyes rendered her mute.

But she needed to speak. She had to tell him, despite her insides shrinking at the possibilities of what he would do if he found out that she was untouched. None of them filled her with elation.

Esteemed men like Zufar preferred women who knew how to please a man. The women he'd dated before were all experienced. Sophisticated. The history books she'd scoured in the library had even contained sections on how prospective brides were tutored in the art of pleasing their husbands. She knew nothing except what she'd read in romance books years ago. And even those had sounded unrealistic.

Dejected, Niesha lowered her gaze to his shoes. Zufar had seemed aroused by their kisses, but this was far more than mere kissing. Besides, he'd done all the work and now she was terrified he would find her severely lacking.

'Speak,' he commanded, the directive firm and implacable.

'I don't… I'm not…'

'Niesha.' The dangerous edge to her name sent another skitter of alarm along her nerve endings.

She raised her head, compelled by his voice. His face was a taut, unreadable mask, but she imagined she glimpsed hunger in his eyes. That bolstered her a little.

'Tell me what worries you,' he pressed.

'I'm not…experienced,' she confessed with little more than a whisper.

A wave of decipherable emotion swept across his face. Slowly his eyes narrowed. 'I require a better definition of inexperienced,' he replied.

'Virgin,' she blurted. 'I'm a virgin. And… I don't want to disappoint you.'

For the longest time, he stared at her, his eyes a deep bronze that saw right to her soul. When his eyes conducted a searing scrutiny from her crown to her toes, Niesha was painfully reminded that she was naked from the waist up.

'The only way you will disappoint me is if you fail to tell me how that is possible.'

Another fierce blush swept over her skin.

A sound rumbled from him. Once again he seemed fascinated by her blush, his gaze following the tide of pink as it suffused her skin. When his gaze reached her face, he stared deep into her eyes, waiting for an answer.

'I would have thought it was simple enough. I've never been with a man,' she confessed in a hushed voice.

Niesha was shocked by the naked possessiveness that lit through his eyes. A moment later it was gone, but the searing flame of it remained, heating up her blood as she stared hypnotically at him; as she watched his nostrils slowly flare in a show of frayed control before he sucked in a deep breath.

'You're twenty-five,' he breathed. 'And you've never been with a man?'

Even though she was dying to hide from his all-seeing eyes, Niesha forced herself to maintain eye contact. 'No, I have not.'

His breath punched out. A single clench rippled through his jaw before he cupped her elbows. 'Then you will be mine. Only mine.'

The ruthless, irrefutable possessiveness in those words flattened her lungs. She was struggling to breathe when he drew her arms decisively away from her body, exposing her to his eyes. Caught in a web of sorcery he wove so effortlessly, Niesha let her arms drop, trembling before him as his eyes settled on her breasts.

Another rough sound ripped from his throat. 'You are truly exquisite.'

She couldn't have moved if her life depended on it. With his eyes and his words and his commanding stature, he captivated her. She stood trembling as he firmly tugged the gaping dress over her hips.

It dropped to her ankles. He lifted her effortlessly out

of the tangle of silk and lace. She should have felt vulnerable in just her panties and heels but something about the way he looked at her body sent a thrill of power through her. Maybe he wasn't as unaffected as she'd first thought.

She had very little idea of what making love with him would fully entail, but for now something about her pleased him enough to remain before her, his eyes tracing over her skin as he leisurely explored her body.

Abruptly he swung her around to face her away from him, drawing a gasp from her as his fingers circled her waist and pulled her back into the heated column of his hard, toned body.

They stayed like that for endless seconds before he notched his head into the curve of her neck, his lips tracing over her skin. Slowly, his fingers wove into her bound hair, and began to tug out the diamond pins securing the elaborate knot. One by one he discarded them until her hair cascaded over her shoulders and down her back. 'Incredible,' he breathed again.

Between her thighs, heat built, powering up into unbearable levels as he sifted his fingers through her hair, indolently, as if he had all the time in the world. Only when he was satisfied did his hand drift over her shoulder to the slope of her chest.

Without warning he cupped one breast, his hand a warm bold caress as he gently fondled her.

At her gasp, he grazed her neck with a teasing bite, even as his fingers began to toy with her nipple. Her knees turned liquid but he easily held her up.

'Mine,' he rasped hotly in her ear.

Her soft cry gave way to a helpless whimper as he mercilessly teased her nipple, stoking relentless fire in her belly she knew wouldn't be assuaged until he gave her more, more, *more*. Fully attuned to her need, his other hand cupped her other breast, torturing both peaks with expert tugs.

In that moment, Niesha was convinced she would explode. 'Oh!'

'Does my little hellcat like this?'

Her head dropped forwards as flames of hunger singed her whole being. 'Yes,' she sobbed helplessly.

He gave a soft laugh as he continued to caress her. Behind her, she heard the rustle of clothes but feared that her senses, already overloaded with new, unbelievable sensations, would send her over the edge if she looked at him.

So, letting her imagination run wild, she conjured up what Zufar looked like. But even that fevered imagining left her breathless. Hungry.

The driving need to experience the reality of him brought her head up. But before she could turn, he was touching her again, his fingers sliding beneath the waistband of her panties and firmly pushing them over her hips. Just like her dress, they pooled around her ankles and he lifted her clear of them. Then he turned her around.

Of course, her imagination had fallen far, far short.

Magnificent.

Bronzed from head to toe, there wasn't an ounce of fat on his sleek, muscled body. He could have been hewn from marble blessed by the gods themselves, he couldn't have been more perfect. The hard, hairless planes of his chest were woven into a tight six-pack, before arrowing into defined silky hair that framed an impressive manhood that jutted proudly from his body.

Niesha's jaw dropped. He was beyond impressive. So much so her body flamed with a new, intensely searing hunger as her gaze drifted down his powerful thighs to his feet and back again to that place between his legs that she couldn't pull her fascinated gaze from.

'You like what you see, little one?' he enquired with more than a touch of male arrogance.

Even as the question dropped from his lips, his manhood continued to swell. She watched, her breath completely locked in her lungs. There was no way he could fit inside her.

Accurately deciphering her thoughts, he stepped forwards. 'You needn't worry. I'll take care of you, *habibti*.'

He gave her no time to dwell on what was coming. Powerful arms swept her off her feet, laid her down on the bed and he levered himself over her. Then, excruciatingly slowly, he lowered himself until his hard chest brushed against her sensitive nipples.

At her wild tremor, one corner of his mouth lifted.

The wildness intensified when he dropped down and sealed another kiss on her lips, while his hands roamed freely, possessively over her body, leaving no part of her skin untouched as he explored her thoroughly.

Niesha had no idea how much time passed before he began kissing his way down her body.

Sensual lips trailed from her collarbone to the valley between her breasts, dropping torrid, open-mouthed kisses on her skin before cupping her breasts and fondling her. Hot murmured words she couldn't decipher dripped from his lips before he captured one tight peak in this mouth.

A tiny scream tore free from her throat, her back arching off the bed as sensation like she'd never known rippled through her body. He rolled his tongue over her nipple, sucking her deep into his mouth before releasing her, only to start the torture all over again. He repeated the gesture on the twin peak, leaving her delirious and whimpering when he freed her to trail kisses over the skin above her belly button.

'Be calm,' he ordered thickly. 'You have my promise we will do this again. For now, I must taste what is mine.'

When she fully grasped his meaning, Niesha gasped, and attempted to close her legs. Surely he didn't mean…?

'Yes,' he insisted gruffly.

Powerful hands held her easily captive, clamped on her thighs as he slowly, insistently laid her bare.

His gaze snagged hers for a moment, and then his eyes

dropped to her most intimate place. The fiercest, wildest blush she'd ever experienced threatened to swallow her whole as a deep rumble emitted from Zufar's throat.

'Truly exquisite.'

Niesha was spinning at the power of those two words when his head dropped and he slicked an expert tongue over her needy flesh. A long moan ripped free. She shuddered wildly, even as every cell in her body clamoured for more. Zufar delivered, leisurely exploring her as if he owned every inch of her.

Which he did, she thought dazedly.

At some point, Niesha stopped blushing, the blissful sensation of what he was doing to her overcoming embarrassment as she gave herself over to the magic of his tongue. He teased, nibbled, explored, and then concentrated with single-minded focus on that bundle of nerves at the top of her sex.

Just when she thought there could be no sensation as thrilling as this, he suckled her with steady pressure that detonated a volcano deep in her pelvis.

She cried out, her whole body tightening for one soul-shaking instant before her world erupted in a billion fragments. Convulsions tore through her as bliss blinded her. An eternity passed. Or it might have been one enchanted minute. Niesha had no idea of the passage of time as she was fully engulfed in pure sensation.

Gradually she became aware that her fingers were curled into Zufar's hair, holding on tight as the world slowly began to right itself. She was also aware that his breathing was uneven as he trailed kisses against her skin.

It occurred to her that, far from the tightly controlled man who'd carried her into his bedroom, Zufar's demeanour had altered. He was just as caught up in the fever as she was.

And he'd been that way from the moment she'd mentioned her virginity. Or was she reading too much into it?

She had no time to dwell on it because he was kissing his way back up her body. When they were face to face, he lowered himself onto his elbows, stared deeply into her eyes for a moment before he fused his mouth to hers. The taste of her on his lips should have embarrassed Niesha. But all it produced was a decadent triumph.

She'd done something right. He wasn't pulling away. He didn't look disappointed.

If anything, there was an edge to his kiss, an aggression that spoke to a need that matched the one rekindling inside her.

When the need to replenish their breaths forced them apart, his fevered eyes seized hers. 'Touch me,' he commanded gruffly.

Her hands trembled wildly, from the strength of her release, and from the nerves that were resurfacing. But the need to feel the warmth of his skin beneath her fingers overcame the nerves.

Just as he'd done to her, she drifted her fingers down his neck. Over his Adam's apple. His tight swallow and groan told her he liked it. Emboldened, she continued to touch him, caressing the hard muscle of his pecs before trailing her hands down his stomach to settle on his hips.

Zufar's breathing turned harsh and uneven. With not quite steady hands, he pulled her thighs apart and settled between them. His thick length settled between her folds. Her very wet, very needy folds.

As another wave of embarrassment hit her cheeks, he smiled down at her. 'Do not be embarrassed by your eagerness for me,' he murmured. 'Spread your legs wider,' he commanded.

She complied, her heart pumping like a runaway racehorse. The broad head of his manhood nudged her flesh and Niesha's breath strangled in her throat.

'Be calm,' he instructed again.

She forced herself to breathe even as her fingers bit into the hard muscles of his arms.

Zufar inhaled sharply then pushed inside her.

The sharp pain took her completely by surprise. She cried out.

He kissed her, hard and swift. 'Hush,' he soothed gruffly. He withdrew slowly, then pushed inside her again.

Hot tears welled in her eyes as pain rippled through her again.

Above her, Zufar's jaw clenched tight, his breathing ragged as he stared down at her with dark, ferocious eyes. 'The pain will ease.' It was a directive, as if he had power over her pain too.

For some absurd reason, she believed him. And gave a jerky little nod.

As if that action had triggered something inside him, he gave a rough groan and penetrated her to the hilt. Another shaky cry tore free as tears slid down her temples. And then just as abruptly as it had arrived, the pain disappeared.

'Tell me how you feel,' he rasped.

'I… I'm fine,' she replied softly, and then realised she was.

Above her, he continued to watch her with hawk-like intensity, dark gold eyes scrutinising every expression. After a moment, he drew back, and pushed back in.

Niesha gasped at the new sensations dancing through her bloodstream. With shallow thrusts, Zufar possessed her, his eyes watching her every move as he joined their bodies.

Her moans fusing into one litany of need, she shut her eyes when Zufar lowered himself over her. His breath washed over her face as he lengthened his thrusts, drawing even more exquisite pleasure from her body.

'Wrap your legs around me,' he instructed.

An instant after she obeyed, she gasped as his next thrust drew a sharper, more intense sensation from her. With a grunt of carnal satisfaction, he fused his mouth to hers in a bold mimic of what was happening below.

Dear heaven, she'd had no idea it could be this incredible.

The thought barely registered before another charge lanced through her, sending her spinning even higher.

'Oh… Zufar…'

As if his name on her lips had triggered madness inside him, his thrust grew wilder, pushing her relentlessly towards a pinnacle that far surpassed the one she'd crested only minutes ago.

Her world began to tilt again.

'Niesha, open your eyes,' he demanded.

She pried her eyes open to meet with burnished gold ones. Something about that sizzling connection was enough to send her over the edge.

With a strangled scream, she tumbled from the highest peak of sensation, falling into a never-ending sea of bliss that drew tears to her eyes.

Zufar al Khalia couldn't believe the woman beneath him was the same person he'd met only this morning; the woman he'd dismissed so carelessly. He'd gone into this believing he had his eyes wide open to every angle. Not for one single moment had he believed enjoyment would come into the undertaking. But here he was, unable to deny the surfeit of pleasure rippling through his body. He'd bedded many women in his life, but none came close to the responsiveness of his new wife.

His virgin Queen.

He wondered if it was her complete innocence that added to the thrill of the conquest. More than likely, he concluded. He'd never bedded a virgin, never felt inclined to be the first to stake a claim on a woman. To be honest, the thought of tutoring one to please him had been a deterrent rather than a draw.

But as he thrust into his new wife, Zufar thought of all the ways he could mould her to his liking. How he could teach her to take pleasure in her own body, even as he planted his seed in her womb. They were archaic, primitive thoughts that should have shamed him, but only intensified his pleasure as he let the sounds of her pleasure fill him up. She was his in every way. He stared down at her as her sweet lips parted on another pleasurable gasp, her beautiful eyes glazing over as he crested his own pinnacle.

With a raw shout, he let the sweet taste of nirvana sweep through his body.

It was only as he came down from the unparalleled high that the full effect of his thoughts began to settle in.

Shock ripped through him when he recognised how quickly he'd let temptation sway him from his purpose.

How quickly, like his father, he'd been prepared to set aside his priorities to succumb to desire.

How, for a handful of heartbeats, he'd completely lost sight of just how affairs of the flesh had ripped his family apart.

CHAPTER SIX

SO THIS WAS what true desire felt like. This endless cyclone of sensation. This exceptional feeling of touching heaven.

This—

Niesha's thoughts ceased abruptly as Zufar wrenched free from the arms she hadn't even realised were locked around his shoulders, anchoring her to the present.

The thought that she'd been clinging to him like a limpet doused her with a wave of chagrin. Luckily, he wasn't looking at her. In fact, his whole body was turned away from her, and he was getting out of bed.

Heart still racing a little wildly, she watched him walk, gloriously naked and arrogantly assured in his own skin, away from the bed. But there was tension in his broad shoulders and back that chilled her with each step he took away from her. Her heart rate slowed, a little of that magic leaching from her, then fading completely as he firmly shut the bathroom door behind him.

Okay, what had happened?

She hadn't said anything. Had she done something to provoke that reaction? Minutes ago, he'd seemed…into it. Even now, the animalistic roar of his release echoed in her ears, making her blush anew at the memory. Niesha would have felt ashamed at the throb of feminine power she'd experienced in that moment, if she weren't overcome by his masculine beauty.

But that was ten minutes and a lifetime ago. The aftermath was turning out to be a different story.

Her thoughts ceased abruptly when the door opened and he strode back to the bed. She was so busy searching his expression, she didn't read his intent until he scooped her up.

'Wh-what are you doing?' she squeaked.

His eyes had grown remote, if still a touch darker than usual. They met hers for a split second before he strode, set-faced, towards the bathroom.

'Seeing to your comfort. You must be sore.' The matter-of-fact tone of his reply killed any softness the words evoked, although his touch, when he set her down in the shower cubicle and began to wash her, was gentle.

Why?

The question stayed locked in her throat as her breath shuddered out at his disturbingly intimate cleansing of her body. Niesha withstood his touch even though she wanted to sprint back into the bedroom and draw the covers over her head. It would solve nothing. So she stood there, biting her lip as he took his time to perform his task. Maybe it was no big deal. Maybe he did this for all his—

No. Not going there, she concluded fiercely.

Inexorably, her eyes rose to his face. To the tight mask blocking his every expression from her.

'Is…is everything okay?' She hated herself for seeking the reassurance.

His expression didn't change but she saw his shoulders tighten. 'Everything is fine.'

Tell that to your clenched jaw, she wanted to blurt. She bit back the words before they spilled free.

Maybe this was post-coital etiquette? Even as she pondered the question, Niesha knew she was grasping at straws. She wanted to find an excuse for the hollow sensation widening inside her but, really, wasn't it her own foolish whims leading her astray, again?

As the thought struck she noticed his movements had slowed, his hands gliding fluidly over her flesh. Breath snagging, her gaze flew to his face. His lips were parted, his tongue resting on his lip as he glided a soapy palm over her breasts. Between his thighs, his manhood was stirring into life again. Niesha's senses thrilled anew, the foolish notion that she'd got it wrong almost making her laugh with relief.

In the next moment, Zufar turned away. With almost cruel movements, he turned off the shower and stepped out of the cubicle.

No. She wasn't wrong. She'd fooled herself into thinking she'd pleased him. That he would want her again. But as he'd told her in the living room, he needed heirs—and lots of them, quickly—if they were to be married for only five years.

The need to consummate this marriage had been an essential part of that goal. It had had nothing to do with her. The future of the kingdom depended on it. Nothing more, nothing less.

Zufar was a man who placed his duty above all else. He'd performed it and now the act was over.

Despite the warmth of the shower, a chill settled over her. Growing stiffer by the minute, she concentrated on breathing in and out as he wrapped a towel around himself, then one around her, before carrying her back to the bedroom.

Immediately she fled to the far side of the bed. Then, wondering if she was sleeping on his side, she started to reverse position. Then froze in the middle when it occurred to her that they hadn't even discussed sleeping arrangements.

Niesha knew that besides the previous Queen's private suite in the east wing, there was an adjoining suite next to the King's for the Queen's use. Was she supposed to retire there now and await further summons or return to the east wing? Her hands curling in frustration, she started to move to the edge of the bed.

'Where are you going?' he drawled, his imposing figure looming beside her.

A furtive gaze confirmed his demeanour hadn't changed. In fact, he looked even more remote. 'I don't know which side you preferred or…even if I'm supposed to sleep here?'

His brows gathered in a dark frown. 'Where else are you supposed to sleep?'

She licked her lips, her fingers tightening on the sheets bunched between her breasts. 'In the suite next door? Or back in the Qu… Queen's quarters?' She stumbled over the word, was positive she would stumble over it for a long time to come.

His face darkened further, his jaw jutting out as he stared down his patrician nose at her. 'Is that what you would prefer?' he asked with chilling terseness.

Niesha suppressed a shiver. At this moment, she would prefer to be anywhere but here, withstanding his cold, haughty scrutiny, which he managed to pull off superbly despite being completely naked. 'Isn't that what is expected of me?'

'What would make you draw that conclusion?' he bit out.

'It wasn't a secret that your parents did not share the same bed…' Her words withered to nothing when his whole body clenched into terrifying stillness.

'In case the obvious needs pointing out, I'm not my father. And this is not the nineteenth century.' If she'd thought him remote a minute ago, he was positively arctic now.

For some reason, mentioning his parents had hit the wrong nerve. Niesha, like everyone else living within the palace walls, had heard whispers of the strained relationship between the previous King and his wife, despite the King's utter devotion to her. But with no facts to back it up, she'd attributed it to palace gossip. As for the relationship between King Tariq and his children, it had appeared civil if not outwardly warm.

But from Zufar's reaction…could it all have been an act? A series of royal chess moves designed to fool the general public?

Niesha had certainly witnessed how ruthlessly calculating her new husband could be when he desired a specific outcome. Her current position was the living embodiment of that ruthlessness.

She strove to speak despite the unease flaring through her body. 'I know that…but we both know this isn't a real marriage.'

Sensual lips that had kissed hers only a short while ago twisted in faint derision. 'I've just taken your virginity, Niesha. We have agreed to have children. It doesn't get more real than that,' he pointed out, his voice deeply husky and painfully direct.

Her chin dropped, every skin cell flaming. 'You know what I mean.'

'Do I?'

Her head reared up. 'Yes!' She lifted her hand to her slightly throbbing head and pushed back the heavy curtain of hair. 'Look, we both know I wasn't your first choice. I wasn't even in the running.' If Amira hadn't been seduced by another man she would be here right now. The thought lodged a hard knot in her stomach, but she pushed it away. 'So it's completely understandable if you want to maintain your private quarters.'

He took a step closer, braced one knee on the bed. It took everything in her power not to drop her gaze to the impressive manhood between his legs. A part of her felt bitter jealousy for his ability to be so confident in his own skin, especially when she couldn't even control her own stupid blushes.

Her breath stilled as firm hands captured her chin.

'I ask again, is that what you want?' Piercing eyes probed hers.

He seemed to be fishing for something specific. Something she had no clue about. She blinked, glanced at the tousled bed. Unbidden, the image of going to sleep in the same bed as Zufar, surrounded by his unique scent, his magnificent body, the sizzling mastery of his possession, and waking up with him, loomed in her mind.

Did she want that?

Not if each one ended with him staring at her with such remote, almost indifferent eyes. But then how else would she live up to her end of the bargain? Surely it was better to remain here, ensure the deed was done in the shortest possible time?

'As you said, the quicker we ensure that I'm...pregnant, the better for everyone, I think—' The words stuck in her throat, most likely because they were far too clinical, stripped of any emotion, and it wasn't a true reflection of what was happening inside her.

But he was nodding, as if in complete agreement with her.

It drove home the fact that she couldn't afford to let her emotions run free. Or give into foolish dreams of this union being anything but the stark bargain she'd struck. She was only here because another man had stolen the woman he'd chosen.

As for hoping her child was conceived in contentment and warmth, it was really past time she put those fairy-tale notions behind her. Not when she was the epitome of what came *after* conception.

Abandonment. Loneliness. Deprivation.

All things she needed to ensure never happened to her child, no matter how it was conceived.

He dropped her chin and slid into bed. 'I'm glad to hear it. And for the record, this is what I prefer, too. Tomorrow the palace designer will contact your assistant with a view to setting up a meeting.'

'What for?' she asked.

'To discuss what you intend to do with the suite next door. You can turn it into a giant dressing room. Or perhaps a nursery. Entirely up to you.'

Niesha was grappling with that when he pulled the sheets from her with a firm tug and began to rearrange the covers over them.

'You've had a challenging day. Tomorrow will not be any less so. I suggest you get some sleep now.'

On that none-too-reassuring pronouncement, he turned away and doused the bedside lamps.

Niesha awoke to the breath-stealing sensation of a stubbled jaw grazing her cheek. Still lost in a jagged dream of smoke and fire and screams, it was a relief to awaken.

It wasn't the first time she'd had those dreams. Along with the soft voice that echoed reassurance in her mind in times of distress, the disturbing dreams had also been part of her life for as long as she could remember.

It wasn't a stretch to conclude it was her psyche grappling with whatever dark shadows lurked in her past. That the thoughts and fears she pushed to the back of her mind during her waking hours transmitted to nightmares in her sleep.

Despite knowing this, she still woke most mornings with a panicked, racing heart and a sinking sensation that her past would always remain a pitch-black, desolate landscape to her.

Not this morning, though. Before her anxiety could take hold, firm masculine lips moved along her jawline to the corner of hers.

She shuddered, then opened her eyes to meet dark gold ones that burned with single-minded purpose. For the longest moment, Zufar stared at her. He didn't utter a word. Neither did she.

Then one hand dipped between their bodies to settle firmly between her thighs. At her gasp, his nostrils flared, the only sign that he'd registered her response.

The moment he established that she was wet, needy and more than ready for him, he angled the thick column of his erection and thrust, deeply and powerfully, inside her.

Her husky moan was filled with need and awe, her senses ripping apart at the potency of his possession.

Even when she realised that the only sounds filling the

room were coming from her, his silent lovemaking was still electrifying, perhaps even more so than the night before since her body now knew what to expect.

Minutes later, she found out that even in that she was wrong, that there was a new determination in his lovemaking that robbed her of the little breath she'd managed to sustain.

He captured and pinned her arms above her head, and then, with caged intensity, he thrust relentlessly into her, the formidable power of it driving home one purpose—ensuring she took his seed and produced the heir he wanted.

The small part of her that attempted to shrink back from such a complete but detached coupling was soon swept under the traitorous melting that radiated from her core and took control of her own being.

The tiny cry she gave as she crested the pinnacle of pleasure was soon followed by his suppressed groan as he, too, achieved his release.

Moments later, he left the bed. She heard the muted hiss of the shower and sagged onto the pillows, willing her heartbeat and the tumultuous emotions reeling through her to slow.

She really couldn't afford to lose her mind each time he touched her. Every instinct warned that would be reckless in the extreme. Already his brief absence was triggering a craving for another glimpse of him, and somewhere in the back of her mind a tiny clock was counting down the five years she'd agreed with him.

What would happen afterwards?

Banishment from the palace? Niesha jackknifed into sitting position, realising she should have hammered out more than just parting with her freedom for five years. Would she be allowed to take her children with her? Or would she be once again condemned to a life of loneliness and desolation?

She firmed her lips. No, she wouldn't let that happen. No

matter what, the children she produced with Zufar would be part hers.

But then he was the King, with endless resources to fight her if he so wished.

She was grappling with the future threat when he emerged from the bathroom. And just like that every thought evaporated from her head.

His thick black hair was slicked back from his face, glistening damply beneath the low-lit chandeliers. His arms and chest rippled with sleek muscles as he strode towards the bed. But it was the snowy white towel, knotted low on his hips and framing the divine V of his pelvis, that made her mouth water shamefully.

She held her breath, unable to prise her gaze from him as he sauntered over to the bed.

A moment passed, then two. At his continued silent scrutiny, she dragged her head up. 'Good morning,' she said after swallowing hard.

He raised an eyebrow. 'Is it?'

Her fingers bunched in the sheets, her heart lurching wildly. Had the new day triggered a change of mind? Did he wish to renege on the deal he'd struck? Was he going to chase after Amira after all?

Why that thought left a pile of ash in her mouth when she'd all but demanded the very same thing last night floored her.

She lifted a hand in a futile attempt to ease the sudden sharp ache hammering beneath her breastbone.

'I ask because you were having a distressing dream. It was why I woke you up.'

Her hand dropped to her lap, unsettling relief weaving through her. A moment later, her heart dropped too, slowing to a disturbingly dull thud. Was that why he'd made love to her too? To distract her from her nightmare?

'Oh, I see. Thank you,' she murmured, because, really, what did it matter why he'd woken her? She'd agreed, without force or coercion, to be his brood mare. So why was the reality dampening her mood?

His eyes narrowed on her face. 'Are you well?' he asked abruptly.

Did he mean the nightmare? Or what had happened last night and this morning. Or generally? Again, what did it matter? She nodded jerkily. 'I… I'm fine.'

He gave a brisk nod. 'You will join me for breakfast. After that, your time is your own, save for the hour or so you need to select your staff. My chief aide will provide you with a shortlist.'

The briskness with which he walked away towards his dressing room told her she didn't have time to linger on yet another bombshell dropped so neatly at her feet. She would think about what on earth she would do with a staff later, when she was appropriately dressed.

As she rose from the bed, she spotted the telltale signs of her lost virginity on the sheets and her face flamed all over again. Glad Zufar wasn't around to spot her embarrassment, Niesha located her discarded dress and fled the room before he could return.

Her walk of shame wasn't any less cringe-inducing because she was the Sheikh's new bride, because of course the palace was wide awake and the usual bustle of people that went into making the place run like a well-oiled machine were up and about. Her state wasn't helped when her attendants, headed by Halimah, who looked as if they'd been lying in wait for her, descended on her the moment she entered the main wing of the palace.

Within minutes everyone knew she'd spent the night in Zufar's bed.

Niesha managed to hold her head high as she was escorted back to her rooms.

Again, a stunning array of clothes had been hung out for her, this time lighter linens and soft chiffons in pastel colours. Unsure how long she had before her breakfast with

Zufar, she declined having her hair washed and didn't linger in the bath.

Twenty minutes later, dressed in a knee-length ivory and navy block dress with a delicate lace waistline fringe, capped sleeves, and navy platform heels, she retraced her steps back to Zufar's private quarters. An aide led her into the dining room, where he sat at the head of a long antique dining table, reading a newspaper.

Even performing the mundane task of reading while he ate, he was a spectacular sight, dressed in an impeccable suit she knew had been specially imported from Milan.

When she neared him, he deftly folded the paper, inclined his head in a regal nod and watched as she was seated. She kept her hands folded in her lap and her spine straight, tinglingly aware of his direct gaze as her tea was poured and various dishes placed before her.

'You left my bed before I could show you the less...public passage from my room,' he said with a stiffness that spoke of his displeasure the moment the staff retreated.

Niesha fought the blush that threatened. 'Oh... I...didn't know—'

He waved her response away. 'It is done. And since you won't need to leave my bedroom again in the future, we will not speak about your precipitous exit. Eat your breakfast.'

Niesha stared down at her plate, trying to summon an appetite, while curbing a bite of irritation. Slowly she reached for a piece of toast, buttered it and added a dollop of jam made from dates and honey. It melted on her tongue, but, where she would probably have groaned with the delicious taste, she chewed thoughtfully.

'Something wrong?' he queried after a minute.

'You made it sound as if I needed your permission to leave.'

His gaze scoured her face. 'Or perhaps I wished to spare the blushes that come so readily to your cheeks,' he retorted.

It took great effort not to lift her hands to her hot face. 'I'm sorry if my comportment is lacking.'

Something flashed in his eyes before they regained that remoteness again. 'On the contrary, you're the epitome of a blushing bride. Legions of people across the world lap up that sort of thing, I'm told,' he said lazily.

She barely managed to stop herself from asking who'd told him. Did she really want to know who he'd been discussing her with? Or whether he had an opinion on blushes one way or the other?

But even as she thought that, she felt his gaze tracking another rush of heat to her face. One day she would master her flaw. Today she had other matters on her mind.

'What you said yesterday, about the honeymoon… Is it still happening?'

Steady eyes rested on her. 'Of course. Why should it not be?'

Because he'd planned it for another woman. Under the circumstances, the idea shouldn't have lodged a tiny stone beneath her breastbone but she couldn't forestall the ache. She shook her head. 'I was just double-checking.'

'If you're feeling a little…bruised because I'm taking you where I would've taken Amira, don't be. Like you, she and I had an understanding. The continued prosperity and smooth running of the kingdom comes first. Which is why this trip was always going to be partly a business one.'

She wasn't sure whether knowing she was so interchangeable made her feel better or worse. Or that he wasn't bothering to soften where his priorities truly lay. 'When do we leave?' she asked when she'd smothered the growing hurt in her chest.

'In three days. We will stay at the Emerald Palace for two days, then leave for Europe.'

He went on to name the other places they would be visiting, places Niesha had dreamed of exploring once upon a time. But the joy she'd felt then was severely lacking now.

She finished sipping her tea, nodding when expected, all the while feeling the cloak of loneliness and abandonment encroaching once more.

Would she ever be rid of this feeling? She was tied to one of the most powerful men in the world, and yet she felt…hollow.

'I seem to have lost you.' His hard, abrupt observation prised her from her thoughts.

Before she could respond, a knock rapped on the dining-room doors. An instant later, a ping sounded on his phone. He touched the screen as the door opened, and his private secretary strode in.

'Good morning, Your Highnesses,' he greeted, bowing low before turning to Zufar. 'You are needed urgently, sire.' He didn't say more, but whatever lay behind his words was enough to make Zufar's face tighten.

Without further questioning, he rose from the table. 'I'm afraid I need to start my day earlier than planned. Finish your breakfast. Your aide will be here in half an hour.'

With that, he swept out with all the regal authority and purpose of a true king.

Niesha deflated the moment she was alone. After a few minutes of toying with the fresh fruit on her plate, she rose and went to the window. Outside the sun was blazing. On the palace grounds, the remaining signs of the wedding were being removed. In a few hours, it would be a thing of the past.

Desolation crept closer, wrapping tighter around her.

She realised that somewhere between last night and this morning, she'd let the tiniest grain of hope take root, fooled herself into thinking that the bargain she'd struck with Zufar would immediately go towards filling the yawning hole she'd felt all these years.

But it still gaped as wide as ever.

A throat cleared behind her and she steeled herself not to stiffen.

'Your Highness?'

She turned. The woman dressed in a sharp skirt suit was tall, statuesque, with kind brown eyes and an easy, deferential smile. 'My name is Kadira Hamdi and I'm your new aide.'

Niesha had never seen her before but something about her expression eased the knot inside her. For starters, there was none of the judgement in her eyes that she'd witnessed in Halimah's.

And even though the woman before her was stunningly beautiful, Niesha sensed no malice in her.

She nodded and returned the smile. 'I'm Niesha...but of course you know that...' She trailed off, feeling a little out of sorts. She smothered her unsettled emotions. 'What's on my agenda this morning?' she asked brightly.

Kadira stepped forwards, opened a leather-bound folder and ran her finger down a long list of items. 'We will do as much or as little as you desire, Your Highness, but I suggest we get your honeymoon wardrobe squared away. With your permission, I'll have the three stylists I have on standby meet with us now?'

Niesha tried to hide her nervous gulp with a smile. 'That works for me.'

Kadira's smile widened, before she reached for the phone tucked into her folder. Her fingers flew over the surface for a few seconds. 'If you're ready, Your Highness,' she said with a graceful dip of her head.

Niesha left the dining room, thinking she was headed back to the women's quarters. But Kadira turned down a different hallway, one that led past many doors and into Zufar's private suite.

On entering, Niesha realised it was the one that connected the previous Queen's rooms to Zufar's, the one he'd suggested she turn into a dressing room or nursery. She barely had the time to take in the fact that the previously fully furnished room was now empty before Kadira was leading her through a narrow hallway into another room.

This one was just off Zufar's bedroom and was a dressing room similar to his. Within the space large enough to hold an entire new suite, sumptuous sofas had been set up against one wall, with half of the closet space already filled with designer labels and accessories.

'Whose clothes are these?' she asked, a little more sharply than intended.

Kadira looked surprised. 'They're yours, Your Highness. His Highness instructed your belongings to be moved here this morning.'

Niesha hid her surprise at how quickly Zufar had acted, took a seat, then focused as Kadira continued, 'The rest of the space will be filled according to the seasons once the designers have made their presentations.'

'I understand,' Niesha murmured.

Moments later, the stylists arrived, trailing assistants pushing endless clothes rails.

For the next two hours she was bombarded with choices and suggestions until her head started to throb.

The sheer scale of opulence was staggering, and Niesha was glad she was sitting down. She knew another woman in her shoes would have jumped for joy at being so totally immersed in wealth and privilege but, in that moment, she would have given all of it away for a crumb of her past, because she knew that even dressing in the most luxurious clothes and jewels wouldn't dull the persistent ache in her heart.

She was about to ask for a reprieve, or a cup of tea, when a sharply voiced command preceded Zufar's majestic entrance into the room. Everyone stilled for a second, before executing a curtsey, which he acknowledged with a sweep of his hand.

'Leave us.' The command was brusque.

The room emptied in seconds. For a full minute he didn't

speak, just paced in a tight, inflexible line that spoke of his military training.

'Is…is something wrong?' she asked, after watching his jaw clench a few times.

He stopped abruptly and looked at her. 'Yes, we'll have to postpone the honeymoon.' The tightness behind his words drew unease but it was the way he loosened his tie a moment later that caught her attention.

She'd never seen Zufar even a little bit dishevelled, and that included the moment he had found out his betrothed had disappeared through a window only hours before they had been due to wed. Now she watched as he released the first two buttons of his shirt with an angry flick of his elegant hands.

'Oh?'

'Only by a few days, perhaps a week.'

'May I ask why?'

He exhaled harshly. 'It seems one scandal in twenty-four hours isn't enough for my family,' he said by way of explanation. Ice-cold anger bathed his words and she watched, utterly fascinated, as he clawed a hand through his dark hair, upsetting its usually neat order.

He paced to the end of the room and abruptly reversed course.

Was it something to do with Amira? Unable to stand the suspense, she spoke. 'Zufar…'

He froze, his eyes meeting hers across the wide space at her use of his name.

Nervous at the intensity of his gaze and the unsettling need to ease his angst, she slicked her tongue over her upper lip and plunged ahead. 'Can…can I help?'

Surprise flickered over his face even as his gaze lowered to lock on her mouth. After a moment, he lifted his head.

'I'm being blackmailed,' he pronounced icily.

She gasped. 'What? Is it about Amira?' she forced herself to ask.

He frowned, then his jaw rippled. 'No. It looks like her choice was definitive. I've seen security footage of her leaving the palace, which confirms she went of her own free will. I will no longer be wasting time and attention on her.'

The cold dismissal sent tremors through her, probably because of the quiet fury that lingered in his voice when he spoke of her. Perhaps he wouldn't take her back but he wasn't as unaffected as his words suggested.

'Unfortunately, the new set of issues involves my sister.'

Niesha refocused, and frowned. 'Princess Galila? What did she do? Is she okay?'

Zufar exhaled another breath full of ire. 'She's in the middle of what can politely be termed as a hissy fit. One she's blindly refusing to admit is the result of her own actions.' He started pacing again. 'Apparently, she saw fit to get blind drunk at the wedding reception and let loose a few family secrets to a complete stranger,' he snarled as he reached the far wall of the dressing room and reversed direction.

'What secrets?'

Zufar eyed her with narrow-eyed ferocity. About to preempt a response to mind her own business, she swallowed her words as he slowly advanced to tower over her. He seemed to be weighing his options. After a moment, his fist unfurled and he lowered his formidable length into the sofa next to her.

'You're part of this family now. If this gets out it will be better that you are armed with a response rather than caught off guard.'

It hurt a little to know the only reason he was confiding in her was because he didn't trust her to react properly in public.

But then she reminded herself that she was barely twenty-four hours into this marriage. To Zufar al Khalia she was little more than a stranger thrust into his life by exceptional circumstances.

Niesha composed a nod, her spine straightening as she returned his gaze. 'Very well.'

She waited.

For several heartbeats he assessed her. Then, 'She revealed that our mother had an affair with Sheikh Karim's father over three decades ago.' He took a deep, hissing breath. 'That the affair bore a son. The same son who took Amira yesterday. So Karim not only knows my family's secrets, but he's been made aware of the existence of his half-brother.'

Niesha's jaw dropped, then her heart dropped lower. 'What?'

He didn't respond, letting the shock waves sink in.

She wasn't aware how protectively she'd held the bubble of a happy-ever-after dream until Zufar callously burst it with his words. The royal family she'd spun her teenage dreams around was nothing more than a broken façade.

But…it was a façade that was affording her a glimpse of the not quite perfect humanity behind the thick veil.

Like her…

Niesha wasn't certain why that thought settled deep inside her. Surely she wasn't comparing herself to them? Her past was broken too, and had plenty of missing chunks. And yet she couldn't dismiss that seed of kinship taking root inside her.

'So your half-brother stole your fiancée?' she murmured, shocked.

Anger darkened his eyes, right before a low, bitter laugh emitted from his throat. 'Because he believes my position in this family should be his.'

'That's what the note meant by *birthright*?' Was that why Zufar had wanted to win the skirmish yesterday at all costs? The thought drew another cold tremor through her.

'Yes. And I believe it was a move I neatly countered and even bettered,' he said with throbbing satisfaction, confirming her suspicion.

Had she, and to some extent Amira, been perfect pawns in their game? Niesha was thankful that too many emotions swirled through her for the statement to pierce any harder. Instead she focused on the reason behind his initial anger. 'So what does this blackmailer want? Money?'

Zufar's head went back as if the reminder greatly vexed him. Which it did, if the harsh breath he expelled was an indication. 'Would that it were so. Sheikh Karim of Zyria has enough of that for it not to be his goal. He's after something else entirely.'

Niesha swallowed a gasp. The kingdom of Zyria was Khalia's direct neighbour, with shared borders and a long history of shared traditions. The magnitude of Zufar's mother's betrayal expanded in Niesha's mind. A few things began to make sense, like the haggard pain she'd glimpsed in King Tariq's face over the years.

'Your father knew, didn't he?' she asked.

After a moment, Zufar nodded. 'Yes.'

The confirmation only further shattered her rose-coloured glasses. But on the flip side, she felt a little closer to Zufar even though she knew such a feeling would only ever be one-sided.

'So if Sheikh Karim doesn't want money, what does he want?'

Zufar's jaw clenched tight until the vibrating muscle turned white. 'He wants my sister's hand in marriage. Immediately.'

Her hand flew to her mouth. 'And are you going to give your blessing?'

He shrugged. 'I have limited options. Scandal must be avoided at all costs. At least if they pull it off, my people will be happy. Two weddings within weeks of one another? Anyone would think heaven itself was smiling down on us,' he mocked bitterly.

Her heart twisted, but she clung to her composure. 'And will Galila agree?'

'She will if she wants what's best for the family,' he said curtly.

Silence descended, and then she cleared her throat. 'Can I do anything?'

Again he seemed surprised by her offer. One corner of his mouth lifted, but any trace of mirth was wiped clean an instant later. 'A guarantee that I'll have peace for at least twenty-four hours would be greatly welcome,' he breathed.

This close, his scent wrapped around her, triggering a yearning to move closer, to feel the heat of his skin against hers. Then she reminded herself exactly why he'd woken her this morning and her spine stiffened.

'I can guarantee that *I* won't be the cause of any unwelcome distraction in that time.'

A strange expression crossed his face before he abruptly stood up, did up his buttons and straightened his tie. When he was done, it was almost as if the brief glimpse behind the wall of royal duty hadn't happened.

Niesha wasn't sure whether to be thrilled or terrified that she'd seen the man behind the mask. And she didn't want to examine why. She watched him stride to the door, and then, unable to stop herself, she followed. 'Zufar?'

He stiffened. Then turned, one eyebrow raised.

'What are you going to do about…your brother?'

A fierce light blazed in his eyes. Then it was gone. 'He intended to disrupt my kingdom with his actions. When the time is right, he'll be dealt with appropriately.'

Meaning what? Revenge? Punishment?

'I will see you tonight.'

He left her shivering where she stood, fairly certain she wouldn't be able to withstand another bombshell.

Infidelity. Betrayal. Revenge. Was this what being an al Khalia was like? To think she'd rhapsodised about and envied them once upon a time!

She was still rubbing her hands down her chilled arms when Kadira knocked and entered.

Moments later they were back to discussing her wardrobe for her now postponed honeymoon.

And then it was time to choose from the list of tutors who would lecture her through her child psychology course.

One filled her with dread. The other with a quiet joy.

Niesha took a deep breath and vowed to cling onto the latter with everything she had.

CHAPTER SEVEN

THE ONE WEEK Zufar had accommodated to broker his sister's marriage while juggling his duties before leaving on his honeymoon turned into two.

It could've been because he received a summons from his father, which he kept postponing simply because he didn't wish to deal with Tariq. Their last meeting had ended with stiff, cold words that still rankled, and the simple truth was Zufar didn't know whether he would ever forgive his father for abdicating.

But his sister's sudden impending marriage needed explanation and whether he liked it or not his father was owed one.

Today was the day he'd made the trip to see Tariq. As he'd suspected, it hadn't been an easy one. Probably because his father hadn't once asked about state affairs or even about Zufar himself. He wore his grief like a cloak and looked even more shrunken than he'd been the last time Zufar had seen him. Or perhaps Zufar's unease was because, despite everything, a small part of him regretted cutting his father out of his wedding. He told himself he'd done it for a good reason—to keep the atmosphere stress-free and his citizens happy on his wedding day.

Out of sight out of mind, after all.

The pat statement rang hollow inside him, driving him from his desk and into a restless pacing of his office. King Tariq might have taken his absence from his son's wedding with pained stoicism but he'd taken the news of Galila's marriage to Sheikh Karim worse. The reminder that his father had once upon a time doted on Galila had further unsettled Zufar. It occurred to him that now his mother was dead, perhaps his father would want to reconnect with the children he'd disregarded for so long.

Zufar hardened his heart against the strange yearning triggered by that notion. There was no room for sentiment. His father had chosen his path, his actions forcing Zufar to choose his.

With the smooth running of the kingdom his priority, he had no space to accommodate might-have-beens.

What was done was done. And for the first time in for ever he had a moment's peace. Even Galila had finally accepted the consequences of her actions.

Zufar didn't know whether to succumb to the silly tradition of touching wood or raise a glass of cognac in honour of that rare peace. As to whether it would last was a debate he wasn't prepared to enter into right in this moment.

He arrived at the window overlooking the rose garden that had once belonged to his mother, and he clenched his teeth as the peace threatened to evaporate.

Many times, he'd toyed with having the rose bushes uprooted.

But he'd kept it as a reminder that loyalty and dedication to duty were far more valuable than the false love his mother had claimed to have for him in front of strangers, and the icy indifference she'd shown to him and his siblings behind closed doors. As for the man who'd occupied this office and this throne before him? Tariq al Khalia had been so locked in his obsession he'd failed to see his children, had forgiven his wife's infidelity, even going as far as to hide the full consequences of her actions right up until the past had crash-landed into their lives in the form of Adir and almost destroyed everything in its path. Until any hope of keeping this family together in the wake of his mother's death was gone for ever.

And then he'd fled, uncaring of the devastation he'd left behind.

Zufar's insides twisted with bitterness and a pain he

wanted to will away with every ounce of his being but had found over the years was near impossible.

That too was a salutary lesson, an abiding reminder to stay away from foolish feelings and keep his trust circle to a party of one.

Those reminders had served him well, would continue to serve him well when it came to the subject of Adir. He would need to be dealt with, of course. Zufar's intelligence chief had pinpointed where Adir had gone into hiding in his desert kingdom but Zufar was in no hurry to pursue his brother. Revenge was a dish best served cold, after all.

Plus, he had a honeymoon to embark upon.

The thought of the woman who was now his Queen, his *wife*, triggered a different sensation in Zufar.

The rose bushes faded from view, his mind's eye conjuring up a vision of shy, quiet strength and surprising beauty that clenched a muscle in his belly.

At every turn his new bride surprised him. He hadn't held much in the way of expectations from the woman he'd plucked from obscurity. Even though her lack of pedigree hadn't bothered him as much as it had his councillors, he'd had reservations about her ability to rise to her position. But she'd taken on the role with an intelligence, poise and dignity that had surprised everyone, including him.

Unlike her predecessor, his mother, Niesha was not filling her diary with appointments with designers, magazine photo shoots and gossip-mongering luncheons. In fact, the occasional demand on her time for anything other than palace duties drew the small press of her lips he was beginning to recognise as signifying her displeasure.

The one thing that made her eyes light up was any activity involving children. And when it was time to take lessons from her tutor.

There were other times when he glimpsed strong emotion in her eyes, too, although after their wedding night she'd attempted to hide those emotions from him. Another earthy sensation shifted through Zufar, his manhood responding to his thought.

Those early-morning hours together were becoming an addictive means of waking her up from her nightmares. They might be sharing a bed in order to produce an heir, but that hour before sunrise was fast becoming a routine he didn't wish to abandon.

He sucked in a breath as his blood sang with fire and the pressure behind his fly thickened. His wife might have been innocent when he took her to bed, but she was swiftly gaining the status of the most memorable bed partner he'd ever had.

He frowned inwardly as the reasons for the need to awaken her each morning sliced through his mind. Niesha claimed not to remember the subject of her nightmares, and he believed her.

Nevertheless it was a problem. One that might need addressing sooner rather than later. As was the subject of her past. All his investigators had been able to dig up so far was that she'd grown up in an orphanage on the outskirts of his capital city.

The last thing he needed was for other skeletons to fall out of his proverbial closet, but it seemed her past was a blank no one could fill.

The knock on his door in that moment was a half-blessing, freeing him from thinking about the enigma surrounding his new bride. Besides, he could do with not inviting problems where there were none, so he turned abruptly from the window.

'Enter,' he called.

Niesha entered, and he couldn't help but stare. He took in her slender form, his eyes lingering on the shadow of her cleavage, the neat little waist he'd gripped to hold her steady as he lost himself in her body, and the curve of her hips that could even now be cradling his child.

For the first time since his clinical discussions of heirs

and legacies, Zufar allowed himself to wonder what their child would look like.

He frowned, pulling himself from the brink of useless daydream as she drew closer. Dressed in a burnt-orange dress that complemented her colour superbly, with her hair pulled up into some elaborate knot, she more than held her own as a queen.

And even though he'd availed himself of every inch of her body only a handful of hours ago, a gnawing hunger began to beat a restless, relentless beat through him.

She stopped before his desk, spine straight, head angled as if she'd spent a lifetime learning comportment rather than a scant two weeks, and looked him straight in the eye, sending the rush in his blood higher.

'I was told you wanted to see me?' she asked.

Zufar forced himself to focus. 'Yes.' He indicated the chair before his desk and waited for her to sit. 'I wanted to inform you that we leave for our honeymoon tomorrow. But before we do, there's one engagement today that needs to be filled.' The reason why that engagement had now fallen on Niesha made his mouth tighten. 'I need you.'

Her eyes widened a touch before they swept to the window, avoiding his gaze. He found himself wanting to capture her chin and redirect her attention to him. He blunted the need.

He couldn't afford to indulge in carnal pleasures when he had a kingdom to run.

You have a fifteen-minute window of free time, a voice whispered insidiously in his ear.

He pushed it away, striding to his desk and settling himself behind it. 'Galila's departure has left a few engagements unfulfilled. I've delegated most of them, but I need you to handle this one,' he said briskly.

'Oh, I see. How can I help?' There was a briskness to her tone that drew a frown from him despite his own effort to display the same demeanour. He liked her softer, Zufar realised.

She caught his frown, and a moment later her face was the serene mask she'd been presenting to the adoring public since she first stepped out in her role as his Queen two weeks ago. That his people had taken to her was an understatement. Everywhere she went she was met with bunches of flowers and adoring crowds. But that mask was for the public. Zufar was a little irritated that she was maintaining it when they were alone.

'Your schedule is free for the next few hours, I believe?' he enquired.

She nodded. 'Yes. It is.'

'Good. This is an opening ceremony at a local children's hospital. Galila was supposed to have attended but of course circumstances have changed.' His sister was currently in Zyria, Sheikh Karim having wasted no time in whisking her away the moment Zufar had given his agreement.

Niesha picked up the sheet he slid across the desk, scrutinising the page before setting it back down. This time when she looked at him, a genuine smile was in place. She was pleased, as he'd known she would be when the suggestion of being surrounded by children came up.

Again, he found himself wondering about his own future offspring, whether his son or daughter would be cherished by Niesha the way he'd never been by his parents. Zufar was a little taken aback to realise that hidden behind the gratification of certainty that his own child wouldn't be neglected or visited with indifference was a thread of jealousy.

Was he really jealous of his own unborn child?

'I'd be honoured to attend. I'll try not to let you down,' she said with a small smile that drifted away all too quickly.

He looked closer and saw the faint shadows beneath her eyes. 'They were expecting a princess. They're getting a queen. The honour will be theirs, I am sure of it.'

Her lips parted, as if she was going to respond, then she pressed them firmly together again.

Zufar wasn't entirely sure why his unease deepened. Rounding his desk, he drew a finger down her cheek. 'Are you well?' He noted that his tone was abrupt and felt a little irritated with himself.

She drew away under the pretext of rising to her feet. 'Of course. I had better go and get ready for this.'

He frowned as she started to walk away. 'Wait.'

'Yes?'

He strode towards her, the soft and alluring scent of her perfume tugging at him. 'I've had to add a few more appointments to the schedule on our honeymoon. It seems the lure of my Queen is too much for dignitaries to resist. I'd advise you therefore not to overtire yourself. We have a busy couple of weeks ahead of us.'

Her lashes swept down, the long silky length brushing her cheek. 'I'm glad I can be useful. It is my role here after all, isn't it?' she enquired softly with a smile that didn't quite reach her eyes and a note in her voice that further grated.

His eyes narrowed on her face but for the life of him, Zufar couldn't dig beneath her serene demeanour. The realisation that he wanted to know what was bothering her jarred him hard.

He was the King. He didn't deal in emotions.

'Yes,' he affirmed. 'It is.'

'Then I'll be ready.'

He went with her to the outer door, waved away the guard and opened the door himself. Then he stood watching her walk down the wide hallway, again struck by the dignity and grace in her stature and the smiles and reverence she commanded in her wake. He had no doubt she wouldn't let him down.

The first speech she'd given had been so in tune with his own vision that he'd wondered whether she'd conscripted his private secretary as her speechwriter. The discovery that she'd written the speech to his army veterans on her own had been a stunning surprise.

All of that though didn't explain the withdrawal he glimpsed frequently in her eyes.

Zufar returned to his desk, unable to shake off his frown or unease. For the first time in his life, he had a problem whose solution was eluding him and the reality of it jarred.

He had a wife who was shining in areas his own mother had severely lacked. At the thought of his mother, his mood plummeted. But try as he did to dismiss her from his thoughts, he found himself circling back to the woman who had given birth to him and then treated him as if he was an inconvenience.

Sure, there had been times now fading from memory when she'd bestowed a kind smile and a gentle touch. But that had been a long time ago, possibly even figments of his imagination. As he'd been prone to wondering lately, had those moments of brief affection been because she couldn't be with Adir, the child she'd truly loved?

His fingers tightened on the edge of his desk.

Was that it? Adir had spoken about the letters his mother had written to him in his youth. Letters declaring her love for him. That revelation had driven home the grating fact that all her devotion had been reserved for the child she'd never been able to claim as her own, with nothing left for her remaining children.

The unpalatable thought pierced him but it wasn't so easily dismissed on recollection of Adir's fury at their mother's funeral. Had their mother's love for her bastard son eventually faded too, usurped by the wealth and prestige she'd craved more than anything else?

Enough!

It was no use dwelling on his mother and a fruitless past he needed to move on from. Zufar planted his elbows on his desk and attempted to dig into the mountain of work await-ing his attention. But concentration was at a premium. Perhaps he should've touched wood after all, he mused bitterly.

When his private secretary knocked, Zufar tossed down his pen.

'Your Highness, your next appointment has been cancelled. The foreign minister's daughter was taken ill suddenly. I have sent flowers.'

Zufar's mouth twisted at his relief.

His foreign minister was an obsequious man, prone to rambling for an hour on an issue that required ten minutes. Reluctant to return to his sour thoughts, he rose from the desk.

'Free up my appointments for the next three hours,' he said, even before he'd fully made up his mind.

'Immediately, Your Highness. Can I arrange anything else for that time?'

'Inform my wife's motorcade not to leave without me. I'm attending the ceremony with her.'

His private secretary hid his surprise well, made a quick note on his tablet, bowed and hurried away to do his bidding.

Ten minutes later, Zufar waited in the limo as her bodyguards escorted Niesha to the car. For the several seconds it took for her reach him, he stared, once again arrested and a little stunned that he'd ever imagined her plain.

Sunlight glinted on her thick, luxurious hair, which had been rearranged into another attractive knot. The sea-green dress she'd changed into hugged her slim torso before flaring at the waist, the skirt showing off shapely long legs balanced on designer heels. A pulse of satisfaction went through him as he spotted the emerald necklace he'd given to her two days ago circling her neck.

It was part of a larger collection of jewellery that had belonged to his grandmother, and, even though the emerald was the smallest of the lot, it was eye-catching on Niesha and suited her outfit perfectly.

She was truly exquisite, he observed with a curious catch in his chest and a slowly elevating heartbeat.

When his gaze rose again to trace her delicate cheekbones and wide, generous mouth, renewed hunger punched through him.

He hurried to adjust himself or risk embarrassing both of them as the driver held the door open for her.

She slid in and froze, her eyes widening in surprise and then suspicion. 'What are you doing here?'

'I found myself free of obligations.'

'So you decided to come to a ribbon-cutting ceremony?'

He shrugged and reached out to secure her seat belt. 'I'm in danger of losing my position as the most popular figure in Khalia,' he mused dryly.

She didn't return his smile. 'There's no danger of that, and even if there was, you're not vain, so there must be another reason for your presence,' she said, her eyes growing wary as the motorcade left the palace grounds.

'A compliment slapped away by suspicion. I don't know whether to be pleased or wounded, Niesha.'

Her face remained set in lines that suggested she wasn't too pleased by his appearance.

'What's really going on, Zufar? Do you not think I can execute my duty properly?' she asked with a trace of hurt in her voice.

'I wouldn't have given you this responsibility if I didn't think you could handle it,' he stated, a little put out by the need to explain himself.

'Then why? Don't forget I saw your itinerary in your office.'

He'd kept his schedule free to spend time with his wife. It was that simple. And that complicated, Zufar realised.

'There may be questions about Galila.'

'Questions you don't think I can handle.' It wasn't a question but a flat statement.

For a moment, he wished he'd stayed in his office after

all. It was certainly an odd feeling to know his presence wasn't required. Unsettling still to acknowledge that he wasn't wanted. That brought back memories he'd dwelt on for far too long already today.

'I don't believe I owe you an explanation of how I use my time,' he added, his voice emerging a touch more tersely than he'd intended.

He caught her wince and her pinched face, and suppressed a growl.

For several minutes they travelled in silence. Then she reached into her handbag and pulled out a sheet of paper. 'Well, I'd intended to read through my speech in the car, so if you don't mind…?'

'You may practise it on me, if you wish.'

Her breath caught faintly before a wave of colour flowed into her cheeks. It took every ounce of control he could muster not to touch her in that moment. 'Are…are you sure?'

'Of course,' he replied.

She stared at him for endless moments, then gave a small nod. After straightening the sheet, she cleared her throat. And then she began to speak.

Zufar listened. Watched her. Struggled not to get lost in her husky, melodious voice. Not to get lost in the powerful message of support, the strong empathy and even the self-deprecating jokes she managed to slot in so effortlessly.

It took a few beats to realise she was done, and staring at him, eyes wide and wary.

'You wrote that by yourself in three hours?'

She immediately averted her gaze, looked down at the paper. 'Is it that bad?' Her voice was a little unsteady.

Before he could stop himself, he reached across and captured her hand. 'It's that good.'

She gasped. 'Really? Are you sure? I always worry that I'm gushing a little too hard. Or not enough.'

His thumb stroked back and forth across her hand, a strange need that had nothing to do with sex mounting higher inside him. 'There's a perfect amount of gush. But I would nix that last joke at your own expense. You can keep that one private.' *For me.*

She nodded, then began to rummage in her handbag. He reached into the sleek compartment next to him and offered her a pen.

The smallest smile curved her lips as she took it. 'Thank you.'

A yearning to see a wider, longer-lasting smile hit him hard, but he settled for watching her amend her speech. When she was done, he took her hand again. She made no move to withdraw it, and, finding that he liked touching her silk-smooth skin far too much, he kept his hand where it was right up until they arrived at the hospital.

An excited hum of surprise went through the sizeable crowd as he stepped out. Then it turned into shouts of adoration when Niesha joined him on the bright blue carpet. 'I believe my assessment is proving accurate,' he murmured.

Her smile as she waved to the crowd was warm and open. 'I'm just a passing fancy. You'll regain their total devotion before the month's out, I'm sure.'

He wasn't sure why that transitory statement rubbed him the wrong way. Perhaps it was the reminder that he'd placed a ticking-clock clause on their marriage, one that was already chiming much too loudly for his liking.

He shrugged the thought away and accompanied Niesha as she approached the crowd. As with her smile, her greeting was warm and engaging, although Zufar noticed that she gravitated towards children and mothers with small babies, taking time to draw a smile or laugh before she moved on.

Almost automatically, because such occasions were bred into his bones, Zufar expertly navigated the crowd until it was time to go inside.

They were given the tour, the hospital staff beside themselves to be graced by two royals. Again Niesha lingered with the children, especially the disadvantaged ones, listening to them and reading them stories that drew smiles even from the sickest children.

When the time came for her speech, she delivered it with grace and eloquence, drawing immediate and enthusiastic applause when it was over.

But even as he experienced a satisfying swell of pride, he couldn't shake the niggling thought that, though his wife seemed to be settling into her role as his Queen, perhaps she was also counting down the time until the five years were up.

'You're frowning,' observed the deep voice.

Niesha looked up from the medical webpage she'd been reading, a little startled by Zufar's sudden appearance.

From the moment they'd taken off four hours ago, he'd been ensconced with his advisers at the front section of the stunning royal plane, leaving her with her own smaller staff. Her meeting to go over her itinerary had lasted barely an hour, after which she'd dismissed her staff and found a quieter area towards the back of the plane.

She'd needed a moment or three with her thoughts but had declined Kadira's suggestion that she head upstairs to the master bedroom to rest.

The thought of sliding into bed, with Zufar in such close proximity, sent several traitorous tingles through her body, a state she couldn't seem to block no matter how much she tried.

Besides that, there was also the fact that last night she'd noticed a little spotting when she'd taken a shower. But this morning there'd been no trace of it. She'd debated whether to tell Zufar and decided to keep it to herself for now in case it was a false alarm.

Deep down though, Niesha knew the reason she was keeping quiet was because of the possibility that if she was pregnant, Zufar, with his duty done, might instigate separate bedrooms after all. Since that first time they'd made love, that remoteness had remained, even though he managed to skilfully draw sensations from her she'd never thought possible. He was an undeniable expert in the bedroom, and a huge part of her was terrified that she'd already grown addicted to her husband's touch.

Very quickly their time in bed, especially in the dawn hours when he drew her from a restless sleep, had become the highlight of her day. And try as she might she couldn't find the strength to give it up just yet.

So she closed her tablet and the page that gave dire predictions for spotting during pregnancy, uncrossed her legs and attempted to school her features. Thankfully, when she raised her gaze, his was on her legs. A moment later, probing eyes met hers, and his eyebrow quirked as he awaited a response.

She grimaced. 'I unwittingly clicked on a link while I was reviewing a list of charities. I told you not everyone was enamoured of me.'

It was a smaller, safer truth in a greater list of things on her mind.

He sank onto his haunches, surprising her a little, and then set her heartbeat soaring by bringing his masculine perfection even closer. His clean, musky aftershave drifted over her, sending vivid images of how shamelessly she lost herself in it when they made love.

'Do yourself a favour and ignore them,' he dismissed offhandedly. 'You don't need the headache, and I don't want an overwrought wife on our honeymoon.'

'I like to think I'm made of sterner stuff than that.'

'Then why do you have shadows beneath your eyes?'

She stiffened. 'Is that your way of telling me I look a mess?'

'It's my way of saying you should've taken your secretary's advice and gone upstairs to bed.'

She wasn't even going to ask how he knew that. 'Are you

here to order me to bed?' she retorted, cringingly noting the huskiness in her voice.

His eyes blazed for a moment before they cleared. Rising gracefully to his feet, he held out his hand. 'That is precisely what I'm doing. We don't land for another three hours. I'll make sure you're woken before then.'

Disappointment followed hard on the heels of the breathlessness that seized her. She was so busy trying to hide it she let herself be pulled up and tugged up the stairs.

The bedroom took up the whole smaller top deck of the plane, and was so dreamily, jaw-droppingly beautiful, Niesha would've been completely lost in it had Zufar's riveting presence beside her not commanded her attention.

She barely heard the door snick shut behind her, but she was intensely aware of his overwhelming presence, the dizzyingly broad width of his shoulders as he drew her towards the bed. Her heart began thundering as he plucked the tablet from her hand and deftly tossed back the coverlet on the king-sized bed.

The jacket of the stylish navy trouser suit she'd worn for the flight came off neatly under his ministrations, leaving a cream silk camisole that suddenly felt too hot against her skin. Her nipples were beginning to pebble and that dragging sensation had started low in her belly.

Niesha shook her head when his hands went to her hair, intent on removing the diamond clip holding it up. 'I really don't need help undressing. Nor do I need to rest at all. I'm f—'

'You're not fine,' he interrupted. 'You spent the night tossing and turning.' The grim set to his face told her he wasn't pleased. 'Another nightmare?'

It was easier to nod to that than admit that her suspicion of her new condition was what had disturbed her sleep. 'I'm sorry if I bothered you.'

He dismissed her apology with a wave of his hand, and stepped forwards with renewed intention of freeing her hair. This time he succeeded. 'How long have you had them?'

She steeled herself against the clutch of pain confessing the truth brought. 'For as long as I can remember. I think the only thing that will stop them is a full account of the years I lost before I ended up in the orphanage.' She wasn't sure why she let that slip but once it was out there, she couldn't take it back.

He stilled. 'Perhaps you should consider reconciling yourself to the possibility that you might never know,' he suggested after a moment.

Hurt lanced through her. Her heart thundered louder as she took in his grim expression. Would this flaw in her lineage reap consequences down the line? Make her a damaged queen? 'You think I haven't tried? That I want my subconscious to keep dredging it up every night?'

His eyes narrowed. 'Calm yourself—'

Hurt built up higher. 'That's easy for you to say, isn't it? You've had your whole life documented a few hundred different ways from the moment you drew breath. All you need to do is pluck a book off a shelf and you can refresh your memory on even the tiniest detail. Well, I'm glad you can be so glib about me forgetting my past but you'll excuse me if I don't feel the same!'

'Enough, Niesha. I won't have you distressing yourself,' he commanded with a bite to his deep, masterful voice.

But she wasn't in the mood to heed this warning. 'And I won't have you ordering me about, telling me when to go to bed or telling me how to feel!'

Perhaps it was the reality that she might be pregnant that sent her emotions into free fall. Or the dire predictions for her spotting she'd foolishly looked up on the Internet. She'd done it as a means of alleviating her worry but had ended up even more distressed.

Because thinking about the child she would possibly be having nine months from now, she'd been confronted with the fact that one day her son or daughter would ask about her past. And she wouldn't have an answer for them. One side of their family tree would be full to brimming with generations of history, and the other side, *hers*, would be woefully empty.

Zufar started to raise his hand.

She shook her head wildly, knocking his hand away. 'I don't want your sympathy. Or your directives. I want... I want you to leave me alone!'

He completely disregarded her request, strong hands gripping her shoulders to pull her into his hard, brick-wall body.

One hand was splayed on her back while the other captured her nape, trapping her against his impressive length. Before she could protest, both hands began a languorous kneading, digging with gentle pressure into muscles knotted tight with tension.

She parted her lips on a gasp that never made it because he was kissing her, his tongue delving between her lips to boldly stroke her tongue.

The resulting effect of the outer caress and the inner melting was so wonderfully divine, she moaned helplessly. Then kept moaning as he deepened both caresses, rending her mindless as her knees weakened and she sagged against him.

The floating effect continued even after he'd laid her on the bed and levered himself over her without breaking the kiss. His thighs bracketed hers as he continued to hold her tight against his body, ravaging her lips, flooding her whole being and especially her sex with warmth and desire and so, so much hunger.

This.

This was the addiction she already feared she would never be free of.

With a strangled cry, she spiked her fingers into his

hair and threw herself into the kiss, her body writhing against his.

She was fairly sure he didn't remain as removed or as silent this time. Or perhaps the muted growl she heard might have been the hum of jet engines.

Niesha didn't really care.

All she wanted, all she *craved* was for him to keep wrecking her with his potent kiss, his magic hands. He cupped her breast, moulded her flesh before mercilessly teasing its tight peak.

'Zufar…' She gasped.

The plane hit a pocket of deep turbulence, rudely jarring them apart.

For an eternity Zufar stared down at her, his breathing harsh, his face a tight mask of unbridled hunger. Hunger he mastered before her stunned eyes seconds before launching himself off her to stride several steps away.

'Zufar…'

He rounded on her, his face under even tighter control. 'My apologies,' he bit out thickly. 'I didn't mean for things to get so carried away. It won't happen again.'

She wasn't sure whether the chill that descended on her was because he was apologising for touching her or for the hint of self-loathing she caught in his voice. Both, she suspected.

The reality that their lovemaking was really only about duty for Zufar lanced like forked lightning through her. Every anguished cell in her body wanted to curl up in a ball. But she forced herself to remain contained, to rise and force her weak legs towards the door she hoped led to the bathroom. 'No need to apologise. You were looking for a way to calm your hysterical wife. Don't worry,' she threw over her shoulder, 'I'll be the picture of composure by the time we land.'

With that she thrust the door open, glimpsed the porcelain sink and shower stall, and rushed inside, locking the door behind her.

She avoided her gaze in mirror as she splashed water over her wrists and face. Then, knowing she couldn't go out and face him, not just yet, she braced her back against the door, wrapping her arms around her middle as she fought the tears that were determined to fall.

Niesha wasn't sure how long she spent in the bathroom, but by the time she emerged he was gone. Yet relief was nowhere in sight. Not when the dawning suspicion that, far from being a thing of the past, her childhood crush on Zufar seemed to have resurfaced, and, much stronger this time, now loomed like a spectre on her horizon.

CHAPTER EIGHT

TRUE TO HIS WORD, the incident on the plane didn't happen again. Nor did Zufar make any attempt to touch her either during the night or in the early hours of the morning as he'd previously done.

By the sixth day of their honeymoon tour, Niesha was beginning to think she was one of the unfortunate few women who wouldn't experience the most intimate part of her honeymoon. And while a greater part of her desperately struggled with the loss of his touch, a tiny, self-preserving part of her urged her to count her blessings.

She hadn't been able to completely expel the niggling voice that whispered she was much more invested emotionally than she was willing to admit. Because it couldn't be true. Not so soon. Not so foolishly.

So she pushed the voice away, joined Zufar for breakfast each morning before they made whatever appearance in whatever museum or charity or luncheon they were supposed to attend, where she gazed adoringly at him, waved at the crowd and pinned the smile on her face until the photographers had their money shots.

After that he had her driven back to whatever splendid hotel or villa or mansion they were staying at while he went off to conduct business, and she was supposed to spend endless hours getting ready for another evening function.

Tonight, it was a ball being thrown in their honour by the Khalian Ambassador to Italy. They'd arrived in Venice last night and visited all the main sights this morning. After Dubai, Prague and London, the magnificent sights were beginning to blur into one. But Venice had been truly breathtaking, something she wasn't going to forget in a hurry.

But as she dressed in a sweeping, strapless dove-grey silk gown, overlaid with soft chiffon mesh, into which delicate butterflies had been sewn, Niesha's heartbeat began to thud faster.

Her period still hadn't arrived.

And she really couldn't hold back from telling Zufar any longer. For all she knew, he had the exact dates of her monthly cycle memorised. Was that another reason for his sudden lack of interest?

She tried to breathe through the heavy, unbearable weight that pressed on her chest as Halimah settled the small diamond tiara on her head. Apparently it was customary headwear for all overseas Khalian-hosted functions.

After the second day, she'd given up keeping track of protocol when it came to her attire and jewels and let Halimah take over.

Like now, she tuned out a little as she was primped and made up. But her smile of thanks was genuine, as were the butterflies fluttering wildly in her stomach as she left the suite and headed to the living room.

Zufar stood at the glass window of their villa, his gaze hovering in the middle distance as he nursed a cognac. For a moment she was struck genuinely dumb at the magnificent figure he cut in his tuxedo.

Truly, no man had the right to look this good, this powerful, this rawly masculine. And yet the evidence was right there before her eyes. Irrefutable. Dangerous to her senses.

She inhaled shakily and audibly, enough to drag him from wherever he was. He swivelled to face her, and Niesha wanted to groan with the indecency of his breathtaking face.

She swallowed the sound, curled her fingers around her minuscule clutch to keep from doing something foolish like reaching out for him as he approached.

He didn't speak. Not immediately. Instead, his gaze rested for a long time on the tiara, then conducted a lazy inspection of her from head to toe. 'You look exceptionally beautiful,' he breathed.

The faintest hint of cognac and mint wafted over her face and she wanted to close her eyes, taste him from the source. Instead she locked her knees. 'You don't look so bad yourself.'

Her words sounded stilted, even to her own ears. He didn't react, merely inclined his head before handing off his glass to a hovering attendant and holding out his arm. 'Shall we?'

The sleek speedboat they boarded took them smoothly down the Grand Canal and beneath the Rialto Bridge before traversing a series of smaller canals. Their destination was another architectural masterpiece that took her breath away.

The Chiesa Palace was owned by Zufar but loaned to the embassy for its residence. She knew from absorbing royal history that it had been painstakingly restored from a crumbling heap to its former glory, including the stunning cathedral windows, the priceless paintings that had almost perished during wars and floods, and the chandeliers made of crystal and Murano glass.

Everything in sight glittered and gleamed as they stepped onto the red carpet and greeted the long line of guests await-ing their arrival.

Halfway down the line, her heel caught in the carpet and Niesha stumbled. Zufar immediately caught her, righting her with a sharp look.

'Are you all right?' he murmured, ignoring the guest in front of them waiting to be greeted.

'Yes, I'm fine,' she said, somehow managing to keep the smile pinned on her face.

A moment later, Zufar's hand settled on her back. The branding heat of his hand and the act itself was so unset-tling, warmth flushed through her.

She wanted to lean into him, absorb even more of him.

Which resulted in holding herself stiffly until they were in the stunning reception room of the palazzo.

'You...you can let go of me now.'

Tawny eyes scoured her face, as if he was searching for something. A moment later, his hand dropped.

Immediately she wanted his touch back. Cursing her traitorous body, she slid into diplomatic mode, smiling and conversing, and even managing to waltz with Zufar without letting her emotions slip.

But it was a drain on her senses. So the moment they returned to their villa, and had a moment of privacy, she gathered her courage and faced him. 'Zufar, we need to talk.'

His face tightened, and he stiffened as if bracing himself for a blow. 'To my knowledge those words either herald catastrophe or something...different. I've yet to experience the latter but do go on,' he rasped.

'It's up to you how you view the news that I think I'm pregnant.'

As Niesha was beginning to recognise, the wheels of royalty and privilege were programmed to turn so smoothly and efficiently, she barely noticed their motion.

Since becoming Queen, in her every waking moment, she only had to lift a finger for her tiniest request to be put into action. And sometimes even that wasn't necessary, a seemingly telepathic connection of the staff accurately deciphering her desires before she knew about them herself.

So she shouldn't have been surprised when a team of physicians trailed into their living room suite moments after their arrival in Paris the next day.

She was sure that had it not been after midnight when she'd voiced the possibility that she might be pregnant, he would have summoned them to the palazzo in Venice.

The sensation that her world was spinning out of control wouldn't abate. Heart racing, she pulled the lapels of her elegant silk lounging wrap more firmly around her as a suited

Zufar approached where she stood on the terrace, trying in vain to distract herself with the view of the Eiffel Tower.

'The doctors are here,' he said.

'Do we need to do this now?' she hedged, unable to stop the scenarios that reeled through her head, all ending with the unassailable fact that if she was confirmed pregnant, her honeymoon would be over.

True, her supposed honeymoon had been filled with accompanying Zufar to endless engagements and smiling through luncheons and state dinners when she would rather be curled up with a book in one of the quieter rooms of their royal suite.

But during those events, she had a front-row seat to the daily life and work of the man she'd married. No longer did she have to watch him on a TV screen or gaze at glossy, still pictures in a magazine.

She'd watched in real life as he'd negotiated a trade deal over pre-dinner cocktails with little more than a handful of sentences. She'd listened, stunned, as he'd given his frank opinion on a decades-long border dispute between bitter enemies, only to see it implemented days later. Last night she'd looked on, her heart melting, as he'd charmed the eight-year-old daughter of his ambassador.

Who cared that he barely said more than a handful of words to her throughout their engagements? Fine, she cared. No one liked being ignored.

But still, those times she spent with him, secretly hoping she would absorb even a little of his effortless ability to govern and charm? Niesha…liked it, she admitted reluctantly. Watching him navigate the sometimes choppy waters of diplomacy was a sight she wasn't ready to be rid of despite the dangerous waters her heart waded into.

She didn't need to be a genius to know that the moment her pregnancy was confirmed she would be whisked back to Khalia. If he wasn't touching her on their honeymoon she could guarantee they would resort to separate beds, like his parents, on their return. On the other hand, if her pregnancy wasn't confirmed then…

The idea that she was hoping she wasn't pregnant just for a chance to stay in Zufar's bed for a little longer struck her in equal parts with shame—for being so weak—and with a hunger she couldn't dismiss.

'It needs to be done, according to royal protocol,' he pronounced, in answer to her question. There was no gentleness to his tone, only a firm recital of purpose and duty. 'I'm assured it won't take long.' At her continued hesitation, he beckoned with a commanding hand. 'Come.'

Little one.

He hadn't used the endearment since their wedding night and even as she mocked herself for the absurdity of missing it, she couldn't deny that its absence left a small hollow inside her.

Firmly, she pushed that sensation away, then forced herself not to dwell on the fact that his hand dropped to his side when she approached him, instead of reaching for hers as he did when they were out in public.

Those moments were for show, she reminded herself. Zufar and Niesha al Khalia had been hailed as the world's most photogenic and romantic royal couple. She barely managed to stop her lips from twisting.

If only they knew.

So, as she'd trained herself to do, she went to his side, making sure to keep a small distance between them as they re-entered the living room.

There were three physicians in total, two male and one female, all of middle age, and a younger male intern who bowed as they approached.

'I'm Dr Wadya. We will not keep you very long, Your Highness,' the female doctor promised with a smile.

A little more at ease, Niesha acknowledged other introductions and took a seat on the sofa. Zufar took his place behind her, one hand resting lightly on the seat a hair's breadth from her shoulder. When she was instructed to, she removed her wrap, handed it to an attendant hovering nearby, then resisted the urge to run her sweaty palms down the thighs of her silk slip dress.

Try as she might, she couldn't stop her racing heart. Not when she, and everyone in the room, were holding their collective breaths at the possibility that she could be carrying Zufar's heir.

The drumming in her ears precluded her from hearing what was being discussed. In a way it was a blessing because she could temporarily forget that her life was being planned and plotted around her.

Still, she heard the sharp inhalation from the older male doctor, Dr Basim.

'What is it?' Zufar enquired sharply.

The man's pale-faced gaze was fixed on the birthmark on her forearm. He gave a slight shake of his head, but remained silent, his focus on the pink starfish mark that resided on the inside of her arm just below her inner elbow.

She frowned, her heart lurching as she looked at the faces of the doctors.

'Is something wrong?' she asked.

As if dragged from a stupor, Dr Basim's rose gaze from her arm. 'I'm sure it's just a coincidence,' he said.

'What is a coincidence?' Zufar bit out. 'Explain yourself, if you please.' The statement was less request, more directive.

'I don't wish to jump to conclusions, Your Highness,' the doctor said. 'I merely thought I recognised the mark on Her Highness's arm.'

Tense silence descended on the room. Niesha's breath strangled in her throat as everyone remained frozen in place.

Zufar moved, his elegant hand flicking in a subtle command that got everyone moving. The young intern approached with the equipment and swiftly set it up.

Niesha barely acknowledged the process, her heart racing now for a completely different reason. The moment they were done, Zufar dismissed everyone save for Dr Basim.

'How do you recognise it?' she blurted, unable to keep the question inside.

Dr Basim shook his head. 'It's nothing. I don't wish to alarm you, Your Highness. My apologies.'

She wanted to protest that it wasn't nothing, not when his reaction had been so strong. But one look at Zufar's closed expression and she held her tongue. Numbly, she watched Dr Basim prepare to leave.

She wasn't sure why she jumped up and trailed him as he left the living room. But as they approached the door, she knew she couldn't let it go. Something was wrong. 'So, what now?' she asked, watching the doctor.

Dr Basim paused and turned around. 'Your Highness?'

'How long before we know whether my wife is pregnant or not?' Zufar slid in.

It wasn't what she had meant to ask, but she held her breath all the same. 'The blood tests will reveal if there's a pregnancy within a matter of hours, Your Highness.'

Zufar nodded.

She watched the doctor reach for the doorknob. 'Wait.'

Beside her Zufar stiffened. 'Niesha? What is it?' he enquired softly, even though the set of his jaw showed that he was as puzzled by her reaction as she was herself.

'I have some questions,' she addressed Dr Basim. 'Can you please stay for a few more minutes?'

As the royal doctor, he couldn't very well refuse, and she was selfishly counting on that.

Acutely aware that Zufar followed closely behind, she returned to the living room. Then before she could lose her courage, she faced the two men. 'What do you know about me?' she asked Dr Basim boldly.

The doctor's eyes widened, and he slid a quick glance at Zufar. But Zufar's narrow-eyed glance was on her face. It remained there for a long time before he turned to the doctor. 'Answer my wife's question.'

Dr Basim hesitated. 'Your Highness…'

Niesha shook her head. 'You have my word that you won't be in any trouble. I only wish to know what you thought when you saw the mark on my arm. You recognised something about it. Am I right?'

Zufar tensed even harder, then he redirected his gaze to the doctor. 'Did you?' he demanded.

Dr Basim's unease grew.

'Please… I need to know.'

She stared down at the starfish mark on her arm, which had started to throb and burn as if yearning for its secret to be set free. Something inside her told her to push the doctor. Something unstoppable.

Zufar turned to the older man. 'Is she right? Do you know something?'

Dr Basim took a deep steadying breath and then slowly nodded. 'Perhaps I do.'

She lunged forwards before she could stop myself. 'What?'

'Before I emigrated to Khalia, I was a citizen of Rumadah.' He named the small country nestled in the most southerly point between the Middle East and Africa, known to many as a desert paradise, rich in oil. The only other facts she knew about the small kingdom were those she'd read in glossy magazines.

'Go on,' she urged with a voice that croaked a little.

'I had the honour of being the royal physician, right up until…' He paused, a wave of anguish unfurling over his face.

'Yes?' Zufar prodded impatiently.

Dr Basim cleared his throat. 'The royal family were on a private family holiday when tragedy struck.'

Zufar stilled, his whole body assuming the appearance of a granite statue. His eyes darted to Niesha before returning to the doctor. 'You were the royal family's personal doctor?' he pressed.

'What were their names? What happened to them?' she cried, unable to keep her emotions bottled.

Eyes reflecting pain met hers. 'As far as I am aware, Your Highness, a tyre exploded and their vehicle veered off a bridge while they were visiting a resort in Zyria. It burst into flames on impact and the whole family perished.'

She staggered backwards, swaying on her feet. The next moment Zufar was in front of her, taking her by the elbows and placing her in the seat. 'Stay there,' he instructed firmly under his breath.

Turning around, he faced the doctor again. 'I vaguely recall the incident but what has it got to do with my wife?'

The older man's gaze dropped to where she was still absently rubbing at the birthmark. 'The King's five-year-old daughter had the exact same birthmark as Her Highness. It was what made me think that there could be a connection...' He stopped, realising the enormity of his words. 'Or it could just be a coincidence.'

'You don't think so, otherwise you wouldn't have reacted so strongly,' Zufar countered.

Dr Basim spread his hands in apology.

The rock that lodged itself in Niesha's chest threatened to choke her, cutting off the air to her lungs and any possibility that she'd, *at last*, found some answers.

The hope she'd wildly entertained turned to ash in her mouth.

She dropped her head and fought the tears that stung her eyes. Words had lost meaning the moment he'd mentioned the bridge. The accident he spoke of had happened in Zyria. According to the matrons, she'd been found wandering in a ravine in Khalia.

Nowhere near a bridge or a resort.

Besides, the thought that she could be associated with royalty was absurd. Because surely if that was the case, other members of her family or *someone* would've come looking for her?

'When exactly did the accident happen?' Zufar probed.

Dr Basim's gaze grew thoughtful. 'Twenty years ago.'

Her heart lurched again, but she shook her head. It wasn't her. It couldn't be. The truth was, she would never know her real family. She needed to accept it, especially now that she was possibly pregnant with her own child. She needed to look ahead, forge a future for her children without clinging to the past.

She summoned a smile at Dr Basim. 'Thank you for your time. That's all I wanted to know.'

She caught Zufar's frown, but he dismissed the doctor with a casual wave of his hand. She remained frozen in the seat as they walked away. Once again her hopes had been dashed. She would never really know who she was, where she came from or if she belonged to anyone.

Even now, despite her title and the ring on her finger, she didn't belong. She was just a vessel to carry al Khalia heirs.

It should be enough.

It is enough, she affirmed to herself. But the reassurance rang hollow, the pain in her heart not letting it take root. The anguish of knowing she would never find answers wrapped itself around her heart, squeezing every last bit of her hope out of her.

She attempted to straighten her face as Zufar returned, and swallowed when he placed himself directly in front of her. The look in his eyes was intently speculative, drawing a small shiver across her skin. 'What?' she asked.

'You may be carrying my child. The need to discover your past burns strongly but it would please me greatly if you didn't distress yourself unduly over it.'

A laugh scraped its way out of her throat. 'You heard what the doctor said. These…people perished in Zyria. I was found in Khalia. There's no connection.'

His eyes darkened a touch and his mouth pulled in a firm line. His whole body thrummed with tension. 'Nevertheless you are disappointed. And emotional. I may not have experienced what you're going through but that doesn't mean I don't empathise.'

Her eyes began to prickle all over again. 'Thank you.'

He nodded. 'And while you may not believe there's a connection, I will instruct my investigators to dig a little deeper with the new information we have. When Dr Basim returns, he'll provide the additional information we need.'

She inhaled sharply, astonishment bursting through her. 'You want to help me?'

'Why does that surprise you when my investigators already attempted once?'

Her shrug didn't quite hit the mark. 'I don't know,' she floundered, 'maybe because you said you preferred me to be a blank slate?'

His face closed, and then he nodded. 'I don't want any surprises, but I also don't want you to distress yourself over the question of your past.' His eyes dropped to where she was rubbing her birthmark. 'It's a matter that needs to be resolved one way or the other. I wish it to be sooner.'

Because of the baby.

Her heart thudded dully inside her. Everything needed to be smooth so nothing disturbed any pregnancy, now or in the future. She wasn't sure why the offer bruised her. She should be glad he was putting his considerable resources and authority behind the quest to find her past.

Still she shook her head. 'There's nothing to find,' she said flatly, unable to rouse any enthusiasm for the task. 'I asked the matrons at the orphanage for years and they had no clue what happened to me before I was found near that ravine. I was miles away from civilisation and no one came forwards then or afterwards. It's a waste of time.'

His lips compressed. 'With respect, I have a little more clout than your matrons.'

She nodded. 'I know, but I still don't want you to waste your time.'

'Because you are afraid of further disappointment?'

A burst of anger propelled her to her feet. 'What's that supposed to mean?'

'Calm yourself, Niesha,' he warned silkily.

'You're doing it again,' she snapped.

His eyes narrowed. 'And you're getting agitated. It's not good for your condition.'

She laughed. 'What condition? We haven't even verified that I'm pregnant yet,' she exclaimed wildly.

'But you know. Don't you, Niesha?' His voice was like the softest, most potent magic, weaving its way through her as he caught her by the shoulders. 'You know you're carrying my child.'

Helplessly, she swayed against him. 'Our child. It's *ours*.' She had no past to claim, but this…*this* she would claim.

He captured her chin, propelled her gaze to his. The stark possessiveness that gleamed in his eyes stopped her breath. A heartbeat later, his hand dropped to splay over her flat belly, and his chest expanded in a long inhalation. 'Indeed, it is ours. And we will *both* make its well-being our priority.'

There was something so final in those words that she shifted on her feet.

'Enough fretting,' he commanded thickly without raising his voice. 'Stay.'

Perhaps it was the electrifying effect of this touch, or the deep timbre of his voice. But she stilled, unable to look away from the gold depths as he gazed down at her.

His eyes raked her face a moment before he swung her up in his arms. With quick, sure strides he went down the wide hallway into the master suite. She thought he would leave her there, and her pulse rocketed wildly as he drew back the sheets and joined her in bed.

But all Zufar did was press a kiss to her forehead before

drawing her into his arms. 'I've cancelled our appointments for the day. You will rest until Dr Basim returns.'

A part of her wanted to protest at his high-handedness. But really what was the use? He was the King. And she… she was cocooned in warm, powerful arms, her thoughts already beginning to drift away, as if reacting to his directive. With a sigh, she snuck her arm around his waist, rested her head on his shoulder and let her senses succumb to nothingness.

She would need her strength for when Dr Basim returned with further disappointment and heartache. Until then…

She was pregnant. Of course she was.

Zufar's seed had most likely taken root on their wedding night. Her heart sang wildly with a mixture of joy and apprehension as she listened to the doctors' instructions on how to take care of the royal baby in her womb.

She glanced at Zufar as the doctors rattled on about vitamins and healthy eating. Besides the initial gleam that lit his eyes, his face was an inscrutable mask. As for her, she couldn't stop her gaze from darting to the briefcase Dr Basim had brought with him.

It stood beside his chair, offering dangerous hope she couldn't stem.

A noise echoed through the room. When Zufar's eyes narrowed on her, she realised it'd come from her.

'That will be all,' he said abruptly. 'Thank you. Dr Basim, you will remain.'

The others bowed and filed out. Sensing suspense wouldn't be tolerated, the doctor reached for his briefcase. 'Your Highness, I've consulted my old notes. We'll need to do further tests, of course, but the blood type I have on file matches yours. And I've gathered pictures of all royal skin markings including the Princess and your…um… King Nazir's. The one of the Princess is an identical match to yours.'

King Nazir. Her father. Maybe.

A jagged whimper left her throat. Zufar's warm hand enfolded hers, lending her much-needed strength. 'What... what was his...their full names?'

Zufar answered, 'Your father's name is...was... King Nazir Al-Bakar, Sheikh of Rumadah, and your mother was Queen Ayeesha. If the records are correct you also had an older brother, Jamil, who perished in the crash. Your own name is Princess Nazira Fatima Al-Bakar, named after your father.'

Nazira not Niesha.

She had a name. A history. But she was still all alone.

Her cracked heart broke into further pieces at the thought of the parents and brother she would never meet, never share a smile or a joke with. Never confess her worries to or share theirs. 'How did you know?' she croaked.

'I did some research of my own while you were asleep.'

'A-and?' Her voice shook horribly but she was past caring.

'And you are the exact likeness of your mother,' Zufar delivered with a deep, low voice. 'In hindsight, it's astonishing how the similarities could've been missed.'

Shock continued to reel through her. In some distant corner of her mind, she knew she was crying but she couldn't help her tears. 'Because no one was looking for a pr-princess in an orphanage. Or in a chambermaid's uniform.'

Silence throbbed as her words seeped into their very bones. A moment later, Zufar handed her a handkerchief.

She dabbed her eyes, then refocused on the doctor. 'You said you'll need to do further tests?'

'Your blood type is rare. So was your father's. Because of that we kept samples in storage in case they were needed for surgery. Comparing yours to his won't be a problem.'

'But how can they still be in storage twenty years later?'

'The laws of your kingdom prohibit the destruction or disposal of a king's property for twenty-five years in case of his sudden death and no heir apparent. But besides the blood, there are other forms of DNA we can test. With your permission, of course, Your Highness.'

Niesha nodded numbly, shock holding her prisoner. 'I… Of course. You have my permission.' She bit her lip, unable to contain what was happening to her. 'But…how is it that I ended up in Khalia and not Zyria with my family?'

Zufar's hand tightened on hers. 'The place where the tragedy happened was very close to the border with Khalia, separated by a deep ravine. I think you were thrown clear when the accident happened and you wandered off.'

'What? But I was only five years old.'

'I only met you a few times, Your Highness, but you struck me as very determined, even at such a young age. You may have gone to seek help and got lost. Or you may just have been disorientated, the trauma wiped from your memory by the time you were discovered,' Dr Basim said.

Niesha realised then that she would never truly have all the answers she sought. But there was one deep, burning curiosity she could satisfy. She licked her dry lips and nodded to the sleek tablet lying on the coffee table. 'Can I see… Do you have pictures of my family?'

'Of course,' Zufar said, reaching for the tablet.

Seconds later, she found herself staring into eyes that looked so much like her own, further tears welled. Her mother was delicately beautiful, like a rare flower. Her father stood tall, broad-shouldered in traditional clothes. His eyes were darker than hers but, within the depths, Niesha recognised herself. Her soul.

She moved to another picture. In this one, a candid shot probably taken in between more scripted ones, her parents were staring at each other with such utter devotion that the camera was an intrusion. Her gaze moved to her brother and her heart began to break all over again.

Jamil.

Eight at the time of his death, he bore all the hallmarks of turning out just like their father.

Lastly, she located a picture of herself as a child. She wore a deep lavender dress with a white ribbon tied at the waist. The ribbons were replicated in her hair and she was beaming at the camera, leaning forwards with the eagerness and impatience of a five-year-old. Her hands were propped on her knees, and there, clear as day, was the starfish imprinted on her skin.

At the sight of the birthmark, another sob escaped.

'Niesha.' Zufar's voice held a throb of concern, but she waved him away.

'I'm fine, I promise.'

She scrolled through until she found a video interview of her parents. They were about to celebrate some event and had given a few minutes to a reporter. Fingers shaking, Niesha hit the play button. Her father was speaking, his deep, baritone voice authoritative but warm.

And then her mother spoke.

Niesha gasped, a deep trembling seizing her body as she listened to her mother's voice. The voice she carried in her head. The voice that soothed her in times of distress…was her mother's voice.

'Mother…'

She didn't feel the tablet slipping from her fingers.

Or the tight curse from Zufar before he caught her in his arms.

All she felt was blessed darkness.

CHAPTER NINE

SHE WOKE UP propped against soft pillows, the thick coverlet pulled up to her chest.

'What happened?'

Zufar's mouth tightened and his darkened eyes scoured her face. 'You fainted after hearing your mother's voice.'

Memories rushed back, buffeting her with profound sadness. But beside that emotion there was a curious warmth, a lessening of the hollowness that had been part of her life for so long.

Her mother's voice.

It had stayed with her all these years, assuring her that she wasn't truly alone. That she was loved.

Tears began to well again, but she blinked them back, if for no other reason than because she was sure any more tears would make Zufar confine her to bed indefinitely. She couldn't allow that, not when there was so much more to learn about her family. About herself.

Absently, she noticed her wrist being tugged and turned her head to see Dr Basim taking her pulse. She held her breath as he finished up.

'Well?' Zufar demanded.

'She's fine, Your Highness.' Dr Basim smiled at her. 'As long as you take it easy, the episode shouldn't happen again.'

'It shouldn't have happened at all,' Zufar stated with a near growl.

'I'm fine. Really.'

'So you keep telling me. And yet the evidence tells a different story.'

Dr Basim tucked his stethoscope away. 'I'll leave you to rest.'

'Wait,' Niesha rose off the bed, only to be firmly tucked back in by Zufar. Her glare merely bounced off him. She redirected her gaze to Dr Basim.

'Can we… Can we keep this confidential? I don't want anything to get out until…in case it's a false alarm.'

The doctor smiled. 'I'm almost certain it won't be, Your Highness—'

'Nevertheless, I want your word that nothing about this will get out until we have an answer one way or the other. Zufar… I mean, Khalia can do without the upheaval right now.'

Beside her, she saw her husband's imperceptible stiffening. 'You're thinking about me? My people? In this moment?' There was a trace of astonishment in his voice.

'They're my people too, aren't they? They deserve better than to have another bombshell thrown in their laps.'

An emotion shifted across his face, gone before she could read it properly. 'You forget that our marriage ended up being less of a bombshell and more of a welcome celebration.'

'And I'd like to keep it that way for as long as I can, if you don't mind,' she said.

Again something gleamed in his eyes, arresting her focus, not that she needed much to take her focus from Zufar's face. Everything he did, every breath he took seemed to captivate her in some way.

In all ways.

She wasn't sure how long they stared at each other.

A discreet cough reminded her the doctor was still in the room.

Zufar was the first to regain himself by standing and sliding his hands into his pockets. 'You will do as my wife says. Keep the circle of trust small and tight. Report directly to us once you've done your tests.'

The doctor executed an elegant bow. 'Of course. It will be exactly as you wish.'

'A private jet will be chartered to fly you to Rumadah today. We're returning to Khalia tonight. You have forty-eight hours to present us with your findings there.'

The doctor bowed again and left. Zufar crossed the suite to the phone and picked it up.

Unable to lie still, Niesha rose and padded to the window. Through the window of their presidential suite in the heart of Paris, the Seine glistened sinuously in the sunshine and the spear of the Eiffel Tower looked almost close enough to touch.

But this time the view didn't hold as much appeal. Alternate waves of heat and cold surged through her as she wrapped her hands around herself.

'I suspect I'll have a fight on my hands if I suggest you return to bed but I have ordered an early lunch for you and you will eat something.'

She rounded on him, her heart pounding. 'What if I'm not this…this person? What if all of this is a wild coincidence?'

'It's not,' he replied. 'The pictures alone prove your connection. Besides, you were the only one unaccounted for following the accident. You were most likely presumed dead because no one expected a five-year-old to survive such an incident.'

Another shiver danced down her spine. A moment later, warm hands cupped her shoulders, then drew down her arms.

'You are the Princess. It's time you start believing it,' Zufar commanded, his deep voice sending a different sort of shiver through her.

The small laugh she gave held a touch of hysteria. 'I don't know that I can. It all feels so…overwhelming. And so messy for you.' She gave a pained laugh. 'Perhaps you would've been better off going after Amira, after all.'

His hands tightened fractionally. 'I've found that it's useless dwelling on things we cannot change.'

Her insides shrank a little that he didn't issue a firm de-

MAYA BLAKE 155

nial of any desire for his ex-fiancée. Because deep down it was what she'd been selfishly, hungrily angling for.

'As for things being overwhelming, you proved that you can handle overwhelming when you married me three weeks ago.' That odd note she'd heard a little while ago pulsed through his voice, but, scrutinising his face, Niesha couldn't decipher his thoughts.

'If my name really isn't Niesha, do I have to change it?'

'I expect you can do whatever you please. You are the Queen of Khalia. And soon to be confirmed as the rightful heiress to the throne of Rumadah.'

She gasped. 'But...how will that work?'

For a single moment, his jaw clenched tight, and Niesha was reminded that whatever happened to her would also cause Zufar, and more importantly Khalia, huge upheaval.

The very thing he'd striven to avoid by marrying her.

'With very careful strategising,' was all he said before he released her.

Before she could speak, a member of his staff wheeled a trolley onto the grand terrace, where a table had been set for two.

Despite her inner turmoil, Niesha forced herself to finish the vichyssoise starter. She was eating for two, after all.

She saw the gleam of approval in Zufar's eyes as she tucked away a good portion of pasta with rich creamy sauce and French bread. When she was done eating, she placed her napkin on the table and attempted to enjoy the view.

'Would you like to go out?' Zufar asked abruptly.

She returned her gaze to him and watched the sunlight dance over his glossy hair. 'Where?' she asked warily.

He shrugged. 'Wherever you please.'

'I thought you'd cancelled all our engagements.'

'I did. But I won't have you cooped up in the suite, climbing the walls. We're not scheduled to fly for another few hours. If you wish to go out, we will.'

She wanted to point out that they were in a fifteen-room

suite, hardly a space that evoked a coop. But her eyes lit on the tower again, and she nodded. 'I'd like that. Thank you.'

He rose and held his hand out to her. Pulse jumping into her throat, she placed her hand in his, absorbing the tingles that raced up her arm as she let him help her up from the table.

In their bedroom, he walked her to the dressing room. 'I'll summon your attendants.'

She grimaced. 'Can you not? I'd like to dress myself for once without all the fussing.'

He hesitated, then gave a regal nod before heading for his own dressing room.

The off-shoulder design of the maroon jumpsuit came with wide palazzo pants that made it look like an elegant day dress. The outfit was a little more casual than she'd worn for any occasion during her honeymoon but even before she slipped it on, Niesha knew she would love its easy comfort.

She'd watched Halimah and her attendants closely enough to expertly apply light make-up and twist her hair into a stylish bun in minutes. Deciding on simple diamond earrings, she slipped them on. Then she slid her feet into blood-red heels that matched her belt, scooped up oversized sunglasses and a clutch and left the suite.

As always, Zufar was waiting for her in the living room. He'd swapped his suit for a softer pair of grey trousers coupled with a light blue shirt over which he'd worn a jacket two shades darker than his trousers. His tie was gone, in its place a silk scarf tucked neatly into his collar. Handmade loafers completed his outfit and she stared, thinking he could easily have stepped off a magazine cover. As he drew nearer, she saw the House of al Khalia monogram embroidered on his jacket pocket. She wanted to say that he didn't need it.

Every inch of him shouted his regal status.

In the lift down, he drew a pair of sunglasses from his pocket and slid them on. The moment they stepped out into the sunny reception, Niesha knew what she wanted to do.

'Can we walk for a while?'

'Not unless you want to be mobbed.' The ever-present paparazzi loitered outside.

She grimaced. 'Then I'd like to just drive around, if you don't mind?'

He nodded. 'It will be as you wish.'

They set off in a smaller convoy.

From the back of the limo, she tried to forget her turmoil and just bask in the sights. But it proved impossible.

Strong hands captured her twisting fingers. 'It will be all right.'

Different words, said by a different voice but both owned by people she knew she was emotionally heavily invested in.

She would never get to meet her mother or hear the real-life version of the sweet words she'd whispered in her ear.

But Zufar was right here, a temptation she'd told herself to resist the moment she'd set eyes on him as a romantic teenager with her head in the clouds. Temptation she knew could decimate her when she took his name and accepted him into her body.

His tempting words were the ones she needed to be wary of because Zufar would never see her as anything other than a replacement for another woman. A woman he hadn't cared about enough to go after. If he'd found it so easy to discard Amira, what hope did she have of ever finding anything deeper with him?

When her feelings grew too much to contain she tried to prise her hands away. He held on tight. 'Tell me what troubles you.'

'I'm scared,' she blurted before she could stop herself. But self-preservation stopped her from expounding.

To her surprise, he nodded. 'I know. You'll recall I, too, have been in your shoes.'

'You've been pregnant?'

He looked startled for a moment, before his mouth curved

in a smile. It was the first genuine full smile she'd seen on his face. And it floored Niesha completely.

'No, that is a privilege you will enjoy on your own.'
Smooth.

So smooth, she felt a little of her agitation drift away. And when he meshed his fingers with hers and drew her head onto his shoulder, she went with her insides melting, her heart pounding and her head telling her she was just ten kinds of fool for leaving herself wide open for further heartache.

'Niesha. Wake up.'

The low, deeply voiced command tickled the shell of her ear.

With a small shiver, she blinked awake, and realised she was draped all over Zufar.

She jumped but didn't get very far as the arm clamped around her tightened. She raised her gaze, about to murmur an apology for falling asleep on him, when she noticed where they were. 'We're at the airport?'

'Yes. You fell asleep in the car. After we drove around Paris for two hours I thought it best to come straight to the airport.'

'I've been asleep for two hours?'

Tawny eyes gleamed at her. 'Clearly you needed the rest.'

The thought that he'd driven around with her even though she'd fallen asleep shouldn't have touched her, not after the stern warning her head had issued her heart.

And yet, she found herself softening against him, the decadent desire to melt into his warmth sucking at her. She told herself she would only give in for a minute. Or two.

When his gaze dropped to her mouth, she added one more.

But the kiss she yearned for never came.

Without taking his eyes from her, he gave a casual flick

of his wrist, and the door was thrown open, ending the private moment that only she had wanted more of, it seemed.

Zufar stepped out, and held out a courteous hand for her.

Niesha placed her hand in his, struggling to reconcile the man who'd driven around the streets of Paris just so she could take a nap with the man who had clearly seen her invitation and declined it.

The baby.

Of course, it was all to do with the baby. How could she have forgotten?

At the first opportunity, she drew her hand from his, vowing never to repeat her mistake. Besides, with her future in turmoil, the earlier she learned to stand on her own two feet, the better.

She ignored the sharp look he sent her and hurried to board the plane.

For the duration of the flight, she stayed in the bedroom with her tablet for company. By the time they landed in Khalia, she'd devoured everything she could find on her family. And shed a few tears along the way.

Zufar scrutinised her face as they stepped out of the plane but didn't comment. The ride to the palace was also conducted in silence, but when they approached their bedroom, she couldn't hold back any more.

'So what happens now?'

'Once we have irrefutable confirmation, my special council will meet with yours and we'll take it from there.'

It wasn't what she'd wanted to know, but discussing their bedroom arrangements when two kingdoms stood to be plunged into uncertainty felt trivial.

'What do you mean, take it from there?'

He shrugged. 'You will appreciate that this is a unique situation for both of us. We'll need to strategise the best way forwards.'

'You're speaking but not really saying much.'

He dragged a hand through his hair, the first sign that the

circumstances they found themselves in weren't straightforward. 'I can't give you an answer I don't have. Not without further investigation.'

'Investigation?' she echoed.

'All signs point to the fact that Rumadah needs its rightful ruler back on the throne. It hasn't had one for two decades.'

'Because a new one couldn't be crowned for twenty-five years,' she added, recalling what she'd read about her country's constitution on the plane. According to the laws, a missing heir to the throne couldn't be ruled out until twenty-five years had passed. In that time a twelve-member council, the same that had served the last King, would rule the kingdom.

In another five years, she would've lost her birthright.

But was it one she wanted, if it meant what she was beginning to fear? Because how could she claim her Rumadian birthright and still remain Queen of Khalia? Zufar's wife?

Her insides shook at the mere thought of walking away from him. It seemed more impossible now than ever. Because the loss of her family wasn't the only reason she'd cried on the plane. She'd also cried because she'd finally accepted that she was in love with Zufar. And painfully accepted that that love would never be reciprocated.

'Perhaps we shouldn't jump the gun just yet. This could all be an elaborate hoax,' she said, more in hope than expectation.

The look in Zufar's eyes told her the same. 'A few days ago I urged you to reconcile yourself to never discovering your past. That landscape has changed and delivered everything you hoped for. Perhaps you should reconcile yourself to this blessing?'

She flinched at the trace of censure in his voice. Before she could respond, he turned from her. 'I need to catch up on a few engagements. Don't wait up for me.'

The last statement was both a blessing and a curse. He

intended to find her in their bed when he deigned to return but he didn't care whether she was awake or asleep now that she was pregnant?

Niesha was rubbing at that agonising spot in her chest when the doors opened again and Halimah and the rest of her retinue descended on her.

She forced herself to respond that, yes, she was happy to be back, and that, yes, her honeymoon had been everything she'd dreamed about as they helped her undress and ran a bath for her. She withstood their attention for as long as she could, until she felt as if her face would break if she smiled one more time.

They respectfully retreated when she asked for privacy. With a sigh, she sank into her lavender and jasmine-scented bath. Immediately, a few dozen questions crowded her mind.

Zufar had suggested she be grateful to have her birth-right back. But would everyone else feel the same? Would her people even want her once the inevitable announcement was made?

With no definitive answers in hand, she ate a light dinner and went to bed early.

If Zufar came to bed at all, he was gone when she woke, and when Kadira arrived, she was told His Highness had instructed her workload be kept light until further notice.

If he wanted to set tongues wagging about a possible pregnancy, he couldn't have done a better job, she thought with a bite of irritation. All day, Kadira slid smiling, speculative glances at her. And Halimah and her attendants joined in as they helped her prepare for bed.

Again, she didn't see Zufar, even when she woke in the middle of the night.

When she next woke, it was with a heavy, pounding heart.

Today was the day.

Dr Basim had been given forty-eight hours. Whatever happened, she would have a choice to make.

* * *

His wife, his Queen, who carried his heir, was herself an heiress to another kingdom. Even though Zufar had known it was inevitable the moment he'd clapped eyes on the pictures of Niesha's parents, he wasn't ashamed to admit a small part of him had hoped that the information would be proved wrong.

Dr Basim and a team of doctors in Rumadah had proved conclusively that Niesha, or Nazira, as she was being addressed in his conference room, was the rightful heiress to the Rumadian throne.

Not that he'd wished for her past to remain a closed chapter to her, but this situation was not at all what he'd anticipated or remotely wanted.

With their reports, however, another bombshell had been dumped into his lap. One that demanded immediate remedy.

He watched the councillors who had accompanied Dr Basim bow and scrape before Niesha. Watched her shy, smiling acknowledgement, and the eagerness with which she absorbed every morsel of information they delivered to her.

For the most part, her seeming return from the dead was very welcome news indeed. And with each moment that passed, he could see the wheels turning in the councillors' minds regarding how to swiftly reclaim their Queen.

A few cast furtive glances towards him, wary of his silence.

The simple truth was that to vocalise his true feelings would've shocked them all. The churning in his chest that had begun long before Niesha's past had been revealed, and which had grown considerably since the revelation, exploded into gut-clenching proportions as he watched them slowly sink their claws into the woman he had claimed for himself.

Or attempted to claim.

Behind his back, his fists curled, his whole body tensed

up in battle mode. The thundering of his blood hissed that, regardless of his acceptance of her birthright, he wasn't about to let her go that easily.

You may not have a choice.

He ignored the voice that had been growing louder. By his own bargain, he'd placed an exit clause on their marriage. Whether he chose to accept it or not, a termination date could very well be on its way back to bite him.

He noticed his own councillors sending him questioning looks, but for the first time in his life, he didn't have ready answers available. He hadn't had them back in Paris when the thought had first occurred to him that he might lose Niesha.

'Your Serene Highness, we will need to make an announcement soon. When can we expect you to return to Rumadah?'

This came from the chief councillor, a cunning old man who'd been eyeing Zufar since they entered his conference room.

'Return?' Niesha echoed.

'Of course. Once the announcement is made, your people will wish to see you, to reassure themselves that you are well.'

'She is well, as you can very well see.' Zufar attempted to modulate his voice, but knew he hadn't succeeded when more eyes turned wary.

'Of course, Your Highness, and we will be grateful to you and to your people for ever for taking such good care of our Queen.'

'But...?' he trailed softly. There was a *but*. It was written on all their faces.

'But...with a thousand pardons, her rightful place is back in Rumadah. Her people need her.'

Simple words.

Heavy, life-altering words, as he very well knew.

Not too long in the recent past his own councillors had

pleaded with him in the same manner, urging him to save Khalia after his father's abdication.

Even now, his people needed him. Khalia might have regained her rightful position as a powerful state to be reckoned with but Rumadah had merely trundled along, no one stepping up to make the bold decisions that would take it from a game player to a shot caller.

Without a bold leader to ensure its considerable power was harnessed in the right way, it risked falling into apathy or, worse, into enemy hands. From the research he'd done himself, Zufar knew that the oil-rich country had only stayed on an even course because of its substantial deposits.

A glance around the room of ageing councillors delivered the hard truth that it was only a matter of time before the situation altered for the worse. They needed a true leader, a visionary, who would rule with a firm but compassionate hand.

Someone like Niesha.

His wife.

His Queen.

The mother of his unborn child.

It was impossible.

It was also inevitable that a decision needed to be taken. And soon.

He turned and looked at the two dozen people in the room.

Niesha sat at the head of the table, nodding and making comments where necessary, but he knew her head wasn't in the game. How could it be, when they were all speaking at once?

Over their heads, her gaze snapped up. Wide amethyst eyes met and locked on his, and something deep and profound moved in his chest. *That* sensation had also been escalating, confounding him at the oddest moments.

But far too soon, her gaze dropped away from his as she turned to address the man seated to her right. Whatever he was saying to her wasn't good because after a few minutes she paled a little, even as she nodded.

Enough.

Realising he hadn't vocalised the word, he spoke again. 'Enough.' When he had their attention, he went to Niesha, placed his hand at the back of her chair. 'Give us the room,' he ordered, stamping his tone with implacable authority. 'I wish to speak to my wife in private.'

The councillors looked a little surprised, but one by one they filed out.

'Thank you. I needed a break,' Niesha murmured.

'Then you should've asked for one.' Realising his voice was still brusque, he modified it. 'This must be overwhelming for you.'

'Despite their collective age, they're like a pack of over-zealous wolf pups, all with sharp teeth they don't know can hurt.'

Her description couldn't have been more accurate. He also remembered that pups grew into adulthood, some into alphas who relished a challenge. 'The trick is to train them early, show them who's in charge. Yours doesn't need to be the loudest voice in the room, but it needs to be the final authority.'

The look she gave him was filled with gratitude. As much as he welcomed it, Zufar yearned for another look. One whose absence made the band around his chest tighter by the day.

'I need to write these things down, don't I? To remember them for later.'

'You won't need to. You're their Queen. Leadership was bred into you from birth.' And soon, if her councillors succeeded, she would take it and herself away from him.

She sighed and lifted a hand to rub her temple. A moment later, she straightened her spine, a resolute look settling on her face.

How could he not have spotted signs of her breeding from

the moment they met? Royalty was stamped into every fibre of her being, every drop of her blood.

'You wanted to talk to me?'

Words eluded him for a moment as the combination of delicate jaw, sensual mouth and alluring eyes flattened him. But he forced himself to focus. He'd cleared the room to give her breathing space but there was another subject that needed discussing. 'Dr Basim hasn't told them you're pregnant. Is he planning on telling them?'

It would be one way to force her quicker return to Rumadah. A risen-from-the-dead queen would please her people. One expecting a royal heir would be euphoric.

He wondered whether it was a card she intended to play.

She laughed. 'I've barely managed to get their names right.'

Her self-effacing response didn't please him. 'It's customary to keep news of pregnancy under wraps for the first trimester,' he pressed.

She blinked, then rose and went to stand before the floor-to-ceiling windows. Framed against it, she looked almost delicate. But her spine was straight, her resolve absolute. 'I'll tell them when I'm ready.'

Relief and the breath he hadn't realised he held burst through him. She burst it a fraction of a second later.

'Half of the advisers are returning tomorrow. The other half leave on Friday. They want me to accompany them when they return to Rumadah.'

When had these arrangements been made? While he'd been tuned out, feeling sorry for himself? 'Friday is three days away,' he growled. 'We just returned from our honeymoon. I can't leave again so soon.' Especially when he didn't have an answer on how to stop the freight train he could sense heading his way.

Her lashes swept down, veiling her expression. 'I understand. I'm sure I'll be fine on my own,' she said.

That vice threatened to squeeze every last breath out of him. 'I see. And how long will you be gone?'

'Three days. Maybe four.'

The prompt answer froze the blood in his veins. 'Was that the plan all along?'

Her eyelashes lifted. 'I beg your pardon?'

'Use my duty to my people against me?'

She gasped. 'Zufar, I don't know what you're talking—'

He stared down at her, the inevitability of loss continuing to suffocate him. 'And what happens after that?'

Her eyes widen. 'What do you mean?'

'Do you intend to commute back and forth between your kingdom and mine?'

Her forehead gathered in a delicate frown. Then she shrugged. 'This is all new. I don't have the answers, Zufar. But I think you know that I owe it to my people to at least let them know who I am.'

A part of him felt shame for her hurt, but it wasn't enough to overcome the terrible anguish scything its way through him. He despised the feeling. Enough for him to approach her, despite his vow to refrain from touching her.

She had enough on her plate without his ever-growing hunger for her saturating the atmosphere between them. It was a decision he'd made in Prague after watching her sleep, seeing the shadows beneath her eyes, and knowing that he was partly to blame for it.

For the first two weeks of their marriage, he'd never let a night pass without making love to her, his need so great it had confounded him even then. That need had grown into unbearable proportions by the time they'd arrived in Prague.

When the demands of his duties had kept him way from the marriage bed for that first night, he'd watched her for signs that she'd missed him the next morning. There had been none.

The idea that the carnal weakness was on his part alone had brought him up short. And when, night after night, Niesha had made no attempts to reach for him, he'd had his answer. He'd roped her into a bargain to provide him with an heir, but was that all it was for her? Was that the only reason for her welcoming him into her body?

Perhaps that was the reason she could speak so freely of leaving him behind for four days.

'If that's the plan, you'll need to rethink it because it won't be sustainable,' he bit out.

She paled a little, but continued to hold his gaze boldly. 'What are you saying, Zufar?'

'I'm saying that even the shortest of separations has a habit of growing. It's not healthy for any marriage. My parents led separate lives, my mother lived in the east wing and my father lived in the west. Even under the same roof, their marriage was a sham. I do not wish this for myself.'

'I agree, but—'

'I know what I want and it certainly did not involve living in separate countries.'

'So you wish me to renounce my birthright?' she demanded with a hint of tears in her eyes.

Ice gripped his nape hard. 'I'm saying that hard choices need to be made.'

'And you want me to be the one to make them?' Her eyes brimmed, her mouth trembling for one second before she pursed it.

He wanted to lift his hand to her face, brush away her tears, but that would be giving in. For as long as he could remember his father had given in to his mother's every whim, making himself deeply miserable at every turn. Zufar had vowed never to leave himself that vulnerable. But…was it already too late?

'We had an agreement,' he threw at her.

She took in a heavy, shaky breath. 'And I am not reneging on it. I'm only trying to find a way—'

'A way to do what?' He knew he was being unreasonable, but for the life of him, he couldn't stop. He was floundering, hurting her, hurting himself in the process but there didn't seem to be a life raft in sight, and with every moment that passed his anguish strangled him, making him hold tight to the one thing that he knew he couldn't hold onto.

Niesha.

'You promised me five years,' he repeated, as if that would make her fall at his feet, and give him everything he wanted. When really, a greater part of him wanted it to be the other way round. But how could he, without leaving himself desperately exposed?

Slowly her regal head lifted, her eyes condemning him, challenging him to remain obstinate, to keep standing in her way. 'I don't recall signing any piece of paper saying you owned me for five years.'

He wasn't sure why that statement both shocked and made him proud. He had already admitted his flaw in striking that bargain. A part of him applauded her for jumping through that wide loophole.

'I'm aware that all we had was a verbal agreement,' he stated. 'But I still wish you to stand by it.'

Her shoulders sagged a little, but in the next moment she pulled herself back up. 'Don't push me, Zufar. You might not like the consequences.' After a moment, her gaze softened. 'But if you let me work this out on my own, perhaps we can find a solution that works for both of us.'

The only solution he wanted was her here under his roof, in his bed, at his side, bearing his children, loving them the way his mother had never loved him.

'Three days. That's all I ask. Surely you can give me that?'

Could he? Already he felt emptier than he'd ever felt in his life, and she was standing right there in front of him.

Zufar didn't know where he found the strength to nod. 'Of course. Go with my blessing.'

The realisation terrified him that despite everything he'd said he meant it. Because wasn't that something his father would have done? Ripped out his organs if his mother had asked?

'Thank you,' his Queen said, her gaze searching his.

For signs of his obsession, perhaps?

He clenched his jaw, attempting to neutralise his expression. 'You'll let me know of your travel plans once they're finalised?'

She nodded.

He left her in the conference room, calmly walked out even though he wanted to bellow to the skies; to rip himself inside out just so he could reach the pain inside that was decimating him. The walk to his office was the longest he'd ever taken.

Once he was there, he strode to his desk and sank into the chair.

He couldn't even take three days of separation. How would he take a lifetime? Because he knew that was coming too. Unless something changed drastically, Niesha would be out of his reach even before their child was born.

He slammed his fist on the desk, his thoughts churning a thousand miles an hour. Sunset came and went and still he had no solution. When the door to his office opened without announcement from his private secretary, he nearly snarled.

He managed to bite it back when he saw Malak framed in the doorway.

'I'm hearing all sorts of juicy gossip about you and your new bride, brother,' Malak drawled.

'You know very well what's happening. Your private secretary received the same memo I sent to Galila and Father.'

Malak shrugged as he strolled over to the drinks cabinet and poured two fingers of cognac into crystal glasses. Returning to Zufar's desk, he slid one across the smooth surface. Then he sprawled himself in the chair across the desk.

'I have to say, your new wife is turning out to be quite the surprise, isn't she? I admit, I wasn't very impressed in the beginning, but—'

'Watch yourself, brother,' Zufar warned.

Malak held up one hand as he sipped his drink. 'No disrespect meant, brother. But I'm not the one who harped on about wanting some peace and quiet around here, only to turn around and start tossing dynamite like it was a party favour.'

'Did you come here to make a specific point or are you just here to annoy me? If it's the latter, then bravo, you are succeeding.'

Malak laughed. 'I came to offer you whatever help you need. I may be the selfish playboy the tabloids like to portray me as, but underneath this handsome exterior lives a semi-decent heart that's bleeding for you right now.'

The words were laced with so much amusement, Zufar's irritation mounted. 'You claim you want to help, but all I see is you sitting there drinking my cognac.'

Malak waved a gracious hand. 'Tell me what you need and I will do my best to give you a simple yay or nay.'

Zufar stared into the amber shadows of his drink, two words ticking over and over in his head. *Three days.* He'd agreed to three days. Would she come back? What would he do if she didn't?

'Or I can leave you to brood into your drink?' Malak suggested.

Zufar stood and paced to the window, that feeling of being turned inside out surging to breaking point. He tossed back his drink, then his gaze dropped to the rose garden below his window. He stared at the perfect flowers, his thoughts churning.

After several minutes, his brother joined him, his gaze zeroing in on the same place. 'Why didn't she love us?' Malak asked in a thick, heavy voice.

Zufar was unprepared for the question, just as he was unprepared for the canon of the pain that shot through him. He'd thought he was over that, or at least had suppressed it enough not to feel the agony of his mother's indifference any more.

He shrugged. 'Because she was incapable of it. Ultimately, she couldn't love anyone but herself.' Perhaps it was a flaw he needed to come to terms with, and move on.

Niesha wasn't like that though.

She loved children. She would love their child with the same passion with which she loved his people. The same devotion with which she loved her people enough to threaten to walk away from him and his crown to serve them again. That kind of selflessness was humbling. Inspiring.

How could he stop her from pursuing that, from giving to people who would love her back, and welcome her with open arms the way his people had done?

Malak sighed. 'I wish he'd done something.'

'Who?'

'Father. I wish he'd made a decision one way or the other. Demanded that she love him and us, or leave her. Instead of trailing after her all those years. Instead of making us live each dreadful moment with him.'

'I don't think it was that simple,' Zufar found himself explaining. 'Maybe he was left with very little choice.'

His brother sneered, turned and started walking away. 'Whatever. I'm over it. Anyway, it's been a good talk. If you decide you need me after all, you know where to find me.'

Zufar barely heard him leave. And as he stared into the bottom of his glass, he found his thoughts veering in another direction.

To his father.

CHAPTER TEN

NIESHA STOOD IN front of the plane door, waiting for the attendant to open it. Unlike the flight to Europe, this one had been short and nerve-shredding, her emotions swinging between what awaited her in Rumadah and what she'd left behind.

The last three days had been alternately perfect and horrendous. The coordinated news of her real identity had been greeted with another wave of happy frenzy across the world, the short interview she'd given to explain her unfortunate absence accessed over a billion times online. That had been her public life.

In private, she'd remained in turmoil.

Even though he'd given her his blessing, Zufar had stayed away from her, and in the rare moments when they'd met, his gaze had chilled her. He still came to their bed, but it was only to sleep, with his back to her and a mile between them. When they needed to communicate, they did so via their private secretaries.

That was how she'd found out he'd granted her access to his royal jet to make this trip. That was how she'd found out he'd gone on a whistle-stop tour of his kingdom and wasn't expected back before her departure.

Their conversation in the conference room had left her bruised and hollow and heart-wrenchingly convinced that her days with Zufar were numbered. It was why she'd thrown herself into this visit.

When he was out of her life, at least she would have this, her new life, to fall back on. The more she'd absorbed about her heritage, the more she was certain she wanted to claim her birthright. Her parents had loved this kingdom and dedicated their lives to it. How could she walk away?

In a way it was easier that Zufar had laid down an ultimatum.

No. It wasn't.

She would have preferred a different ultimatum. One that made loving and dedicating herself to both kingdoms possible. But she knew it was another dream she needed to let go of. Just as she knew she would need to reconcile herself to letting Zufar go.

Divorce.

That was what one of her advisers had cautiously suggested during their meeting in Khalia.

Divorce the man who hadn't meant to be her husband in the first place so she could be free to fully embrace her destiny.

Such an easy suggestion. With such catastrophic consequences for her heart, her soul, every breath she took from here on out.

'We're ready, Your Serene Highness,' the Rumadian attendant said softly, with a blinding smile and shining eyes that hinted of tears. 'And if you'll permit me to say, I'm so happy you're here,' she gushed.

Niesha returned her smile, then her heart lurched wildly as the door slid soundlessly open and sunshine poured into the doorway.

Momentarily blinded, she blinked a few times, smoothing her hands over her royal blue wrap dress before stepping forwards. Immediately, a deafening roar went up over the sound of the still-whirling jet engines.

The lump of emotion wedged firmly in her throat grew as she caught sight of the crowd beyond the barricades set up on either side of the plane.

She paused for one full minute to wave before she slowly descended the stairs.

She'd been briefed on the protocol.

Her council of elders would be the first lined up on either side of the red carpet. Beyond that the senior members of the military...*her* military, would be next in line. Then a few prominent ministers and dignitaries.

So she was startled when a figure broke away from the line and approached the bottom of the steps.

Niesha gasped as the unmistakeable figure of her husband materialised in front of her. 'Zufar...what are you doing here?' she whispered as he stepped forwards and took her hand.

'It is my right as your husband to be at your side, is it not?' he returned.

She kept a smile pinned to her face as he raised her hand and kissed the back of it. Peripherally, she heard the crowd go wild.

'Welcome home, Your Highness,' he intoned deeply.

She took another step down, their height disparity forcing her to look up at him. His face was a perfectly neutral picture of regal discipline, his eyes giving away none of his feelings.

'I don't understand...'

'You don't need to. You're perfectly capable of doing this on your own. But I'm here nevertheless.'

For how long? she wanted to demand. But she'd already broken protocol, albeit through no fault of her own. He took a single step to the side and stood tall and proud and royal, but out of her way.

With a nod, she stepped onto the carpet, widening her smile as the chief adviser held out his hand.

'We are so very fortunate and honoured that you have returned to us, Your Serene Highness. Welcome home.'

All through the greeting of her statesmen and military, she was acutely aware of Zufar's presence one step beside her.

How had he got here before her?

Why was he here?

Was he staying?

The questions tumbled through her mind over the next few hours. At some point it struck her that she'd become an expert at compartmentalising because she managed to talk and walk and respond easily to conversation, even while her insides churned.

But everything fell away the moment they left the State House and approached Nazir Palace, the home she'd lived in so very briefly before losing it all.

Unlike Zufar's hilltop palace, Nazir Palace sat in the centre of the city, right on the doorstep of the people. In fact, hundreds of citizens and tourists were strolling through the public grounds as her motorcade entered the gates and drove through secured gates to the private front door.

Niesha struggled to remember any aspect of her home during the grand tour. Nothing came to mind, not even the toys left in the same position as the day she'd left and never returned. When she said as much, she received sympathetic murmurings.

'You will make new memories, I'm certain, Your Serene Highness,' her chief adviser said with a gentle smile.

Niesha wasn't unaware of the gentle pressure coming her way. Or the way Zufar stiffened each time the subject of her return was casually dropped into conversation.

When they reached her parents' bedroom it all grew too much. 'May I have a moment alone, please?'

'Of course.'

The room emptied immediately, save for Zufar. He walked by her side as she walked through the bedroom suite, touching her father's discarded tiepin, inhaling her mother's silk scarf that still faintly held her scent.

In their dressing room, she picked up her mother's hairbrush, gasping when the faintest memory materialised.

'I remember her...this room. She would sit me on her lap and comb my hair with this brush.' The last of the words dissolved into a sob.

Beside her, Zufar held out his handkerchief.

She took it, her gaze snagging his for a moment. 'Thank you.'

He gave a stiff nod. 'You are strong. You can do this.'

A moment later she was alone. As alone as she'd been from the beginning. As alone as she would be when Zufar left as abruptly as he'd appeared.

You will be all right.

She wanted to laugh. She wanted to cry and scream and throw things. But she bottled it all up because she was a queen. *Twice over.* And queens didn't break down into uncontrollable hysteria.

She reminded herself of that as she gave another interview and expressed her joy to be back home. It came in handy when she danced in Zufar's arms and he held her courteously but stiffly that night at a ball thrown in her honour.

And she reminded herself *many times* of that, the next morning, at the breakfast meeting with her chief adviser.

'As I have said, I will give you an answer in due course once I've given the matter more thought.' She picked up the tea and sipped it, her heart alternately joyful to be sitting in her mother's favourite breakfast chair, drinking from her favourite tea set, and heavy because once again Zufar had made himself scarce the moment they were alone.

'If it is a matter of pride, Your Serene Highness, please be assured it is not necessary. No one will judge you. We are simply thrilled that you are back. But we want you back permanently and as soon as possible. Your kingdom needs you. And the only way to extricate yourself from all things Khalia, we strongly feel, is by divorce.'

Icy water drenched her veins. But a numb part of her had already seen this coming. Wasn't that what Zufar himself had suggested in his own way a few days ago? He'd spoken of hard choices needing to be made. And when it came down to it, wasn't a dissolution of a marriage that was doomed to failure anyway the only option?

'You want me to divorce my husband in order to assume my birthright?'

'At the moment, it seems to be the only course open to us, Your Serene Highness.'

The boulder-sized pain that lodged itself in her chest made it hard to breathe. The joy of being back among her parents' things faded, her hands trembling as she set her teacup down.

'Very well.' She stopped, those two words birthing a thick sob she had to swallow to keep down. 'I understand—'

She froze as Zufar stepped onto the balcony. The look on his face chilled her to the bone.

'I'm guessing I'm no longer needed here, in that case,' he said, his voice edged with soft deadliness. 'Perhaps you wish for me to make myself scarce?'

'Zufar—'

He batted her words away in that unique way of his. 'You can save your words. I came to say goodbye. You have saved me the tedium of saying a more permanent one at a later date.' His gaze dropped to her stomach before rising to her face again. 'But be assured, Your Highness, that what is mine will remain *mine*.'

The shock of his words rooted her to her chair. Her world turned grey as he executed the perfect military turn and disappeared from view.

From her life.

Another sob threatened to escape. With every cell in her body, she wanted to let it rip free. She contained it as she'd never contained anything else in her life.

She was a *queen*. Queens didn't break.

'Wait! You're what?'

Zufar stared at his brother. 'Which part of it do you need repeated?'

Malak stared at him, shock and apprehension written all over his face. 'All of it. Better yet, let's just pretend everything you said was a joke. I can appreciate the odd joke when—'

'It's not a joke, brother. You said you wanted to help. This is what I need from you.'

Malak snorted. '*Help* means handling a difficult meeting in your stead, or picking out a gift for your wife when you run out of ideas. *Help* doesn't mean tossing your throne in my lap, telling me you're abdicating and expecting me to take your place.'

'Not expecting. Requesting. And the throne is too heavy to toss so you'll just have to settle for sitting on it.'

His brother exhaled noisily. 'I'm glad you're okay with cracking jokes. That means you're not that far gone. That you still have time to—'

'My mind is made up, Malak.' He injected the conviction of his decision into his words.

Once he'd come to the realisation that it was his only option, it had been surprisingly easy. The greater battle of winning his wife's heart was yet to come.

'You really mean it,' Malak observed with a stunned look. At Zufar's nod, he threw out his hands. 'What the hell? I don't want it either.'

'But you will take it because this kingdom is important to both of us. And our people need you too much for you to walk away.'

Malak opened his mouth to protest. But a full minute passed in silence as he breathed in and out, his gaze locked with Zufar's.

Zufar saw the moment duty overcame individualism, when the mantle of responsibility settled firmly on his brother's shoulders. It had been exactly like that for him.

'Okay. I accept.'

He rounded his desk and held out his hand. 'Godspeed.'

Malak pulled him into a hug. 'Same to you, brother.'

* * *

Five hours later, Zufar stood looking at his father, wondering for the umpteenth time if the visit had been wise. He didn't know. In fact, he wasn't sure about a lot of things any more.

But one thing he saw—and recognised—was the pain of loss on his father's face. It was similar to the one currently clawing deeper roots into his heart.

Was this what it felt like to have something right in front of you and lose it so completely, leaving only a gaping wound?

Because he'd lost Niesha. His foolish attempt to join her in Rumadah to mitigate the looming loss had failed miserably.

'Why have you come here, son?'

Son.

Another wrench of agony joined the endless symphony of pain slashing his heart. Zufar couldn't remember the last time his father had called him that. If ever. Or perhaps he had called him that but Zufar, too wrapped up in his own bitter loneliness, hadn't noticed?

He tried to shake off the feelings but they wouldn't leave him. What else had he missed while he'd been busy feeling wronged and aggrieved? Looking into his father's eyes now, he thought he saw a plea that looked like his own. Even a wry understanding.

As if he saw something Zufar didn't.

For some reason that observation both soothed and terrified him. For so long he'd harshly denounced anything to do with his father. But what if the wrongs he'd condemned his parent for were imprinted in his own DNA after all? What if he'd been predestined to repeat the same sins?

Or…what if they weren't wrong at all? Just an extremely misguided obsession but one that could have been mitigated with the right partner by his father's side?

Again he tried to shake off the disturbing thoughts. They

persisted until he realised he hadn't answered his father's question.

'Father, I have some news to share with you.'

Niesha walked into Zufar's library, her heartbeat drumming madly in her ears. She'd come straight from the airport to the palace, the urge to speak to him after an excruciating twenty-four hours without him, paramount.

He was sitting elegantly cross-legged on a large, stripped antique sofa, a book on Khalian history balanced on his knee.

As usual, the sight of him arrested her, slowing her steps as she absorbed his virile essence. He was in one of her favourite rooms of the palace but the books might as well have been candlesticks for all the attention she paid to them.

He looked up, his gaze slowly raking her from head to toe before reconnecting with hers.

'You have returned.' The observation was deep, husky, lethal to her senses.

She gave a jerky nod, then ploughed ahead before she lost her nerve. 'We need to talk.'

He tossed the heavy book to one side and stood. 'I agree,' he said. 'But first I need you to take a look at this.' He picked up a bound document from the coffee table as he came towards her.

She went cold, her heart shredding into smaller pieces. Surely he hadn't drawn up divorce papers that quickly?

'What is it?' Her hands shook as she took the papers he held out to her.

'Take a look,' he commanded softly.

She gathered the nerve to look down at the document. Then her heart dropped to her toes. 'This is… No, it can't be,' she said, although a terrified part of her just *knew*.

'It is exactly as you see, little one,' he murmured.

Niesha gasped, that small endearment she had missed

so much momentarily overcoming the momentous, life-changing document she held in her hands.

She searched his face, desperately wanting to know if any of this was a cruel joke that would further pulverise her bleeding heart. But as usual, Zufar's expression was an enigma that challenged and thrilled her at the same time.

But it didn't stay that way for long. As she searched deeper, his eyes grew lighter, his expression clearing to leave ferocious resolution. 'Read the document, Niesha,' he urged again.

Her gaze dropped to the weighty document. At the top of the first page, the heading blared loud and clear—*Petition For Abdication*.

'No,' she breathed again. 'You can't do this.' Her whole body shook as chills went down her spine. 'You can't!' she repeated fiercely.

'I can, and I have,' Zufar replied.

She shook her head. 'No, I won't let you do this.'

He reached forwards and brushed his knuckles down her cheek. 'My fierce Niesha. You cannot change what is already done.'

She flung herself away from him. 'You cannot abdicate. You should've checked with me, Zufar.' Her hand trembled as she waved the paper at him. 'This is unacceptable.'

He merely smiled. 'You will reconcile yourself to this too, *habibti*, because there's no going back.'

'But your people. Your kingdom—'

'Will always be my people and my kingdom. But I will not be their King.'

'Just like that? But why?'

'Because I realised that no amount of power or privilege is worth losing you. My place is with you. By your side. I'd give up a thousand kingdoms for the chance to spend a lifetime beside you.'

Hope flared wide and bright through her heart. 'I... I don't know what to say.'

'Say you're not still considering divorcing me,' he implored, his jaw clenching tight as he waited for her answer.

'Saying that would imply I considered it in the first place.'

The grim smile tugged at his mouth. 'I heard you, Niesha. I'm not ashamed to say it was the worst moment of my life.'

'Then I wish you'd stayed a moment longer because you would've heard me decline the suggestion. I admit it did cross my mind, but only because I thought you wanted it.'

'When did I give you that impression?'

'When you said there were hard choices to be made. I thought you meant going our separate ways.' Her eyes fell to the paper. 'But you meant this, didn't you?'

He gave a single, solemn nod. 'Yes.'

She swallowed, unable to fully accept the enormity of what he'd done. 'We should've talked about this. Your people will hate me for driving you to this.'

He leaned forwards, brushed his lips over hers. 'They will not. They will throw themselves wholeheartedly at their new King.'

She frowned. 'Their new King?'

He nodded. 'Malak will take my place. The council has already met with him. They're preparing his coronation speech as we speak.'

The progress he'd made without her having any inkling staggered her. She dropped to the sofa, her hand going to her head. 'Zufar...'

He was with her before she'd finished saying his name. He dropped down onto his haunches, his hands settling on her thighs. 'Whether you accept me or not, I will not retake my throne. That is now in my past. I aim to dedicate myself to the future.'

A desperate sob broke free. 'Your future is here with your people.'

'No, my future is with you, by your side, the only position I will accept.'

'But you'll lose everything, Zufar. Your title, your—'

'The only title I wish to assume is that of husband. Lover. Father. If you'll have me.'

'I can't believe—'

'Believe it, little one. For so long I've lived in misery and bitterness. You shone a light into my life where there was only darkness. When I realised my feelings for you had deepened I fought it. I believed, based on what I'd witnessed from my father, that loving you would make me weak. But I watched you loving everyone you came into contact with, watched them fall under your spell and grow stronger because of it.' He reached for her hand, bringing it up to his lips to kiss her knuckles. 'I'm a stronger person today than I was yesterday and that is because of you. How can I resist craving more of that? More of you?'

'Oh, Zufar, you have no idea how much that means to me.'

'I have a fair idea. I want to be a father to our children. I want to grow old with you.' His jaw tightened for a second. 'But before that I want to strike a new bargain with you.'

'A bargain,' she echoed faintly.

'Yes. If you'll have me, if you'll stay my wife, I promise a lifetime of loving you.'

She gasped, then launched herself at him. His arms immediately folded around her, wrapping her tight against him as she fell off the sofa and into his embrace. She didn't care that they both knelt on the carpet. And she definitely didn't care that she was sobbing.

'Is that a yes?' he demanded, his mouth dropping tiny kisses against hers.

'It's a yes. It's an absolute definite yes. But on one condition.'

He tensed slightly, leaning back to look down into her face. Then he gave one of those very regal nods she adored so much. 'Whatever it is, I agree.'

'Promise me you'll never make such life-altering decisions without discussing it with me first?'

'Niesha, you stepped up to be my Queen when I demanded it. It was my turn to return the favour. Rumadah needs her Queen.'

Her happiness dimmed a little. 'Are you sure, Zufar? Absolutely, irrevocably sure? Is there a cooling-off period for abdication? Can we take it back?'

'Hush, little one,' he said, then dropped a longer kiss on her lips. 'There's no going back. There is only going forwards.' One warm, bold hand splayed on her stomach, gently cradling their baby. 'Besides, this project is going to be a full-time one, I suspect.'

She sighed. 'You will be a great father, Zufar, but I don't want you to be just a father. Our coming together may have been a little unorthodox, but without you I would never have found my family, or claimed my birthright. You've helped me in ways that you can never imagine. I don't want you to give up your life here for me, and I came back to tell you just that—that I'll stay in Khalia and be your Queen if that is the only way to hold onto you. I selfishly want a lifetime with you too. But if you think you'll be happy in Rumadah with me, then I want more for you.'

'It shall be as you wish.'

She shook her head. 'You don't understand. I don't want you to just be my husband. I want you to be my King.'

Shock flared through his eyes. 'Niesha, you don't have to.'

'I want to. Just as you wanted me by your side as your Queen, I want you by mine as my husband and my King. That's another non-negotiable condition.'

A wider smile curved his mouth. 'I get the impression there will be a few conditions along our journey through life.'

'You drove a hard bargain when we met. I learned from the best.'

His hands framed her face, his thumbs caressing her cheekbones as he stared deeply into her eyes. 'Even back then, without knowing why, I knew I couldn't let you go. You were in my heart, in my blood, and I didn't even know it.'

'But you know it now?'

'Without doubt or regret.'

'You're in every fibre of my being too. And I wouldn't want it any other way. I love you, Zufar.'

'And I love and adore you, my magnificent Queen.'

EPILOGUE

'Is HER SERENE HIGHNESS ready for her next present?' The words were whispered against her nape, right before warm kisses rained on her bare skin.

Niesha—or Nazira, as she'd reverted to calling herself—laughed. 'You can't keep showering me with gifts, Zufar. One was enough. Twenty is beyond excessive.'

'I have no idea where you got the impression that I have twenty gifts for you.'

She chuckled. 'I'm sorry to inform you that your private secretary caved under pressure from mine.'

Zufar's head dropped onto her back and he groaned.

She laughed harder. 'In his defence, I think he has a crush on her.'

'Well, if my secret is out, then you'll have no choice but to accept.'

He rolled her over and tugged her into his arms. Nazira draped herself over his wide chest, deliriously happy to watch as he reached beneath his pillow, and brought out a small square box tied with ribbons. It was the sixth one he'd given her today and it was barely morning. He'd woken her with deep, intoxicating kissing, and proceeded to take her to heaven and back. As a start to her twenty-sixth birthday, it had been second to none.

And then the presents had started. That Zufar intended to keep to his promise to deliver twenty presents for all the ones she'd missed was evident.

While she was happy to let him because it pleased him, she was content just counting her blessings.

Just a few short months ago, she'd been drowning in loneliness and despair.

Now, she had regained her past, been crowned a queen and, best of all, was tied for life to the husband of her soul.

She accepted the box, and gasped. The diamond pendant was a replica of her birthmark, the starfish the same size as the mark on her arm. And on the back were the names of her family, etched into the white platinum. 'Oh, it's gorgeous.' Tears brimmed in her eyes as he nudged her upright and fastened the necklace.

'I thought you might want a symbol of how you found yourself,' he murmured. 'And the inscription will keep your family with you, always.'

'Oh, Zufar, just when I think I can't love you any more.'

He drew her back into his arms, then demonstrated that there was another way she could love him more.

After they caught their breath, she reached for the folded piece of paper on her beside table. 'I have something for you, too.' She handed it over and watched him open it.

'This is the guest list for my coronation.'

She held her breath. 'Yes.'

His gaze dropped to the sheet. She knew the moment he spotted the addition. 'You want him there? Are you sure?'

She nodded. 'I reached out to him a few days ago. He responded yesterday with an acceptance.'

Zufar remained silent for a moment and then he nodded. 'If you're happy to have him here, then I will welcome Adir and attempt to put the past behind us.'

She smiled, her heart bursting because she knew it had taken a great effort for him to say that. 'And you're not sore because he stole your intended?' she teased.

'*You* were my intended. The one my heart truly wanted. If Adir is happy with Amira, then I'm happy for them both.'

'I love you, Zufar.'

He kissed her long and deep, until her insides melted. 'Keep saying that to me and I will be your slave in this life and the next.'

They stopped talking for a long time after that.

An hour later, as Zufar watched his wife dress for the start of her birthday celebrations, his breath caught all over again.

He couldn't believe how life-changing loving her had been for him. Gone was the bitterness and misery that had clung to him before he met her. He'd accepted her proposal to make him King mostly to honour her, not because he wanted the position.

For the privilege of loving her and being loved by her in return, he would have happily lived in her shadow for the rest of his life. His acceptance had made her happy.

His upcoming coronation in two weeks wrung happy smiles from her each time she spoke about it. Who was he to deny her any of that? His heart grew to bursting as she dropped the towel on her way to the dressing room and he caught the small swell of her stomach. His cup had truly run over, and he couldn't wait to hold their son in his arms.

He'd foolishly thought he wanted a polished stone to pass off to his people. What he'd been blessed with was a gem that shone brighter than the brightest star in the sky.

For as long as he lived, he vowed to ensure that radiance never dimmed.

* * * * *

MILLS & BOON

Coming next month

CONSEQUENCE OF
THE GREEK'S REVENGE
Trish Morey

'Going somewhere, Athena?'

Breath hitched in her lungs as every nerve receptor in her body screeched in alarm. Alexios!

How did he know she was here?

She wouldn't turn around. She wouldn't look back, forcing herself to keep moving forwards, her hand reaching for the door handle and escape, when his hand locked on her arm, a five fingered manacle, and once again she tasted bile in her throat, reminding her of the day she'd thrown up outside his offices. The bitter taste of it incensed her, spinning her around.

'Let me go!' She tried to stay calm, to keep the rising panic from her voice. Because if he knew she was here, he must surely know why, and she was suddenly, terribly, afraid. His jaw was set, his eyes were unrepentant, and they scanned her now, as if looking for evidence, taking inventory of any changes. There weren't any, not that anyone else might notice, though she'd felt her jeans grow more snug just lately, the beginnings of a baby bump.

'We need to talk.'

'No!' She twisted her arm, breaking free. 'I've got nothing to say to you,' she said, rubbing the place where his hand had been, still scorchingly hot like he had used a searing brand against her skin, rather than just his fingers.

'No?' His eyes flicked up to the brass plate on near the door, to the name of the doctor in obstetrics. 'You didn't think I might be interested to hear that you're pregnant with my child?'

Continue reading
**CONSEQUENCE OF
THE GREEK'S REVENGE**
Trish Morey

Available next month
www.millsandboon.co.uk

COMING SOON!

We really hope you enjoyed reading this book. If you're looking for more romance, be sure to head to the shops when new books are available on

Thursday
4th October

To see which titles are coming soon, please visit
millsandboon.co.uk

LET'S TALK
Romance

For exclusive extracts, competitions
and special offers, find us online:

f facebook.com/millsandboon

📷 @millsandboonuk

🐦 @millsandboon

Or get in touch on 0844 844 1351*

For all the latest titles coming soon, visit
millsandboon.co.uk/nextmonth